FOAL

THE BETTER MAN

THE

*B*ETTER MAN

A NOVEL

Anita Nair

PICADOR USA
NEW YORK

For Bhaskaran Nair, my father
(A better man has never walked this earth)

And for Sunil, Unni and Maitreya
(Better men in the making)

Library of Congress Cataloging-in-Publication Data

Nair, Anita.
    The better man / Anita Nair.—1st Picador USA ed.
        p.   cm.
    ISBN 0-312-25311-7
    1. Friendship—Fiction. 2. Middle-aged men—Fiction.
    3. Malabar (India)—Fiction. I. Title.
    PR9499.3.N255 B4   2000
    823'.92—dc21   00-027420
                                                    CIP

First published in India by Penguin Books
First Picador USA Edition: June 2000

10 9 8 7 6 5 4 3 2 1

Acknowledgments

As much as writing produces the most satisfying moments of my life, this book wouldn't have been such a joy to create if these people hadn't constantly and consistently cheered my progress. I owe much to:

Jayanth Kodkani, literary barometer, sounding board and very good friend for steering me towards the writing of this book and then reading every word I wrote.

Laura Susijn, my literary agent, for her hard work and encouragement. And most of all, for her complete faith in me and my writing.

Jayapriya Vasudevan and Amrita Chak of Jacaranda Press, publishing consultants and more, for countless cups of coffee and confidence. And more specifically, for shepherding me through the writing of *The Better Man*.

George Witte and Carrie McGinnis of Picador USA who offered valuable inputs, as did Karthika V.K. of Penguin India.

Sumenta & Franklin Bell, George Blecher, Tarun Cherian, Amy Eshoo, Antonio E Costa & Tanya Mendonsa, Elizabeth Valsala, and Dr Raphael Parambi—friends who made a difference. And Dr Amardeep Kainth for counsel, legal and otherwise.

Charlene and Peter Ganga for their affection and their hospitality in New York City, time and again.

My father Bhaskaran for helping me research various aspects of this book, my mother Soumini for adding to my store of folklore and trivia, and my brother Sunil for sharing my love for minutiae and the absurd.

And Unni, husband, critic and editor-at-home, and Maitreya, son and vociferous one-man cheerleading squad. For their love and laughter. For putting up with my sunny days and stormy hours. And for letting me be . . .

I would like to thank the Virginia Center for the Creative Arts, USA for their hospitality extended to me. *The Better Man* was completed in the summer of 1998 while in residence at the VCCA.

Part I

1

A Reason to Be

Perhaps you have seen me. Perhaps you have not. On most days you can find me glued to the side of some sun-speckled, age-spotted wall. A human lizard with brushes for claws and a can for a tail.

Do you see this ladder, Mukundan? Do not dismiss it as a ramshackle contraption that will someday break my back. Step on it, and you will know for yourself that these bamboo poles and splints still have a lot of life left in them. I had this ladder built to my specifications many years ago when I decided to come to this village and create for myself a new persona. That of a painter.

Look at the rungs. Each one of them is narrow enough for my feet to find a grip and broad enough to not hurt them after a while. I prefer perching on ladders to standing on the ground. When I am ten feet above everyone else I do not have to worry about how I behave. I can stick my little finger in my ear, turn it and squiggle it till I feel sheer pleasure squirm down me. I sigh. I smile to myself. I hum. I make faces. I declaim. No questions asked. No need for explanations. And so long as the pace of my hands keeps up a steady rhythm, no one cares.

There is no reason why you should have heard of me. I am a man of no outstanding virtue or singular genius. There are others in this village of Kaikurussi whose talents far exceed mine. Like Vishnu, the priest who at dawn and dusk can arbitrate on your behalf with the pantheon of gods and at other times can cajole your catatonic radio to burst into boisterous, raucous song.

Then there is Power House Ramakrishnan. Visiting relatives are taken at least once by their hosts to see the high brick wall and imposing metal gate, in this village of bamboo fences and makeshift gates. More than the house though, it is the man who is the landmark. 'He was just an ordinary man like you and me. Until the day a lottery ticket was thrust into his hand. He didn't want it, he could barely afford to pay for it. But look how it changed his luck,' the relatives are told.

Power House Ramakrishnan's palm, they say, has the most unusual lines criss-crossing it. How else do you explain the overnight transformation of a man's fortunes? From petty shop to Power House. From penury to conspicuous prosperity. Even though more than ten years have passed since the day a lottery ticket effected his metamorphosis, the people in the village still haven't ceased to marvel at Power House Ramakrishnan's incredible stroke of luck.

I am not even in the class of Shankar, the tea club owner whose combination of a glass of steaming tea and fragrant beedi smoke has the effect of a truth serum. While the rest of us flounder in a swamp of speculation, he alone is privy to what really happens behind closed doors in this village.

Nor am I like Postman Unni or Barber Nanu or the village crier, Pavitran. How can anyone claim to not know the man who delivers their mail—money orders, letters, tax notices, and wedding invitations? Or the man who trims their hair every third week? Or the man who announces the local panchayat orders and all other events held by it, from house-tax collection camps to vaccination visits, as he walks through the village tom-tomming his drum?

As for notoriety, even that eludes me. That is an honour that the doctor at the Primary Health Centre has reserved for himself. For when you enter his room after having waited patiently in line all morning, he will greet you with a calculating gleam in his eye, quickly assessing your ability to pay. After hearing your heart beat, pulse tick, and blood pound, he will point to the two vials laid on a tray and tell you, 'The medicine on the left is what the government provides. It is free, but I can give you no guarantees as to how long it will take to cure you. The one on the right is what I recommend, but it will cost you some money. Which one is it to be?'

Then there is Che Kutty. Che Kutty's brand of healing is liquid forgetfulness. He advertises this by placing on his shop veranda a full bottle of toddy crowned with a red shoe flower. He wasn't born Che Kutty, but in his younger days he greatly admired Che Guevara, and so every thought he had, every sentence he mouthed, was distilled from the philosophy propounded by his idol. Soon his friends began to refer to him as Che Sivan Kutty. Over the years his real name was discarded, and he became Che Kutty.

In another country, in another time, he would have staged a revolution, probably even have been a highly paid guerrilla. But here in Malabar, all that Che Kutty could do was continue with the family business. Perhaps he sought consolation in the fact that what he dealt in was the common man's drink and by disbursing it, he was helping reduce the profits earned by the bourgeoisie who peddled Western imperialist spirits like whisky, brandy and rum. Now all that remains of his leftist leanings and militant youth is a beard that resembles the guerrilla leader's mangy tufty one, and the single lock of hair that falls irreverently onto his forehead.

There are some who claim that Che Kutty hasn't completely relinquished his past. Or, why else would he choose a red plastic pot (red being the colour of revolution) to upturn on a pole and place outside his toddy shop? Why not a green one or a blue one? Besides, there was no need for such a graphic symbol when on a signboard the legend 'Toddy Shop' was clearly and boldly written. Even an idiot could read it. In fact, every child after just a few days of learning the primer felt compelled to gawk at the signboard day after day on his way to school and back, and practise aloud his newly acquired skills, reading out the white letters on the blackboard.

Night after night, month after month, the men of Kaikurussi flock to his shop to fill their bellies and numb their minds with Che Kutty's fresh coconut and palm toddy. But if toddy alone won't suffice to diminish the extent of your suffering, and if you have a reference, he'll bring out from the back of his shop glasses of 'the other one'. What makes Che Kutty's 'the other one' distinct, apart from its being illicit, is the extra that goes into the distilling process. So, if the Jesus Christ mix has you flat on your back for three days, the Bride will make your head droop till the effect of the hooch wears off. The Knock-an-elephant-down will knock you off your feet and the Lean-on-me will make you grope for the wall in a matter of minutes.

While everywhere else they might add caterpillars, batteries and rat poison to the vats that bubble over wood fires in secret hideouts, Che Kutty's 'the other one' is pristine, pure and powerful, spiced with tranquillizers, hypnotic drugs and barbiturates made by respectable pharmaceutical companies. Perhaps that is why Che Kutty is a much sought after man. A man's man, who for a price has the cure for sore hearts and bruised egos.

And yet, it is I alone, thin man, ordinary man, paint-splattered, soda-bottle-spectacled, bristle-haired man who can help you. But for that you have to trust me and give yourself to me.

They have a name for me in this village. They call me Painter Bhasi.

Behind my back, in the shadowed lanes, on the benches in Shankar's Tea Club and the fug inside Che Kutty's toddy shop, amidst the crowds that fill the temple ground on the pooram day, they refer to me as One-screw-loose Bhasi.

Smirks, secret winks and hushed laughter are the coinage that denominates my standing in this village. They look at the insignificance of my features and assume they know me. They look at the tools of my trade and think they have fathomed my mind. My advice is never solicited. My opinions are mostly ignored. All I am considered fit for is just dipping a brush into a can of paint and slapping it on, this way and that.

I can see the look in your eyes too. The puzzlement that creeps into most people's minds when they realize I am not who they think I am. And as they get to know me better, I know they speculate about my past. The common consensus is that a feckless woman is the reason why plain Bhasi became One-screw-loose Bhasi. And that it was a broken heart that brought me to Kaikurussi.

Some nights, after a long, tiring day, I don't sleep too well. I wake up in the early hours of the morning and lie on the bed staring at the blackness outside. There is to that hour a certain eerie quality that encourages the emergence of forbidden thoughts, filling me with a longing for I-don't-know-what. I ask myself what I am doing here, playacting as a painter with a diminutive for a name. For there was a time when I used to be Bhaskaran Chandran. The sun and the moon. A time when I thought I could make something of my life.

I shouldn't have given up so easily.

I have a college degree in botany and a postgraduate degree in English language and literature. I have a piece of paper that states I qualified with distinction in the study of plants. And a certificate of merit issued by the university honouring me as one of the ten rankholders in mastering the intricacies of the English language. But it wasn't enough. There came a time when I knew that if I wanted to cling to the last fragments of self-respect, I would have to leave.

And so I fled to Kaikurussi, this village. There is nothing here that would make anyone come looking for it. It is the birthplace of neither a Mahatma nor a movement. There are no craft forms originating from here to fill Government Cottage Emporia shelves. No miracles have ever happened here. In fact, nothing of significance ever happens here to anyone.

I knew that here I would find respite from my inadequacies. There would be no reminders, no peer pressure, no expectations that I perform. Or succeed. I could be just another one of the villagers going through the motions of living till they are buried or cremated in their backyards.

You may find this hard to believe, but there are those who seek me out again and again. At first, when they arrive at my doorstep, they ask for me haltingly. Voices muffled under an epidermis of doubt. Bodies shrouded in hopelessness. I can see the questions in their eyes and hear the doubts that swirl around in the can of their minds. Does he know what he is doing? Is he really capable of healing? Are you sure we have come to the right house?

I do nothing to reassure them. I don't feel the need to do so. They seek me out, coming to me when they have lost faith in everything else. Bringing me bodies and minds that have been neglected, mistreated, and sometimes even abused. And it is these that they expect me to turn whole again.

I make no promises. I never have to this day. I am not dealing in the conventional principles of contrary effect. My learning is not based on slicing parts of the human anatomy or exploring the tenacity of life on a glass slide. I do not capsulate healing with compounds and equations packed into little pink and blue gelatin caps. At first I studied my science of healing to fill the long hours between returning home after work and going to sleep. But soon I had mastered it well enough to dispense health.

The human body has a natural in-built capacity to heal itself. To safeguard against trauma and disease. All I do is reinforce that natural vitality. I don't work miracles. I don't wave a wand to kill diseases. I simply find a remedy for the body to fight that disease.

But with you, Mukundan, I knew a difference. I felt the portents of a sign. My time had arrived.

Eight years ago I was in the train that tried to cross the Perambavu bridge and never did. I was late reaching the Ottapalam railway station and almost missed the train. Which is how I found myself in one of the last compartments. The Quilon railway station was just a furlong away from the bridge. The engine ran across the bridge; the compartments followed. Then the bridge snapped as if it were made of matchsticks instead of iron and steel. The waters parted, and the cries of horror rose in a giant wave as the front and middle sections of the train sank into the bottomless abyss of the Ashtamudi Kayal. A snake crushed beneath a farmer's plough, leaving its rear end thrashing and buckling in shock.

Who was to know what happened? Did any one of them have a premonition of disaster, a strange discomfort, a hollow feeling in the pit of the stomach, an eyelid that fluttered furiously? The women who were found with combs in their hair had been grooming themselves to embark at the station; the men gripped their attaché cases on their way to work; the children who had fought for the window seat clung to the window bars tenaciously. Why was it that they were taken and I was spared? What decree of destiny said that their lot was to be buried fathoms deep in waters that were neither sea nor river, while mine was to walk away, shaken but virtually untouched?

For days divers searched the underwater gardens of mangled metal. Silvery fish glided in through window bars easily, while taciturn crabs pulled at the flesh of corpses. The divers watched helplessly. The waters were deep, and

they were mere men. And there the train and its
vacant-eyed, bloated passengers would have remained but
for the pulley workers of the Beypore shipyard, who came
in and hoisted up the remains of the train and its passengers.

And now, in the workings of my deliverance, I see a grand
pattern emerge. I know that I have been chosen to bring
forth from the churned-up mud of some wrecked psyche a
luminous and complete mind. A whole being that perhaps
even God wouldn't aspire to create. And that everything
that I have done leading up to this moment—the decision to
come to Kaikurussi, the knowledge I have been steadfastly
acquiring, my success with difficult patients, all of it has
been in preparation for this day.

How was I to know that today would be the day? When I
woke up in the morning, it seemed no different from any
other day. All I knew was that I had been sent for to inspect
the blistering walls of your house and quote an estimate.
And so I presented myself to you as Bhasi, the painter. I
wish we had met as equals. I have learned to disguise myself
to assure my customers about my jobworthiness. If I don't,
I'm considered too expensive or too stupid. So I wear what I
am expected to. A paint-splattered shirt and a hideously
flowered lungi reeking of turpentine.

Every day in the evening when I return to my home—the
plot of land that houses my herb garden and my dreams, the
first thing I do is take that repugnant shirt off and leave it
hanging on the clothesline outside. You might find this
ridiculous and fanciful, but to me every paint stain that I
add to my shirt further intensifies the darkness that fills my
soul.

When I reach home, I like to pick up my little son and toss
him in the air. I like to do so without wondering if someday
he will be as brusque and callous with me as one of my
customers was towards his father in my presence. I like to lie
in the easy-chair and watch my wife clean the rice. And it
bothers me that I begin to worry if she's planning a tryst

with my handsome neighbour. Damaged lives fill my world as much as flaking paint does.

What better captive audience than a painter with no assistants? A painter whose opinions are reputed to be as suspect as the wall he's been hired to paint? And so the owners of those walls stand by my side, seat themselves on a stone, or position themselves in a spot in the shade, keeping a constant eye to ensure that I don't dawdle, daydream, or drag the brush lazily so that three days of painting stretch to a week. As I work they fill my ear with grievances nursed, illnesses braved, and family feuds battled. In the manner of the wall I'm painting, it is expected of me to soak in their woes without speaking a word in return. By the time I have finished painting a house, there is little that I don't know about the people living in it. At least a lizard on the wall can choose to disappear when it wants to.

But with you, Mukundan, I broke a rule. I realized that I could maintain no such distance, no clear-cut compartmentalization. In you, I saw a friend and a customer. A patient. Someone whose healing had to be aided. You needed me. And so when I saw you, I was filled once again with the radiance of hope. I knew that you were the one great happening that destiny had given me. A perfect instrument to demonstrate to the world that Bhasi the painter, that One-screw-loose Bhasi, was put on this earth with a mission to accomplish.

The revelation came to me as I stood contemplating the neglected walls of your house. It was as if you and your walls had become one. I looked at the cracks, the degradation of strength, the silent creeping in of mouldy hopelessness, and wondered at what must be the condition of the inner walls, the inner man. And I knew as I caressed the sad walls that these could be repaired. You can be healed. Then I looked at the extent of the peeling, the flaking, and the cracks and asked myself, Where do I begin?

There is something you need to know about me before I

go on. I have no pretensions to being an artist of any sort. But every wall I have revived to life I have looked at with as much awe and tremulousness as Michelangelo must have felt when he gazed up at the bare ceiling of the Sistine Chapel. I like to understand the temperament of my wall before I even run my fingers over its surface. I look at it, ponder over it, and at times even dream about it. And it is only when I know exactly what the wall needs and what I ought to do that I begin work. For this they point a finger at me in the village and remark in voices tinged with annoyance, He's a good worker but he's slow. Once he starts a job, he takes forever to finish.

If fluidity is the plasma of paint, then fear is the plasma of your life. A fear that seems to know no extent. Neither a beginning nor an end. A fear that seems to course through you, like the road that runs through this village. Dividing everything in you into what you could be and what you are not. As I attacked the walls of your house with handfuls of coarse coconut fibre that removed the surface grime and the past that clung to it, I tried to understand how I could achieve the same with you. To peel the scabs off your festering soul and let the fear seep out, I need to know what it is that binds you in such terror.

Tell me, Mukundan. Tell me what it is that haunts you so. Tell me of the darkness that clouds your life. Tell me why you fold your handkerchief in eight precise squares. Tell me why it is that every strand of coconut fibre has to be heaped in one place when I finish with it. Tell me how it is that you have chained yourself to the clock. Tell me what makes perfection so important to you. Tell me why you have about you the smell of a hunted animal.

Tell me. For therein lies your escape. Your hope, and someday your happiness maybe.

2

The Reluctant Native

Once upon a time Mukundan had a life that in no way resembled the hell he had been exiled to. As a government employee all his working years had been spent in the living quarters provided for him. The rent had been negligible and the comforts many. When a fuse blew, he called the electrical department. If the tap dripped, the civil works men fixed it. The apartments were not palatial, but they were convenient. Since he shared his with other bachelors, whom he carefully chose, he was never lonely.

Besides, there was the Club Library, over which Mukundan ruled as its librarian. When Mukundan took charge ten years ago, the library consisted of a hundred books of torrid passion, most of them with pages that were either missing or ripped through. The earlier librarians were men who had to be coerced into taking up the job and therefore resented having to give up two hours of their evening three times a week. Most often they pleaded illness or a social commitment as an excuse and stayed away. So the library functioned sporadically and sometimes remained closed for weeks at a time. Hardly any books were bought and when they were, the quality of their contents was suspect.

Mukundan changed all that. He had taken up the post on a sudden whim but soon began to enjoy it. Something about running the library appealed to the meticulous side of his nature. He insisted on the library being allocated a budget to buy new books every two months. He personally went to the bookshops to scan their shelves and put together a selection of reading that would uplift tired minds and nurture young ones. For every James Hadley Chase, Sidney Sheldon and Wilbur Smith he had to include, he compensated with Irving Stone, Agatha Christie and R. K. Narayan.

He had window bars installed so that books didn't disappear mysteriously. He bought bookcases with glass doors so that the books could be looked at without being handled by grubby hands. He organized a filing system that was practically foolproof, and if someone held on to a book for too long, he thought nothing of accosting them wherever he saw them and demanding it be returned. He charged a late fee and made no exceptions, not even if it was the general manager's daughter. When he discovered that fourteen-year-old boys were borrowing books with pictures of naked women on the cover, he drew their parents' attention to it. He steered adolescent girls from Mills & Boon romances to Pearl S. Buck and Nevil Shute.

To Mukundan the library took the place of a family and allowed him to don the role of head of a household. He cared for it and provided for it, and unlike human beings it demanded little from him and claimed no rights.

It wasn't that he particularly loved books or reading. In fact, all he read was magazines. The truth was that Mukundan shunned books with the fear of a man who thinks that within their pages he will find startling and unsavoury glimpses of himself. When Mukundan was thirteen, he discovered the manifest power of the written word. An abridged edition of *David Copperfield* was given to him by an English teacher. 'Whether I shall turn out to be the hero of my own life, or whether that station will be held by anybody else, these pages must show.' Mukundan read these words with a beating heart. His mouth went dry, and he felt his insides quiver with the certainty of knowing. Mukundan realized that this was what he would like to do for the rest of his life. Write. Make words express the dictates of his mind. With words, he could rule kingdoms, swim treacherous currents, bring tyrants to their knees. I will be a writer, he told himself again and again, hugging the thought with a furtive joy.

For a while Mukundan was an inveterate scribbler. He tore pages from the middle of his class notebooks so that no one noticed the missing sheets, and filled them with words. He copied down long passages from books he chose randomly in the school library. But since the school headmaster favoured the classics, Mukundan found himself confronting the masters of literature. He tried rewriting the Brontës and Dickens, Goldsmith and Chesterton, in his own words, but when he finished, they glared back at him with annoyance. Why don't you leave us as we were? What makes you think you can do better? they questioned scornfully. He chewed his lip, sucked on the end of the pencil, and persisted till the day his father found the hoard of pages.

'What is this nonsense?' Achuthan Nair asked peering at the pages. 'All the people of the village were at the fountain, standing about in their depressed manner, and whispering low, but showing no other emotions than grim curiosity and surprise. The led cows hastily brought in and tethered to anything that would hold them were looking stupidly on, or lying down chewing the cud of nothing particularly repaying their trouble, which they had picked up in their interrupted saunter . . . ,' he read aloud. 'Who wrote this?' he demanded.

'Charles Dickens,' Mukundan mumbled uncertainly, looking at his mother who was hovering by the doorway to rescue him.

'So what is all this?' Achuthan Nair persisted, scanning the remaining half of the page. 'They were all there. The people of the village stood at the fountain whispering, curious, and surprised! The cows hastily brought in and tethered to anything that would hold them looked stupidly chewing the cud of nothing . . .'

'I think it is school homework,' Paru Kutty began. But Achuthan Nair silenced her with a stern glare. Stay out of this, his eyes said.

'I was trying to write like he did,' Mukundan whispered.

'Well then, it reads like a précis and nothing more. Don't you have anything better to do? Or is it that you fancy you are a writer?' Achuthan Nair asked with a malicious grin, wagging his finger. 'Let me tell you, boy, banish that thought from your mind. No son of mine is going to waste his life trying to be a writer. Do you understand?' he barked.

'Yes,' Mukundan said in a voice hollow with despair.

'What do you understand?'

'That I shouldn't waste time trying to be a writer.'

'Good. However, since you seem to like fiddling around with a pencil and paper, from this evening onward, after you have done your homework, you can do some writing for me. But this will be the kind that will help you in your adult life,' Achuthan Nair said, tearing the sheets into several pieces.

Then Achuthan Nair pounced on Paru Kutty. 'He must have got this vagrant streak from your family. Didn't you have an uncle who went away to someplace in Tamilnadu to study music? No one in my family has ever had any pretensions of artistic ability. And let me tell you how glad I am about that. We are a family of capable and hardworking men. Not namby-pamby creatures rattling away lines of useless poetry or drawing pretty pictures or strutting around towns and villages bleating. What is the use of it all?'

Later that night Paru Kutty sat beside Mukundan as he lay in bed staring at the beamed wooden ceiling. She took his hand in hers and said quietly, 'Never mind what your father says. If you want to write, you go ahead and do it.'

'How can I?' Mukundan tried to choke back the sob that

clutched at his throat. 'If he finds out, he'll be furious.'

Paru Kutty stroked his brow, wishing she didn't feel so helpless. 'Perhaps you can write when he's gone out or is busy with his accounts,' she said.

'It's impossible. He is sure to find out, and then you know what will happen,' he cried. Achuthan Nair didn't take kindly to anyone questioning his authority. Or what he called doing things behind his back.

'Amma,' Mukundan asked in a troubled voice, 'why is he never satisfied with anything I do? Why is he so angry with me all the time?'

'Ssshh . . . ,' she comforted him. 'You mustn't talk about your father in that manner. He is not really angry with you. He just wants you to grow up to be like him. Strong and capable. When you have a son of your own, you too will find that you want him to be like you.'

Mukundan turned away from her to face the wall. He knew she was just mouthing those words to make him feel better. His mother was as intimidated by his father and as much a butt of his ire as he was.

Every evening Achuthan Nair dictated letters for Mukundan to write. By the time he was seventeen and ready to leave home, Mukundan knew how to hit the perfect note of supplication in every letter he wrote. He knew what to say when asking for leave, how to beg for a sanction, what phrases to use when seeking a favour. And so the emotion that Mukundan had meant to drain into his stories found expression in the letters he wrote.

When Mukundan turned eighteen and was waiting for his Pre-University exam results to be announced, he heard of an opening for a clerical post in an explosives factory in Trichy. For a week Mukundan toyed with the idea of asking his father permission to apply for the post. In the end he decided he would apply anyway and see what happened before he discussed it with anyone. And so Mukundan penned the best letter he would ever write. For it helped him escape the father and life he hated with a single-minded passion.

Mukundan never again wrote anything but letters and official reports. That side of him, he knew, was dead for ever. And he didn't think he could revive it. Nor did he ever read a novel again. He seldom touched a book except perhaps to dust it or move it from one place to another. When he began to live alone and no longer had to fear his father's wrath, Mukundan still couldn't bear to read a book. It caused too many inexplicable emotions to surface. But a magazine with its pictures and sterile words evoked no such feelings. It demanded neither involvement nor any space in his life.

Mukundan met Narendran when they were both appointed as lower division clerks in the explosives factory at Trichy. As the most junior clerks in the section, they sought each other's company. And when they discovered that they had many things in common including the fact that they were both from Malabar, a friendship developed. It was so much easier to reminisce in one's own language than in the stilted textbook English that the two of them spoke. A camaraderie developed, which endured even after Mukundan was transferred to Bangalore. Through sporadic letters and official tours they kept alive their relationship.

Mukundan saw in those foolscap double-spaced typewritten sheets the flourishing of dreams and the abundance of hope that graced Narendran's life. He learnt of the grand plan Narendran had charted for himself. In anticipation of his retirement and return to his village, Narendran had already sent his wife and daughters back to Malabar. The daughters had been admitted to colleges, and feelers had been sent out to prospective bridegrooms. When Narendran returned to the old ancestral house his wife had inherited, he would sink some of his pension into the remodelling of the house so that it resembled a modern bungalow, at least from the front. Then he would get the daughters married off. Once all such responsibilities had been taken care of, Narendran intended to enjoy every minute of his retired life. He and his wife would travel a bit. Visit the Taj Mahal, see the sun rise at Kanyakumari, and if health permitted, even go on a trip to Benaras. But as people who had been away from the village for so long, it was necessary for them to establish themselves there. Renew old family ties. Revive forgotten friendships.

Two years ago Narendran had been transferred to the same Bangalore explosives factory where Mukundan worked. The other room in Mukundan's house was vacant, so he invited Narendran to share his quarters. As their retirement day drew closer, all their conversations led to just one subject—life after retirement. Mukundan didn't know what he was going to do. But one thing was certain. He was not going back to his native village. He considered buying a small plot of land in Bangalore and settling down there. After all, he had lived in Bangalore for more than twenty years. But what would he do in a house all by himself in a new neighbourhood? No matter what his friends said, he knew that once he left the service, it wouldn't be the same.

When Narendran asked him to come with him to his village and make his home there, he agreed. Narendran told him of the plot of land next to his that Mukundan could buy. It even had a small house on it. All that he would need to do was make a few modifications and redo the wiring and plumbing. And Narendran and his wife and children would be there anytime that he needed help. Over many drinks late into the night, they planned their future. Or at least, Narendran made plans and Mukundan listened.

Narendran wanted to start a typing and shorthand institute in a shed in his compound. 'Eight second-hand typewriters and a few tables and chairs are all that we require,' he calculated. 'We could give shorthand lessons and teach some basic bookkeeping,' he added. 'I can see it in my head. "Jai Bharath College of Commerce" written in big bold letters on a blue board with a yellow border.'

He looked at Mukundan and asked, 'You will help me, won't you? Apart from bringing in an income, it will keep us occupied.'

Mukundan nodded. He had thought of setting up a little lending library. He had adequate experience in running one. And it didn't require any real commitment from him. But he knew Narendran would balk at the idea. Narendran liked people and noise and life teeming around him.

Mukundan wasn't too sure about hearing the click-click of typewriters all through the day or having to be chained to an office routine, but he was willing to be a part of any plan. He was so grateful to Narendran for rescuing him from having to go back to Kaikurussi.

A few months before they retired, Narendran began to suffer from headaches that twisted his face into a grimace and his fists into rock. He was irritable all the time and quarelled at the slightest provocation. And Mukundan began to worry whether he was making a mistake by choosing to become Narendran's neighbour in the near future.

One Saturday night when he returned from the library, he found the apartment empty and dark. Mukundan waited till midnight before he went looking for Narendran. When he found him, it was by the side of the road in what seemed like a drunken faint. He dragged Narendran home and put him to bed. In the morning he waited for Narendran to emerge from his room with a sheepish grin. The words were all ready in his head. But Narendran remained in the sanctuary of his room, or so it seemed to Mukundan. When he could bear it no longer, Mukundan—who was a great respecter of privacy—broke his own rules and rushed into

Narendran's room, where he found Narendran lying on the bed staring at the ceiling.

'You overdid it last night,' Mukundan said in a stern voice.

'I didn't drink last night,' Narendran said.

'You don't expect me to believe that, do you?' Mukundan snapped. 'You should have seen yourself. How could you?' he asked, letting his anger show in his voice. 'How could you behave like one of those labourers in the factory? If you wanted to get drunk, you should have done it at home. When I saw you lying by the side of the road in a drunken stupor, I was so ashamed. And as I hauled you all the way back home, I kept praying that we wouldn't meet anyone we know. Imagine what they would have thought of us!'

Narendran turned to look at him. His eyes were wet and his voice cracked when he spoke, 'I swear by everything I hold precious, I didn't drink a drop of alcohol last night. I don't know what is happening to me. I just know something is wrong.'

As they sat in the doctor's waiting room, Narendran suddenly asked, 'Do you think I'm going to die?'

'Don't be silly. You will be fine. It's probably just very high blood pressure,' Mukundan tried to reassure him.

'All these years I kept putting off things saying I would do it when I retired. And now I no longer know what is going to happen. I'm scared, Mukundan, I'm frightened that I'm going to die before I begin to live. Why do we do this to ourselves? Why do we waste time so? I wish . . .' He stopped in midstream as if even talking about it was pointless now.

Mukundan sat there with his head bent, not knowing what to say. He was scared too. It was not just the thought that his best friend could be ill, but knowing that if something happened to Narendran, he would be all alone in this world.

Eight months before they were due to retire, Narendran died of a brain tumour that filled almost his entire skull.

Mukundan was devastated. He didn't have the strength to make any more plans.

And so when he retired in midsummer, on the last day of May, he returned to the village that he had tried to stay away from all his adult life.

As the taxi leaped and dived over the narrow road that wound around the hill, Mukundan felt his stomach churn. A feeling that had nothing to do with the suspension of the car and everything to do with the uncertainty of what was waiting for him at the end of the road. Vasu, the driver, a Kaikurussi man, took great delight in pointing out to him what he thought were sights of significance. 'Do you see that pond over there? Last week a bus fell into it. Luckily no one was hurt.'

A few minutes later, he slowed alongside a gate. Through the dense foliage, Mukundan saw a house painted blue. Vasu looked over his shoulder and murmured, 'Poor Hamsa, he thought all his problems were over when his son found a job in the Gulf; the boy used to send him money regularly. Then one month there was no news from him. No calls, no letters, and no money. The next week the boy came back'—he paused and then continued, relishing the expression on Mukundan's face as he whispered—'in a coffin.'

When Mukundan grimaced, Vasu met his eyes in the mirror. 'One thing I have learned about life is you can never be sure of anything. When you think you've settled it all, something happens to turn your life upside down. Take yourself, for instance. Did you ever think you would come back to live here? All of us thought you would sell the old house and settle down elsewhere in some town.'

'I almost did,' Mukundan blurted out and then bit his

tongue in annoyance. He didn't want anyone to know that he had nowhere else to go. Instead he defended himself from all such gossip in the future by saying, 'Why wouldn't I come back here? This is where I was born, after all. This is where I belong.'

Vasu's eyes narrowed for a moment, and he opened his mouth as if he were about to say something. Then he paused as though he'd changed his mind and steered the conversation away.

It began to rain. A flat, hammering rain that drummed on the roof of the car in an urgent, monotonous beat. The windshield wipers like frenzied devotees in a temple began to wave their arms briskly in time with the rhythm of the rain. Mukundan hastily rolled up the car window and sat there cocooned in its stifling interior. He had forgotten the capricious nature of the Malabar monsoon. Of rain that waited for clothes to be hung out on lines to dry, for children to set out to school, and for people to leave their homes without an umbrella before it came hurtling down from nowhere. Persisting vigorously till everything was wet and sodden before it stopped with the same abruptness with which it had begun. 'Looks like the monsoons are early this year,' Mukundan said as Vasu began to wipe the clouded windshield.

'No, no, it's on time. The first week of June was what the newspapers said. Every year the monsoons begin on the day the schools reopen after their summer vacation,' Vasu laughed. His voice droned on. Mukundan wished Vasu would stop treating him as if he were a tourist who had to be shown all the attractions of the village to be persuaded to stay on.

He slowed alongside a huge metal gate into which ornate letters that said POWER HOUSE had been welded. 'You have heard of him, haven't you?' Vasu asked in a voice that seemed still awestruck. 'Power House Ramakrishnan. He won the lottery some years ago.'

Mukundan nodded. Once upon a time his house had been the only one to sport a metal gate. Now every house seemed to have one, contending with one another as if to see whose could be bigger and more ornate. Except for the gates and the terraced houses that seemed to have sprung up overnight, the landscape had changed very little since he had seen it last.

The long-abandoned limestone quarry that stayed filled with water all year round, lay serene and unruffled. Even on the hottest days, its waters were icy cold. The road ran alongside the quarry pool, a slithering grey snake between lush paddy fields fringed in the distance by the Anangan Hills. Grim and granite faced, the Anangan range sometimes grumbled, sending showers of pebbles and loose rocks down its slopes. And the people in the village would look at each other in trepidation and say, 'Seems like Anangan's waking up.'

The road went up a steep slope and then, a few yards after Mukundan's gate, ended abruptly in a stretch of gravel and mud with patches of tar in between. 'Someday soon they are going to finish building this road. When they do, it's going to link Shoranur and Mannarkad, and you can be sure nothing's ever going to be the same again,' Vasu's voice rattled along with the car. When they stopped, Mukundan felt his stomach descend to his knees.

He tried to delay going in as much as he could. If he chatted with Vasu, he would linger on, scratching his head, patting the car's roof, standing on one foot and then the other as he voiced his opinion on everything that was happening in the village. But it seemed that on that day even Vasu was in a hurry. He pocketed the money Mukundan gave him, jumped into the car, and called out as he began reversing the vehicle, ' If you need the car, just leave word at Shankar's Tea Club. I'll get the message.' Then he was gone with a loud honk.

Neeli, with dusty feet and clutching a broom, stood in the

shadows that cloaked the house. She cleared her throat and murmured, 'Krishnan Nair has had to go home. There's been an accident in his family. He said it could take a week to ten days, but he'll be back as soon as he can. The key is on the beam, he said.'

He tried to catch a glimpse of her face but Neeli stayed steadfast in the corner. There had always been a Neeli hovering in the shadows cast by the house. He wondered if it was the same Neeli who had been there many years ago. His mother's errand girl and confidante. When his father had left the house to live with his concubine, it was Neeli who had consoled his mother. When Paru Kutty had confided in Neeli how scared she was to be by herself in that huge old house, Neeli had offered to keep her company in the night. And she had, until that last night.

Then Mukundan caught a fleeting glimpse of the young body—the slender waist, the muscular haunches, and the tilt of her breasts—and knew that yet another Neeli had come in her place.

It was the sixth night of his vigil. He dared not close his eyes. For as the night intensified, so did his fear. He knew they were there, lurking in corners, crouching in shadows. He had often heard their tread as they climbed down the steep wooden staircase. A creaking of the old wood as if it were in pain. The splintering of silence that stretched only as long as they descended into the narrow, dingy staircase room. He wished he knew what it was that they searched for in the empty rooms that lined either side of the corridor.

Some nights he thought he saw them come rushing down the corridor that ran through the length of the house. From somewhere behind him, he heard Ammuma's toothless gums mouth, 'Mone Mukunda.' Her fingers swept through his hair and caressed the back of his neck. When he turned to look for her, she had dissipated into a shadow the moonbeam threw off the wooden slats in the window.

Mukundan sat on the terrace with a bottle of rum, waiting for the dawn. An ice bucket kept him mute company. He did not miss making conversation. But he would have liked the comfort of another human presence. He clinked the ice in the glass and gulped down a mouthful of rum. Khodays XXX. He had brought back from Bangalore enough stock to see him through the first few weeks. Except that suddenly the rum seemed to have lost its ability to suppress the fears the house spawned in him. For all that it did for him, he might as well have been sipping black coffee.

Lightning darted from behind a cloud shaped like a buffalo's head. There was no thunder. Just zigzags of light that tattered the sky. A bird screamed, flapping its wings, slashing the air with a few thwacks. The bamboo copse at the bottom of the garden began its strange music. He heard the wind as it came wailing down the hillside through the trees, shaking the tiles on the roofs and lifting the dust off the ground. All around him was darkness, murky and intimidating. And yet it was the inside of the house that filled him with greater dread.

This was the house he had been born in. In its rooms and in the cashew groves around it, he had spent his childhood. Long, silent days as he plotted and planned his escape from the confines of its walls and the tyranny of his father. And then, when he thought he had left it behind him forever, he had to return. Now this was his home, though he knew deep in his heart that it would never ever feel like home.

Mukundan heard a noise. A scurrying of feet as if someone was searching for something. He had left all the lights on. Every single bulb burned, but the voltage was so low that there was just a pool of yellow in the middle of each room. The rest of the room was immersed in shadow. The force of the wind rose, and the electric wires hissed, metal serpents that slithered through the air. Venomous sparks spewed from them. Suddenly the power went off.

He switched on the torch and swung it this way and that, throwing arcs of sharp light. There was a candle on a saucer and a box of matches beside it in the room that opened onto the terrace. All he needed to do was to walk inside. Just a matter of four ordinary strides.

Mukundan tossed the last of the rum down his throat. He tried to get a grip on himself. What am I scared of? he tried to rationalize. Stealthily a thought crept into his mind: Remember what happened to your mother. The same could happen to you too.

The first drops of rain fell. He huddled in his chair and prayed for the rain to go away. The fine drizzle pierced his clothes with the intensity of a thousand needles. The rumble of thunder rattled the glass panes in the new section of the house. If he stayed there any longer, he would get soaking wet. And so he crept in, clutching the bottle in one hand and the torch in the other.

Mukundan put the bottle on the table and groped for the box of matches. His hands were shaking so badly that he fumbled. He struck a match, and the candle popped to life. But above the acrid smell of burnt sulphur and melting wax, he could sniff a sweetness in the air. Of a cheroot burning. The kind that only one man he knew had smoked. His granduncle, Balammaven.

He took a deep breath. This cannot go on, he told himself. I can't spend the rest of my life creeping through this monstrous house expecting something to pounce on me from its dark depths and swirl me away into a black vortex.

A moth appeared from nowhere. Its magnified shadow flitted across the walls. He walked resolutely to the nearest room and pushed the doors open. The twin planks of wood resisted at first and then parted unwillingly, making known their displeasure with a shrill moan.

It was the room in which Balammaven had spent most of his life. There was a lingering fragrance of tobacco. The four-poster he had slept in had been pushed into a corner, and in another corner were his armchair and a wooden bureau he had kept his clothes and other possessions in. Mukundan swept the room with the torch. The beam rested on the ornately carved headboard of the bed. The chiaroscuro of light brought alive a mural of evil faces that stared at him. He focused the beam hurriedly elsewhere. There was nothing in there except the mustiness of neglect. When he closed the doors behind him, a muted whisper followed him, slithering through the crack between the wood planks: 'Don't go. Come back in here, son.'

'No!' He heard a scream. When he realized the strangled cry was coming from his own throat, he stopped. Don't be a fool; Balammaven died half a century ago. There is nothing in there. It's all in your mind, he told himself over and over again. It seemed to help. For the rest of the rooms upstairs made no attempt to hold him back. He wandered through the top floor of the house, opening all the rooms, one by one. When each and every door lay wide open, the rooms exposed to air and the tall flame of the candle, he decided to go downstairs.

The staircase fell steeply. Made entirely of the finest teakwood, cut from their own garden, it stood almost twelve feet high. Each of its steps was barely nine inches wide. Even an average-sized foot fit into it with great difficulty. There was a knack to climbing down this staircase that was more than a hundred years old. He seemed to have forgotten how. So he held on to the narrow banister rail and traced each step with his big toe before putting his foot down on the next. From the open window in the room above a gust of wind came rushing down and almost snuffed out the candle. He let go of the rail to cup the flame and nearly fell down the staircase. Just as his mother had all those years ago.

By the time Mukundan recovered his footing, the wind had swept the flame away into a little puff of smoke. He felt the hollowness within him come back though he knew there were just eight steps left. What on earth had made him take the candle instead of the torch? He cursed himself for his stupidity as he hurried down as fast as he could in the dark. When he lit the candle, portraits of fierce-faced beings stared down at him grimly. Chottanikara Bhagawati, Kadampuzha Bhagawati, Narasimhan, Hanuman, and Mukundan's dead ancestors. Then he caught sight of an old calendar of the Mahatma, framed by his father in a fit of patriotic fervour, and felt comforted by its ordinariness. There was no reason to feel fear in here unless he was going to let the work of an artist with a macabre imagination scare him out of his mind.

Mukundan walked down the long, dark corridor that had been haunting his thoughts for the past six days. It led into the dining room. As he crossed the threshold, something cold caressed his cheek. 'What?' He jumped and dropped the saucer. A blob of hot wax landed on his foot. But the searing heat did not even register. For the room ahead, he saw, was peopled with shapes.

The dining table stretched, eating up most of the room. There were ten chairs, tall and stately, hovering around the expanse of teak. In the corner was a tallboy on top of which a lantern had always rested. Mukundan inched his way toward it, striking one match after the other. The lantern wick was brittle with disuse. He shook the lantern and heard the faint lapping sound of kerosene swishing at the bottom. He held the match to the wick till it caught fire. The scent of freshly dug earth filled his nostrils. The overpowering fragrance of crushed grass and mounds of dormant soil newly dug. When he turned, he saw them. Sitting there watching him, immobile, silent, but with accusing eyes. All five of them. Balammaven, Ammuma, and his three cheriyammas. Their faces turned toward him, their arms resting on the table. Watching.

'Leave me alone,' he screamed, and slumped to the floor.

And then the whispering began. 'How can we? You are the one holding us back. How can we leave without her? Set her free and we'll leave forever.'

The whispers died. When he opened his eyes, there wasn't anybody there. He sniffed the air for the loamy scent; instead he could only smell the damp that was everywhere in the house. He pulled out a chair and sat with his head in his hands. His legs felt weak and he needed a drink.

Mukundan retraced the way he had come, back to the stairwell, past the ferocious-faced divinity and the glum ancestors. The dining-room door slammed shut. He had forgotten how powerful the draft could be when it funnelled through the corridor. He felt his way to the staircase. He needed to go back upstairs for the bottle and the torch. But mostly for the bottle.

He touched the wall by the stairs and felt a warm stickiness on his fingers. Almost as if in a dream, he slid his fingers over the spot once again, and something warm and moist slid down into his palm. He raised his fingers to his tongue. The rusty taste of blood filled his mouth. Blood that had been coursing through veins moments ago. And he remembered what they had told him about his mother. Of how she had smashed her forehead against the banister as she fell, splattering the wall with her blood and filling the house with her anguish. A low keening echoed through the room. Of a woman gasping for life as her blood drained away. Of agony that went beyond physical trauma. He felt his knees buckle.

A long while later he drifted back into consciousness. When he opened his eyes, he saw her. She was perched halfway up the staircase. She looked as she did when he had seen her last, a month before she died. Her long hair, streaked with silver, was coiled into a loose knot at the nape of her neck. She was wearing a spotless cream mundu and veshti with a narrow green-and-gold border. The hakoba blouse with its gently puffed sleeves made her arms seem even more frail. The ruby earrings glinted sedately, while in her nose a lone diamond sparkled.

The evening before he left for Shoranur to board the train to Trichy, she had clutched at his arm and pleaded one more time, 'Take me with you, son. I am so unhappy here.' Mukundan had hesitated before he replied. His mother no longer tried to hide how terrified she was of his father. When he was a boy, she had tried to shield him from Achuthan Nair's cruelty. She had tried to make him believe that tyranny was simply another expression of love and concern. Not any more. Now when she spoke of her husband, it was with a bitterness that made Mukundan, as much as he detested his father, cringe.

'How can I, Amma?' he had said, gently loosening her fingers from his arm. 'I share a room with another bachelor. I can't just take you there and expect him to move out. Give me a little time, and I'll find us a house we can live in.'

'Amma,' he whimpered now and reached out for her. 'Amma, I am here.'

She moved her face so that it emerged from the shadows. Her eyes glittered; but there was no warmth there, only a remoteness. When she spoke, her voice was cold and grainy. 'Where were you when I needed you? You could have rescued me, but you chose not to.'

The night whirled around him. This isn't happening to me. It is the rum. I'm drunk, I know I'm drunk. He began reciting the names of the months. January. February. March.

'Mukunda!' Her voice rang through the room. 'Look at me. Do you think you can wish me away just as your father did? This time I won't leave until I'm ready.'

'You don't exist!' he screamed at the apparition. 'You are just a creature of my imagination. My mother died thirty-seven years ago. Why would she come back now?' Beads of sweat ran down his face.

It laughed. The creature that claimed to be his mother

burst into loud, harsh laughter. 'Here, touch me and you'll know if I exist,' it said, and held out its hand to him.

Mukundan's fingers crawled through the air, and when his skin collided with its, he felt a stillness swamp him. A sensation that had more to do with death than life. Suddenly its hand clamped around his wrist and pulled him forward till his face was almost touching the face that was his mother's and yet not hers. The rage and venom etched on it made it as hideous as a monster's.

'See this,' it moaned. 'See what you and your father did to me.' And as he watched in horror, it moved from the shadows, and he saw what was his mother's dying face. The temple on the right side had caved in; the skull was smashed, blood and brains oozing. The stench of decaying flesh rose from her, and suddenly bile filled his throat. He began to retch. Then the creature began to drag him up the staircase. 'No, Amma, let me go,' he begged.

But the fiend went about its task with the vigour of one in whom resentment had been building for ages. When they reached the top of the staircase, it said in a hollow voice, 'I want you to know the fear I felt when a hand smashed into my back, pushing me down. I want you to know what I saw when the floor reached out to slam my life away. I want you to feel the anguish I felt as I realized I was going to die before my time.'

'Amma, don't!' he screamed as he went hurtling down and the floor swung up to meet him.

When he awoke, through one of the half-open windows he could see the pale fingers of dawn wiping all traces of grey from the skies. The air was wet with rain and above the din of the crows, a crackling rose. The temple loudspeaker. Mukundan felt a tremendous sense of relief when he realized that he had survived the night.

The floor was cold beneath him. He dragged himself to

the window and held onto its bar for support as he levered himself up. He hobbled down the corridor to the new section. This was the only place in the house where he knew for certain that there would be no memories to haunt him. He closed the door behind him, shutting off the rest of the house and its tumultuous spirits.

In this room was everything he held precious. His books, his collection of tapes, his electric kettle, his gold watch, his Smith Corona typewriter, and an old maritime map. Also a framed photograph of all the members of his department taken at his send-off party. And his cane armchair painted a turquoise blue.

He didn't need the rest of the house. He could live in comfort in this new section he had arranged to build three months ago. Tonight, Mukundan swore to himself, he would drag in a bed from one of the downstairs bedrooms, make it with his own bed linen, drink himself senseless, and put an end to the memories that were tearing him apart.

The red light on the electric kettle glowed. The power was back. He filled the kettle with water from a pitcher. He needed a shave and a cup of tea before he could think about what to do next. He examined himself in the mirror. There really was only one word to describe his looks—average.

He was of average height, average build, and his facial features were average too. Eyes that were neither too big nor too small. Framed by eyebrows that weren't bushy or sparse. A nose that wasn't hooked or flat. Even the pencil-line moustache with its stray grey hair, which he touched up with an eyebrow pencil, did only what it was meant to do. Fill the space between the upper lip and the nostrils without attempting to create an impact. With his black-metal-rimmed spectacles, he looked what he was: a respectable middle-aged man.

Anyone asked to describe Mukundan would have found

it very difficult. There were no moles or scars. Nor any particularly exceptional feature that gave him a distinct identity. When he had been much younger, he'd had a certain charm brought about by the amalgamation of youth and pleasant features. Now he saw before him a man with tired eyes, a slackening mouth, and leathery skin blotched with grey stubble. He still had a good head of hair though, and as he traced his hairline he spotted the bruise. The skin was broken. He touched the clot and felt the swelling around it. How had he got it?

He took his clothes off. There were purple bruises on his calves. Suddenly he felt the familiar knot of fear tighten within him. Had he in a drunken stupor missed his step, fallen down, and dreamed it all? Or had something happened here the night before? He returned to the room and slumped into his chair, hugging his knees to his chest. What was he going to do?

Outside he could hear the brisk movements of the broom as Neeli swept the ground. All presence of life had to be banished from the front yard. Tufts of stubborn grass that reared their green heads through the rocklike earth were ruthlessly tugged out and thrown onto the same heap as the dried mango leaves and twigs. It was ingrained into Neeli, and several Neelis before her, that the first chore of the day was to sweep the front yard clean. Everything else could wait. For to let grass, weeds, or anything green flourish in the front yard was to tell the world that here was a home that had no hope; here was a family plunged in debt; here was desperation and unhappiness.

Mukundan ran his fingers through his hair and thought bleakly of a dream he used to have. Of a well-laid-out garden and a manicured lawn where he would sit and drink the day's first cup of tea. Like everything else, he could see that dream too crumble into dust. Except that in his front yard, there was no room even for dust. For when Neeli finished sweeping the yard clean, she would mix cowdung and water and sprinkle it all over the ground to settle the dust.

He poured hot water into a cup, added some sugar, put a tea bag into it, and waited for the tea to seep. For the water to turn a murky brown. For the day to move on.

3

The Craggy Face of Steadfastness

Later in the day Mukundan Nair watched from the window as Krishnan Nair came trudging up the hill. In his saffron-colored mundu and grey half-sleeved shirt, he could have been just another old man. Until you saw the expanse of his shoulders and the jut of his two upper incisors. They stuck out of his mouth like twin boulders, grimly hanging onto his jaws from where their companions had long since fallen.

As a young man the fleshiness of his face and the abundance of hair on his upper lip had camouflaged to a certain extent the magnificence of his teeth. But as he grew older and his cheeks sank in and he took to shaving his moustache off, the teeth seemed to acquire a prominence that overshadowed the rest of his personality. Krishnan Nair's teeth conjured up images of tenacity, of a stubbornness of purpose. So much so that the villagers had taken to referring to anything immovable or unshakable as Krishnan Nair's teeth.

They might never have helped him bite a thread off, let alone tear a piece of food, but they were a legend in themselves. Several generations of children grew up fearing the jut of his teeth. When a child persisted in shoving his thumb into his greedy mouth in spite of blandishments followed by warnings, his mother would refer to Krishnan Nair's teeth and say, 'Do you want to look like that? Then go ahead and suck on your thumb. See if I care.'

Krishnan Nair made sufficient noise opening and closing the metal gate to give notice of his arrival. He walked up the steps leading into the new section and began to dust the top of the low wall that enclosed the veranda. Mukundan watched him in silence. He knew that the old man was as uncomfortable with the situation as he was. Once upon a time they had been friends. As a boy, he used to tag behind Krishnan Nair, who had a hero's body and the manner of a child. Mukundan could talk to him, confide in him and question him without having his head bitten off, as his father was prone to do. And now here he stood, at a loss for words. What was he supposed to say?

'So what was the problem at home?' Mukundan began and stopped abruptly. It sounded like a grouse to his own ears. 'I hope it's all sorted out,' he amended, trying to sound as amiable as he knew how.

'My grandson fell out of a moving bus. We had to rush him to a hospital in Thrissur for surgery. They discharged him only yesterday,' Krishnan Nair said. He ran a finger over the top of the waist-high wall that edged the veranda and dusted it methodically with the towel he always had with him. Indoors it hung over his left shoulder, and outdoors he tied it around his head like a turban to shield himself from the sun. He perched himself on the low wall and looked around with interest.

'How have you been coping?' he inquired.

'Not too well,' Mukundan replied. 'But Neeli's been a great help,' he added as an afterthought.

Krishnan Nair sat up straight. 'What do you mean?' he barked.

'Well, she's been cleaning and dusting, sweeping and washing, and has managed to get the house in some order.'

'What? You shouldn't have let her,' he said worriedly, coming closer to the chair Mukundan was seated on. 'She's a young woman, and you know how people talk around here. And how could you forget the existence of the Macchilamma? Don't you know that when the mother goddess chose to make the macch inside this house, her home, she laid down certain conditions? A lamp in the granary all day and an offering of fowl's blood once a year. She is a fierce goddess and is offended easily. She has to be treated with respect and caution. If you anger her, she will not rest till the blood of someone in the family flows. So you need to be careful whom you let into the house.'

'My father doesn't believe in segregating people by their caste. He has always let everybody in—as long as they are clean,' Mukundan retorted, stung by the old man's censure.

For the first time since Krishnan Nair had walked in, he looked into Mukundan's eyes. A long moment later, he said quietly, 'A lot of things your father did and continues to do are not right.'

As he spoke Mukundan saw a queer sadness creep into Krishnan Nair's eyes and spill into his voice. Instinctively he knew that Krishnan Nair was talking about his father's abandonment of his mother.

For a while Krishnan Nair didn't speak. His great teeth, now yellow with age, glinted like ivory in the sunlight. Then he pulled himself together. Mukundan could almost see the mental shrug. 'Well, now that I'm here, you don't have to worry. I'll handle everything.'

Mukundan looked up in surprise. He hadn't expected Krishnan Nair to resume his old role. Krishnan Nair had always been the caretaker of the house and the many acres of paddy fields the family had owned. Some years ago, when Mukundan had come to the village, on his way back from an office tour, he had sold all the paddy fields to Power House Ramakrishnan.

Power House Ramakrishnan had always lived on the fringes of poverty and had never owned anything of significance in his life. When a lottery ticket changed him into a rich man, perhaps the richest man in the village, the first thing he decided to do was to acquire land. So when he heard rumours that the paddy fields were up for sale, he sent an emissary with an attaché case full of money to settle the

deal on the spot. In one stroke, he saw himself rise to the
ultimate rung inhabited by the people who ate the rice
harvested from their own fields. Moreover, by buying the
land that for generations had belonged to Mukundan's
family, he would be buying himself a position in the village.

Krishnan Nair had been heartbroken by Mukundan's
decision. But Mukundan had adamantly refused to
entertain any discussion on the matter. He had given
Krishnan Nair five thousand rupees from the money he had
received for the land. Krishnan Nair had given him a
withering look and asked, 'Is this my pension for devoting
all my life to the land? How could you give up your heritage
so easily?'

Mukundan had paused in the middle of his packing and
said, 'What am I going to do with all this when I die? Can I
take it with me? Do I have children for me to safeguard my
heritage and keep it intact for them?'

The old man looked at Mukundan's face searchingly.
Sometimes he still saw in him traces of the boy whose spirit
had been bruised and battered by his callous, domineering
father. 'It's not too late, even now. You could marry and
have children,' Krishnan Nair had said.

Mukundan had mumbled, 'It is much too late to talk of
all that now. Who will give his daughter to a
fifty-two-year-old man? And, if the purpose of the marriage
is progeny, then she will have to be young and of
childbearing age. Let's not talk about pointless things.'

Now all that was left was the house and the two acres of
land around it. Krishnan Nair was seventy-eight years old.
He needed rest, not the stewardship of a house older than he
was. Mukundan realized that as much as he needed
Krishnan Nair, he owed it to him to refuse his offer.

'I'll take care of the house,' Krishnan Nair repeated.

'I don't think so. It'll be too much for you to manage,'
Mukundan said, thinking of the rooms that seemed to
absorb dust by the minute; the long, dark corridors that

housed many a representative of the insect world; and the endless things that had to be done to keep the house habitable. Like an insatiable female ghoul, it would drain Krishnan Nair of his blood, draw out his marrow, and ultimately kill him.

Krishnan Nair continued to sit there dangling his legs. Mukundan wondered what it was he wanted. Was Krishnan Nair waiting for some money to be pressed into his palm before he left? He made a quick calculation and realized he didn't have enough change. He decided to ask Krishnan Nair to come by after a day or two. He cleared his throat.

'Please,' Krishnan Nair whispered. 'The only thing left in my life are memories. When I am in this house, they cascade into my mind, one after the other. When I'm here, it seems like I am back in time when your mother was alive and this house was what I thought paradise would be like.'

Mukundan blinked. He felt his throat constrict. 'I didn't say you are not welcome here. I just thought it would be too much for you at your age,' he said hastily.

'I will be all right. I'll find an elderly Nair woman who can come in every day to cook and clean inside the house. And Neeli can do all the other chores.' Krishnan Nair's voice brightened once he realized he wasn't being asked to leave.

'What about your wife? Won't she object?' Mukundan asked.

'She doesn't care one way or the other,' Krishnan Nair mumbled as he walked down the steps. He had already slipped into the skin of the caretaker. All Mukundan had to do was let him do what he did best.

Late in the evening, as Mukundan went around switching on every single light in the house, Krishnan Nair followed his trail. When the last bulb was glowing, he nodded his head in approval. 'This house has been asleep far too long. The last time there was so much light and life in here was when your mother was alive.'

Mukundan smiled in surprise. He had been certain that the old man would grumble about the electricity bill and the thoughtless extravagance.

When they returned to the new section, he hovered by the doorway waiting to be invited inside. He looked at the room, the bookshelf crammed tight with books, the music system swathed in a cover; the armchair and the bed covered in a yellow-and-red block-printed sheet. Mukundan flicked a piece of lint off the pillow and smoothed the sheet. He opened the cupboard and took out the bottle. 'Will you have a drink?' he asked Krishnan Nair.

'A small drink,' the old man indicated with his thumb and forefinger.

Mukundan walked into the dining-room alcove where the fridge hummed like a giant beast slumbering, breathing heavily. One of the first things he had unpacked had been the fridge. He filled the ice bucket with cubes and rinsed out two glasses. He put it all on a tray, went back to the room and settled down in his armchair.

Krishnan Nair covered the mouth of the glass with his palm when Mukundan began to spoon out the ice, 'No, not for me. I don't like to ruin the taste of good rum with water.'

He sat on the edge of the bed and cupped the glass in his palms. The night sounds crept into the room. Crickets that sounded as if they were sharpening knives. The swish of whips as leaves rustled. The devil bird that shrieked poo-ah, poo-ah! He seemed totally unperturbed by the murky gloom that lay thick in and around the house. Mukundan swallowed a mouthful and felt it burn its path down.

'When you have the whole house, why have you crammed all your possessions into this one room?' Krishnan Nair's voice intruded into his thoughts.

Mukundan peered into his glass and feigned indifference. 'I'm not too comfortable elsewhere in the house. I haven't been used to a lot of space in the houses I've lived in. The factory quarters were never palatial. Living room, two bedrooms, kitchen, bathroom. And,' Mukundan added shamefacedly, ' I like to have all my favourite things around me.'

Krishnan Nair nodded. 'You were the same as a boy. When you got something new, whether it was a school textbook, a whistle from the pooram stalls or an odd-shaped stone, you slept with it beneath your pillow,' he said. When his drink was over, he rose from the bed. 'I'll fix your dinner. You take your time over your drink. Don't rush it or you'll be drunk before you know it.'

Mukundan heard him flip the towel he wore over his shoulder as he walked down the corridor. It was as if he were a callow adolescent once again and Krishnan Nair the man he used to be: strong, capable, and in control. Mukundan wanted to tell him, Look at me, I'm an old man too. You don't have to protect me any more.

The smell of eggs cooking wafted into the room. His stomach rumbled hungrily. He went in search of the aroma. Krishnan Nair smiled wryly as he inspected the contents of the dishes on the table. 'Why don't you sit down? I'll serve,' he said.

Mukundan pulled out a chair, and another one alongside. 'Join me,' he said. When he saw the hesitation in the old man's eyes, he lied, 'I can't eat alone.' Krishnan Nair stirred the kanji thoughtfully. Then he slid into the chair beside Mukundan and began pushing the dishes in his direction. He watched Mukundan as he ladled the gruel into the shallow white enamel dish with its blue rim. 'Try the eggs,' he urged. 'I brought them from home; they're not the tasteless poultry farm variety.'

The eggs had been scrambled with chopped onions, green chillies, ginger and curry leaves. Coconut oil glistened on every morsel, and in the white porcelain dish the creamy yellow morsels seemed the most delicious food Mukundan had ever seen. When he praised the simple dishes, Krishnan

Nair gleamed with pride. 'I've asked for a woman to come in from tomorrow. When she does, the food will be much better. I'll ensure that she cooks just like your mother did.'

Krishnan Nair went about his ablutions as silently as he could. Mukundan heard the rolling out of the grass mat and the flat fall of the mattress on it. The slicing of air as he stretched out the sheet. The muffled thumping of the pillow. And then the long drawn out yawn that echoed in the cavernous innards of the corridor. Krishnan Nair had said that was where he would like to sleep. 'I don't like ceiling fans or table fans or any fan, for that matter. It's much too noisy and if I sleep in a room where there is a fan on, I catch a cold,' he said eyeing the whirring blades of the fan suspiciously. 'If I leave the window open at the end of the corridor, I'll get a nice breeze and I'll sleep well. I don't know how you sleep under that thing. It's the same in my house. My children can't sleep without the fan on.'

Mukundan clicked the light off and got between the sheets. A cool breeze blew in through the half-open window. His eyelids drooped. Tonight he was determined to sleep, to make up for all those other nights he had stayed awake.

He closed his eyes.

A loud shriek pierced the silence of the night. A few seconds later, the laughter began. Demonic peals that rang through the room, reverberating from all sides, filling his head, clamping his throat so hard that he couldn't breathe. He reached for the door to escape from what he knew was coming next. But the door wouldn't budge. The huge wooden wedge had slipped into the sleeve and no matter how much he shook it or pounded on it, the door stayed stuck. Then he saw the figure, the flash of the diamond, the eyes that burned with anger, and he began to scream, 'No, Amma, let me go!'

Mukundan woke up shaking, to find Krishnan Nair crouched near his bed.

'What happened?' Krishnan Nair asked gently.

Mukundan sat up. His hands were trembling, and he felt sweat running down his face.

'What's wrong?' Krishnan Nair asked again.

When Mukundan could speak, his voice came out in a croak, 'It's been the same every night ever since I came here. They wait for me in the corridors. I don't know if I'm dreaming. Or if I really see them.'

'Who is "they"?' Krishnan Nair whispered.

'All of them. Balammaven, Ammuma and the cheriyammas. But at least they don't hate me like she does.'

'Who is "she"?' he asked, stroking Mukundan's head.

'My mother,' Mukundan whispered, burrowing his face into the pillow. 'She sits on the staircase every night waiting for me. No matter how much I try not to go there, she lures me to the stairs and then she blames me for what happened to her. She says I could have prevented her death. As she speaks, she gets angrier and angrier. Night after night, she tells me she wants me to know what she went through and so she drags me to the top of the staircase and pushes me down. I wake up screaming.

'It seems so real that I don't know if it really happened. Or did I dream it all? Sometimes even in broad daylight I catch glimpses of her wandering through this empty house,' he ended and felt more hunted than ever.

Krishnan Nair rose from his haunches and went to stand by the window. At his age, he still stood tall and erect. When he turned to speak to Mukundan, there was pain in his eyes. 'Your mother could have prevented what was happening to her. The heartbreak. The humiliation. But she chose to remain a victim. So don't go about feeling guilty for what happened to her.'

'When I came home, she asked me to take her away. She said she was unhappy, and she wanted to be someplace far

away from where he was. But I didn't. I was scared of my
father. I didn't have the courage to confront him. So I made
excuses. I said I would have to wait till I was allotted a
family quarter. I left her here all alone at his mercy,'
Mukundan said, anguish thickening his voice.

'You were young. Just a boy pretending to be a
grown-up. Your father is a formidable man. Even at this
age, I am filled with a strange nervousness and find myself
stammering and faltering when I speak to him. So how
could you, a mere boy, have had the courage to oppose him?
Anyway, how could you have known what was going to
happen here?' They say when it is time for a soul to leave, it
goes and nothing can hold it back.'

'In my dreams, she tells me that she wasn't ready to leave.
She blames me for her death that she says happened before
it was meant to.'

'Have you ever heard anyone say, "I'm happy to die
now"? Your father is almost ninety years old. Ask him if
he's ready to die yet and he'll say no,' Krishnan Nair said
quietly. 'Only the hopeless and the enlightened await their
own death.'

'What about the rumours?' Mukundan persisted.

'Who knows what really happened? Her death was
something you and I couldn't have prevented, no matter
what we did. So why then should you blame yourself or
even feel responsible for not being here with her? Go to
sleep. I'll wait here by your side till you do. And don't
worry, I'm in the room next door.'

Krishnan Nair sank into the armchair. In the pale light of
the moon, only the contours of his still-muscular body were
visible. As a young man he would till the soil until his
rippling muscles glistened with sweat. His palms were
ridged with callouses, and his shoulders rivalled the expanse
of the plough he wielded as if it were a frail toy.

Krishnan Nair had had the strength to make the most
barren of lands blossom. His face was now bathed in

shadows. Mukundan looked at Krishnan Nair and wondered what it was that bonded him to this house and its inmates. And he wondered if he would feel the same way if he knew. . .

4

The Mountain That Was As Flat As a Football Field on Top

From behind the Pulmooth mountain, the sun peeped out surreptitiously. The trees were wreathed in cobwebs of gossamer mist; the paddy fields shivered in the chill of the dawn breeze and the cocks waited anxiously in their coops. One by one the cocks raised their heads and searched the air for the warmth of the sun's lips. Unable to contain their impatience any longer, they puffed their chests, stretched their throats, and crowed lustily, beckoning the sun to make intimate contact with their proud red combs.

The sun took a deep breath and began its morning chores. With a long-handled sunbeam, it dusted the veils of mist off the trees. Then it set about warming the paddy tops before knocking on the doors of the various coops. The air filled with a faint throb that grew in intensity as it came down the hill: Duk. Duk. Duk. The thumping of Majid's Royal Enfield Bullet as it wound its way down the dirt road to his house. Parrots raked the skies with their screeching, and doves gurgled from within the hollows in the walls of the well.

Shankar removed the wooden planks with which at night he turned his tea shop into a matchbox. As the planks went down, the sun darted in crumbling the mask of the night. Shankar liked to watch the sun frolic in the tea shop.

He took out the two wooden benches and positioned them at the entrance. He hung up the plantain bunches which the sun eyed lasciviously. He tuned the radio for the early morning news broadcast. Minutes later the samovar began to hiss. Shankar's Tea Club was open for business.

Shankar rinsed out the glasses and arranged them in sentinel rows. The sun, tired of caressing the plump, inert contours of the plantains, turned its attention to the glasses. Born coquettes, the glasses sparkled when the sun flirted with them. A fickle admirer, however, the sun disappeared when the first bus from town ground to a halt outside Shankar's tea shop. Shankar walked to the bus to pick up the bundle of newspapers that arrived in the bus every day, and plonked it on the counter from which he surveyed his domain.

Shankar's Tea Club stood at the crest of the hill. Opposite it were the few shops that catered to the needs of the village. A fish shop that sold various kinds of dried fish. An all-purpose store that stocked rice, sugar, tea, oil, bolts of cloth printed with gigantic flowers in oranges and mauves against lush green leaves, notebooks, batteries, and even condoms. A rice mill, the barbershop, and a little cubbyhole in which the lone tailor of the village cut and sewed. The last three shops were all housed in the building Hassan had built some years ago when he came back from Kuwait for good during the Gulf War. A hundred feet away, as if distancing itself from all such commercial activity, stood the post office.

Achuthan Nair had always believed himself to be a progressive soul. Long before the village had even heard of a new-fangled idea, he would have assimilated it into the fabric of their lives. When a post office was sanctioned for Kaikurussi, he took it upon himself to make everything possible to hasten its arrival in the village. He built a two-room house at the bottom of the garden and this, he decreed, would house the Kaikurussi post office. No one dared ask why not somewhere else more convenient to the whole village. And from that hub soon, one by one, the rest of the shops sprouted.

Many years later, when the people who ran the two buses that plied to and fro between Kaikurussi and the town came to inspect the route, they looked at the motley collection of shops and jeered, 'The city, ha!'

The name stuck. It rolled off the tongue easily. It was so much simpler to say, 'I'm off to the city for a tea and a beedi' than 'I'm going to the shop opposite Shankar's Tea Club for a beedi'. If Shankar resented losing his landmark status, he hid it well. After all, as people waited for the bus, they strolled in for a cup of tea and some gossip.

The house stood halfway up the hill, crouched on the land like an old man bent over. Aging by the minute, but seemingly indestructible by time. Mukundan looked at the house and tried to fathom what it was about it that disturbed him so. The cobwebs had been pulled down, the dust swept away, the floors mopped, and the woodwork made to gleam. And yet the house continued to wear the look of a chronic sufferer. Its gloom enhanced by the trees that crowded around it like commiserating aunts. A beard of unkempt grass almost thigh-high covered the terraced hillside that was broken only by gnarled old trunks of trees that neither bloomed nor bore fruit.

For a moment Mukundan thought the house raised its hooded eyelids and peered at him. Now that I have you in my clutches once again, there is no way you can escape, it seemed to say with diabolical pleasure. He shook his head in annoyance and told himself not to be silly. He decided to go down the hill. There was a certain pleasure in breaking off a dried old branch from a tree nearby and swinging it like a machete through the grass as he tried to trace a forgotten path.

'Why don't you use the road?' Krishnan Nair called out. Mukundan pretended not to hear him and walked on.

The grass scratched his calves as he stumbled over the

stones. Suddenly the hill became steeper, ending abruptly in a high precipice of mud. Beyond it was a deep ditch. Alongside, the road ran on less dangerously. He wished for a moment that he had chosen the road.

The fields were everywhere. Endless shades of green that stretched into the horizon on one side and the foot of the Pulmooth mountain on the other. Speckled only with the bright blouses of the women as they stood ankle-deep in water-logged mud and pulled out the young paddy plants. When a breeze blew, the tops of the paddy rippled and turned the sheets of sedate jade into gleaming splashes of emerald. He knew that soon the sun would disappear behind thick grey clouds that would frown down unrelentingly. Then it would be time to seek the dry confines of the house. Until then he would stay here and look at the view he had banished from his memories for many years now.

Mukundan leaned against the trunk of an old tamarind tree. His left foot firmly planted in the mud, his right one sidling, in the manner of a furtive crab, on the dune-like indentations of the bark. For the past one week, he hadn't strayed from the boundary of the house. He had examined everything and everyone from a distance. It was as if he knew that if he were to let in a wave of warmth or a sense of bulk, then he would lose this dreamlike trance he had drifted into. In this hazy world, there was no room for cumbersome thoughts.

He turned the leaves over with his stick. When his eyes lit on a grey curve, he lazily pondered, Was it a twig or a dried leaf?

He looked around him thoughtfully. What is it about age that shears everything around of its grandeur? It was as if by simply growing old, he had dwarfed the universe and robbed it of its awe-inspiring qualities. Even the Pulmooth mountain was no longer that huge mountain that reached into the sky insurmountably.

There was a time when the wooded slopes and steep paths of the mountain were forbidden to him. 'Little boys are not allowed to climb the Pulmooth mountain. For once you have climbed it, then in the eyes of the village you are a man. Which means they will expect you to do manly things,' Krishnan Nair had told him each time he begged to be taken along on the eve of the harvest festival.

He had to wait till he was twelve before he was allowed to join the men when they trudged up the mountain on the day before Onam. The muscles in his calves had ached as he trekked up, but he had refused all offers of help. He had waited for this for a long time, dreaming of the day he would scale the Pulmooth mountain and see for himself the wonder of the mountaintop; he had heard the men describe it time and again. And then when they were on top of the mountain, he felt a sweep of disappointment cloud his vision. It was as flat as a football field.

'Do you see that?' Krishnan Nair pointed out to him a strip of water that slimed through the brown fields of the neighbouring village several miles away. 'That's the Kunti river.'

Mukundan didn't know what he had expected to find there. But in his imagination the top of the mountain had been a peak that spiked high into the sky beyond everyone's reach. A needle's point that only he would be able to scale. And he dreamed of the villagers describing his valiant efforts to his father. Of how Achuthan Nair would ruffle his hair affectionately and say to him, 'I'm proud of you, my boy. Who did I say I'm proud of?'

Mukundan along with the rest of the village knew that Achuthan Nair ended every conversation with a question. The listener was meant to answer the question so that Achuthan Nair knew for certain that the gospel truth of his words had been understood by the inferior intelligence of the person standing before him. But this time Mukundan would have gushed happily, 'Of your son. Of me.'

The flat brown plain almost made him want to cry. He swallowed and retorted, 'It looks like a gutter to me.'

Krishnan Nair placed a hand on his head and swivelled him around to face him. 'It is all in your mind. If you want to look around you and see mountains, forests, and oceans, you will. Or else you will see little mounds of earth, sparse bushes, and piddling streams.' A peacock screamed and rose in the air.

Mukundan moved away from the rest of the men and went to sit on a cashew tree bough. And as he sat there, he watched the magnificence of the landscape grow. There was a world beyond the valley he lived in. A world he would someday escape to. Far away from his father. Far away from the village.

The next time he climbed Pulmooth mountain, Meenakshi went with him. They had sneaked out in the afternoon so that Meenakshi could see for herself this splendid world he had described to her. By the time they reached the top, sweat was running down their backs and they were panting with thirst. But they forgot all about parched throats and aching legs as they looked down on the rest of the world. In a voice hushed with awe, Meenakshi whispered, 'Someday, I'm going that far.' And she pointed to the horizon that shimmered in the heat.

'Me too,' he whispered back.

They sat in the shade of a cashew tree catching their breath. 'Do you think that life will be different elsewhere?' Meenakshi voiced the doubt that had niggled in his mind ever since he had glimpsed heaven from the top of Pulmooth mountain.

'I don't know,' he said thoughtfully. 'But it must be infinitely preferable to this.'

'I guess we will never know until we leave.' Meenakshi stood up. It was time to go back. If they were missed and someone found out what they had been up to, there would be endless recriminations and accusations.

They ran down the hill. A boy in a pair of khaki shorts that owed their existence to a pair of trousers long discarded; a girl in a skirt patterned with flower sprigs, a shabby pink blouse, and two long shiny plaits. At the bottom of the hill, they stopped for a drink of water from a well by the paddy fields. The water was cold and sweet. They gulped down mouthfuls, sluiced their faces, hands and legs and then by silent consent went back separately.

Other children had brothers and sisters, companions to share their giggles and nightmares with. The wonder of a peacock's feather, the triumph of bringing down a mango with one perfectly pitched stone, the agony of scraped knees and splinters under the skin. Mukundan had Meenakshi—his girl cousin once removed; companion and soul mate. They crawled together as babies. They paddled together in the pool and when they were a little older, they learned to swim together. Diving from the top of the stone wall, slicing through the water and surfacing at almost the same moment from different corners of the pool. When they were three years old, Ezuthachan, who ran the local primary school, was invited to conduct their vidyarambham ceremony. With a gold ring, he traced the sacred letter *Hari Sri* on their tongues and guided their forefingers through a plate of raw rice to form the letters that invoked the blessing of the gods. By word and deed, they were deemed fit and old enough to acquire learning. And so together they began studying the alphabet, sharing a book and a necklace of consonants and vowels. They recited the multiplication tables and long poems about steam engines in one breath. They knew each other's bodies and minds as well as they knew their own.

And then suddenly one day they were considered to be too old to spend so much time in each other's company. Mukundan was given a room to himself. He was asked to put aside his short pants and switch to a mundu. He was encouraged to bathe with the rest of the men and asked to stay away from the pool when the women bathed. As for Meenakshi, she was forbidden to go wandering around the fields and cashew groves as she once used to in Mukundan's company. 'Put aside your books and fancy talk. It is time you learned to cook,' her mother nagged. She frowned whenever she saw them huddled together and invented excuses to separate Meenakshi from Mukundan. When Mukundan came looking for her, she would whisper into Meenakshi's ear that it didn't matter whether the leaf fell on the thorn or the thorn fell on the leaf, it was the leaf that was hurt for life. So sprang a distance between them, which they furtively tried to bridge. And because their meetings were so infrequent, they began to function as two separate beings.

For the first time in their lives, they had secrets from each other. His dreams were no longer hers. Her plans no longer his. When they met, they never had enough time to say everything they wanted to. The first few precious moments were spent trying to regain the closeness that they once had. It was frustrating for the two of them, and they weren't old enough to understand it or even know how to handle it, and so once in a while they fought. Mukundan never won those fights. His need to be with her was more than hers. They fought in whispers but there were times when he couldn't control his anger. Then he would seize her arm and press his fingers into its softness, enjoying seeing the pain fill her eyes with salt. Sometimes she would let him draw his secret vicious pleasure from her pain. Sometimes she would raise her foot and expertly kick him in his balls. Painful enough so he would let her go and light enough to cause no real injury. But their differences, like their plans to escape, were a secret.

5

Seeking to Escape

Meenakshi never managed to escape. At first Mukundan was the one who was going to take her away. A tacit understanding they had arrived at as an aftermath of several humid afternoons spent together. It was to be the reward for the times she let him grope the curves of her breasts and tease the nubs into nibbly nuts that invited his tongue, taunted his mouth, and flared his already itinerant senses. Once, a hundred times, a thousand times.

Behind the haystacks and beneath the dense foliage of the tamarind trees with their teardrop leaves that danced around them like yellow butterflies, he bruised her lips with his. Tasting the tartness of the cashew apple juice there. Running his tongue on the teeth of her need to flee the confines of their world.

When Mukundan left Kaikurussi, Meenakshi dwindled into a memory he preferred not to dwell upon. Thinking of her aroused many emotions, chief among them guilt. It was easier to relegate her into some corner of his mind that he rarely visited.

When he met her next, it seemed to him she had done the same; dismissed their adolescent fumblings as a part of the growing-up process. There was no bitterness, no reference to the past, no dredging up of forgotten promises. But when his palms sought to span her waist, she held them between her hands and thrust them away gently murmuring, 'No, Mukunda.' And when he persisted, 'No.'

Thereafter, each time he saw her, she had donned a new role in life. She was forever seeking an avenue of escape. But somehow it eluded her.

When he came home for the first time after he was appointed as a lower division clerk in an explosives factory in Trichy, she was nowhere to be seen. 'Where's Meenakshi?' Mukundan asked his mother.

'I don't know what's wrong with your cousin . . .' his mother began, lowering her voice, worry crinkling her forehead.

His father who walked in just then threw up his arms and scowled furiously, 'I want no mention of that brazen hussy in this house. She's caused more trouble than ten elephants on a rampage. As for the humiliation . . .' He ground his teeth and walked away.

Meenakshi had become a Naxalite. Armed with books on revolutions and driven by the mythical powers of Stalin and Lenin, Meenakshi had pledged to cleanse the earth of bourgeois vermin. And her first target of attack was Achuthan Nair—Mukundan's father, her uncle. Feudal landlord. Tyrant. Master of oppression.

She and her group incited the labourers to rebel. When that didn't work, haystacks were set ablaze; cows let loose in ready-to-be-harvested paddy fields and irrigation ditches gutted with mud. To them Achuthan Nair was the system, and these were some ways of upsetting what he represented. Mukundan often wished that instead they had taken a sickle and slaughtered his father.

Pulmooth mountain was where they held their secret meetings. Meenakshi went up the mountain late in the evenings and huddled with the rest of them around the flickering flames of the fire. She thought she had finally found companions who would help her escape.

Elsewhere Naxalites were sending out ripples of fear. Policemen were butchered, landlords killed in broad daylight; grain-laden barns went up in flames, and sons of rich merchants were kidnapped. No one dared question Meenakshi. She wore the threat of violence as a halo.

Achuthan Nair had given instructions that she was to be humoured and not irked. 'Let her do what she wants, come home when she wants, consort with whom she pleases. Just ignore her and that way we'll come to no harm.'

But Achuthan Nair really had nothing to fear. Meenakshi's group, though driven by ideals, was not bloodthirsty. None of them had witnessed an atrocity, let alone suffered any kind of injustice. They had no moral outrage to fuel them. They liked the idea of taking on the system while they sent out applications for jobs in faraway places. Besides, there was Meenakshi.

When she was angry, her bosom swelled even further, making her waist seem smaller than ever. The firelight threw a sheen on her skin that already had the gloss of well-polished teak. They were mesmerized. She preached hate and anger; it could have been love and charity for all they cared. For her, they were willing to lay down their lives. So what were a few haystacks?

Then Meenakshi fell in love. Balan was just two inches taller than she was. But he had fine features and the strong supple body of a Kathakali dancer. When Mukundan came home for a cheriyamma's funeral, she was still a bride who couldn't believe her fortune.

'He said,' she confided in him, when they had a moment to themselves, 'that he would come to fetch me as soon as he's found a house we can rent. Right now he stays with a relative, and there's no way he can take me there. He wants me to travel with him when they go on performance tours. Mukundan, I'm finally going to escape this prison.'

Balan never came back. The Kathakali troupe he worked with went to Europe. When they returned, he stayed back in Delhi where he was invited to teach in a famous dance school. Often his picture appeared in newspapers and once there was even a lengthy feature about him. But it contained no mention of Meenakshi. There were no letters, no guilt money, and no attempts to keep up the pretense that they were still married. All Meenakshi had were fleeting memories of the days they had spent together and a child that was the result of the few passionate nights.

Meenakshi stonily rejected the sympathy of aunts, cousins and neighbours because she realized that it was self-congratulatory. When people spoke to her about how best to deal with an errant husband, she knew they did so with a gladness of knowledge that no such trauma would visit their own lives. She pretended to listen with great humility while heaping a thousand curses on their heads. May a freak storm drown your hay! May your grandchild turn into a murderer and rapist! May your brother hang from the gallows! May your husband be bitten on his penis by a scorpion when he squats to urinate behind some bush!

'How can I abandon my mother?' she said in a flat, dull voice when Mukundan met her next, five years later. 'And there's the child to think of now. If I stay on at home, we'll manage. We don't have to worry about a roof over our heads and food when we are hungry.'

He looked away, not wanting her to see the pity in his eyes. She was proud, and his sympathy would only offend her. Mukundan was sitting on the post office wall. In the vacant room next to the post office, Meenakshi had carved out a place for herself. Painting it albumen white, duplicating the security of the womb, maybe, she had tried to take control of her life that, until now, had shown every sign of being as brittle as an eggshell.

Authorized by the panchayat, she was paid a small stipend to run a crèche. She had chosen to extend it to include slightly older children. Meenakshi was more educated than most other women in the village. When they sent their children to her, not only did she get them used to a school-like regimen in preparation for the year ahead, but she also wrought a minor miracle by teaching them their alphabet. It freed mothers of this most irritating of tasks that would test even the most enthusiastic of dispositions and gave them the time to go about their chores or lie around doing nothing. In return, they paid her a small fee that helped supplement her income.

He watched Meenakshi as she stirred milk powder into a cauldron of simmering water. The milk powder was a gift from the government of some milk-rich nation for the malnourished, milk-hungry children of India. Most of it went into making tea, coffee, Horlicks and Ovaltine in restaurants and tea shops. Of the remainder that was left, some had found its way into Kaikurussi, and thereafter into Meenakshi's Balawadi, as the crèche was called.

A stench of rancid milk rose from the bubbling liquid. 'How do the children drink it?' Mukundan sniffed as she filled the glasses.

Meenakshi smiled. 'The alternative is kanji. How many glasses of rice gruel can a child drink without gagging? This at least tastes like milk.'

The children, including Mani, her son, took their glasses and drank the milk without protest. Over the children's heads their eyes met, and this time she looked away. 'Have you heard from him?' There, it was out, the question that had been hovering on his lips, an impatient bee ready to sting.

Her face turned blank. What you can't see you won't know. 'No,' she said, turning to wipe the milk moustache from a child's face.

Mukundan expected her to clam up, instead she continued as if she were reading out the weather bulletin. 'Vasu met him at the railway station two years ago. When Vasu asked him if he would be coming down to visit us, he said he was leaving for Delhi in two days' time and that he would try. Or else he would come the next time he passed through Shoranur.' When her eyes met his, they were furious. Mukundan realized with a pang that she probably had to answer this question every few days. 'Satisfied?' she spat out.

Meenakshi ran the crèche until Mani was old enough to go to school. Then she gave it up and set about becoming a shopkeeper. The albumen white walls were replaced with a businesslike blue. Mats were shunted back home and on the floor where once children lay, voluptuous golden bananas basked. Glass jars appeared, and instead of the alphabet charts on the walls, calendars of film stars were mounted.

Once a week she travelled to the town and stocked her shop. Bangles, ribbons, buttons, toffees, notebooks, pencils, batteries, embroidery threads, needles, headache remedies, tomatoes, eggs. Women wandered in for a box of matches and stayed all afternoon talking. They told her of husbands who came home drunk, of meddling mothers-in-law, of tight-fisted relatives. Meenakshi listened to it all. Very seldom did she offer any advice. Mostly she let them untangle their lives by themselves. She knew that if she kept them talking about themselves, they would forget to ask her the question she dreaded the most: 'Any news from him?' In the process she acquired a reputation for sagacity and wisdom. In time people forgot that she had ever been married or that her husband had abandoned her. And as the years passed, Meenakshi forgot how to smile with her eyes. Her lips would widen, the dimples would appear, but her eyes were dead. It was as if they had given up and knew that she would never leave.

Meenakshi. Of the fish-shaped eyes, and tiny waist. Of the honeyed tongue and ice-cold heart. Since he had returned to the village, he had yet to meet Meenakshi. Mukundan wondered what had kept her away. The chill of the morning was dissipating quickly and it was time he went back. When he turned for one more look at the horizon that was a silvery blue now, he heard his name being called. 'Mukundan.'

The voice was soft and familiar. He pivoted hastily and

looked straight into the aged eyes of Meenakshi. 'I was just thinking of you,' he said in delight.

'Yes, I know,' she said quietly. 'When I saw you looking into the distance, I was sure you would be thinking of the old times.'

His gaze faltered. Mukundan didn't want to be reminded of the past. Of when he had captured her waist within the circle of his palms and nuzzled his face in the skeins of her thick and gleaming hair. If she had mentioned it on purpose, he was determined not to show her that it had disturbed him. Instead he made an effort to sound as normal as he could and asked the polite nicety that was expected of him. 'So, how have you been?'

She murmured, 'As is to be expected.'

'What kind of an answer is that?' Mukundan demanded.

Meenakshi didn't say anything. They walked back to the house together in silence, and when they reached the low wall that enclosed the yard around the house, Mukundan noticed the man standing a little away in the shadows. He sucked in his breath in shock. 'What is he doing here?' he whispered fiercely.

She patted his arm as if he were the one who needed consoling. 'He fell ill. Tuberculosis of the spine. He couldn't dance any more and when they abandoned him, he remembered that I existed.'

Meenakshi had received a letter from Kotakkal some weeks ago. Balan had written to her pleading for forgiveness, beseeching her to at least visit him. For several days she kept the letter close to her, tucked into her blouse by day, beneath her pillow at night. Once in a while, as if she couldn't believe in its existence, she would unfold the letter and read it, trying to seek in the spidery writing the reason why he had sought her after so many years. A part of her wanted to rush to his side. To forgive and revive the dead marriage. To know once again the protective feel of a husband's arm thrown around her. To wake up in the morning and see him sleeping by her side. To lavish love and tenderness so that he would never leave her again. But there was another part of her that wanted to ignore the letter and punish him for all the years of loneliness he had caused her.

When Meenakshi went to Kotakkal, she saw a decrepit old man. Instead of the flamboyant paints Balan had worn as a second skin for so long, they had smeared his body with foul-smelling poultices. And she thought of the man that he used to be. The virility of Bheema, the sensuality of Krishna . . . She saw how weak and lonely he was. The men there did their best to heal his body. But they ignored his ego. No one told him how great a dancer he was or how his talent was so rare that it could only be God's gift. That was not part of their job. And so for the first time Balan realized he was nothing without his ability to dance.

'Don't you realize that he's going to be a burden on you for the rest of your life?' Mukundan's voice rasped, careless of the hurt he would inflict if overheard.

She pushed an errant strand of hair behind her ear and snapped wearily, 'So what's new?'

'But this time you had a choice.' Mukundan didn't know why he was arguing with her. It was her life. If she wanted to wear a millstone for a pendant, who was he to question her? Don't tell me you were planning to resume some of that old excitement, a little voice inside him taunted. Shut up, shut up, he elbowed the thought away.

She was staring at him. Her eyelids didn't flicker. His did and lost the battle. 'I know,' she said quietly. 'This time I could have said no. Which is why I said yes.'

Mukundan was baffled. Try as he might, he couldn't understand this girl companion of his. Where did it come from, this streak of steel that ran within her, straightening her back, tilting her head high, and sealing the cracks in her much-broken heart?

'Mukundan,' she broke into his contemplation about her, 'I have to go. I'm taking him to the Ayurvedic centre for a.

massage.' She paused as if she were trying to make up her mind, and then she said softly, 'I'll be back in the afternoon. Alone.'

He watched the two figures go down the road between the gleaming fields. The frail-spirited, meagre man and the ample-hearted, comely woman. That was the curse on Meenakshi. She was the one who would always need to be strong.

'How long do you plan to sit here?' Krishnan Nair sounded annoyed.

Mukundan smiled at him, trying to wipe the frown off his forehead. 'Meenakshi was here.'

'I know,' he sighed.

He looked at Krishnan Nair speculatively. He had to get rid of him for the afternoon. There was no way he could revive old fires with an audience. And old fires were what the afternoon's rendezvous was about. The long-drawn call of the oriole echoed through the air. Moments later the answer came from another bush. Thickets, bushes, bamboo clump, all of these seemed populated by forlorn birds filling the space with songs of loneliness. Suddenly a streak of brown flashed through the low branches of a tree that had draped itself over the low wall. An oriole. Sighting an oriole was a sign of good fortune to come.

How does good fortune come your way? Does it call on you in a soft familiar voice? Or does it steal into your home and drape itself around you like an invisible halo? Or does it fall into your lap and beg to be taken? Mukundan wondered where Meenakshi and the promise of her still-beautiful body fitted. Should he ignore what seemed to him was a blatant overture, a flirtation that bore the promise of fruition?

When he was what was considered a marriageable age, he was never certain of what it was he wanted in a woman. Beauty, intelligence, eloquent conversation, charm, grace . . . It was so much easier to consort with lesser women—on an hourly basis—while he waited for the perfect woman to come his way. There was no promise of happily ever after, no fear of disillusionment. When he met attractive women, he let their greed to grasp as much fulfilment as they could flourish. Most of these women—secretaries, office assistants and once even a schoolteacher—were just a few years younger than him, married and bored with their lives. They enjoyed him pursuing them, even wooing them discreetly. His affairs rarely went beyond a few clandestine couplings. But while it lasted, he revelled in the feeling that he was sexually interesting.

As Mukundan grew older, he realized his chances of finding the perfect woman were getting slimmer. They were all married or didn't care to tie themselves to a forty-year-old. So he advertised in the matrimonial columns, but the responses that came were from sad-looking, defeated women seeking to escape from the ignominy of spinsterhood. Remaining single seemed infinitely preferable to this. Besides, he had his friends, and he wasn't exactly lonely.

But when Mukundan hit the fifty mark and met a woman he would like to have been involved with, he found himself trying to see himself through her eyes. And, very often, he realized that she saw him as a nice old man; somebody helpless and probably impotent. A man she could talk to without worrying if he would pounce on her.

For many months now there had been no woman in Mukundan's life. Partly because he had built yet another line of defense against love—his fear of hurt. He created it out of fear as he watched Narendran die. He couldn't bear to lay himself open to such anguish once again.

But here was Meenakshi. Bearing the promise of her still magnificent body and handsome spirit. And a tag that read—No strings attached.

Mukundan waited for her. To avoid an embarrassing confrontation, he invented an errand that would keep Krishnan Nair out of the house all afternoon. The old man had left, grumbling to himself that he couldn't understand what the haste was all about. Or why he had to go right away to inquire about painting the house when it was raining.

Mukundan set about organizing the room for his tryst with Meenakshi in the afternoon. He covered the bed with a bright sheet so that it looked more like a divan, plumped the cushions, pulled shut the curtains so that the room was bathed in soft shadows. And then he put his favourite music on.

When Mukundan heard the latch lift, he reclined on the divan pretending to read. He didn't want her to know how eager he was.

She hesitated on the doorstep. He continued to keep his eyes on the book. She cleared her throat. He looked up and smiled, a half smile he had practised in front of the mirror. A bit of vagueness, as if he were surprised. A hint of sexual promise but mostly immense delight. She stared at him for a long moment and said shortly, 'Why do you look so surprised? I did tell you I was coming.'

He wiped that expression off and tried another òne. The worldly man making time for the old, forgotten provincial friend. Look, I'm very busy; I can hardly spare the time, but for you, anything . . .

She came in and sat on the bed. This was going all wrong. She was supposed to opt for the armchair when he—with another switch of expression, this time tender but mildly amorous—would say, 'Come here. Sit beside me. It's been so long.'

She looked at her palms for a moment and said, 'I need to talk to you. Could you please turn the music off?'

He sighed. This is what came of playing Mukesh's golden melodies. No one here knew how to appreciate it. He should have put on Yesudas, and she'd probably have swooned in his lap by now. He switched off the music and then, through the shadows, his fingers inched their way toward her. Mukundan cleared his throat. The words were all ready on his tongue—I need you too. But she continued in the flat tone that seemed to have become her spoken tone, 'I haven't met the targets for this year. I was wondering if you could help me.'

'What?' he yelped.

She turned in surprise, saw his fingers splayed in midmotion, and whispered, a horrified sound, 'What did you think I was coming here for?'

Mukundan felt blood rush to his face. 'What do you mean?' he stammered, trying to sound convincingly indignant.

'We were young then. A boy and a girl. We had no one else but each other. But I'm married and a grandmother. I know what every one in the village thinks, but I have been faithful to my husband. And I'm not going to change that, not even for you,' she said angrily, and then, as if she could no longer bear to be in the same room as him, she stood up to leave.

'I'm sorry,' he pleaded. 'I don't know what came over me,' he mumbled shamefacedly, 'what did you want to see me about?'

She opened her mouth to speak, then closed it again. For many minutes they stayed like that. Finally she walked to the door, saying, 'It can wait for another day.'

Mukundan watched her leave. Distress clung to her, dishevelling her near-perfect features into an untidy clutter. She had been slandered enough, and he had just added his bit to it. As she went through the gateway, Krishnan Nair came into view. He said something to her but she ignored him and walked past quickly.

He gave Mukundan a strange look and chortled, 'So Meenakshi's found her next victim, huh?'

'I don't understand,' Mukundan began. But Krishnan Nair gave him a disbelieving look and said, 'Are you telling me she came here and didn't sell you a policy?'

'I don't understand,' Mukundan repeated stupidly.

'Mukundan, that woman is an insurance agent. She's forced almost everyone in the village to take a policy they don't need. From Power House Ramakrishnan to Barber Nanu, she's spared no one. Perhaps the only two people in this village who are not insured are your father and I. You just wait! She's going to come to you with a quivering voice and a sob story of how if she doesn't meet her targets, there won't be money for food or Ayurvedic oil massages for her nincompoop husband. Don't tell me I didn't warn you.'

He shrugged and walked into the house while Mukundan stood there slumped in thought. So that was what it was all about. A sales pitch for an insurance policy.

6

The Echo of the Wooden Clogs

Mukundan was four years old when he first saw his father. Achuthan Nair had left for Burma when Paru Kutty was three months pregnant. At first she was supposed to accompany him. But when he saw the alarming frequency with which she threw up and heard her complain of tiredness every few hours, he decided she was an encumbrance he could do without in a distant land. 'I can't be saddled with an invalid for whom I'll have to be responsible every minute of the day,' he told a snivelling Paru Kutty.

She did her best to convince him that it was just the effect of pregnancy, but he wouldn't listen.

In fact, he turned it around as a point in his favour and snapped, 'Have you thought of what you'll do when the baby is born? Here you have people to do everything you want. From washing your soiled clothes to bathing you and feeding you. You can't expect the same luxury of life elsewhere, and that too in a strange place. I think it would be best for you to remain here.' He glowered at her and added as an afterthought, 'Tell me, why would it be best for you to remain here after the baby is born?'

Mukundan had been playing with a kitten when a dark shadow loomed in the periphery of his vision. He looked up and saw a tall man swathed in black. His moustache twirled upward like angry question marks, and his eyes echoed the same fierceness of thought. Who are you? they seemed to snap as they darted around the room. Mukundan was frightened by the man he recognized as his father from the framed picture that hung in his mother's bedroom. 'Come here,' the man said awkwardly. Mukundan clutched the kitten to his chest and ran to stand behind a pillar. 'Come here, son,' the man beckoned once again. But Mukundan stood rooted to the place. When the man came towards him, he bawled loudly, 'Amma!'

Paru Kutty walked into this strange tableau where father and son stood separated by the expanse of the room and four years of time. At first she was too surprised to speak. There had been no intimation from him informing her of his arrival.

'How? What?' she stammered, overwhelmed by a jumble of feelings on seeing her husband suddenly.

He shot her an angry look and greeted her after four years of separation with a growl. 'What have you done to him to turn him into a pathetic creature like this?'

'He must be frightened by your clothes. He hasn't seen anyone wearing a suit. He's never seen anyone who looks like you,' Paru Kutty apologized. 'Monu, go to your father,' she cajoled.

But Mukundan wouldn't listen. He hid behind her, wrapping his arms around her legs. Achuthan Nair stood there furious, his lip curling in disgust at the mass of tears and sniffs before him. And a little hurt that his own son should reject him so. In time Mukundan began to accept Achuthan Nair as his father. But the tone of their relationship had been set in that first meeting.

When Mukundan was eight years old, Achuthan Nair decided that he had had enough of working for white-skinned imperialists and returned to Kaikurussi. He folded his suits, wrapped them in fine muslin, and stored them in a trunk scattered with mothballs. He gave his expensive calfskin shoes away to a schoolmaster in Shoranur and used his ties to halter calves with vagrant tendencies. He took to wearing a handspun dhoti and a white half-sleeved shirt. From the sartorial splendour of the past, all he retained was a pair of wooden clogs which he had worn in Burma. In Kaikurussi he wore them as a testimony to who he was: Here is a man who has seen the world. Here is a man who is to be respected. Here is a man whose authority is not to be questioned. The wooden clogs seemed to echo these declarations with every step.

Mukundan learned to read his father's mood from the sounds the clogs made. In the mornings, if he dawdled in bed, the clogs began to beat a steady time on the polished floor of the front room. So, even as he cringed his way down the stairs, he knew that his father had his opening speech for the day ready. The subject: How discipline in life shapes a man's destiny. The lectures always ended the same way, with a pointed accusation and a raised finger that quivered with the righteous fury of a prophet's sceptre. 'What is the point in your having grown as big as a buffalo? You don't have a scrap of discipline or responsibility in you. You will never make anything of your life. All you will be fit for is ploughing the fields!' he would bellow, pausing only to question, 'Tell me, what will you be fit for when you grow up?'

And Mukundan would reply, hurt and shame thickening his voice, 'To plough the fields.'

'Don't hang your head like a thief. Look at me when I talk to you, you swine. What do they teach you in that school of yours?' Achuthan Nair demanded one morning.

'About China,' Mukundan replied hoping it would please his father.

'What?'

'The Chinese invented paper and steam engines. China is famous for its tea and silk. The longest river in China is the Hwang Ho,' Mukundan recited disjointedly.

'Paru Kutty, is this boy insane?' Achuthan Nair asked the wooden rafters of the room. 'Don't they teach you any arithmetic?'

'They do,' Mukundan mumbled, knowing what was

coming next.

'So then tell me the answer to this problem. A group of forty-five people set out on a walk from Kara in Upper Burma to Imphal in India. On the way, six died of exhaustion, one of snakebite, and one was swept away in a river. However, four new babies were born during the course of the walk. So how many were they when they reached Imphal?'

Mukundan chewed his lip. Why did his father always try to trap him?

Achuthan Nair felt the familiar ire rise in him when he encountered stupidity. No son of his could be such a dunce. 'Why are you taking so long?'

'Forty-three, father?' Mukundan asked hopefully.

'Forty-three? Are you asking me or telling me?'

'Forty-three. No, forty-two,' Mukundan corrected himself hastily.

The cane swished through the air as Mukundan had known it inevitably would. He yelped in pain as the blows fell and then could hold it back no longer.

Achuthan Nair saw the growing puddle on the floor and sprang away in disgust. 'Paru Kutty!' he hollered at the top of his voice. 'Look at your wonderful son, snivelling and standing in his own piss. He can't even take a few blows on his skin without piddling in his pants. If he ever had to walk through the jungles of Burma, how on earth would be survive it?'

When the Japanese invaded Burma during the Second World War, Achuthan Nair was part of a group that walked to safety through the jungles. Achuthan Nair never knew how he had survived that walk. The jungles were full of unknown terror; the skies criss-crossed with danger, and the rivers ran fraught with malevolent currents. But survive he did, and he was determined to teach his son to survive too, if he ever had to fight for his life.

'If you wish to survive, you need to think of yourself first,' he drummed into his son day after day. 'The moment you start thinking of others, there is no way you'll ever reach anywhere. In this world no one can be responsible for any one else. Protect yourself first. Then, if it doesn't involve risking your life, you can help someone else. A survivor is someone who is selfish. There is nothing to be ashamed of in it. Anyway, I think selflessness is a much overrated virtue. Who is a survivor?' He demanded of his son wondering if the dunce understood any of what he had taught him about the skills of surviving.

'Someone who is selfish,' Mukundan murmured.

On most evenings, when he came back running all the way from school, the clogs would be making impatient noises. Tap, tap, tap, silence. Tap, tap, tap, silence. A staccato rhythm that said, Where have you been, you vagabond? It's been more than an hour since the school bell rang. What have you been doing all this while?

Mukundan had tried to explain the presence of compulsory sports in his school timetable. But Achuthan Nair accepted no such explanations. 'I send you to school to study. Not to play. I want you here exactly thirty minutes after the last bell rings. Do you understand? So tell me, how much time do you have to get back home after the school bell has rung?'

Mukundan would stand there before him, hanging his head. He didn't know what to do any more. If he didn't attend the compulsory sports, the drillmaster caned him in assembly next morning. If he didn't reach home on time, his father caned him. All he knew was that a caning was certain. At least the drillmaster restricted himself to delivering three sharp, stinging blows on his open-faced palm. But with his father, the caning stopped only when the cane snapped.

At night the clogs kicked aside anything that lay in their path as Achuthan Nair made his way to the pond for a bath.

By the time the clogs strode back, snapping twigs underfoot and stamping on dried leaves, dinner had to be ready on the dining table. The rice had to have steam rising from it. The curry had to be piping hot, the pappadums crisp and glistening with oil, and the water in the glass moderately warm. Only when Achuthan Nair had dined was the rest of the family allowed to eat. Some nights when Mukundan was almost fainting with hunger, Krishnan Nair took him into the kitchen and fed him stealthily. They kept their ears cocked for the sound of the clogs as he made little balls of rice, dipped them in curry, and put them into Mukundan's open mouth. This way there would be no evidence to suggest any flouting of authority and transgression of rules. The sight of a used plate, Krishnan Nair knew, could invite a kick with those clogs. And the poor boy was beaten enough already.

When Mukundan earned his first salary, he took home a pair of leather slippers for his father. Achuthan Nair wore them once and put them aside, complaining that they bit into his feet and caused blisters. Two years later when Achuthan Nair built his own house and moved into it, he left his wooden clogs behind. They had served their purpose, and he had no more use for them.

Forty-nine. An age when most men are worried by the stiffness of their knees and their inability to digest a full meal rather than the diminishing demand of their penises for satiation. An age when men begin to wonder if hot flashes of desire will ever again come their way. The age when Achuthan Nair discovered lust.

Ammini was half his age and lusciously curved. When Achuthan Nair went on his morning rounds of the fields he owned, she followed him with pitchers of cold buttermilk spiced with crushed ginger and lemon leaves and scented with her fragrance. When he had slaked his thirst, she offered him her body to do with it as he pleased. In return she expected him to hand over the keys of the big house and make her its chatelaine.

Mukundan's mother Paru Kutty waited in the silence of the big house with the aging cheriyammas. Too proud to show her agony and too frightened to stand up to him and demand to know what was going on. The aunts, as afraid of him as she was, crouched in the farthest corners of the rooms. In time they dropped dead one by one. When the penultimate aunt died, Achuthan Nair looked at the house with its rooms that echoed like plundered vaults and remembered his promise to his Ammini. 'I'm tired of having to visit Ammini in her house. The whole village knows about Ammini. So I might as well bring her here,' he told his wife matter-of-factly.

Paru Kutty emerged from behind the ultimate living aunt, shrugged aside years of cowardice, squared her shoulders and said, 'No.'

'What do you mean "no"?' He frowned.

'I said "no". I'm willing to live with the shame of your taking a mistress. But I'm not going to let you flaunt how little I mean to you. I am your wife and I insist you treat me with the respect due to me.'

'And what if I don't?' he sneered as his fingers bit into her upper arms. She swallowed the pain and murmured through clenched teeth, 'Then it'll be over my dead body. For as long as I'm alive, I will decide who lives in this house and who doesn't.'

In all the years that he had been married to her, Achuthan Nair had never heard her use that tone with him. Like Ammini, his mistress, the whole village was awed by his moustache ends that curled in the air and his voice that boomed with authority. In their eyes, timid and shy Paru Kutty had long ceased to be the rightful owner of all the property. Achuthan Nair, basking in their adulation, had forgotten it too, until Paru Kutty reminded him. And so in a fit of pique, he bought his mistress a piece of land directly opposite Paru Kutty's house and built a house there.

In the evening, when he had settled the accounts for the day, he would bathe, put on fresh clothes, and walk down the steps, cross the dirt road, step over the stile nimbly, and stride up into his mistress's arms.

The ultimate living aunt sipped at gruel, twisted a piece of cloth into a knot all day, talked to her sisters, who had merged with the shadows, and disappeared into herself. However, to Paru Kutty, she was a living presence. A creature that breathed even if its soul was showing distinct signs of restlessness. Then one day the pale, wraithlike ultimate aunt gasped and closed her eyes. Before she wandered away to the place from which her sisters beckoned, she clutched her niece's hands and croaked happily, 'Paru Kutty, don't worry, we won't leave you here all alone for too long.'

For six months Paru Kutty lived alone in the house surrounded by memories, ghosts, and an all-consuming desire to get even. It was as if she wanted revenge for the years of tyranny Achuthan Nair had subjected her to.

After the harvest, when the labourers brought in the paddy, she allowed only what had come from her inherited fields into the macch. 'I have no storage space for other people's grain,' she snapped when Krishnan Nair asked her, 'What do we do with the rest of the paddy?'

She stared at him for a moment, and then calling Neeli, whose loyalty she knew lay completely with her and who she knew would carry out her orders without hesitation, she said, 'Leave it outside her stile. After all, that is his house now.'

To the horrified amazement of the village, mounds of paddy were dumped on the dirt road near the stile. Golden brown grains that were soon coated with dust. Paru Kutty wouldn't even let them heap the paddy on the palm-leaf mats. Everything that was hers would remain hers. As for the rest, she didn't care what happened to it. Paru Kutty couldn't have chosen a more public way of declaring battle.

But Mukundan's mother was no general. She didn't have a strategy, a battle plan. And she suffered for it.

For the first time in twelve years Paru Kutty invited her second cousin to visit her. Ever since Devayani had married and gone to live in Shoranur, Achuthan Nair had forbidden her to have anything to do with her cousin. 'She might be your relative, but her husband is a first-rate scoundrel. I don't want people like him coming here. Who ever heard of any decent man running a cinema tent? I have to think of my reputation.'

Paru Kutty had never dared to provoke him, though she knew that Achuthan Nair resented Devayani's husband only because he was successful. And perhaps more important than Achuthan Nair could ever hope to be. As the owner of the only cinema tent—Murugan Talkies—in Shoranur, everyone in the village and in the surrounding villages knew of Devayani's husband and looked up to him with a certain awe. After all, he was the man who was responsible for bringing alive their favourite matinee idols on a white screen. And surely some of the magic of the cinema world was bound to wrap itself around him. Achuthan Nair, Paru Kutty knew, hated sharing his position of 'man of the world' in the village, and Devayani's husband posed a dire threat.

So Devayani and her two sons came to Kaikurussi in a car that her husband drove expertly, scattering chickens and people to the sides of the road. For a whole week the house and the garden echoed with the exuberance of two boys frolicking. Pebbles rattled on rooftops. Wood thumped as they ran up and down the stairs several times a day. Doors slammed. Water splashed as they hurled the bucket into the well. The pulley screeched as they tugged at the rope to haul the full bucket of water up. Loud-pitched laughter. Incessant chatter. Paru Kutty felt the house vibrate with Achuthan Nair's displeasure from across the road and revelled in the feeling.

When Devayani and her children left and Paru Kutty was alone once again, she took to dousing the lantern that lit the veranda and blowing out the gleaming brass lamp that hung from a chain hooked onto a rafter, plunging the front yard into darkness. Though Achuthan Nair had moved out of the house, he still continued to bathe in the enclosed pond at the bottom of the garden. She knew he had to pass that way, and she hoped someday he would stumble and fall. Once he tripped over a root. From the next night onward, he lit a blazing torch fashioned out of dried coconut leaf fronds and swung it in the air as he walked past, as if to taunt her with its drizzle of sparks: Go on, do your best, you can't do anything to hurt me.

An almond tree Achuthan Nair had planted near the gate was razed to the ground. In its place Paru Kutty planted a champakam plant. But only after she was dead and gone did it burst into bloom, scenting every night with a dense, cloying fragrance. And in an ironic twist of fate, it was into Ammini's house that the fragrance of the flowers wafted every time the breeze blew.

Paru Kutty left her husband's few remaining things in the house untouched. He had no use for a pair of battered wooden clogs, some old ledgers, and a barometer that had stopped working. Or he would have taken them with him. However, to her, they represented the man who had once lived there, and she showed her animosity, her contempt for him by letting them gather dust. When one of Devayani's sons began to play with the wooden clogs, at first she had wanted to protest. Then she watched him strut around in the wooden clogs and saw a grim parody of the man who had once sought to weigh down the house with his authority. 'Take them with you to Shoranur,' she said, hoping that Achuthan Nair would sense their absence when he came across next.

On his rare visits to the house Achuthan Nair hardly noticed the dust or the neglect. Instead he regaled her with tales of what he and his mistress did in bed, outside it, on the staircase, in the barn. Of how Ammini was a real woman, responsive to his needs and understanding of his demands, unlike the cowering, weak, lifeless creature he was married to. Mostly she pretended not to hear him. But when he had left, she would bury her face in her lap and weep so noisily that Krishnan Nair hovering outside would come to the doorway and try to console her, mumbling, 'Now, now, why do you let him affect you so? Calm down, wipe your tears, you are going to make yourself ill weeping like this.'

Then one morning, at the crack of dawn, she fell down the staircase and lay on her face in a pool of blood. Till Krishnan Nair found her.

Achuthan Nair never brought his mistress home. She refused to live in a house she said was the homing place for Paru Kutty's distressed soul. And so what Paru Kutty couldn't accomplish in life she did in death. Settled once and for all the humiliating threat of possibly having to share her husband with another woman under her roof.

The house remained closed except for those rare times when Mukundan went visiting. And since he never stayed for more than two or three days, he ignored Krishnan Nair's repeated pleas to do something about the house. Mukundan never saw his father unless he came across to the house. 'Don't you want to see your father before you return?' Krishnan Nair said the first time Mukundan went home after his mother's death.

'No,' Mukundan said.

'You shouldn't be so stubborn. After all, he is your father,' Krishnan Nair persisted.

'So what? Do you expect me to forgive him for what he

did to my mother?' he had snapped. Krishnan Nair never again mentioned it. But from the next time onward, Achuthan Nair, as if to remind him that he still hadn't given up his claim on the house or Mukundan's life, took to coming in early and planting himself in the armchair.

When Mukundan walked in, Achuthan Nair would pretend not to notice him. Many minutes later he would mumble with a dismissive nod of his head, 'So you're here.' And Mukundan would affirm quietly, 'Yes, I'm here.'

After that there would be silence until Mukundan opened the small suitcase he had with him. Achuthan Nair's eyes would rake the contents, settling only when they found what they knew were for him. Fine cotton undershirts. A long-sleeved woollen shirt. A blanket. A torch and always a tin of fragrant chewing tobacco. Apart from the money orders Mukundan sent dutifully every month, he took with him an offering of sorts every time.

'Why do you bother?' Krishnan Nair asked him once. 'He has everything he wants and he can afford to buy anything else he needs.'

'I know,' Mukundan said. 'But he is my father. And he expects me to do my duty as his son.'

How could he tell Krishnan Nair that he was still trying to find a way into his father's heart? And that he hoped to buy affection with these bribes that he knew pleased his father immensely. He was always trying to measure up; trying to please. But Mukundan had yet to see any difference in his manner toward him. Nothing Mukundan ever did satisfied his father. He accepted the gifts in the manner of a god accepting homage to his greatness.

Some nights when Mukundan had had a lot to drink, the bitterness would swell in him and he would thump his fist on a table, against a wall, against anything that was as hard and devoid of emotion as his father was, and cry, 'Someday I'm going to make you weep. Someday I'm going to make you beg me to love you.'

7

One-screw-loose Bhasi Stakes His Claim

His skin was a brown sheath stretched tight against a rock-bed skull. Millions of raindrops and countless sweepings of the wind had wiped it clean of wrinkles, lines and all other effects of living. A rock worn smooth with aging. You may bore into its depths but you won't find an arterial spring of sweetness. Far inside the layers of rock, there does exist a molten core. There is nothing sweet, pink or sugary about this inner liquid. It is all fire and steam, lava waiting to erupt. Eagerly seeking victims to sear, burn, and reduce to ashes. That is who he really is.

The outer man wears his dignity with the grace of an urn excavated from some long-forgotten civilization. Even his ears add to the image. Like handles on either side, they stick out from his head with a frieze of grey tuft embedded in the inner curve. Foster child of silence and slow time. But there it stops. From the cheeks downward, age seems to have caught up with this clever quarry. Cheeks once padded with muscle and teeth caved in, pushing the jaws to resemble a cavernous corridor. The mouth, like a whore's, is fixed in a perennial moue.

His large trunk is that of an aging palm tree, bristly but still hard and muscular. Only his eyes remain the same. Deep brown swamps of arrogance giving nothing away. Reflecting no emotion. They could be the eyes of a dead man or a murderer. The eyes of Achuthan Nair. Mukundan's father.

Across the room he sat in an armchair with the authority of ownership. His walking stick was hooked on the back of the chair. His hands, long, bony, and capable, gripped the handles of the armchair. Had those hands wound round his mother's neck with the same effortless ease, secure in the knowledge that he was above all rulings of the law? Mukundan wondered. After all, he was king even if he had been ousted from this kingdom. He was withering, but even now no one dared meet his eyes or hold his gaze.

Earlier in the evening Achuthan Nair had stood outside his house across the road and rumbled, 'Mukunda, Mukunda.' Mukundan had rushed to the gate feeling that familiar sense of unease in the pit of his stomach.

'Come here and help me cross the road,' he had hollered impatiently. As Mukundan went to his side, Achuthan Nair raised his walking stick and Mukundan cringed instinctively. From the time Mukundan could remember, whenever his father raised a stick, it always landed on his back. It took Mukundan a moment to register what he had done and he straightened, hoping his father hadn't noticed the effect he still had on him. But as he gave him his arm, he met the older man's eyes and he saw the triumph there. Achuthan Nair knew the power he had over his son.

With an exaggerated gesture, Achuthan Nair planted the stick in the ground and slowly stepped over the bamboo stile. 'These steps feel like mountains,' he said as he walked up the steps to the veranda. 'I asked you, what do these steps feel like?'

Mukundan noticed how studiously he avoided the new section and instead chose to go toward the main veranda that had been the formal living room when he had lived here. Achuthan Nair had an uncanny knack of taking time in his hands and twisting it around so that no matter where he was, he continued to be master of the situation.

'Like mountains, I know,' Mukundan mumbled.

'Indeed. What do you know? You're just fifty-eight years old. How can these steps seem like mountains to you? You were always a weak creature,' his father mouthed with distaste.

They continued to sit there in silence. Mukundan was as tongue-tied as ever in his father's presence, who did nothing to encourage a conversation. Anyway, what could he say to this man who first abandoned his wife and then, it was suspected, got rid of her to make another woman happy?

Father, how is your dead mistress's daughter—my stepsister? Are she and her family well? Do you think about your dead wife, my dead mother, and gloat with pride that you killed her and got away scot-free? Do you, Father, do you?

Achuthan Nair's glance went through the house. A little child searching for the hidden biscuit tin. What did he expect to find? Does he see what I do, Mukundan thought, a mammoth house resounding with emptiness? Or was it peopled with memories in his mind?

'You need a woman in here,' he said flatly.

'Krishnan Nair said he'll find one.' Mukundan murmured.

He gave him a withering look. 'I didn't mean a servant. I meant a wife for you. Tell me,' he snapped, 'what did I mean by a woman?'

'A wife. But I'm too old to think of marrying now,' Mukundan protested. You should have thought of this thirty years ago, he seethed. But you were too busy fucking your mistress to think of your son then.

Achuthan Nair's mouth stretched into a grimace. 'You should have married. What were you waiting for?'

'You. I was waiting for you to let me become a man,' Mukundan said under his breath.

And then, as if the thought had just crossed his mind, his father asked, 'Were you expecting me to find you a wife? I've never believed in that sort of nonsense. Every man has to find his own woman. At least, I did.'

Which one?

Mukundan took a deep breath. Once again he had failed to please him. If he had taken it upon himself to marry, his father would have found fault with everything. The girl's looks, her ancestry, her family tree . . . And now that he hadn't, he was a man who couldn't even find a woman of his own.

Father, do you want to know whether I can make love to a woman? Will my sexual exploits make you accept me as a man and not as the weak, sexless creature you make me out to be? Mukundan's big toe wrote frantically on the floor.

'Don't encourage that woman to come in here. I saw her swaying in earlier this afternoon,' he said a little later.

'Who?' Mukundan pretended not to understand.

'Who else but that creature Meenakshi. She's a leech. Once she finds a soft spot, she'll cling till she's sucked you dry.'

Tock. Tock. The sound of knuckles cracking broke his thoughts. Time captured in a bone and then released. Tock. Tock. For a moment, he stared at the turtle-like head across the room, and then a slow realization came over him.

What am I doing here, he asked himself. Accusing eyes stared at him from all sides. Dead ones. Living ones. Aging ones.

This was not how he had planned to live for the rest of his life. His father was never going to die. He would continue to live just so he could flash his power over Mukundan with malicious glee. As for the rest of them, what did they care? He was an outsider. Achuthan Nair's city son, reluctant native, misogynist, misfit . . .

Mukundan lay on the bed staring at the ceiling. He had waited all morning for his father to summon him. But he hadn't. It was almost as if the old man was drawing a certain perverse pleasure from playing this cat-and-mouse game with him. The dull throbbing at his right temple had turned into an angry hammering. Why hadn't his father come today? Was he ill? Mukundan turned on his side and clenched his teeth. Doing this, he discovered, helped. The tautness of his jaws coursed up and strangled the pain.

Most afternoons he had a headache. The humidity, the oppressive silence, the stirrings of his father's presence caused it. After the first day Achuthan Nair had taken to coming over by about eleven in the morning. As soon as he was seated in the armchair he had usurped for himself, Mukundan would retreat to some corner of the house or burrow into the security of his room. Like a sixteen-year-old, he went behind the house to smoke, washing his hands and mouth later to erase the smell. He hid all the magazines that had scantily dressed girls as centerfolds and walked up to the gate when it was time for the postman to come. Achuthan Nair had little regard for Mukundan's privacy and had taken to opening his mail if it fell into his hands.

He would stay on for lunch, and late in the afternoon, after a short nap, Mukundan had to see him across to his house. I wonder why he does it, Mukundan sighed. Doesn't he trust me to be by myself in the house all day? Or could it be that he doesn't want me to forget that he is still lord and master even if he no longer lives here? Or was it nostalgia for the house that brought him back here?

Having him in the house exhausted Mukundan. They didn't share anything apart from the width of the steps that led up to the veranda. And yet, he left Mukundan feeling limp and drained. There had always been a chasm between them. The death of Mukundan's mother had only further deepened this ravine of mistrust. Mukundan couldn't forgive him for abandoning his mother and humiliating her. As for Achuthan Nair, he couldn't get over the fact that Mukundan was more his mother's son than his.

Krishnan Nair came to the door at half-past three. How easily they had settled into a routine. Two old men in an ancient house pussyfooting around the face of the clock. Counting the passing of days by tearing the date sheet of the Co-operative Bank wall calendar that hung in the dining room. Day after day.

Mukundan sipped the tea Krishnan Nair had made for him. He had learned to not complain when the cream in the milk coated his tongue. He had tried to make Krishnan Nair understand that he liked his tea black with a slice of lime. But Krishnan Nair dismissed it, saying that the time would probably come when he discovered that he had diabetes. Until then he should drink his tea like normal people did. Mukundan told himself: He's doing it out of affection, this drowning of tea in milk and sugar, and that he should be grateful for it. So he spooned some mixture into his mouth and crunched it noisily.

'Bhasi is here,' Krishnan Nair said when he thought Mukundan had finished. By now he was used to Mukundan's little eccentricities and knew that he always left an inch of tea at the bottom of the glass.

'Who?' Mukundan asked. He was in no mood to embark on yet another conversation on life after the road came into being. Almost everyone he had met so far brought up the road after a few minutes. The promise of the road to come. Every few hours he was told about it as though it was the mantra that would transform the sleepy little village into a bustling metropolitan city. Things would change when the road was finished. Life would be different when the road was ready, he was constantly being assured. Once the buses began to ply, he wouldn't miss the comforts he had been used to. There were just fourteen kilometres left to be completed. One of these days the sanction would come through. All he had to do was be a little patient.

The road meant nothing to Mukundan. He looked at the few mounds of tar on what was no more than a dirt track.

He didn't think the work on it would ever be completed. When he was in his early teens, he had heard of a bridge that was to have been built across the Bharathapuzha river to link Mayannur with Ottapalam. There had been a great deal of excitement when the Ottapalam Minor Bridge Committee had been set up. His father had read about it in the newspaper and hmm-ed and ah-ed all morning about how the bridge was going to change the lives of several villages.

The bridge had found its way into the first Five-Year Plan. Nine Five-Year plans later, it still remained unbuilt. Mukundan smiled to himself, thinking of the silent protest the people of Ottapalam and Mayannur made month after month. A human chain across the half-kilometre breadth of the river. And yet the bridge remained a blueprint filed away in some dusty cabinet somewhere.

'The painter!' Krishnan Nair said impatiently, breaking into Mukundan's thoughts. 'Painter Bhasi,' he explained, miming a brushstroke.

Bhasi was standing by the side of the house looking at the wall intently, as if written on it were the secret to happiness. He was a frail-looking man with skin the colour of coffee and hair that stood up like the bristles of a brush, dressed in faded paint-splashed clothes. From him came a faint reek of turpentine mixed with the woodsy, burned-leaf fragrance of beedi. When he drew closer, the waft of yet another fragrance came Mukundan's way. He saw the jaw clench and unclench rhythmically and wondered if the painter had a drinking problem. Or why else would he try to camouflage his breath by chewing mint leaves? Mukundan recognized most faces in the village, but he had never seen him before. Mukundan cleared his throat.

Bhasi peered at Mukundan from behind the thick lenses of his spectacles. Mukundan stretched his lips to simulate a smile of sorts and grunted, 'Huh!'

The painter grunted back and asked abruptly, 'Are you troubled by piles?'

'What?' Mukundan burst out in surprise that slowly turned into rage. He wondered if the man was mad or plain drunk. What sane man would dare presume such liberty in their first meeting? And that too with a prospective client.

'If you do, the cure is growing right here beneath your nose,' Bhasi said pointing to the clumps of a weed that was everywhere. Brown rambling stems, tiny ovate leaves that responded to touch by coyly folding themselves, little vicious thorns and a pink feathery blossom. 'Lajjalu. The "shy one" in Sanskrit. *Mimosa pudica*, in Latin. Its action on small vessels is implicated in its hemostatic property. The juice of its freshly crushed leaves is used internally and externally to cure piles.'

'Can we get to the subject of painting this house?' Mukundan asked in irritation and began to walk to put distance between himself and this painter whose breath smelt of mint and his mind of madness.

'There is a lot of work to be done on these walls.' After being subjected to all kinds of skirtings, hedgings and pre-mumblings before the real issue was broached, Mukundan was surprised to meet someone who didn't feel the need for any social preamble. He tried to read the man's eyes, but it was like looking into a room through a frosted windowpane. Mukundan pulled a handkerchief out of his pocket and wiped his brow. The hot tea was making him sweat.

'Yes, I know,' Mukundan mumbled, folding the handkerchief meticulously so that he didn't have to meet Bhasi's eyes. He didn't want him to know that he had neglected the upkeep of the house because he had never intended to live there.

'There is a lot of damp locked within the walls. There are hairline cracks and there is mildew. Do you see this?' He pointed, scrubbing at a spot with a handful of coconut fibre. Beneath the haphazardly slapped-on whitewash, an almost pustulent looking surface emerged. 'The neglect goes deep within,' he said, wiping his hands. It occurred to Mukundan that he was making a point, though it didn't necessarily pertain to the wall. He felt a twinge of irritation, and the sight of the coconut fibre that Bhasi had dropped carelessly on the ground added to it.

'Could you throw it on to the heap of dried leaves beneath the coconut tree?' Mukundan said brusquely.

Bhasi gave him a strange look but did as asked. As they walked around the house examining the extent of work that needed to be done, he said in a grave manner, 'I will need to scrub the walls, cleanse it of its past. Grime, fungi, and the—' Abruptly his expression changed. He grinned impishly and continued, '—the artistic failure of previous painters.'

He stopped abruptly by the side of the front veranda and caressed the wall as if it were a woman who sat downcast, streaming rivulets of pain. 'When that is done, I will seal the cracks and heal it with primer. Only then will I begin to paint the walls. It seems to me that the great sadness within this house has seeped into the walls.'

Mukundan felt a glimmer of fear for this man. Who was he? 'Where are you from?' he asked curiously.

'I came to live in this village some years ago,' Bhasi said, wiping his glasses with the corner of his shirt. Without his glasses his face acquired a mystique that was hard to define. His eyes were large and clear, light brown in colour. Luminescent eyes that seemed to mesmerize, making Mukundan feel naked and vulnerable.

'Oh!' he mumbled as he walked away to the side.

'Who can fight destiny?' Bhasi's voice crept from behind. 'Today of past regrets and future fears; tomorrow—why, tomorrow I may be myself with yesterday's seven thousand years,' he quoted.

Mukundan turned in surprise. Bhasi searched his face and then continued with a knowing look in his eyes that made Mukundan break out in a sweat once again. 'Tis all a chequer-board of Nights and Days. Where Destiny with men for pieces plays. Omar Khayyam,' he explained. 'Do you like poetry?' he asked abruptly.

Mukundan swallowed in amazement. He didn't know if he liked poetry. Not if liking poetry meant memorizing large chunks of it and reciting it. But he didn't want to admit it. Not to a painter, even if he was more astute and better read than him. So he smiled and grunted once more.

'When can you start?' Mukundan asked, trying to fill the awkward silence that suddenly seemed to have sprung between them. He wondered if Bhasi thought he had overstepped his boundaries.

'Two weeks from now when the monsoon is over,' Bhasi said walking towards the gate.

'You didn't tell me where you are from?' Mukundan asked again, suddenly reluctant to see him go.

Bhasi smiled. A smile that radiated kindliness, and a warmth that Mukundan could almost sense on his skin. 'I'll tell you everything you want to know when I come back. After all, we are going to spend a great deal of time in each other's company.'

Mukundan stood there feeling faintly breathless. Something about Bhasi's voice sent a shiver down his spine and raised the hair on his arms. It was as though he had stepped in and decided to take control of Mukundan's life.

Part II

8

The Landscape of Perpetual Succour

I can see the word form in your head. The devilish dance of the letters as they leap and turn, swirl and pirouette on the floorboards of your mind. E-x-i-l-e.

But I am not an exile.

Let me tell you, an exile is a creature who, in spite of being banished from his land, never ever manages to sever the ties with the place where his umbilicus lies buried. A pitiful being, who combines one part memory and two parts imagination to create a land so magical, so unique, that he can never truly belong to the present—to the land that now offers him refuge. For such is the power of the past. So that when some familiar scent comes his way, he feels his guts twist and strangle themselves in misery and longing; his throat fills with spider eggs of nostalgia that hatch by the minute, climb up into his eyes, and run down his cheeks leaving behind watery trails.

There is no room in my life that houses my past, a shrine I retreat to when things don't go right for me. A sanctum where I stand and chant the mantra—someday when I return to the land of my ancestors, all this will change.

When I decided to make my home in Kaikurussi, I said to myself: This is my land. This is my home. This is the life I choose to live.

Don't curl your lip in disbelief, Mukundan. Or is it that you ask yourself what kind of life Painter Bhasi, One-screw-loose Bhasi would have had anyway. It isn't as if he renounced a life filled with the promise of respectability and riches and chose this. A painter's life is very much the same whether he lives in Kaikurussi or some place else.

Maybe I should describe to you what my life was once like, and who I used to be. I swore never to reveal my past to anyone. But when I let myself get involved in your life, Mukundan, I broke a rule. And thereafter I have been breaking, one by one, all the dictates I had set for myself in my new life.

This is not easy, the delving into the past that I had wrapped in many layers of blankness and hidden in an unused drawer of my unconscious. But I will try. For I would like you to understand why I, Painter Bhasi, One-screw-loose Bhasi was ordained to heal you.

Look at my hands. Calluses ridge the fingertips. Deep dark lines run a wayward course dividing my palm into an archipelago of worry. Once these hands did nothing more strenuous than flick a page. In place of a brush I held a piece of chalk, and with it I filled a blackboard's surface with the extent of my knowledge.

I was a teacher. Once. Fifteen years ago. Not a teacher in some lower primary school, but a lecturer in a college. I taught undergraduate students. Ideal College wasn't exactly the institution I would have chosen to launch my academic career. After all, it was only a parallel college where, by simulating the teaching process of an actual college, we prepared students to appear for the university examinations as private students.

I told myself this was just the beginning. Someday soon there would be a vacancy in a good college. But until then there was a certain challenge in trying to instill if not love then at least an understanding of literature among students with absolutely no aptitude for any kind of learning. Over and over again, I was told that I shouldn't digress from the prescribed texts in any manner. There was no need to burden them with any extra learning. As it was, it was going to be difficult to ensure that they got their degree at the end of three years.

But I wasn't willing to accept that. I told myself I could penetrate the lardlike indifference of my students and reach the sinews of their minds to fill them with knowledge. 'Don't be foolish,' the principal, a taciturn man, advised me. 'Do you think they are interested in who Keats was or how Shelley died? They don't care. All they want is a paper that says they have a BA.'

'This apathy is precisely what I'm trying to fight,' I argued. 'Don't we, as teachers, have a responsibility to do more than just teach the prescribed course? I'm determined that they should have more than just a degree in their hands when they leave, three years from now.'

The principal smiled. But there was a warning in his eyes when he said, 'If you insist on finding out the hard way, then that's your choice. But I want results. My college has a reputation for delivering degrees. I won't let anything jeopardize that!'

I took a deep breath and stilled the angry words in my head. I would show him exactly what I meant, and then perhaps he would understand.

Do you remember what it was like to be twenty-three?

The glorious certainty of that age when everything is bathed in the yellow light of hope and nothing is impossible. When the future stretches ahead, unbounded by the peripheries of time and mortality. When youth, as if it were the tungsten filament in a lightbulb, draws on the power of your conviction that life is what you make of it.

By the end of the first year I had made some progress. From being automatons that mechanically copied in their notebooks every word I mouthed and every letter I wrote on the blackboard, they began to put down their pens and listen. Once I knew I had their attention, I wooed them with a casual affection tinged with irony.

For the one fundamental truth that I had learned over the years was that affection openly given is never valued. It is seen as commonplace; it is treated with little respect and is seldom reciprocated. Instead, if it is to be bestowed as a rare gift, then its value rockets sky high and it is cherished as a precious jewel. And so I speckled my classes with sarcasm, with caustic jokes and, once in a while, to ensure that I had a firm place in their hearts, I overwhelmed them with gentle displays of caring.

She wasn't beautiful or particularly vivacious for me to notice her in the wave of faces that greeted me every day. She was just one among the thirty new students in the first year BA English class. While I did teach English as a subject to the BA economics and history classes, I reserved my best efforts for the BA English students. When I was with them, I tried to forget that these were the dregs of the scholastic world, considered to be unworthy to qualify for even the lowest of the low degree courses—English literature. In colleges in Kochi, Kozhikode, Chennai and Bangalore, I have heard that a seat in BA English is much sought after. But here it is only people who fail to find admission to other degree courses who settle for English literature. And, it was among such student chaff that I found her. My golden grain of hope.

A month after the start of the academic year in June, while correcting a test I had set for the class, I found one paper that for the first time in my twenty-six months as a parallel college lecturer filled my mind with a strange excitement. Here was my prize student. Here was the instrument that would prove to the world that talent could be taught.

Thought by thought, word by word, I had drilled my students almost by rote the answer to the question that appeared in the university exam paper year after year: Discuss the character of Cordelia from King Lear. The test was simply to ensure that their spellings were right, the quotes appropriate, and the grammar correct. But she had attempted to tackle it all by herself

As in a necklace of crystal beads, through the peregrinations of her mind ran a delicate line of lyricism, threading astute insight with great compassion for the character of Cordelia. So that when I came to the end of the page, I felt as though bewitched. More than anything else, I wanted to know who she was, what had brought her to this classroom with its flaking walls, shaky desks, and canopy of disdain.

Omana. A name without a face. A name that I branded on the inner side of my lips so that I could savour its feel with every sound my mouth uttered. Omana. Omana. I said it a thousand times, feeling it pervade my senses. I thought if I said it enough times, my spirit would recognize hers with no need for any formal introduction.

The next morning in class, I searched the faces before me as I discussed the merits of the test papers. Then I mentioned one paper specifically—Omana's. And in the third row from the last by the aisle, I spotted a quiet flush of pride, the stealthy dance of joy, and the condensation of agitation on an upper lip. Omana, beloved girl, my heart leaped.

Unlike other men of my age, I had never been in love. Ever. Very early in life, I had circled the threshold of my heart with handfuls of sawdust. I didn't want love crawling in like a cortège of ants carrying on their backs the aftermath of so tumultuous an emotion. Hurt. Anger. Betrayal. Anguish. Sleepless nights. Long empty hours. The taste of ashes in my mouth. The sting of salt in my eyes. And yet, all it took was a few glistening drops on an upper lip to wash that circle of defense away.

I began courting her the only way I knew. With words. There was none of that slipping a note in between the pages of a book or waylaying her in some dark alley with a love note. That was what adolescents and celluloid heroes did. I chose to make my declaration openly, unashamedly, but with a great deal of subtlety. I took to writing quotes, mostly love poems from world literature, on the blackboard. Quotes I would discuss in the class while my eyes followed her every movement. Faithful hounds forever hoping for a careless glance thrown their way.

What was it about Omana that turned me into a lovesick idiot? I wish I knew.

Maybe it was just that I was lonely.

I had no family to speak of. My father, a toddy tapper, had fallen in love with my mother, the village astrologer's daughter. One night they had eloped, knowing that they would never again be welcome in either home. When I was sixteen, my father fell from a coconut tree and broke his neck. He lay at the foot of the tree whose trunk he had gripped with his thighs as if it were a woman's body. For many years the tree had known the passion of his heave and thrust as he scaled it day after day. One morning, like a woman who had lost interest, it loosened itself from his embrace and carelessly thrust him away to his death.

My mother never recovered from my father's death. In the evening when the wind rustled the coconut leaves and filled the night with whispers, she would go to the doorway and plead with him, 'I'm so lonely and lost without you. All I think of is the time when I'll be with you once again.' Then she would turn to us and say, 'Can you hear him call me?' Five years later she followed him, to the place from where my father had been sending her frantic messages.

I have two older brothers. My eldest brother works as a lineman with the electricity department. My second brother works as a fitter in a factory in Coimbatore. My father, if he had been alive, would have forced me to go to the polytechnic. He believed that a man who knew a trade would never starve. But I wanted more than just food in my belly; I wanted respectability. I wanted a title before my name. I wanted people to look at me and say, There goes Mr so-and-so.

I lived with my elder brother and his family. They didn't

make me feel unwelcome, but my status in the house was of a paying guest. It was expected that someday I would leave.

The little property we had was divided after my mother's death. My eldest brother kept the house. My second brother got the piece of land behind the house, and I was given a small plot adjacent to the house. I sold my piece of land to my eldest brother and used a portion of it to fund my studies and pay my keep till such time as I began to earn. The rest of it, a few thousand, was locked away in a bank account for the next fifteen years. Some years ago I broke the deposit and used it to buy the land I live on now.

Maybe it was that I thought I glimpsed a superior intellect in Omana. A mind that I knew would match mine in every way. Omana, I thought, was capable of stoking alive the embers of my love for her even when our bones cracked with age and our skins veined like dried leaves.

Sometimes I think it was simply the effect of her hormones singing their siren song.

But more than anything else, I think I was attracted by the thought that I could play God. Here was someone I could mould to show the university dons that they had made a mistake. By shunning her as a student. By not hiring me as a lecturer in a regular college. A private student taught by a parallel college lecturer would gather the university honours in three years' time. Through her destiny I would control mine.

I was so wrapped up in the newness of my feelings, the overwhelming need to make her understand these strange and wondrous sensations she aroused in me, that I spared little time thinking of whether she cared for me in the same way. My love was so total, so radiant that I was sure she could only feel the same for me.

But Omana had no intentions of being my beloved. She had her future all mapped out neatly for her. Sudhir, her cousin. A home in Dubai he was meticulously putting together, piling kitchen counters with gadgets, nonstick pans, and unbreakable plates. Heaping in cupboard drawers, tins of Yardley powder, glass vials of perfume spray, frothy nylon nighties, and strands of 24-carat gold. At the end of the year, they would be married and then they would leave in a shining airplane, cutting through the clouds to the promised land and happily ever after.

Meanwhile she indulged her femininity by lapping up my adulation. Maybe it made her feel powerful. She encouraged me just enough to keep me hanging on in hope. And yet, with restraint, so that I was forever asking myself, Does she, doesn't she?

She doesn't, they told me. With snickers. With pitying looks. With casual references to 'Omana's fiancé in Dubai'. But I continued to woo her till the day she waited for me to finish my lecture. 'Sir, I'd like to speak to you,' she said.

'Yes, of course,' I said, wondering what it could be.

'Not now. Could we meet after college?' she asked, not quite meeting my eyes. For the rest of the day, I hurried through my lectures, willing the clock hands to gallop, the college bell to ring on its own.

I waited for her in the classroom that was swathed in long grey shadows. I stood there leaning against the table, my arms crossed. My palms were damp with perspiration, and my tongue felt wooden. She avoided looking at my face as she walked into the room. 'Yes,' I whispered. I cleared my throat and asked once again, 'Yes, Omana, what is it?'

She clutched some books to her bosom. Armour protecting her from my marauding eyes. 'They are talking about us,' she mumbled, her eyes glued to the grimy floor.

'What?' I asked, unable to comprehend her words.

'They are saying all kinds of things about you and me,' she said.

'Ignore it. Don't let stray gossip bother you so much,' I said.

'How can I?' Her voice rose with the tilt of her chin. 'How can I ignore what I hear everywhere I go? At the bus stop. Down the corridors. Among the back benches. They are all saying that you and I are having a love affair.'

'What do you want me to do?' I asked quietly.

'I don't know. I don't want any of this gossip reaching my fiancé's ears. I just want these stupid rumours to stop. I'm getting married in a few months' time.'

'Married!' I yelped. 'What about your degree?'

'I'll write the exams privately. Which is why I didn't join any college. My father is just waiting for my eighteenth birthday to fix the marriage date.'

I felt a great weight of sadness descend upon me. I wanted to take her in my arms and plead, 'Look at me. Do you think anyone else will love you as much as I do?' I began to walk towards her.

She moved a step back. I looked at the face I had singled out for attention day after day, the features that had entwined themsleves around every nerve in my body, and saw only fear there.

I stopped in midstride. I looked around me helplessly. I needed time. Time to show her how much I loved her. Time to make her fall in love with me. Time to bridge the chasm between teacher and lover. 'What is the hurry to get married? Why don't you finish your degree course first?' A frantic note crept into my voice as I sought some method to make her stay on. 'You are so talented. I was banking on you to bring honours to this college. That essay you wrote was one of the best I have ever read. And you are going to let it all go to waste, simply to play house.'

'I didn't write the essay,' she said.

'What?'

'I found it in a students' guide I bought in Trivandrum. It is written by a Professor Kurup from Gandhiji university,' she said, flushing.

I closed my eyes. I didn't know what I felt. Hurt. Betrayal. Anger. Humiliation. A fool. And then, like little rivulets after a thunderstorm they gushed into my heart from different directions. Flooding me with a rage I could barely restrain. 'How could you do something so devious? Passing off an essay written by someone else as yours! Tell me, do your friends know what you did? They must think I am such a fool. They are probably laughing at me,' I groaned.

'They laugh at you anyway. Do you know that the boys in my class count the number of times you look at me?' she said. 'As for all that poetry you recite—"Art thou pale for weariness, of climbing heaven and gazing on the earth, wandering companionless"—I don't have to make a fool of you. You do it all by yourself.'

That was when I lost my temper. If she had left me my self-respect, I am sure that I would have recovered in time. The pain would have become bearable. But no, she had to rob me of my dignity, and that I couldn't accept. In rage, in hurt, in recklessness, I retaliated the only way I could think of then. I wanted her to feel how I felt. If not in love, in hurt we would be companions.

I grabbed her arms and pulled her close. Then I ground my lips against hers. 'Take this,' I bit into her lips, holding her tightly to stop her from escaping my embrace. 'Take this as a gift from a teacher to a pupil. A wedding gift. A congratulation gift for having made such a prize fool of me.'

And when I had had my fill of violating her pride, I let her go. She burst into tears and rushed out.

I heard voices outside. I went to sit in my chair. There would be repercussions and recriminations. But I didn't care. She deserved it. She deserved to be punished, I told myself a hundred times. The taste of her mouth, the feel of her tongue struggling against mine, the rubbery fullness of her lips, mixed with the bile that rose into my mouth again and again. An unpleasant viscosity that wouldn't go away no matter how many times I washed my mouth.

When the rage died, realization dawned. I hated to admit it to myself, but I was ashamed of what I had done. I shouldn't have let rage rule me. And then I was afraid.

Would Omana tell her parents about what I had done? What would my students think of me once they knew the whole sordid story? Would they ever respect me again? I felt unsure of my teaching skills. I no longer knew whether I could trust my instincts. I had so desperately sought a miracle in my life that when Omana appeared on my horizon, I had pounced on her as the stairway to the fulfillment of my dreams.

I didn't think I could go through once again with another student what I had with her. The seed of hope, the sprouting of interest, the careful nurturing of talent, the endless waiting for it all to bear fruit in the form of academic honours.

I felt tired. I felt lonely. I felt desperate. What was I going to do?

Early in the morning I went back to my classroom for the last time. The bareness of my life loomed from behind the blackboard, hung from the rafters, and crawled under the benches. There was nothing left for me here.

When the bank opened, I withdrew all my savings and caught a bus to Kochi. I thought of my father, who had clung to his dignity with the same tenacity with which he had clung to the coconut tree trunk day after day. He had done it without a title before his name. He had done it effortlessly. He had done it because he knew a trade that told the world who he was and what he was capable of, without having to constantly prove himself. I finally understood the wisdom of his words. I decided I too would learn a trade.

One day, after I had been a painter's apprentice for seven months, I was walking down M. G. Road in Ernakulam. I wanted to buy a shirt. I thought I saw something I liked in a window. I went in and asked to see it. Boxes were pulled down and shirts pulled out. Shirts in blue, green, and white. Shirts with collars, without collars. Half sleeves. Full sleeves. Two pockets. One pocket. But nothing I saw made me want to take it home. As for the one in the window, they didn't have it in my size. Half an hour later I said no and walked out.

And suddenly I realized that I had said no without worrying that I had caused offense. At twenty-five I had finally become an adult. I had learned to put myself first. Not to bow and buckle to any pressure. To overcome a childish need for the world's approval.

I was ready to be on my own. All I had to do was find a place to start my life as an adult.

I decided to start my search from Shoranur. To the north were Kozhikode, Kannur and Kasargode. To the south were Kochi, Alapuzha and Kottayam. Somewhere there would be a place where I could live life the way I chose to.

I got into a bus. 'Where are you going?' the conductor asked.

'Where does this bus go?' I retorted.

He gave me a sidelong glance and said, 'Kaikurussi City.'

'Give me a ticket to Kaikurussi City,' I said, going to sit by a window. Kaikurussi City. I had never ever heard of it before.

The bus filled, and in a few minutes' time we were off. I kept my face resolutely towards the window. I didn't want to be inveigled into a conversation with anyone. Soon we left the main road behind and turned into a road that climbed and ran down, curved and circled and turned this way and that with a wantonness that made me catch my breath.

Stop names were called aloud. 'Vellapadam', 'Mannur', 'Karthiayini's Gate', 'Lenin's Gate'. I smiled. What kind of a place would this be where Karthiayini and Lenin lived side by side?

Every few minutes the bus would stop, and the passengers would trickle out. However, nobody got in. It was as though we were travelling to the world's end.

The smell of hay ripening slowly in the sun ran up my

nostrils. The clear skies made my eyes smart. I felt happy. The bus ground to a halt. 'Kaikurussi City!' the conductor called out, lighting a beedi. 'Ssh, ssh,' he hissed as I stepped out. 'We start back in one hour's time. This is the only bus, so you'd better be in it if you want to get back to Shoranur today.'

I looked around. Kaikurussi was a little hollow surrounded by several hills. The road we had travelled upon ended abruptly a hundred feet away from where the bus stood. There was a stillness in the air that made my heart beat faster.

I went into the tea shop and sat on a bench. I drank my tea quietly. There were several curious looks coming my way, but I pretended not to notice. Finally the tea shop man asked me, 'Whose house do you want to go to?'

'I don't know anyone here,' I said.

'Oh, so you got into the wrong bus, I see,' he smiled.

'Something like that,' I said.

'What is there to see here?' I asked.

'Nothing.' He laughed. 'There is not even a river running this way. Just fields, wells, a mountain, and distant hills.'

I smiled. Nothing. I liked the sound of it. I paid for my tea and went outside. A little further down the road was a huge boulder. I walked towards it. There was moss growing on the boulder. I felt the fur of time beneath my palm. A streak of blue whizzed past. A kingfisher that had learned to fish from the depths of a well. My soul danced.

Here is where I would live. Here where time stood still on the back of a boulder. Here where I need never know the anguish of life passing me by. Here where all roads ended and rivers dared not run through. Here I could be the man I had become. No past. No future. Simply a man of the present. Painter Bhasi.

And now I have you, Mukundan. Haunted and tormented by a million ghouls.

In the system of healing I have evolved, the examination of the patient has little to do with physical palpation. I do of course start with making a note of anatomical characteristics: Pale delicate skin. Fine features. Worry lines. Restless, with quick, darting movements.

But it was your mind that I had to fathom. For only when I understood what drove you to such unrest, to such distress, could I begin to prepare the remedy that when administered would cause the healing powers to respond. A remedy that would probably at first cause a brief and mild worsening of your state before it was assimilated into your system. Releasing an energy that would cure and heal your spirit.

But how was I to decide whether to use the shrub that smells of a sweaty horse or the unique Brahmi? Should I seek the power of the pepper or create a bitter concoction of bitter melon and a mineral salt?

I tried to read the workings of your mind. Your fears, your likes, your dislikes. But you were like a snail refusing to be coaxed out of your shell of solitude. You ignored all the overtures I made, resisted every attempt of mine to make you reveal the hoard of deep-rooted anxieties that lie buried in you.

I knew I had to be patient. I began to weave myself into the fabric of your everyday existence. So that when the time came for you to seek me out, I would be there. Willing to listen. Undeterred by the most macabre of confessions. Ready to respond to your plea for help. As Painter Bhasi. As One-screw-loose Bhasi. As the impresario of your destiny.

9

The Village Voice

Mukundan stretched languorously, unwilling to leave the comfort of the bed. Every minute seemed like another. He could stay in bed all day, lulled by this feeling of timelessness. No hurry to go any place, no one to meet. The sun slipped in through the window bars and prodded his eyelids open impatiently. A gentle breeze blew in, pregnant with the fragrance of frangipani.

He picked up the tabletop calendar and looked at it thoughtfully. It was July already. More than a month since he had returned to Kaikurussi. A month in which he had done precious little. With a little pang of surreptitious guilt he realized that he had made absolutely no effort to create a new life for himself.

He rubbed his stubble-flecked chin. A queer restlessness roamed through him. He fumbled for the pack of cigarettes and the matchbox that were tucked away in the top drawer of the bedside table. He lit one and inhaled deeply, letting the smoke trail the restlessness and emerge through his nose in twin jets. He propped the pillow up to enjoy his smoke better. Mukundan had never smoked in bed before.

Across the road, Barber Nanu would be sitting in front of Achuthan Nair, ready to give him a shave. Mukundan had given his father a set of disposable razors and asked him to try them. 'You won't ever have to worry about being nicked by the usual razor blade,' he had said.

But Achuthan Nair had disdained it as new-fangled nonsense and insisted on the barber visiting him every morning. He had his own silver-and-ivory-handled razor and a matching brush with bristles that with years of use was so flattened that it resembled a powder puff more than it did a shaving brush. All that Barber Nanu was expected to bring with him was the strop leather, the knife, a piece of alum, and the village gossip. 'Now that he hardly steps out, having the barber shave him every day is his way of keeping abreast of the village news. You would be surprised to hear how well informed he is about the happenings in the village,' Krishnan Nair had tried to soothe Mukundan's ruffled feelings.

Mukundan stubbed out the cigarette and stood up. Just because he had retired from service didn't mean he had retired from life, he told himself sternly. From this morning he was going to make a conscious effort to regain control of his life.

He took a deep breath and tried to touch his toes. Then he held his hips and jumped. He flapped his arms and swung them over his head. A few beads of sweat began to dot his face. For today, this would suffice. After breakfast, he decided that he would make a foray into the village. He would visit Shankar's Tea Club.

In the complicity of the night, the men of Kaikurussi might choose to congregate at Che Kutty's Toddy Shop. But during the day it was Shankar's Tea Club that was the nucleus of the village. In fact, Che Kutty himself dropped in at least a couple of times for a cup of tea and a smoke. Shankar didn't reciprocate the gesture as frequently, but he too was known to visit Che Kutty's establishment once in a while.

Mukundan took out a cream-coloured bush shirt. He stood in front of the cupboard and let his hands glide over the pile of trousers longingly. A mothball rolled out. Perhaps he should just give them away. God knows when he would don a pair of trousers again. In the village, wearing trousers would alienate every one. Not that there weren't men who didn't wear trousers. All the young ones and the men who held jobs in the nearby towns wore only trousers. But he was neither young nor did he hold a job. The villagers expected him to wear a mundu, and so he would.

Dressed, he admired himself in the mirror. He didn't look too bad. In fact, the shirt and mundu suited him very well indeed. He had about him the air of a mature, dignified man. A natural leader. Someone who had seen the world and understood its vagaries. Rather like his father had been when he returned from Burma. With delight Mukundan thought he looked like a man who could be at the helm of village affairs.

Suddenly he remembered the delicious aromas that filled Shankar's Tea Club at breakfast time. If he was to make his home here, he needed friends. And what better way to win allies than by breaking bread with them? Besides, he was tired of Krishnan Nair's culinary prowess. Krishnan Nair was a good but uninspired cook. Unfortunately his repertoire was limited, and Mukundan had been eating the same dishes with minor variations day after day. In fact, it had come to a point where he thought of the factory canteen food longingly. The kara-bath and the kesari-bath. The puri-sagu. The vegetable pulao and the chapatti-kurma.

Mukundan felt Krishnan Nair's eyes bore a hole in his back as he trudged up the hill. Krishnan Nair was sulking because he had refused to eat the breakfast he had cooked for him. 'What's wrong with this?' Krishnan Nair had demanded. 'Have you ever seen such fluffy iddlies? Taste this chutney, will you? It is delicious,' he cajoled.

'I know, I know,' Mukundan agreed. 'But,' he decided to be recklessly honest, 'I'm tired of eating the same thing day after day.'

'I thought you liked it.'

'I do,' Mukundan sighed. 'But not every day. Anyway, what's happened to the maid you were supposed to find?'

'Maids don't grow on trees,' Krishnan Nair retorted rudely. 'It's not like in the earlier days. Nobody wants to work in homes. They would all rather work at construction sites. There they can flirt with men, take endless coffee breaks and carry home wages every evening. Sluts, each one of them.'

Krishnan Nair was on his favourite diatribe, and Mukundan knew that if he let him, he would keep him there till there was no food left at Shankar's.

'I need to go to the town, to the bank,' Mukundan said as he began walking out. 'I have to arrange for the car. Vasu said I had to tell Shankar one day in advance.'

The sun was high in the sky, taunting all those who walked in its path. Mukundan walked in the shadow along the road that was little better than a cart track. On either side of the road were high banks of mud fringed with slim chattering bamboo and ancient silent trees. A faint breeze fanned his face and he saw butterflies flit around busily. For the first time since he had come to the village, he felt happy.

The intensity of the monsoon had died down. For a few days now, the sun had been out and shining till about mid-afternoon when the dense grey clouds would swoop down from behind the Pulmooth mountain. Sometimes it rained. Sometimes it didn't.

Two or three men gave him curious glances as he passed them. Mukundan let his lips stretch, parodying a smile. They pretended not to see him. Mukundan grimaced angrily. He didn't care. Who were these yokels anyway?

The regulars had already arrived at the Tea Club. When Mukundan walked in, they paused at whatever they were doing and stared. Only Kesavan Kurup, the retired schoolteacher, continued reading aloud the newspaper. Shankar's mouth slackened into a smile. 'What are you doing in the city this early in the morning?'

Mukundan went to sit on one of the benches close to Shankar's counter. 'I thought I'd sample your cooking,' he said with a small smile. The rest of them lost interest. Glasses of strong tea were served, a packet of beedi opened, and the first piece of gossip for the day aired.

'Have you heard from your son this week?' Shankar asked Kesavan Kurup Master.

The schoolteacher peered above his glasses and murmured, 'No, not yet. Maybe I will receive a letter this afternoon.'

'His son is a doctor and works in a place near Goa. He was the first boy from our village to become a doctor. He was a very brilliant student,' Shankar whispered to Mukundan and then, in his usual voice, asked, 'What would you like to eat?'

'Do you have any puttu and kadala curry?' Mukundan's mouth filled with saliva. He had to swallow in order to talk.

But Shankar's attention had already shifted to a point outside the shop. A black Ambassador had just come to a stop at the top of the slope. Shankar eased himself out from behind the bill counter and hurried towards the car. 'What brings you this way, sir?' Shankar's voice carried its effusiveness into the shop and into Mukundan's ear. 'Sir'. Mukundan cringed. Shankar hadn't been so respectful to him when he had walked in earlier. He craned his neck to get a glimpse of this intruder who caused even the phlegmatic Shankar to gush.

The car window framed a long, dark face with gold-metal-rimmed spectacles; the collar of a silk jubbah. A long bony hand covered in cream silk protruded from the window and stroked the side of the car. A heavy gold watch gleamed beneath the jubbah sleeve. The fingers tapped impatiently on the side of the car. On the middle finger was a thick gold ring set with a stone. Power House Ramakrishnan.

Mukundan saw Shankar gesture towards him and say something. Did Shankar expect him to get up and go there to pay homage to that upstart? Mukundan fumed. When Shankar continued to wave his hand, he looked away pointedly.

A few minutes later the car drove away and Shankar returned to the shop. 'Why didn't you come out and meet him? That was Power House Ramakrishnan sir,' Shankar said in a voice still awed, as if the chief minister had stopped by.

'I have met Ramakrishnan,' Mukundan said, refusing to use the prefix 'Power House' that had come to represent in many ways the man's standing in the village. That it had been a brief meeting, Mukundan didn't choose to elaborate upon. The villagers may have been dumbstruck by his aura of wealth, but he had known men more powerful and richer than him.

'He is a good man to know and befriend. Didn't he buy your paddy fields some years ago? You should call on him one of these days,' Kesavan Kurup Master said from behind his newspaper.

Shankar, not to be outdone, added, 'I don't think he'll be back this morning. He's off to meet the new circle inspector. Power House Ramakrishnan sir knows all the important people in this district, and they all think very highly of him.'

'We are lucky he chose to continue living in this village instead of moving to Shoranur or some other town,' Barber Nanu said earnestly. Power House Ramakrishnan was the best customer he had ever had in all his years of barbering. Ever since Power House Ramakrishnan had won the lottery prize and become a rich man, Barber Nanu had been asked to call at Power House Ramakrishnan's house every morning. Besides his daily fee for the shave, Power House Ramakrishnan gave him a sizeable tip every now and then.

Mukundan pretended not to hear them. Shankar suddenly slapped his palm to his forehead and said in a voice that brimmed with great remorse, 'I'm so sorry. I forgot your order. What is it you wanted, sir?'

The 'sir' mollified to a certain extent Mukundan's ruffled feelings. 'Puttu and kadala curry,' he repeated.

When the food arrived, it was nowhere close to what

memory had made it out to be. But at least it was a change from what he had been eating these past few days, and so he continued to eat. Beside, he was ravenous. Between mouthfuls he asked, 'Is the rice flour for the puttu from your home?'

Shankar shook his head. 'All that was in the past. Now I get the rice powdered at the mill. There's no one to do it at home. The only person who still has household help in this area is Power House Ramakrishnan sir. Nobody wants to work in houses any more. They all want to work on construction sites. Houses, houses, that's all you see everywhere. These Dubai chaps, I tell you—' he paused in the middle of his sentence and pointed out the new arrival with a movement of his head. 'Do you recognize him?' Shankar whispered.

Mukundan peered at the old man perched on the other bench. 'Isn't that Mad Moidu?' he whispered back.

'Do you remember what he used to look like? And now look at him in his Dubai lungi, polyester T-shirt, and his gold-plated watch. He thinks he's one of the village bigwigs now. However, everyone still refers to him as Mad Moidu. At least behind his back!' Shankar's contempt for the old man was obvious. But he wasn't considered a good businessman for nothing. He added two teaspoons of tea decoction to a whole glass of sweetened milk and took the glass of tea to the old man. 'Here's your usual paal-chaya,' he said offering it to the old man. ' How come you are late today, Hajiyar?'

Long long ago, when Mad Moidu was mere Moidu, he used to trot on his toes through the village. His feet had mammoth corns that made every step feel like a moment in hell. Moidu didn't dare complain. If he did, there would be someone else willing to carry the basket of tea for the Brooke Bond man who visited several villages in the district. Once when Moidu had gone away for a while, he returned to find his wife had·run away with a wandering puppeteer.

And so Moidu became Mad Moidu.

He set fire to his hut because he didn't want to live where she had once lived, eaten and slept. He sold her goat to the butcher and slit her cat's throat. And when his anger was spent, he sat under a tree for many days till the skies darkened and the monsoon began. Some said he was healed by the stinging rain cascading on to his head and puncturing his skin; by the rainwater puddles that cooled his heels and caused freshly stirred earth to creep between his toes. Some others said it was the passing of time. And there were the devout who claimed that it was the effect of the mullah's prayers that had turned him into his old self.

He found a new wife, fathered several children, and began to trot on his toes once again, carrying head loads of firewood. But the villagers continued to refer to him as Mad Moidu. For, while he might have crossed the line back to sanity, there was no knowing when he might trespass again where he had wandered for a while. Madness, once it had taken root, they believed, like fear, like tuberculosis, like water hyacinth, can be contained but never completely erased.

'*Hajiyar*, indeed!' Mukundan spluttered. 'Since when has Mad Moidu become a much-venerated man in the village?'

'Ever since he went on a haj pilgrimage a couple of years ago, he refers to himself as Hajiyar. However most of us think he didn't go further than Bombay,' Bhasi's voice crept into his ears. Mukundan looked at him in surprise. He hadn't seen the painter come in and sit beside him.

'I come here at least twice a day. This is where my customers leave a message for me,' Bhasi said, blowing into his glass of tea. ' In fact, if you wish to meet someone in Kaikurussi during the day, all you need to do is wait at Shankar's Tea Club for some time. The whole of Kaikurussi will pass you by sooner or later,' Bhasi added with a laugh.

'By the way, I am starting the work on your house tomorrow. Looks like the rains won't trouble us too much any more. I'll be in later today,' Bhasi said gulping his tea down in a hurry.

Mukundan watched him take out his plastic pouch and stuff his mouth with mint leaves. When Bhasi had left, Mukundan turned to Shankar and asked, 'Does he have a drinking problem?'

'That's probably the only problem he doesn't have,' Shankar laughed. 'No one has ever seen him in Che Kutty's shop.' Shankar added in a low voice, 'But then it could be because he thinks he's too good for the likes of us. I don't know if he drinks at home.'

Mukundan shifted uncomfortably in his seat and decided to change the subject. 'Where is he from?'

The tea shop owner shrugged. 'None of us know anything much about Bhasi. At first when he came to Kaikurussi one day, some ten, twelve years ago, we thought he had lost his way. But he never went back.'

Shankar lit a beedi and continued, 'He said he was a painter by trade. That was the time the temple board decided the temple needed to be renovated. He offered to do it for free. They just had to pay him for the material, he said, and that too only when he had finished. He got the carpenter to make him a special ladder, and he painted the temple walls so well that even the usually finicky Namboodiri was impressed and asked Bhasi to paint his house. The Plashi Mana is so huge that it kept Bhasi occupied for several months. What with these Dubai chaps building new houses all the time, he's never without work.

'Some years ago he bought a piece of land, with a house on it, near the temple. Then he married a widow from the next village. Now he is as much a native of this village as you and me.'

Mukundan choked on his mouthful. No matter what anyone said, he was not a native of the village in its true sense. He might have been born here. But that was all. He didn't belong here. And he didn't want to.

The puttu tasted like chalk and the curry was insipid. He didn't feel like eating any more. He washed his hands, rinsed his mouth, and went back into the shop to buy a newspaper. Sipping his tea, he began to turn the pages.

Mad Moidu sucked on his cigarette and sat there deep in thought. 'His son in Qatar hasn't sent the usual bank draft this month,' Shankar offered as if in explanation of Mad Moidu's silence.

When the postman came tinkling his cycle bell, all eyes turned to him. Postman Unni sidled up to Mad Moidu. They watched them conduct a stealthily whispered conversation. Postman Unni gesticulated furiously with his hands. Mad Moidu shook his head emphatically, and finally a slow smile broke on his face. 'Shall I come to the post office around lunchtime?' he asked.

When the postman moved away, Shankar, vested with the authority to question and comment, criticize and approve, asked in his carefully studied careless manner, 'What was all that about, Hajiyar? Has your son's draft arrived?'

Mad Moidu pondered whether to speak the truth or not. But finally the need to impress and cause a ripple among his cronies took over, and he growled, 'Draft! There's no DD. This time, he's sent it as cash in a parcel. Postman Unni said there is a parcel for me. What else could it contain but cash?'

Mukundan got up. He had hoped to establish his presence in the village. He had been certain that the villagers would be grateful to have someone like him with his city manners and knowledge of the outside world in their midst. He had seen himself discoursing on the ways of life outside the village. On American presidents. Battle tanks and sophisticated missiles. Amitabh Bachchan. Drug addiction. New inventions. He had conjured up in his mind an audience enthralled by the magic of his words; seeking his counsel, his opinion. He had thought he could take his father's place. Instead no one even noticed him sitting there. They were all so bemused by Power House Ramakrishnan's arrival and Mad Moidu's parcel of money. Krishnan Nair was right. These upstarts were ruining everything.

Mukundan paid for the meal and told Shankar, 'Will you please tell Vasu to come home tomorrow by nine in the morning? And could you arrange for an English newspaper for me? I want it without fail every day. The *Indian Express* should be fine.'

Two hours later, as Mukundan tried to hide under a mound of rice a piece of almost raw fish that Krishnan Nair had attempted to fry and had forgotten to turn over, Mad Moidu lifted the latch of the post office gate and crept in as silently as he could. There were a few people sitting on the low wall that ran along the length of the veranda. He tried to read their expressions, wondering if they knew why he was there. There were no secrets in this village. He pretended to mail a letter, flapping the lid of the ancient post box noisily.

Mad Moidu dusted a patch on the wall and sat there. He waited for the others to finish whatever they had come there to do. There was a certain pleasure to this waiting, as his mind jumped from one possibility to the other, wondering what the insides of the brown paper parcel would reveal. Apart from the money, what else would there be? He had always wanted a body spray he could perfume his armpits with. He'd always longed for the smell of prosperity to cloak him. Would Suleiman, his son, have remembered?

'Hajiyar!'

Mad Moidu gazed at Postman Unni's face blankly.

'Haji,' the postman sounded as if he was in a hurry. 'Just sign here and pay me five hundred rupees and you can take the parcel home.'

Mad Moidu drew out five crisp hundred-rupee notes

from one of the numerous pockets in his broad belt and handed it to the postman reluctantly. The postman continued to stand there on one leg, grinning foolishly, an expectant crane waiting for its catch. Mad Moidu drew out some soiled notes and thrust it into the postman's palm, muttering under his breath, 'Son of a pig!'

Mad Moidu looked at the package and wished he'd brought a sack along, and one of his grandsons to carry it. No matter how he held it, it peeked out awkwardly, adding substance to the rumour that he was sure was already circulating in the village. Once again, reminiscent of those old days, Mad Moidu trotted on his toes. Eager to reach home, in a hurry to tear open the brown paper parcel and see for himself the treasures from the land across the Arabian Sea.

In the afternoon Mukundan liked to take a little snooze in his armchair. He felt guilty if he lay down to sleep on a bed, but to nap with his feet up on the chair's long armrests was all right. In the sultry heat of the afternoon, it was impossible to sleep for a long stretch. The fan whirred noisily, but it just blew warm air around. Inside the main house the rooms were dark and cool. The wooden panelling and the red oxide floors kept it so. But the new section he clung to with all the tenacity of an embryo in the womb, absorbed heat easily. This is ridiculous, he told himself. I need to start treating the rest of the house as my own. Tomorrow, tomorrow... He postponed the decision. When Krishnan Nair peeped in, he was busily decorating the house in his mind.

'Mad Moidu is here,' he said hesitantly, apologetically for disturbing Mukundan's siesta.

'Why?' Mukundan asked shortly. He was much too comfortable to get up and go out to hear about the wondrous sack of money that had made its appearance earlier in the day.

'He refuses to tell me. He says only you can help him.'

'Why me? There are better men in the village who can help him. Let him go to that Ramakrishnan,' Mukundan snapped.

'He knows that. But if he insists on seeing you, he obviously thinks only you can sort out whatever his problem is,' Krishnan Nair murmured.

Curious now, Mukundan eased himself up, pulled a shirt on, and went out to the veranda where Mad Moidu and a teenage boy waited.

The old man stood up anxiously. 'It is this parcel I received today,' he began without bothering about the usual social niceties that precede a favour asked.

'Yes, I heard about it. What about the parcel of money?' Mukundan smirked.

'That's exactly it. The parcel didn't contain any money. Instead this is what I found,' Mad Moidu said, drawing a Muscle Master from a sack. 'When I took it to the city to find out what it could be, people told me all kinds of things. One fool even suggested it is a currency-printing machine. What does he think I am? An ass? Then Shankar said I should come to you,' he finished lamely.

Mukundan took the Muscle Master in his hands and examined it. How was he to tell this old man that someone had played a trick on him and what he held in his hand was a muscle developer? One of those mail-order items that you paid and took delivery of. Hence the five hundred rupees that he had had to cough up. Moidu's companion, the teenage boy, looked around him uneasily, and Mukundan realized who the perpetrator of this trick was. But he decided to keep his silence.

'Haji,' he began to explain as if he were talking to a child, 'there's been a mistake.' When he finished, Mad Moidu looked even more bewildered.

'So what do I do with this?' he asked querulously.

'Maybe you could donate it to the local youth club. I hear there's a vacant room adjacent to the reading room and library, where the boys do some bodybuilding. And if you gave them a good donation to buy some basic exercise machines, they might even name the gym after you,' Mukundan suggested.

Mad Moidu looked pleased at the idea. The boy didn't.

Krishnan Nair walked in, sighing. 'You shouldn't have suggested that,' he remonstrated. 'This village is ruined as it is, what with that Power House Ramakrishnan swanking around. And now you have put all kinds of ideas into that Mad Moidu's head. That stupid old man is going to be even more full of himself. Haji Moidu Gymnasium, indeed!'

Mukundan settled back in his chair. The thing about life in a village, he decided, was that you could never do anything right. If he had refused to see Mad Moidu, they would have said he was snooty. If he hadn't made a suggestion, he would have been accused of staying aloof. But now that he had, it was the wrong one to have made.

'What are you looking so thoughtful about?' a voice asked.

Mukundan looked up to see Bhasi. 'I came in to drop off the paint,' he said, pointing to the cans arranged by the side of the veranda.

'Oh,' Mukundan said, wishing the painter would go away. 'Krishnan Nair is in there somewhere. Why don't you go to the back door and ask him where you can store the paints?' he said sharply. The painter continued to stand there. Mukundan pretended to doze off. From beneath his eyelashes, he watched the painter give him a strange, piercing look and then walk away.

Mukundan began a letter in his mind to one of his favourite protégés. Back in the factory they knew his true worth and appreciated his guidance.

Dear Anand, he would write. *Trust this letter will find you and all our other colleagues in the Admin. section in the best of health and cheer. As for me, I'm pulling on in this place. I'm slowly getting used to village life. Believe me, it is nothing like what you see in all those Malayalam movies you like to watch on the video.*

I can understand your curiosity as to what I do all day. Actually, come to think of it, there isn't any fixed pattern to my day here. No piercing sirens telling me what time to begin work, what time to eat lunch, what time to return home. It is different, and very often I wish I could return to an office routine. It gave a structure to my existence.

When Mukundan woke up, it was half-past five. His throat felt dry and parched and he could feel the beginnings of yet another headache. The evening stretched ahead, long and empty.

'You look very dull. What is wrong?' It was the painter once again.

Mukundan shook his head. 'I am fine. It is just sleeping at this unearthly hour. I'll freshen up once I have had a cup of tea.'

'Why don't you come to the temple a little later? We are forming a pooram committee today. Power House Ramakrishnan will be the president as always. That way fund-raising becomes easy. You can be sure that he'll shell out a huge sum for the pooram fund. But all the other posts on the committee will be decided this evening. Everyone will be there except Che Kutty. And the only reason he stays away from these late evening meetings is because it is his peak business hour. All the labourers stop at his shop on their way home.'

Mukundan wondered what he could say to extricate himself from this invitation. The Mad Moidu incident had already given him an indication of how his suggestions would be received by the villagers. For a moment he thought of his father with admiration. He had lorded it over the village for so many years, and even now they sought his advice on all major issues. Mukundan wanted nothing to do with any committee where he had to play second fiddle to Power House Ramakrishnan. That man, he decided, was proving to be an infernal nuisance. Couldn't anyone in the village utter a sentence without bringing up his name at least once?

'I have several letters to write,' Mukundan said.

'Well, if you are writing letters, maybe you should write one to the Posts and Telegraphs Divisional Office. Your phone hasn't been working for many days,' Bhasi said.

Mukundan was surprised. The telephone had been installed two weeks ago and had failed to work from the tenth day onward. He had in fact sent Krishnan Nair to the exchange several times. But how did the painter know?

'I have been trying to call you from Plashi Mana, where I have been painting the insides of an outhouse,' Bhasi said, reading Mukundan's mind. 'Not that writing letters is going to be of any use. Bribing the exchange fellow will, though,' he added, as he walked towards the gate.

Mukundan felt a burning anger rise in him. He was tired of everyone telling him what to do. He would do it his way, and he would show them how successful he could be at achieving results. 'Krishnan Nair, where is my tea?' he hollered impatiently.

When he had drunk his tea, he decided to postpone writing to Anand. Instead, he slipped into his typewriter two sheets of paper with a carbon in between, and began to hammer furiously:

8 July, 1997

The Divisional Engineer
Telephones
Ottapalam
Palakkad District

Ref: Telephone number 0492 628343

Sub: Non-functioning of telephone connection

Sir,

I write you this complaint as a last resort to complain of the extreme harassment one of your department employees has been subjecting me to. I am a retired central government servant [a Class I Gazetted Officer] now living in Kaikurussi village, Palavara Taluk. I received my telephone connection on 24 June, 1996. To date, my telephone has been functional only for ten days.

In spite of making several complaints to the local exchange manned by an individual named Shyam M. S., I am yet to receive any response. Every day I am told, he is looking into it. The said individual, Shyam M. S., in fact stated in an absolutely rude manner that if I was dissatisfied with his services, I should write you a complaint.

The local people tell me that no action will be taken unless I pay him a bribe. As an honest citizen who has been paying his taxes regularly and has devoted many years of his life to the service of the country, I consider it unjust and morally wrong. And harassment of the worst sort.

I will be very obliged if you could look into this problem personally and remedy it at the earliest.

Thanking you,
I remain

Yours sincerely
Mukundan Nair

10

When the Pala Tree Burst into Bloom

Mukundan looked up from the letter he was reading and eyed the telephone balefully. Joseph, a colleague from his factory days, had written him a teasing note.

'Who is this woman Valsala who answers the telephone when I dial your number? Have you finally decided to give up your bachelor status? But if you intend to get married, why settle for someone old? Your Valsala doesn't sound very young . . .'

Mukundan picked up the telephone and listened to its hum. Two weeks after he had mailed the letter to the divisional engineer, the telephone exchange man Shyam M. S. had dropped in one morning with a yellow Rexene bag, a handset, and a sullen expression. Mukundan watched him fiddle with the instrument for a while. He felt a slow, mounting pride. His letter to the divisional engineer had done the job. Shyam M. S. had been reprimanded and asked to sort things out before 'that blasted old bandicoot went to the consumer forum.'

The telephone began to work. Except that each time the telephone rang, it wasn't for him. As for all his incoming calls, they went to some house where Valsala lived. But who on earth was Valsala?

Mukundan put down the letter and went outside to look for Bhasi. The painter would be able to tell him who Valsala was.

The painter was perched on his ladder scrubbing the west side wall of the new section. 'Bhasi,' Mukundan began hesitantly, 'do you know someone called Valsala?'

Bhasi stopped the scrubbing and came down the ladder. 'There are three Valsalas in the village. Shankar's little girl is Valsala. Prabhakaran Master's wife's name is Valsala. And Power House Ramakrishnan's daughter-in-law is a Valsala too. Why do you want to know?' he asked with a peculiar expression. 'Is there any problem?'

Mukundan shrugged. 'I can't call it a problem. But it is an embarrassing situation. You see, all incoming calls to my number somehow seem to go to her house, and a friend of mine who called from Bangalore has misunderstood the whole situation. Who is she? He said she sounded old.'

Bhasi laughed and drew out his little plastic packet of mint leaves, 'Old! Now I know whom you are referring to. You should see her. She is quite young. I would call her a young middle-aged woman. As for her voice, it is typical of Kaikurussi. God knows what it is about this village, but all the women here sound old and weary by the time they are twenty-five. I wonder if it is because they feel they are destined to a life-long tedium of chores, a monotony that is more mind-glazing than backbreaking. Do you remember Prabhakaran Master of Kandath House? Valsala is his wife. They live in the master's old family house, quite close to Plashi Mana.'

Mukundan shook his head. 'The name does sound familiar. But I can't say I remember who the person is. I am still in the process of renewing my acquaintances.'

Bhasi smiled. 'You should join the temple pooram committee. That is the best way to get your toehold in the village. Once the pooram committee accepts you, you will discover that things will happen much more smoothly here for you.'

Mukundan looked at the younger man's face with distaste. What did he mean by 'toehold'? I am not an upstart rootless creature like you, he wanted to snap. My family goes back at least six generations in the village. Everyone knows who I am. I don't have to go around building relationships and hoping that I will be accepted.

But Bhasi went on, impervious to Mukundan's displeasure. 'If I were you, I would pay that Shyam what he wants. Then he'll see to it that nothing goes wrong with your telephone line. Everyone in the village who has a phone knows it and has greased his palm one time or another. Even Power House Ramakrishnan with his important friends in important places has had to bribe him. Why don't you too?'

'What nonsense!' Mukundan snapped. 'Why should I pay him to do his job? Isn't the government paying him a salary? It is because people bow down to such pressure that these fellows take advantage. I am not going to pay him anything. If necessary, I'll take it up with his bosses.'

Bhasi began to climb his ladder. Mukundan watched him attack the skin of the walls. Then he too went back inside to begin his letter to Joseph. There was a great deal he wanted to write, including an explanation about Valsala, the young woman with the old voice.

There was something about Valsala that defied description. A lusciously plump woman with a blooming complexion and a head of jet-black curly hair, she attracted attention wherever she went. Men craned their necks to take a second look at her, and women eyed her surreptitiously, wondering what secret beauty treatment she used to keep her hair so black and her skin so radiant.

When Mukundan saw her for the first time, it was her eyes he noticed. One look at them and he felt a freezing of his soul. As if some monstrous hand, cold, clammy and totally ruthless had slithered up his spine. Her eyes were a dense black, remote and devoid of any emotion. A sort of one-sided glass, blurred, inviolable and unreachable, behind which she hid, unwilling to let anyone glimpse the real her. When she spoke, he understood what Joseph had meant by her voice sounding old. It was the voice of a woman who had no more dreams, no more expectations from life. Each syllable bore the hollowness of emptiness, a blankness that matched her opaque eyes until he began to wonder if she was under some spell and was what people referred to as the 'living dead'. A creature whose soul had been destroyed by the Odiyan's powerful magic and yet continued to go through the motions of life till one day some trivial illness caused her to drop dead.

Mukundan walked back from her house deep in thought. Though it was late in the afternoon, the sun continued to burn fiercely. The small sharp stones on the still-to-be-completed road bit into his feet through the leather sole of his slippers. Sweat ran down his brow. He wished he had taken an umbrella. But he had noticed none of the men in the village carried umbrellas no matter how hot it was.

Mukundan felt a strange sense of unease. He had decided to pay Prabhakaran Master a visit to discuss the telephone problem and to rope in support in his campaign against Shyam M. S. But Prabhakaran Master, Valsala told him, was not at home or in the village.

'When is he likely to come back?' he asked, trying to get a better look at her without staring.

'I don't know. He didn't say anything except that he would be gone for a while,' Valsala replied, her face devoid of all expression.

Mukundan got up to leave. When he turned to bid her farewell, she had already gone back inside. He sighed and looked at the huge old house. He thought he heard muffled sobbing coming from within the house. Why was she crying? Where was her husband? Had he, like Achuthan Nair, left her for another woman?

Mukundan wished there was someone he could talk to about the discomfiture he felt. Something was not right in that house. He wondered if he should mention it to Shankar. Then he chased the thought away. He knew what Shankar's answer would be. 'Why don't you mention it to

Power House Ramakrishnan? He'll be able to do something about it. Like I said, he has contacts in all the right places.'

Besides, Mukundan didn't want to lower himself to the level of sitting in the tea shop and gossiping. As for Krishnan Nair, he wouldn't even understand what he was talking about. That left only Bhasi. The painter's response might be strange, but at least he wouldn't bring up the name of that poser. Bhasi was perhaps the only person in the village who didn't fawn all over Power House Ramakrishnan.

Mukundan mopped his brow with his white handkerchief and began to walk faster. He wanted to reach home before Bhasi left for the day. He wondered what the painter knew about Valsala.

Valsala was just another housewife enmeshed in her daily chores, the upkeep of the compound, and watching television every evening. There were no surprises in her life. Even the coconut, cashew and pepper she grew in her garden had ceased to fill her with wonder. They simply followed the course of nature and yielded revenue in proportion to their numbers.

Valsala had never known an awakening of her senses. Not once in her life had a rare and exotic flower blossomed in her yard, filling the air with its overpowering fragrance. Then one night the pala tree at her doorstep at last burst into flower. She thought of how, when she was a young girl, her mother had forbidden her from stepping out into the night when the pala bloomed. 'Tie up your hair and stay inside. When the pala tree's fragrance fills the night sky, the Gandharvas come prowling, looking for virgins to seduce. Once a Gandharva has spotted you, there is no escape. He'll make you his slave with his soft voice, gentle caresses, and sensual magic. No mortal man will ever be able to satisfy you then,' her mother had said in an inexplicable voice, as if she were reliving a memory.

All night, for the first time in many years, Valsala tossed and turned in her bed, breathing in the scent of the pala flowers. Strange sensations coursed through her. Her nostrils flared, her lips parted, her eyes became a little less murky, every pore in her body opened, greedily seeking to fill their depths with this unique fragrance.

The next morning Valsala steeped curry leaves in warm coconut oil and added a pinch of camphor dust. In the twilight, when the oil was green and cloudy, she rubbed it into her hair and then washed it with crushed hibiscus leaves. She lined her eyes with the kohl she had made herself from lampblack, camphor and fine coconut oil. She took out her palakka modiram necklace, from its velvet-lined box that had lain untouched for several years, and clasped it around her neck. Wrapped in a thin mundu, the green and red stones of the necklace glowing, she went to stand beneath the pala tree, spreading her hair out to dry. Still wet from her bath, she let the breeze suck the moisture from her skin with a thousand lips. She stood there rubbing sandalwood paste into her skin, her bare breasts, and thighs. 'Come to me, Gandharva,' she beseeched. 'Can't you smell the fragrance of want in me? Look, the pala has burst into flower. I know you are there somewhere. Seduce me with your soft voice and caresses. Make me your lover, your slave,' she cried into the night.

Sridharan was no Gandharva with godlike looks and irresistible charm. His wooing of her was blatant and arrogant. Here was a woman in whom a secret fire burned. All he had to do was stoke it a bit. He took to dropping in at her house on some pretext or another. It was all perfectly legitimate. He had just bought a plot of land adjacent to her house and he was in the process of planting coconut saplings there.

He came in for a drink of water and stayed for lunch. He came to make a telephone call and left an hour later. He came in to borrow the newspaper and then helped her change a lightbulb. Any woman less naïve, less lonesome, would have seen through him and sent him away curtly. Not Valsala. She delighted in the attention he paid her. He complimented her on the lushness of her garden, and she smiled secretly, knowing he meant the lushness of her body. He praised her cooking and told her that her husband must be the most envied man in the village. He told her silly jokes that sent her into helpless peals of laughter. He had said he loved to hear her laugh.

Most of all he made her feel like a woman. A desirable woman. And every moment Sridharan spent with her made her feel even more discontented.

She looked around her. The house that had held her captive for the last twenty-three years—the kitchen where she had cooked thousands of meals, the dingy blue walls, the old-fashioned furniture—and felt a sob grow in her. When she stepped outside, the coconut, cashew and mango trees became prison walls she could never scale. The pepper vines handcuffed her to the land, and the melon vine bound her to the house. She felt the house and the land were sucking her dry of her youth. But it was her husband who made her want to flee.

He was only twelve years older than she was, but he'd already lost most of his hair and some of his teeth. He looked a feeble old man, and that was what he had become. Preferring kanji to a proper meal of rice, curry and fish. Belching, farting, and forever complaining about the vagaries of his digestive system. Demanding she give him a rubdown first with heated oil and then with a towel soaked in warm water. His face creased into a perennial frown while they watched National Network on the TV every evening, even as she hankered for more. Cable TV operators had looked at the distance separating each house from its neighbours and had given up the idea as non-feasible. The only recourse was to buy a dish antenna of your own. But he wouldn't consent to that. She wanted Asianet and DD4; the gloss of English channels and the glamour of Zee. She wanted twenty-four hours of nonstop viewing and the right to choose.

But he said, 'No. I'm a schoolteacher and not a Gulf-returned man. I can't afford frivolous expenses, and even if I could, I hate displays of ostentation.'

He never looked into her face or tried to fathom her desires. He never felt the curve of her hip or cupped the fullness of her breasts. He never whispered in her ears how beautiful she was or tried to show her with caresses how desirable she was. He couldn't even fill her womb with a child. He was preoccupied with his body, his illnesses, the strain of keeping forty unruly boys under control all day, and staying clear of school politics. Sleep was his only escape, and, curled on his side in a foetal ball, he drifted into a state of blissful non-existence broken only by little snores.

Valsala lay beside him, wide eyed, staring into the darkness and fantasizing about a man who'd thrust her roughly to the ground and make passionate love to her under a starlit sky. A Gandharva whose whispers bore the inflections of Sridharan's voice. A demon lover with the muscular chest and pillar-like thighs of Sridharan.

The lumpy cotton mattress she lay on turned into clods of freshly turned earth. She could hear the crickets urging her on. The fragrance of the night filled her nostrils. She could almost feel the stubble on his chin raze the softness of her skin, his teeth nip her flesh, and the strength of his hands as he gathered her close to him. For a moment, she thought it was him beside her and she turned to the supine form eagerly. When she realized who it really was, she felt more trapped than ever in a bloodless marriage.

I am just forty years old. I don't want to be pushed into old age before it is time. I want to live. I want passion. I want to know ecstasy, she told herself, night after night.

The first signs of change appeared in Valsala's cooking.

She banished the insipid molagushyam from her kitchen. 'I have had enough of these bland parippu-coconut-vegetable combinations,' she told her perplexed maid, sweeping a mound of chopped cucumber away. 'I don't want to see a green papaya, an ash gourd, or a colocasia stalk for as long as I live. Go to the city and see if you can find a breadfruit. Otherwise buy some potatoes and carrots. We will have a masala curry for lunch today. If there is a fish as long as your arm and as thick as your thigh, buy that too.

'I don't want tiny sardines or baby mackerels. Tell the man who brings baskets of fish on his bicycle that henceforth he should save a big fish for me. Sole or pomfret. Seer or cod. Anything big and meaty. And tell the musaliyar that I would like a kilo of mutton tomorrow. It's been so long since I ate mutton marinated in a paste of ginger, freshly ground coriander and pepper, and roasted on a slow wood fire.'

From then on, no matter how much Prabhakaran Master complained of indigestion, Valsala cooked in a frenzy. She revived old recipes and experimented with new ones she found in women's magazines. She speckled her cooking with spices. Throwing in chillies generously, grinding cloves, cinnamon bark, poppy seed and cashew nuts into her gravies. Ghee replaced oil. Pappadums were no longer roasted but deep-fried to a pleasing golden fullness. The house was scented with the richness of excess. Of cravings being satiated. Of forgotten desires blossoming.

It was inevitable that Sridharan and Valsala should become lovers. As it was inevitable that soon Valsala began to long for an intimacy of a protracted nature instead of the furtive caresses and couplings they managed in the middle of the day, late in the evening, and sometimes at the break of dawn. But there were all sorts of reasons why Valsala couldn't just abandon her old life and elope with Sridharan. There was the land she had slaved over and the house she was mistress of—both of which were her husband's. Then there were the retirement benefits he would get when he retired from the Lower Primary School in Pannamanna three years from now. And then there was the sizeable LIC policy Meenakshi had coerced him into investing in. After twenty-three years of marriage, she thought she deserved to have it all. She didn't want to give it up just like that. Nor did she want to give up Sridharan.

11

A Harvest of Discontent

When the police jeep drove into Kaikurussi, a ripple ran through the village. 'The police have come to Kaikurussi! Something is seriously wrong! Or why should they be suddenly here?'

The sight of a policeman was unusual in the village. The nearest police station was eight kilometres away. Only a dire emergency would warrant their presence.

The last time the police had been in the village was during the burning of the Babri Masjid. The violence that had stricken Ramjanmabhoomi, thousands of kilometres away, had been reenacted outside Shankar's Tea Club. A couple of RSS workers had taunted a few Muslim students on their way to the Madarasa. They had snickered, 'Where are you off to, wimps? Tell your mullah that we are not going to let the mosque stand there for too long. We'll tear it down just like we did with the Babri Masjid. Do you think we are going to let you go on living here? We'll wipe you out, each one of you, till we are a fully Hindu land. Why don't you go across to Pakistan? That's where you belong, not here.'

In retaliation the Muslim League workers beat up the RSS men. Suddenly Kaikurussi had become a hot spot of communal violence, needing a full-time battalion of poiice stationed there permanently, complete with tear gas shells and rifles.

But a month later the village settled back into a state of communal harmony, mutual hate and dissension forgotten. The truckload of policemen had proven to be more of a nuisance than they had planned for.

Anywhere else the absence of a man would have gone unobserved. But in Kaikurussi every man was a walking census board. Strangers were noticed, illnesses remembered, births and deaths recorded, and the comings and goings of each resident noted. No one remembered seeing Prabhakaran Master leave. It was as if one morning he disappeared from the face of the earth.

When the police jeep stopped at Shankar's Tea Club, a heated debate was in progress. It had begun with a news item Che Kutty had chosen to read aloud: 'The state government has declared that as part of the Onam festivities, an extra kilogram of sugar is being made available at the state-run fair-price shops—they are trying to buy our votes with a kilo of sugar,' Che Kutty said in disgust, folding the newspaper and slamming it down on the table.

'There is no electricity in the state. There are no jobs for the educated. Rice and kerosene cost the earth. Who do they think we are? A colony of ants to be satisfied with a kilo of sugar?' Postman Unni demanded of no one in particular.

'We should be thankful that we are at least getting a kilo of sugar,' Kesavan Kurup Master said, peering at the newspaper.

'It's all right for you to say that,' Barber Nanu interjected bitterly. 'Onam's just a week away, and I don't know how I am going to raise the money I need to buy provisions for the Onam feast. How can you celebrate Onam without a proper feast? Do you know what the price of bananas is?'

No one answered Barber Nanu. For at that moment a police constable jumped out of the jeep and looked around him inquiringly.

'I think the new circle inspector must have come to the village to visit Power House Ramakrishnan,' Postman Unni said.

The police constable walked into the tea shop and asked to be guided to Prabhakaran Master's house. The kilo of sugar was thrust aside, and its place was taken by the juicier proposition of Prabhakaran Master's plight. Something must have happened to him, someone said. Possibly he's been killed in an accident, someone else added. Or maybe he had embezzled some school funds and run away, a voice mumbled.

When Bhasi, who had gone along as the guide, came back, he said that the police inspector had given Valsala an unusually suspicious look and barked, 'We are here to investigate the sudden disappearance of Prabhakaran Master.'

'What did she say?' everyone at the tea club clamoured to know.

'Nothing, actually,' Bhasi said. 'She simply asked them to come into the house. She didn't seem surprised or, for that matter, perturbed. I wonder who informed them that the Master has not been seen for some weeks now.'

When Bhasi left, Kesavan Kurup Master murmured, 'He must be the one who tipped the police off. I wonder what they'll do to that poor woman?'

There were several rounds of cross-examination, and the house and compound were searched. But nothing conclusive turned up. Meanwhile the school authorities produced a letter written and signed by Prabhakaran Master, asking for sick leave as he was suffering from typhoid. The sub-inspector sent it to the handwriting experts and called in the circle inspector. The circle inspector, who had come in on a transfer and was seeking to make his mark in the department, asked for a fresh round of cross-examination. Sniffer dogs were sent for.

Amidst all this commotion, the telephone would ring and the caller would ask for Mukundan Nair. That's when the police decided that Mukundan was a lead worth investigating.

Circle Inspector Devasiya and a few constables went to Mukundan's house unannounced. One moment Mukundan had been taking a nap in his armchair, and the next minute, he was woken up rudely by the snickering sound of the jeep as it drove up to the doorstep. Bleary-eyed, Mukundan watched them come up the steps. Krishnan Nair was already in a flutter. He stood in the veranda wringing a towel and muttering, 'What's going on? Will someone tell me what's happening? Why are the police here?' Mukundan's heart began to beat faster. He didn't know why. Like any other man, he had committed his share of petty crimes. Peeing in a public place. Ignoring railway station rules and not buying a platform ticket and then slipping out of the station through a gap in the fence. Throwing a stone at his neighbour's dog. But none of it warranted police intervention. He had done nothing wrong. He wasn't guilty of any crime, and yet the sight of the police jeep at his doorstep made him cringe in the manner of a man who had some sordid secret to conceal. He wondered if the police had this effect on everyone. He hid his trembling hands behind his back and went to the doorway.

Circle Inspector Devasiya seated himself in the armchair and glared at Mukundan. Police constables flanked him on either side as if they expected someone to suddenly pounce on their chief and tear him to pieces.

Long years of service with the government had given Mukundan a repertoire of faces to wear when confronting authority. He put on his most humble expression, the one that had always held him in good stead when talking to the GM of his factory, and said quietly, 'How can I be of help to you, sir?'

Circle Inspector Devasiya glared at him some more, his bristly caterpillar eyebrows kissing in the center of his forehead. 'Why are your calls going to 628383?' he growled.

Mukundan sighed and put on his much-harassed-but-I-continue-to-patiently-suffer look and explained to the overbearing policeman his feud with Shyam M. S.

Circle Inspector Devasiya rested his hands on his paunch which—undeterred by the clasp of the impressive steel buckle and belt—rolled out of his trouser waistband. He muttered an eloquent 'H'mm,' as if he didn't believe one word of what he had heard.

Mukundan could see the wheels turn in the policeman's mind as he weighed the impact this case would have in the department, and his possible promotion. Circle Inspector Devasiya got up and began to examine the room, poking his baton behind a stack of cushions, pushing the curtains aside. Mukundan wondered what he expected to find there. Valsala's bra or Prabhakaran Master's decapitated head? Then the circle inspector's gaze fell on a stack of tapes, and his manner changed. 'Are you a Mukesh fan too?' he asked, and his voice had mellowed into that of a long-lost friend.

'Yes,' Mukundan said, bewildered by the sudden change in his manner.

The circle inspector smiled. The transformation was incredible. The wild bison-like face with fierce eyes and angry mouth became almost bovine in its gentleness. Like one of those happy cows shown on chocolate boxes, contentedly grazing on Swiss slopes. He sat on the bed close to the tape deck and began to examine the tapes, humming one of the tunes that the singer had made popular. Abruptly he stopped singing and asked, 'Tell me, what is someone like you doing in a place like this?'

Mukundan stopped holding his breath and asked Krishnan Nair to bring some tea and the Marie biscuits he kept for contingencies such as this. He realized he was suddenly above suspicion. By the time Circle Inspector Devasiya was ready to leave, forty-five minutes later, they had crossed the boundary of acquaintanceship and were racing toward a more effortless relationship.

Mukundan knew he would never presume to call it friendship, but it was something of that nature. Though never for a minute was he allowed to forget in how important a personage's company he was.

Circle Inspector Devasiya picked up a tape and weighed it in his hands. 'Shall I borrow this for a week or two? I don't have this one in my collection,' he offered by way of explanation.

Mukundan managed to beam as, with a pang, he offered the tape to the policeman. 'Please do. I am so happy that I've found a fellow Mukesh fan.' He knew he would never see it again. In return he decided to ask him for a favour. 'Sir, could you please put in a word for me and sort out this problem at the local telephone exchange?' Mukundan asked.

The circle inspector put the tape in his pocket and said, 'No problem at all. Don't worry, he won't be playing any more games with you.' The circle inspector instructed a constable to go and rough up the telephone exchange man. Apart from returning a favour, it was also a good way to demonstrate to the village the extent of his power.

The sniffer dogs came up with nothing. Circle Inspector Devasiya prowled through the compound thoughtfully. Then he noticed that a portion of the fencing separating it from the adjacent plot was really a kind of a gate. All he had to do was lift the bamboo frame to move it. Inquiries revealed that the neighbour was a young man in his late twenties who had bought the plot six months ago and was planting it with coconut saplings. He was also very friendly with Valsala, he learned. Circle Inspector Devasiya went into the plot and stood looking around him carefully. He noticed a line of saplings that weren't as high as the rest. 'When were these planted?' he asked Ayyappan, one of the farm workers, who was digging a ditch.

'Not very long ago,' Ayyappan replied.

'Can you tell me exactly when?' the policeman snapped.

'I think it was about a month ago.'

'Dig them up,' Circle Inspector Devasiya said. He had a hunch, and he hoped to God it was right.

'What?' Ayyappan thought the policeman had taken leave of his senses.

'You heard me. I said, dig them up,' Circle Inspector Devasiya said, pointing to one of the smaller saplings.

Beneath that first sapling, Ayyappan's spade brought forth an object wrapped tightly in a plastic sheet. A severed hand. Ayyappan began to retch, and Circle Inspector Devasiya called for more men to speed up the dig. A harvest of gruesome tubers turned up one by one as the pits produced various parts of Prabhakaran Master. In the last one his blood-stained clothes and an axe, which Ayyappan identified as Sridharan's by a notch on its handle, were found.

All through the digging Valsala maintained a stony silence that was mistaken for shock. As for Sridharan, when the spade threw up the first clod of earth, he fled Kaikurussi. A warrant was issued for his arrest, and the axe, clothes, and dismembered corpse were sent to the lab. Valsala wept and banged her forehead against a wooden pillar. To everyone who came to commiserate with her on her husband's murder, she cried, 'But why did he do it? I treated him like a younger brother, and this is how he repayed my kindness. I knew that he'd had a quarrel with my husband on some encroachment into his land. But this? How can anyone be so inhuman?'

There was a great deal of sympathy for the widow. She was childless, and if the rumours were right, she didn't have much of a family to fall back on. Not that she needed financial help, but at times like these a woman needed the support of her family.

But the axe handle came up with a set of twin prints, Sridharan's and hers. And suddenly she was no longer the poor widow but an evil creature who had killed her husband mercilessly.

Who thought of it first? Who was the one to realize that there could be a solution to this tangle of bodies and minds? What came first? A word or gesture? Or in the desperation of their need, did the thought split into twin streams and channel into their minds at the same time? So that when their eyes met, they knew what had to be done without having to plot, scheme, or devise the deed.

Later on, of course, she said he had forced her into doing it. And that he had been the one who masterminded it and she had been an unwilling accomplice blackmailed into partnering him because in a weak moment she had succumbed to his advances.

But the axe handle bore both their fingerprints. A kind of nuptial knot that bonded them in this unholy union. What about the fingerprints on the axe handle? the police demanded.

Valsala said that she had borrowed Sridharan's axe some weeks ago to chop wood for the kitchen, and so it was natural that her fingerprints should be on it. Everything she said incriminated Sridharan but absolved her. But there were too many things weighing against her. The piece of fencing that hinted at clandestine meetings. Her explanations for her husband's absence. In the end what implicated her well and truly was the leave letter that the school authorities had produced. The handwriting expert said she had written it. The case was solved. All that was left to be done was to find Sridharan.

Circle Inspector Devasiya, who dropped in on Mukundan when the case was tied up and filed, explained what he had pieced together as the 'grand plan'. It was a clever one; its simplicity made it almost brilliant. Both Valsala and Sridharan knew that Prabhakaran Master had almost nothing to do with the rest of the village. His absence would be noticed only after a period of time. So one night, as he slept, curled into a ball as usual, they had crept in. And as one of them covered his mouth, the other one raised the axe. In a matter of minutes, a whole man had been reduced to twelve segments. Easy to dispose of, unlike a whole corpse.

Earlier in the day Sridharan had told his men to dig a line of pits almost five feet deep. He said he had ordered a special variety of coconut saplings, and they needed very deep pits. Prabhakaran Master was put to rest in a line of pits over which a foot or two of mud was shovelled. The next day Sridharan personally planted each one of the saplings and asked the men only to help fill the pits.

Meanwhile Valsala told her maid that Prabhakaran Master had gone to Thiruvananthapuram on official work. He had, she said, walked to Kailiad early in the morning so that he could take a jeep from there to Shoranur and board a train onward. Two weeks later she told the woman that he hadn't yet finished what he had gone there for and would be back only after a month.

Six weeks later, when Prabhakaran Master had still not returned, Valsala would have filed a complaint. She knew inquiries at the school would reveal his letter asking for leave of absence. But it would be construed as a kind of midlife crisis, and he would be the man who had abandoned his wife and run away. Later there would be some mangled body distorted beyond recognition, which she would identify and claim as her dead husband. In ten days' time, their plan would have gone into action except for the interference of a local busybody.

In the days after Valsala was led away in handcuffs, Mukundan oscillated between fear and regret. The sight of his typewriter made him cringe. He hadn't meant for any of this to happen. When he had come back from Valsala's house that day, he had decided to write the letter only so that Prabhakaran Master could be traced. He'd thought that the heartless man had abandoned her. He had been deeply disturbed by what he thought was hopelessness that he had glimpsed in Valsala's eyes.

'Have you seen the newspaper this morning?' Bhasi's voice broke the stillness of the morning.

Mukundan looked up from the cup of tea he had been holding in his hand for a long while. 'What does it say?' he asked absently.

'Murder suspect nabbed.' Bhasi read aloud:

'Murder suspect Sridharan, accused in the Prabhakaran Master murder case, was finally apprehended by the police yesterday afternoon at Vanniamkulam. The accused, disguised as a sanyasi, was travelling in an autorickshaw from Ottapalam to Shoranur. Suspicious of the real identity of his passenger, the autorickshaw driver alerted the police. In a matter of minutes the police were on the spot and arrested Sridharan. Circle Inspector Devasiya said all kudos go to driver Rajan for his prompt action.

'It may be recalled that Sridharan, twenty-nine, along with Valsala, wife of Prabhakaran Master, had brutally killed the schoolteacher in his bed on the night of 14 July at Kaikurussi village. The body was then dismembered and buried in individual pits in a coconut grove owned by Sridharan. The accused had been on the run ever since 8 August when the gruesome murder of Prabhakaran Master came to light.'

'Did you ever think anything like this would happen in Kaikurussi?' Bhasi asked folding the newspaper.

Mukundan stared at the cold tea unseeingly. Then, unable to contain it any longer, he blurted out, 'I wrote that letter.'

'What letter?' Bhasi asked softly.

'I didn't think any of this would happen when I wrote a letter and sent it to the police station. I thought he had deserted her. I felt sorry for her. I only wanted to help her. I didn't want her to go through what my mother did,'

Mukundan rambled.

'Valsala is a cold-blooded murderess. She deserves to be punished. As for writing that letter, you have nothing to be ashamed of. You should feel proud that you were instrumental in bringing a criminal to dock. And that is exactly who she is. A clever and evil creature,' Bhasi said taking the cup from Mukundan's hand. 'Tell me about your mother,' he said. 'Tell me why it is that every lonely woman reminds you of her.'

Mukundan stared at him for a minute. 'My mother. . .' he began and then suddenly stopped. 'I don't know what you mean,' he said, avoiding Bhasi's eyes. Mukundan felt them settle on him. It was like being put under a microscope. He wondered if Bhasi could see through the many layers of self-deceit. He worried that he would find the wriggling secrets buried deep in him.

For a moment he wished it were night. When shadows encouraged the darkness of the soul to venture outside. When he could sit across from Bhasi with a glass of rum in his hands and let its fiery fumes sear his throat and dull the watchful spirit that guarded the secrets of his mind so jealously. When he could let feelings, pent-up for many decades, wash over his listener and leave Mukundan himself feeling empty and light.

For a moment he wished he knew how to confide.

12

A Matter of Hair and a Tug of War

For several days after Valsala was taken into custody, Mukundan remained in deep depression. Then one morning he woke up feeling a great sense of calm. I only did what I believed was right, he thought as he lay on his bed watching dust motes pirouette and bow in a beam of light.

As he stood in the bathroom daubing shaving foam on his cheeks and chin, Mukundan felt even better. He puffed out his left cheek, raised the razor, and cut a clean swath through the foam. Left cheek. Right cheek. Chin. The meticulous flicking around the moustache. And finally, carefully, the throat. The deliberate and methodical movement of his hand restored his sense of well-being. I have to learn to be happy here, he told himself as he splashed eau de cologne on his freshly shaven face. I just need to make the effort. 'I have to be careful that simply because I have begun to live in a new place, I don't let the standards I set for my life years ago slip,' he murmured through clenched teeth, feeling the cologne sting where the razor had caught at his skin.

Mukundan hummed as he bathed. Again and again, he raised the plastic mug brimming with tepid water and splashed it over himself, feeling it slither over his skin like silk. When there was no more water left, he dried himself carefully and then powdered himself with Cuticura talc. Fragrant and fresh, he put on his clothes and went to sit in his armchair until Krishnan Nair called him in for breakfast. He turned the pages of the newspaper, humming under his breath. He felt as if a great weight had been lifted off his chest. He decided that he would tackle the post office issue that morning itself. There was no sense in postponing it any longer. He thought of the letter he had mailed to the Postal Superintendent some weeks ago.

'Sir,' he had written, 'for the past thirty years, the post office at Kaikurussi village at Palavara Taluk has been located in my building. I would like to bring to your attention that while I have put in modern conveniences like a toilet in the building and arranged for periodical repairs as and when necessary, the rent I receive reflects none of this. In this age of inflation and high prices, you will agree that Rs 45 per month can hardly be termed as a reasonable rent.

'As a retired Class I Gazetted Officer relying just on my pension as a sole source of income, I would be extremely grateful if the rent can be raised to match the prevailing market rents in the area.'

Mukundan stood in the post office sticking stamps on an envelope. He looked at Kamban out of the corner of his eye curiously. There was nothing particularly distinctive about Kamban except for the nipple-like mole above his left eyebrow. A frail dark man in his mid-forties, he had a head of sleek grey hair and the pusillanimous expression of a much-whipped dog.

Until two years ago Kamban had worked in the post office at Perinthalmanna. When the postmaster slot fell vacant at Kaikurussi, he requested a transfer and was given it. Every day as he trudged home, he offered a little prayer of thanks that he was back in the village he was born in.

At first the village didn't know how to react to his presence. One half of them kept him at length, going about their business brusquely, afraid that he would take liberties if they demonstrated any signs of familiarity. The other half pretended to look through him, preferring to deal with Postman Unni. But Kamban seldom joined in the gossip the rest of the village liked to carry to the post office. He wore his aloofness as if it were a protective amulet guaranteed to keep away the wrath of all creatures malevolent. When he had to deal with any of the villagers, he did so awkwardly, shrinking into himself as though afraid that they would think nothing of hurling a stone at him, simply for the pleasure of hearing him yelp. Once the villagers realized that Kamban wasn't interested in making any overtures of friendship, they settled into a kind of amicable distance in their relationship in which nothing beyond postal transactions was encouraged.

On an impulse Mukundan decided to invite Kamban home and broach the subject there. 'How about coming to my house for a cup of tea one of these days?' he said in what he thought was quite a casual manner.

For a moment Kamban's eyes widened, the whites of his eyes spilling a secret fear. Then he mumbled, as his hands nervously stacked the files on his table, 'Yes, yes, I certainly will.'

As Mukundan walked out of the post office, Postman Unni shot him a curious look. The kind of look that says, Are you sure you know what you are up to? Later in the day, after lunch, Krishnan Nair hovered around with the harassed look that seemed to sneak on to his face every time he spoke to Mukundan these days. Now what, Mukundan wondered when Krishnan Nair stood before him, diligently avoiding his eyes. 'I hear you invited Kamban to visit you,' he said abruptly.

Mukundan looked up from the newspaper he was pretending to read. 'So?' he asked mutinously, wishing he knew how it was that Krishnan Nair made him feel like a ten-year-old, and an idiotic one at that.

'You should know better,' he said frowning.

'What should I know better?' Mukundan asked, a little baffled. What code of etiquette had he broken with a harmless invitation?

'His father used to come here every morning to empty buckets of shit your father spewed out from his bowels with great regularity,' Krishnan Nair said with the sort of repressed impatience that uncles reserve for moronic nephews. 'And now you expect me to serve his son biscuits and tea!'

'I didn't know that!' Mukundan protested, a little abashed by what he had done. But he was unwilling to let Krishnan Nair know that he knew that he had committed a kind of social faux pas. After all, it was his house.

'Anyway, I don't believe in things like caste. When I was in the factory, my department comprised all kinds of people. Brahmins, Christians, Muslims. As for my boss, he was a Dalit. A Harijan. We all ate in the same canteen, drank from the same tap. We are all the same, you know. Human beings!' Mukundan said, swallowing the memory of the distaste that used to come crawling into his mouth when Shri Ramappa, the section manager, shoved a cigarette into his mouth for a few puffs and returned it to Mukundan coated with his saliva.

The first time Mukundan had refused to share his cigarette, he had been subjected to the brunt of the older man's tongue. Which, tempered by years of oppression and sharpened by newly accorded authority, had an edge that could draw blood with little effort. And Mukundan had stood helplessly in front of Shri Ramappa as he snarled, 'I am sick and tired of men like you who think that being born in an upper caste gives you the divine right to treat the rest of us like animals. Look around you; the world has changed. You are not kings any longer. Here in my office I won't allow any prejudices to rule. So you had better watch out!'

Mukundan didn't dare say anything because he knew Shri Ramappa was vested with the power to wreck his confidential report. So Mukundan stood there staring at his shoes while his mind raged and raved—Listen, you heap of shit, your ancestors cleaned my ancestors' turds, and that is all you are capable of. Moving shit heaps. You are still the same shit cleaner that you were even if you are now dressed in a terrycot shirt and polyester trousers!

But Mukundan didn't think Krishnan Nair needed to know any of this. Instead he declaimed, enjoying the feel of the words as they rattled off his tongue with a fervour he hadn't known he possessed, 'Has not Kamban eyes? Has not Kamban hands, organs, dimensions, senses, affections, passions? Fed with the same food, hurt with the same weapons, subject to the same diseases, healed by the same means, warmed and cooled by the same winter and summer as we are? If you prick him, will he not bleed? If you tickle him, will he not laugh? If you poison him, will he not die?' Mukundan stopped abruptly, unable to remember how the rest of the passage went.

Krishnan Nair flicked his towel as if to get rid of Shylock's wrath hanging in the air and said, 'Fine words. But you should reserve them for your educated factory cronies. Here in Kaikurussi we are all bumpkins with neither your education nor sophistication to be swayed by passionate waving around of the hands. And if you want to live here and fit in, you have to behave like the rest of us do!' Then he walked off with a snort, mumbling, 'If you prick him, will he not bleed? Try pricking him, and you'll have the whole of the Harijan colony and half a dozen politicians at your doorstep demanding compensation.'

For a few days Mukundan avoided the post office, not wanting Kamban to take him up on his impetuous offer. But when Mukundan saw him next, it was as if only he could sense the ghost of awkwardness between them. Icy fingers of embarrassment seemed to slither only on his back. As for Kamban, he behaved as if the words had never been spoken.

There were no omens to foretell the arrival of Philipose. No darkening of the horizon. No sound of a million wings beating through the air. No ominous rustle of paddy as the insect jaws set to making a wasteland of a fertile universe. One day there was Kamban hovering like a gentle spirit in his quiet world. Dispenser of perforated stamp sheets and airmail letters. Keeper of the savings bank. Conduit of people's hopes and despair to the outside world. The lord and master of Kaikurussi Post Office. Then appeared Philipose: hungry as a swarm of locusts and capable of more devastating changes than the seven swarms that turned Egypt into a desert of barrenness.

Philipose arrived in a yellow and black taxi one morning. He stood outside the post office building and touched the top of his head to check if his hairdo was intact. When he was barely twenty-seven years old, Philipose began losing his hair. It fell out in clumps, clung to his towel, and clogged the bathroom drain with great regularity until from his forehead to the top of his head, his scalp gleamed, unmarred by even a single strand. For a while Philipose wore a wig, but false hair triggered an allergic reaction that itched and wept. The doctor swept his hair out of his eye as he wrote a prescription cream. 'You will have to stop wearing a wig. That seems to be causing the allergy,' he advised. 'Anyway, there's no reason to be ashamed of being bald. Most men lose hair sooner or later. Besides, you know what they say about baldness being a sign of wisdom,' he said with what Philipose felt was a very smug expression. What does he know about the wretchedness of being bald? Philipose thought with dislike, staring enviously at the abundance of thick black hair that fell like a crow's wing across the doctor's forehead.

Then Philipose hit upon what he thought was an ingenious idea. He let the hair that edged his temples grow. When it was long enough, he swathed the strands of hair across his scalp this way and that until it concealed his baldness. All he had to do was use a hair cream that would hold the hair down.

Philipose patted his hair and walked into the post office

with the air of a monarch come to claim his throne.

'There was no official intimation,' Postman Unni mumbled when he came to deliver Mukundan's copy of the *Reader's Digest*.

'What is his designation?' Mukundan questioned, wondering if it would be better to raise the rent issue with him.

'I don't know. But I think he is senior to the postmaster. It seems he was transferred to Kannur, but didn't want to go so far, so he managed to wrangle this transfer. This way he gets to keep his promotion, and he can still visit his family in Alwaye once a week.'

'Where is he staying?' Krishnan Nair asked, arching his neck to see if he could catch a glimpse of Philipose.

'Right now he has a room in a lodge at Shoranur but he was making inquiries about renting a room here in the village.'

'Rent a room in the village! Who will rent out a room to a Christian? What is he thinking of?' Krishnan Nair's voice rose to a shrill.

Mukundan went back to lie in his armchair. Poor Philipose, he thought as he closed his eyes and allowed the heat to daze his senses into a stupor. What a village to choose to come to!

In Kaikurussi there were no Christians. There were Hindus. There were Muslims. And in the fringes of the strictly segregated society were the Harijans, a community by themselves. There was no room for Philipose here.

The first day Philipose didn't stay too long. He returned by the same taxi, saying he would be back tomorrow. This, he gestured, was simply reporting for work. Whoever heard of anyone doing any proper work on the day he reported for duty? The postmaster and postman exchanged glances. For the first time that morning, Kamban felt a little less insecure. No one was going to wrest his post office away. Least of all this creature with its glistening Brylcreemed strands of hair, fat moustache, beady eyes, pouched jaw, and hanging belly that the shirt stretched and struggled unsuccessfully to cover. Between the fourth and fifth shirt button, Philipose's belly seemed to assert itself saying, Look here, this is me, the real Philipose. Full of foul-smelling hot air and nothing else.

But the next day Philipose was there before anyone else. So when Kamban and Postman Unni came panting up the hill, it was to find Philipose pacing the veranda, clanging the post box lid as if to keep time with the rhythm of his impatience. When he heard them come in, he looked at his watch pointedly and barked, 'It is quarter past nine. I have been waiting here for more than thirty minutes. I don't care how you ran the post office before, but as of now the post office will be run the way it is meant to be.' 'The way I find it fit' was not uttered, but the implication was not lost on Kamban and Unni.

By the end of the week Kamban resembled a dog with a broken leg. He dragged himself around the post office furtively, afraid to draw the slightest attention to himself. When he spoke his voice came out in a yelp.

Even Postman Unni lost his cocky manner and took to making his rounds with a harassed expression. When Mukundan asked him what the problem was, he thrust his foot into his face. 'Corns!' he mumbled. And there, like Philipose's bloodshot eyes that were forever glued to Kamban, were crimson corn caps dotting the underside of Postman Unni's foot. Mukundan made sympathetic noises. 'This is nothing compared to what the postmaster is suffering,' Postman Unni said with a grim expression as he opened his umbrella.

The fact was that Philipose had taken an instant dislike to Kamban. First of all there was the matter of hair. What on earth did his mother feed him for him to have such a profusion of hair on his head, Philipose wondered. Each time Philipose looked at Kamban, he felt the injustice of life taunt him in his face. Why couldn't he have had hair like that?

Then there was the issue of promotions. Year after year he had seen a junior promoted simply because he was born a Harijan. Year after year he had waited for his turn to come, but there was always someone more 'deserving' than him. And so all the resentment that he had been harbouring towards the department for sidelining him in favour of men he thought were less competent found a vent. Finally one of them was at his mercy, and he intended to exact payment.

There was little he could say to fault Kamban's diligence to duty. But that first day, he had glimpsed Kamban's sense of inferiority, his precarious self-esteem, and realized here was the wound he could probe and twist his knife into. And so it was Kamban who bore the cross of Philipose's wrath. For being blessed with hair he didn't give a second thought to. For being born in a community that Philipose fervently believed had cheated him of what was his lawful right.

At first Philipose chose to pick on Kamban using the post office timings as his weapon. Since the time the post office had come into existence, it had always shut at two in the afternoon. When the post office became a sub-post office and Kamban took over as postmaster, he continued to do the same. There really was no need to keep the post office open after that. Everyone in the village knew it and so there existed a kind of an unspoken agreement between the village and the post office that no complaints would be made.

At five past one the post box would be emptied, the letters sorted out and arranged in individual pouches before being put into the mailbag. It was Postman Unni's job to hand it over to the mail carrier who came to collect the mail from that region and deliver the inward-bound mail for Kaikurussi. By a quarter to two Kamban's desk would be cleared of all objects. And when there were just five minutes left for the clock in the room to strike two, he would shut the windows with a bang. The wood was old, and years of exposure to the sun and rain had made it stiff. Kamban had to drag it in and slam it against the frame.

By two in the afternoon, both men would leave. Postman Unni on his beat up the hill. And Kamban down the road to the Harijan colony that lay on the outskirts of the village. Postman Unni came in usually only by half-past eleven and by the time he finished delivering the letters, it was a quarter to four. Since he was still on duty, it was understood that the post office hadn't closed for the day.

Kamban hadn't made any friends in the village even after so many years. He still didn't have the courage to walk up to Shankar's Tea Club for a cup of tea and a chat. Every day at half-past ten, a little boy ran down to the post office with a cup of tea for Kamban. As for Postman Unni, he preferred to go up to the tea shop.

The first day Philipose accepted a cup of tea at the post office. The next day when the little boy came up to him, he waved him away, 'I'm coming to the tea club. That would be a nice way to meet the locals here,' he said to no one in particular. 'Why don't you come too?' he asked Kamban slyly.

For a moment Kamban felt his heart lurch into his knees. His eyes rolled wildly, and then he mumbled, 'We can't close the post office.'

Philipose read a rebuke in his words. He grunted in irritation and walked away. So later when he saw that they meant to close the post office at two, Philipose seized the opportunity to put Kamban in his place. 'What do you mean, close at two?' he barked in annoyance.

'The post office has to be kept open till five. You can't open and shut it to suit your convenience. I'm surprised no one has complained yet,' he continued, enjoying the mortification that shadowed Kamban's face.

'But we've always closed at two,' Kamban said quietly. 'There really is no transaction after two in this village.'

'Well, from now on we keep it open till five like they do everywhere else.'

'What's the point?' Postman Unni mumbled. 'The mail carrier is here by two, so we can't even have another clearance.'

'That's beside the point,' Philipose said coldly.

Kamban gestured to Postman Unni to quit arguing. Postman Unni looked at Philipose's beefy face and then sauntered out, saying, 'Well, I'm going home as usual at four today because I promised to take my wife to Shoranur for a film.'

Kamban crept back to his table and pretended to write in a file. Philipose cleared his throat. Kamban resisted the feeling that he was meant to look up. When Philipose cleared his throat again, Kamban's pen slid to a halt. 'I say, Kamban,' Philipose's voice boomed. 'This table is not big enough for the two of us. Do something about organizing a separate and bigger table for me.'

Kamban nodded. And so they sat in the post office till five in the evening. At two Philipose had gone off to the tea shop for lunch. 'You can go for lunch at the tea shop after I return,' he taunted, knowing very well that Kamban would rather starve than brave the village's ire.

At five in the evening, Kamban went down the hill almost faint with hunger. Tomorrow he would have to carry some lunch with him. God knows what other changes Philipose had planned in his mind. Kamban felt the post office slip from his hands. And when he heard the honk of the bus at the city, he stopped in the middle of the road. It dawned on him why Philipose had insisted on changing the post office timings: Philipose's bus came at a quarter past five, and he didn't know what to do with himself until then.

The next morning when Kamban walked into the post office, he found that Philipose had appropriated his table. All his things were dumped on an old table with a rickety leg. Philipose had pushed the table against the wall and wedged a piece of brick beneath its game leg. Philipose gave him a wolfish grin and said loudly, 'I thought, why bother arranging for a new table? This one will suit me fine, and you can use that one. It isn't as if it is broken or anything.'

Postman Unni protested, 'But that's always been his table.'

'Did you bring it from your home?' Philipose feigned innocence. 'Is it part of your personal belongings, an ancestral piece, that you should feel such great attachment for it?'

'No,' Kamban muttered unhappily, 'But—'

'Then there are no "buts". Come on, just sort your place out and get to work. Let's not waste time on useless arguments,' Philipose said sternly and set to lighting a cigarette.

Later in the day Postman Unni took Philipose across to Mukundan's house.

'Hello, hello,' Philipose bellowed and walked in as if Mukundan had stretched out both his hands in welcome.

He ran his palm on the smooth teak of the door as if it were a woman's flanks and said, 'Nice house, I must say. You don't get to see too many of these tharavads so well preserved. Most of them are falling apart or are being pulled down. In fact,' he continued with a meaningful look and a guffaw, 'if you demolished this house and sold just the wood, I'm sure you'd get at least fifteen-twenty lakhs.'

Mukundan felt distaste crawl up his mouth for this obnoxious creature who seemed to have made himself at home in his armchair. He murmured, 'Excuse me for a moment,' and walked into the house gesturing to Postman Unni to follow him.

'What is he doing here?' Mukundan turned on Postman Unni furiously.

'That wretched creature. He wouldn't take a no. I made all kinds of excuses, but he wouldn't listen,' Postman Unni apologized wearily. He leaned against the wall and murmured, 'He is so arrogant that it is difficult to get a word in edgewise. If it had been anyone else but the postmaster, he would have smashed the weighing scales on his head long ago and left without a backward glance.'

Mukundan saw indignation tremor through Postman Unni's weedy frame as he began to tell him of the various indignities that Kamban had been subjected to in the past two days.

'Why doesn't Kamban make a complaint?' Mukundan asked, wondering if he should offer to write the complaint out for him.

'It's not as if he says or does anything that could be pointed out as harassment. It is the tone of voice, a twist of phrase—he is a master at subtle insults. Each time he finishes with Kamban, he drains the man of all his dignity.' Postman Unni fell silent. Remembering Philipose's atrocities seemed to drain Unni's vein of loquacity as well.

Mukundan went back to find Philipose inserting a tape into his music system. He took a deep breath and tried to control his temper. How dare he take such liberties?

'I hope you don't mind,' he said with a smile, and Mukundan realized what Kamban must have been going through with his bulldozing ways. 'It is just that I haven't heard any music since I came here. I used to sing in the church choir. And during Christmastime I have always been involved in the carol-singing group,' he continued and burst into full-throated song: 'Oh, come all ye faithful, joyful and triumphant'.

Mukundan didn't know where to look. He saw Krishnan Nair's head emerge like a turtle's, his mouth agape with astonishment. He wondered if his father could hear Philipose from across the road. Mukundan stared at his feet willing Philipose to shut up.

'Could you put the fan on?' Philipose said when he had finished his songbird act. Mukundan saw Philipose pick up the latest copy of *The Week* that he had been reading and fan himself briskly with it. 'Yes, yes, of course,' Mukundan heard himself say.

'I won't take too much of your time,' Philipose said as he poured the tea into the saucer and began slurping at it like a monster cat. Occasionally he would stop to dunk a biscuit into the teacup and pop it whole into his mouth. Krishnan Nair had been so awestruck by Philipose's performance that he had made a cup of tea, arranged half a dozen biscuits on a plate, and brought them simply to get a closer look at this strange and unnerving creature.

'This commuting to Shoranur and back everyday is very tiring. The bus is so unpredictable, and when it does come, it is packed. I am thinking of renting a room in the village.' He paused, waiting for Mukundan to take the cue.

For a moment Mukundan was tempted. The presence of a man such as Philipose, with his braying voice and total disregard for anyone's privacy, would rid this gargantuan house of all the memories and spirits that haunted it. But there was Krishnan Nair, for one, who would probably stage a walkout.

And then there was Philipose himself. In his many years of sharing a roof with other men, Mukundan had instantly come to recognize his type. Like the camel that begged for an inch of space in the Arab's tent, Philipose would insinuate himself into the house. And much in the same manner of the camel, little by little, he would take over the entire house. The first day Philipose would borrow an inch of toothpaste; then Mukundan would find that the razor had been borrowed without as much as a please, and so it would go on till one day he would walk into his room and find Philipose lolling in his bed, probably drunk on his rum. So Mukundan squashed that fleeting thought as if it were an irritating mosquito and pretended not to understand Philipose's broad hint.

Philipose eyed Mukundan balefully and continued, 'This morning as I stood by the window that faces your house, I said to myself, What a fool I am. There is Mukundan Nair living all by himself in a gigantic old house. Why don't you speak to him? He'll be glad to have your company,' he angled, trying to see if Mukundan would bite the bait.

Mukundan stared at his fingers, rubbed his chin, and then said, hoping he sounded sincere enough in his refusal, 'Now, if you had been a Hindu . . . But this is an old tharavad and home to several deities. So we need to be particularly careful about preserving the sanctity of the place. I regret I won't be able to help you.'

'Yes, yes,' Philipose broke in, 'I don't want the wrath of any of your gods descending on me. I should have thought about it. But what about that vacant room next to the post office?' he asked innocently, as if it had just occurred to him.

Mukundan tried to fathom Philipose's face. Had he known he would react in this manner and simply paved the way to renting the room next door to the post office? Or had it been a spur-of-the-moment thing? Postman Unni was right. The man was devious.

'But there's no power there, nor a proper bathroom,' Mukundan said lamely.

'Can't I just take a line from the post office? And I can use the post office toilet. If I feel like a good scrub, I'll draw water from the well. There is nothing more invigorating than a bath in the open air. In fact, the more I think of it, the better I like the idea. It will be just like going into one of those "retreat" places. Simple living and high thinking.' He guffawed so loudly that Mukundan's protests were drowned in his raucous laughter.

'When I came to this village, I wasn't sure whom I should meet or get to know. But in the few days I have been here, I've realized that while there are many upstarts in this village, there is only one aristocrat. The only man I need to meet or know or be friends with. That is you, Mukundan Nair. And I told Postman Unni the same just this morning.

So here I am and I'm putting myself at your mercy,' Philipose added, ignoring Postman Unni's startled face, for he didn't remember having any such conversation. In fact, Philipose, he distinctly remembered, had said that the only person worth cultivating in the entire village was Power House Ramakrishnan.

Mukundan felt a tongue of satisfaction unfurl within him. Here was someone who could distinguish between a true aristocrat and an upstart. He smiled and said, 'If you want to, you can stay in the room adjacent to the post office.'

In less than a week's time, Philipose made the post office building his empire. One half he ruled by day, and the other half he presided over by night. Some nights Mukundan could hear him singing loudly as he threw mugs of cold water over his body. *Mustapha, Mustapha, don't worry Mustapha . . .*

Mukundan wondered what he did all by himself. What did it feel like chopping vegetables just enough for one? How did it feel to fill the evening with an endless retinue of chores, the steaming, the boiling, the straining, and the perpetual washing up? All done in the dull gleam of a sixty-volt bulb. How did he go through the evening with not a word spoken and only a solitary shadow for a companion? At least Mukundan had never known better. But what did it feel like to live alone when one had a wife and children? How did he cope with the loneliness?

In his years of service many such men had shared his quarters. But they had the solace of a routine carefully chalked out to banish any twinge of loneliness. Card games; drinking sessions; long walks—each of these as sacred as any ritual in a temple, not to be deviated from. Poor Philipose had only the comfort of the stove.

In the morning when the post office stirred to life and the brown wooden windows groaned open reluctantly, in the manner of a man who'd like to sleep some more, Philipose sought a victim to dispel the helplessness he felt at night. His narrow eyes often settled on Kamban in his corner. Legs hidden out of sight beneath the rickety table, shoulders slumped, Kamban sat so still that one of the many spiders that inhabited the room seriously considered spinning a web from his nose to the wall.

Kamban had sampled social ostracism in many hues. As a little boy his classmates had avoided sitting on the same bench as he did. He was rarely included in games that ended in a tangle of arms and legs. As an adult he had seen the office peon set aside a separate glass to serve him his tea in. But nothing hurt as much as this banishment into a corner. However, he would have accepted even this quietly, as his lot, until the day Philipose chose to humiliate him in front of the whole village.

After a night of intermittent power-cuts, noisy crickets, and ghoulish mosquitoes set on draining his body, Philipose woke up feeling tired and ill-tempered. It was one of those days when everything seemed to conspire against him. The milk curdled when he boiled it. So he had to drink black coffee, which gave him dyspepsia. Two bulbs blew their fuse, one after the other, so he had to finish dressing in the midnight gloom of a room that shunned light with all the fervour of a photophobic being. But he needed light to arrange his elaborate coiffure. So he decided to open a window. And then, as he wrestled with one of the mulish windows, it chose to turn nasty, slamming into his little finger.

For a moment Philipose felt at one with his maker. That moment when the Romans drove a nail through his palm. Then he began howling in pain as he hopped from one foot to the other, holding his injured hand aloft, 'Where are you, Theresamma, my wife? Bring me ice, a liniment, something to take this pain away! Why on earth did I choose to come to this cursed place?'

They heard him scream as far as the city. Shankar spilled tea over the counter and burned himself in the process. 'I'd never heard anything more scary than that,' he confessed to Mukundan later in the day. 'So I quickly dipped my hand into a jar of cold water and set out to find out who was slaughtering Philipose. I was sure Kamban must have decided, enough is enough, and stuck a knife in Philipose's gut.' Stories of Philipose's tyranny were by then well-known throughout the village, thanks to Postman Unni.

When Philipose realized that neither Theresamma nor her soothing ministrations were available, he felt a furious rage gather within him. He sucked on his injured finger, he hopped from one foot to the other, and looked around seeking someone to blame. He turned and saw Kamban, who had come in early and stood cowering by the door. Philipose felt the wisps of hair framing his face like a lank veil; then he saw the gleaming strands of Kamban's hair slicked back, and a tearing pain ripped through him. He felt the sting of humiliation; the throbbing finger. He bellowed, 'Why can't you do your duties? Why do I have to do everything from sorting the mail to opening the windows? You are lazy and irresponsible, you know, that's what you are. This is what happens when you take useless people and give them responsibilities that they are not qualified to handle. But do the department heads realize all this? No, year after year, they give you promotions, special benefits. While people like me are left lagging behind.

'What are you gaping at? Can't you see I'm in agony? Go get a mug of cold water. Dear Lord, I think I've lost all sensation in this finger. Do I have to teach you even something as basic as this? What do you people do when you hurt your finger? Stick it into a heap of dung?'

As he ranted and raved at Kamban, a whole group of people, including Mukundan, arrived on the spot. And that was how they heard every obnoxious word he heaped on Kamban's head. When Kamban saw the pity in the villagers' eyes and their reluctance to intercede on his behalf, he decided it was time for him to wrest control back.

13

Sleeping Dogs Bite Twice As Hard

When he heard the gate creak open, Mukundan looked up curiously. Who could it be? It was too early for it to be Bhasi. Mukundan stood up in surprise when he saw it was Philipose.

Philipose carried a briefcase and had slung an overstuffed brown Rexene airbag over one shoulder. His shirt was rumpled, his hair was carelessly plastered down on his head, and he had a two-day stubble on his chin. He thrust a key into Mukundan's hand and said in a troubled voice, 'I've had enough. I'm leaving.'

Mukundan frowned, 'Isn't this rather sudden?'

'If I stay here any longer, you'll find me roaming the streets stark naked, talking to myself,' Philipose said pausing in mid-sentence as if to sort his thoughts out. 'Why didn't you tell me that the room is haunted?'

'What?' Mukundan cried in surprise. The post office building was the only place in the village without a past. It contained no memories, no ghosts, except some tattered old posters of film actresses stuck on its walls long ago by Meenakshi.

'I suppose you didn't know about it,' Philipose said wearily. He put down his bags and sat down with his back to the pillar. Mukundan felt pity stir within him. He knew what ghoulish nightmares could do to a man.

Philipose must have sensed the sympathy for he stared at Mukundan with glazed-over eyes. Then he began in a low voice, 'At first, when the cat came in, I thought it would be nice to have a pet. I gave it some milk in a coconut shell. But it ignored the milk and went to sit in a corner and began washing itself. That's when I noticed it didn't have a tail. And I laughed to myself, Well, now I've seen it all. A cat without a tail! How on earth did a cat survive without its tail?'

It was a strange-looking cat. Its fur was nothing like Philipose had ever seen before. Grey ashes sprinkled on black fur. And it had a wart growing on its left temple. Philipose pursed his lips and made inviting noises. But it stayed in its corner eyeing him almost resentfully, as if he had seized some precious thing that belonged to it.

Philipose gave up after a while and went to have his bath. When he returned he found the cat on his bed. 'Shoo, shoo, get away, cat!' he shouted. But the cat wouldn't budge. It continued to sprawl on the bed washing its paws slowly, deliberately, taunting him with its indifference. Philipose stared at the cat for a while wondering what to do with it. He could ignore it and wait for it to go away by itself. Or he could take a stick to it. He didn't know what it was but something about the cat unnerved him.

He went close to the bed, whispering, 'Cat, cat, nice cat.'

The cat narrowed its eyes and looked at him thoughtfully. Its whiskers quivered. Meow, it cried.

Philipose smiled. He was letting his loneliness corrode his sense of the commonplace. What had he expected the cat to do?

He bent over and gently tried to lift it off the bed. The cat screamed and leaped out of his hands. Arching its back, hissing and spitting, its eyes vicious, opaque pools of hatred, the cat flung itself on Philipose. Philipose staggered in surprise and then in pain as the cat's claws raked his chest. 'You little bastard!' Philipose screamed in terror and pain, looking around for a heavy object to fling at the cat. But it had disappeared, and all that was left were angry scratch marks on his chest.

The next night when Philipose had just drifted off to

sleep, there was a knock at his door. He peered through the crack between the doors but there wasn't anyone. He called out aloud, 'Who is it?' There was no answer. Philipose thought he must have dreamed it, and turned to go back to bed. The cat was waiting for him on his pillow. Philipose felt fear escalate through him. He threw the doors open and stepped out into the night. Anything was better than being attacked by the cat. Sometime later, when he peeped in, the cat was gone. Quietly he went back inside and bolted the doors. He drank a glass of water and decided to go back to sleep. And then he found a lump of shit on his pillow. Not cat turds but human faeces.

For the next week, Philipose knew no respite. He was too scared to sleep and even more petrified when awake. All night he left the light on, waiting for he didn't know what to come and terrorize him. For the moment he drifted off into an uneasy slumber, something happened to jerk him awake. Gravel that ghostly hands seemed to fling against the walls. Hammering on the windows. Pots that clattered to the floor all by themselves. Tiles that rattled as though someone were walking on them. And when it stopped, and he thought, the evil spirits had frolicked with him enough and he could return to bed, there, like a calling card each time, a lump of shit would be waiting for him. And then the cat would appear.

He didn't know how it crept into the room. The cat seemed to find its way in through closed doors and windows. It would pad close to him, stare into his eyes, and mew mockingly. The more Philipose looked at the cat, the more familiar it seemed.

'Last night as the cat sat there staring resentfully, I realized who it reminded me of. Kamban. I tell you, Kamban and the cat are connected in some way. No wonder it hated me so much. In the morning I told myself that if I stayed on here any longer, I would lose my mind completely,' Philipose put his head in his hands and began to sob.

As Mukundan stood there helplessly watching him, Philipose rubbed a sodden handkerchief over his cheeks and stood up to go. In a tight voice, he said, 'I am leaving, and I can't tell you how relieved I feel. This is not a good place. It has strange and dark secrets. Only those who can fathom it can survive here. It is not a place for people like you and me. Take my advice: leave this village. It'll destroy you. Get out before it is too late.'

Mukundan stood there watching Philipose shuffle away and wondered how much truth there was in Philipose's tale. Krishnan Nair came to stand by his side. He chewed on his lower lip and said in a thoughtful voice, 'So Kamban finally decided to use his secret weapon.'

'Secret weapon? What are you saying?' Mukundan asked stupidly.

'I heard him talking to you,' Krishnan Nair said. 'What would you have done in Kamban's place? Someone like Power House Ramakrishnan would have hired a few thugs to sort Philipose out. Someone like Che Kutty or Shankar would have gone for his throat. But a man like Kamban simply appeals to a greater power to rescue him. Have you forgotten who Kamban really is? If the Odiyans wanted to, they could have killed Philipose. But Kamban is a timid creature at heart, and he must have decided it was enough to frighten Philipose and send him scuttling away from the village.'

When Mukundan was a child, the Harijans of the village were kept at a distance for more than just their association with excrement. They were feared to be Odiyans. Men who had made a pact with the devil. Men who could snuff your life out if provoked. There were little bronze pots filled with talismans buried all around the house to checkmate the powers of the Odiyans. Young women wore gold talismans around their hips so that even if an Odiayan tried to enchant them, they could resist the pull of his magic. Pregnant women wore black amulets so that they were not lured out of their houses at midnight by the Odiyans who needed the foetus to propitiate the evil forces they worshipped. All through his childhood the Odiyans were a presence that haunted Mukundan every night.

For as long as he could remember, Kamban had worn his ancestry reluctantly. It was not just abhorrence to the idea of cleaning up someone else's excrement. It was the depths into which it made his people sink. It was a dark, rank world they lived in. A darkness of the soul they understood. And so it was forces of darkness they worshipped. Kamban had allowed none of the dark gods to dwell in his heart. All his life he had tried to flee them, but now it was in the darkness that he found redemption for the hurt Philipose had heaped upon him.

The Kamban who had disassociated himself from the stench of the night-soil buckets had also severed all ties with the secrets of the dark world his family had once chosen to reign over. His uncle Chathu was the most powerful of Odiyans. In the village, Chathu's powers as an Odiyan were still whispered about. Of the innumerable virgins he had seduced, creeping into their rooms in the guise of a cat. Of men he had paralyzed for life, appearing as a snake as they climbed a tree. Of homes he had wrecked. Of families he had destroyed. Of people he had turned into blabbering lunatics. Kamban had chosen to turn his back on his uncle until the day Philipose robbed him of his dignity publicly. Then he went knocking at Chathu's door, begged him to intervene with his magic.

Late in the afternoon Mukundan climbed the staircase and wandered though the rooms deep in thought. Ever since

Krishnan Nair had come to stay, Mukundan had ceased to be haunted by his dreams. But Philipose's departure left him feeling uneasy. Could there be any truth in what Philipose had experienced? Could Krishnan Nair have been right? Were there really such creatures as Odiyans?

At the end of the hallway was the granary with a huge wooden chest built into the wall. Mukundan walked into the narrow windowless room and touched the smooth planes of the wood. The rice meant for consumption by the inmates of the house was stored in this chest. On the day his mother had died, she had been carrying a measure of rice taken from this chest. 'She was holding a bowl of rice in one hand and a lantern in the other. She must have missed a step and fallen to her death,' Mukundan remembered Krishnan Nair saying.

And yet, she had walked down the staircase with both hands full almost every day of her adult life. What could have gone wrong that dark dawn? Had she been an Odiyan's victim too? For an Odiyan, he had heard, killed his victims stealthily and sucked the soul away without anyone realizing it. For the next three days, the victim would eat, drink, defecate and breathe. And on the fourth day, he would die of a trivial cause. A slight fever or a fall from a step! They say the only way to know if an Odiyan has cast a spell is by peering into the victim's eyes. For there you will find no reflections. Except a dead plane of stillness.

Mukundan thought of his mother's eyes when she appeared in his dreams. Of the remoteness. Of the cold stillness. Of accusations and the anger her mouth spewed. He felt the back of his neck prickle as if there was someone else in the room. A malevolent being waiting to pounce on him. Mukundan started to walk away and as he reached the doorway, the half-open door of the room slammed shut.

For a moment Mukundan felt black coils of panic swirl around him. Invisible hands pressed down on his chest and squeezed the breath out of him. 'Help,' he screamed sensing an extra presence. 'Help,' he cried and began hammering frantically on the door with his palms and then, just as he thought that he would never escape the creature that heaved and breathed behind him, the door was flung open.

Bhasi stood there with a concerned look on his face. 'Are you all right?' he asked moving towards Mukundan.

Mukundan rushed past him into the hallway and took huge gulps of air. 'She closed the door. She wanted to kill me,' he cried, clutching at Bhasi's hands.

'What are you saying, Mukundan?' Bhasi demanded.

'What is happening there?' Krishnan Nair demanded from the foot of the stairs.

Mukundan took a deep breath and began to hurry down.

'What is wrong?' Krishnan Nair demanded again, agitated by Mukundan's stricken face.

'Nothing. Nothing,' Mukundan said, trying to walk past the old caretaker.

'He felt a little dizzy, that's all,' Bhasi tried to placate Krishnan Nair. 'Come with me. Lie down and rest for a while,' Bhasi said, gently leading Mukundan to his room.

'I have to talk to you. Will you come back this evening?' Mukundan asked. All he knew was he had to talk to someone. Or he would go mad.

Leaning against the parapet wall of the terrace, his mundu tucked between his legs, hands curling round a glass brimming with iced water, Bhasi tried to read the secrets that veined Mukundan's face.

In the course of thirty-eight years of living, Bhasi had chanced upon what he considered a universal truth: That all men are born with two faces. In his growing years, every man lets his environment and temperament determine which one he should wear by day. And it is this face that serves the purpose of a mere scab that is very often categorized so effortlessly as handsome, pleasant, nondescript, or even ugly.

Beneath the thin layer of skin, the everyday mask, there exists yet another face that only the pale silvery light of the moon can coax out. From among the shadows, there emerges one single feature that describes the anatomy of the inner man. One distinct note that reveals the machinations of the soul.

As an example, Bhasi often cited moths. Moths by day, he said, are not what they are at night. In the gentle light of the moon, the drabness, the dusty brown wings, and the bark-like markings are miraculously transformed. Through the layers of the night the moth flies, fluttering delicately woven jacquard wings. An ethereal beauty, a sight so extraordinary that you would want to go down on your knees and pay homage to such magnificence. 'It is all a matter of light and shadow,' he explained. 'In the daylight there are so many things vying for one's attention—a person's complexion, his clothes, his mannerisms, the chair he sits on—'that there is no room for something as tremulous as his soul to emerge.'

During the day Mukundan's demeanour was cloaked in control. In an ordinariness that deceived everyone into believing that he was incapable of plumbing the depths of any feeling. A veneer of shallowness, of a passivity that nothing in the world could shake. And yet, drenched now in the lunar luminescence, what caught at Painter Bhasi's heart was the singularly beautiful shape of Mukundan's lips.

A delicate upper lip crowned a finely etched, voluptuous lower lip. Restraint and sensuality, he thought. A sensitivity that Mukundan sought to hide with that ridiculous pencil-line moustache of his.

And suddenly Bhasi knew that beneath the almost youthful skin that sheathed lightly padded cheeks, the quiet listless eyes framed by thin metal-rimmed glasses, the stubborn chin with the hint of a cleft, and the high forehead, lurked a being so fragile that if he were to help it emerge, he would also have to teach it to live and survive in this callous world.

'Why don't you tell me what is troubling you?' Bhasi probed, crouching at Mukundan's feet.

Mukundan continued to sit in his chair, shoulders slumped, his face desolate, staring stonily into his glass.

'Unless you tell me what it is that is tormenting you so, there is nothing I can do for you,' Bhasi said. 'What is it? Are you just lonely? Did you just want someone to chat to? Is that why you called me over?'

'Have you ever known what it is to be afraid?' Mukundan whispered. 'Over and over again, I find myself wishing I were back in Bangalore, living my orderly life. This place fills me with a strange bewilderment; a queer dread.'

Mukundan gulped down a mouthful of liquid and put the glass down on the edge of the parapet wall. His hands trembled as they lit a cigarette. Bhasi looked at him in surprise. 'Do you smoke a lot?'

'I don't. I gave it up some years ago. But of late, I have started smoking again. When my nerves feel a little frazzled, I find it calming to smoke a cigarette.'

'H'mm. I think I have seen you come into the backyard to smoke when your father is here. Though I find it quite strange why at your age you need to smoke in secret,' Bhasi murmured.

'My father used to whip me in anticipation of the day I would start smoking. I was ten. And I never ever wanted to smoke a cigarette till I felt the sting of the cane on my calves. I thought if he hated it so much, it certainly must be good.' Mukundan smiled. In the darkness, his lips blossomed. Bhasi felt that strange pity surge in him again. How often that lower lip must have trembled and crumpled as a child. How frequently little boyish teeth must have sunk into its softness in an effort to control the tears, the pain from spilling over. If only I had known you then, Mukundan,

Bhasi anguished, I would have been there for you. To soothe and console. To apply a salve to the hurting bruises that still slither snake-like on your calves; white scars that even age hasn't been able to conceal.

Bhasi clasped his palms tightly and stared unseeingly at the floor. He couldn't understand this ache that nagged at his heart. What is happening to me? he thought. What am I going to do with him?

The taste of tobacco nipped at Mukundan's tongue, and the smoke filled his insides, numbing, soothing. 'I know if I were to mention this to any of my friends, they would laugh and dismiss it as nonsense. The less charitable of my acquaintances would smirk that living in the back of beyond has addled Mukundan's mind and turned him into a provincial lout. But you would understand, I thought,' Mukundan paused.

Bhasi blinked. For many days now, he had tried to inveigle himself into Mukundan's closely guarded circle of trust. Several times he had sought to engineer a moment such as this. Yet now he felt a strange reluctance to see Mukundan's secret face unveiled.

What does a man do when he is entrusted with another's past? How does he greet the skeins of memory that are unravelled before him? With concern? With gentleness? Or with silence? And where does he store it all: someone else's sorrow, the burden of one more memory?

He watched Mukundan pour himself another drink. He saw the eagerness that gushed forth. The need to confide. He saw Mukundan's lips quiver with hope. As if by talking about whatever it was that haunted him, Mukundan believed he would be able to exorcise it. He realized with a pang that Mukundan was looking to him to make things better.

Bhasi sipped at his water. It was what he had set out to do. To heal and control. To change and master. There was no going back now.

Bhasi stretched his legs out, leaned against the wall, and waited patiently. He knew that a baring of the soul, like the rising of the tide, couldn't be hurried. It had to happen at its own natural pace. The moon can encourage, the night can aid, and the wind can abet. But first there has to be an all-consuming desire to come forth. Only then will the current swirl and churn thoughts and waves. So that ultimately the land's edge between the past and the present is drowned in a stream of debris: dark, secret, wet, slimy things that for many a year had lain undisturbed in some deep trough of the mind's floor.

'When I left this village many years ago, I tucked all such memories into a forgotten corner of my mind. And there they remained till Kamban dragged them out. The rest of the village is reluctant to talk about what might really have happened. Even Postman Unni, for all his garrulousness, shies away from any reference to the subject. It is as if the villagers want to draw a veil over the circumstances of Philipose's departure,' Mukundan finished.

The wind blew. Wild rogue wind trailing an icy finger down the moon's hip, causing it to tremble and hide behind a cloud. Wicked thieving wind stealing the scent from the champakam flowers and frittering it away. Wanton wind turning hair on the arms into sentinels and unformed thoughts into words.

Bhasi felt the wind wrap his mind with a recklessness. An audacity that he would otherwise have resisted. 'But why does Philipose's going away bother you so much?'

Mukundan looked at him and blurted, 'It's not Philipose's going away. Why don't you understand? It is how he went away.

'When my mother died, the villagers said the Odiyans had murdered her. I didn't know whether to believe it or not. I chose not to. I told myself over and over again that it was an accident.'

Mukundan crouched in the chair, his arms tightly

wrapped around himself as he murmured disjointedly, 'But I don't know what to think any more.'

'Even now, my mother appears before me. She is no longer the gentle woman I knew and loved. She hates me. She hates me for being such a coward. I could have rescued her, taken her away; she begged me to. But I was too scared. I left her here alone. I am responsible for her death as much as the Odiyans. As much as my father who the villagers claimed paid the Odiyans to get rid of her.'

'Mukundan, stop this!' Bhasi's voice rang through the night. Bhasi put his hands on Mukundan's shoulders and peered into his eyes. 'Mukundan,' he whispered fiercely, 'listen to me, I am going to teach you how to escape your past; I am going to help you bury the guilt, the sorrow, the fear that has feasted on you like a leech for years. Mukundan, are you listening? I am going to heal you. Do you trust me? Do you, Mukundan?'

In the silence of the night, a million stars raged. In his anguish Mukundan felt as far removed from the chance of ever stumbling upon happiness as of chancing upon some distant star. A blazing star brother that would guide him through the maze of life.

How can a mortal man seek to change his destiny? How can a mere man twist the cogwheels of heaven to turn another way?

Then in Bhasi's eyes, Mukundan saw the star he had sought in the heavens shine and burn. Mukundan felt its fire reach across and lick at him, charring his uncertainties away. As if in a dream, he stretched out his hands and clasped Bhasi's. Tightly. Fiercely. Clinging to them, as though they were the lifeline he could trust to rescue him from the morass of his past.

Part III

14

A Handful of Water

Time is real.

What isn't are the moments that make it. How does one decide what is real? The truth of life as it is? Or the truth as we determine it to be?

A cauldron of cassava thickens in the sky. The moon has to it the consistency of the powdered root cooking, its surface scored by bubbles that steam from within. In its viscous depths runs the life force, which alone has the power to transform, to transmute, and to change things forever. Liquid turns to solid. Compassion cycles into want.

Greenish bleached moon, stealthy eavesdropper, solitary witness, pale reminder of my moment of revelation, tell me what am I to do? You, who whip oceans into a frenzy, urge the jasmine to bloom, and turn ordinary men into lunatics, tell me what madness is this?

I lie on my side with my head supported by my hand. Thousands of years ago, on a night as luminous as this, Siddhartha lay beside his sleeping wife and child, staring at the sky. Stricken by the enormity of sheer existence. He had chanced upon those signs that told him everything that he had believed to be true was mere illusion. It was in his destiny to seek the meaning of life. It was in his destiny to set out to discover who he really was. It was his destiny to be the Enlightened One.

In Kaikurussi I thought I had found the landscape that matched my mindscape. In Kaikurussi I structured a world of my own. A world where nothing about life could ever surprise me. I found complete peace. For here I knew who I was. And there never rose the need for me to plumb the depths of my own soul as I went about life painting walls and dispensing health.

I have had several patients with ailments stranger than yours. In fact, some of these could be barely classified as ailments at all. And yet I have never felt this overwhelming need to take possession of their lives.

There was Sugu, the tailor from Ongallur. Sugu with long slender hands and delicate wrists. A skin so translucent that you could see the blue veins at his temples. He came to me, plagued by headaches.

'I went to Angamali and had my eyes checked. At the American Hospital in Ottapalam they checked my blood pressure. They even did a head scan, but nothing was wrong. I tried homeopathy, when the English medicines failed to work,' he said spreading a sheaf of reports from various hospitals before me. 'I went to a faith healer. I have made offerings to countless temples and tried all kinds of remedies. I heard about you from a customer.'

Sugu was twenty-eight years old. He owned a thriving business right on the main road. His shop was called Golden Tailors. He specialized in ladies' clothes. Blouses. Skirts. Salwar-kameezes. Sugu's clients liked him, because unlike many tailors, he rarely resorted to exacting measurements. And even if he did, his hands avoided all contact. But the clothes would fit perfectly.

He had never had a sexual encounter in his life. He said he felt no such urge. He had resisted all attempts by his family to get him married. Sugu said the mere thought of lying next to a woman nauseated him.

There is a beautiful word for self-fulfillment in Sanskrit: mushti-maithunam. A word that robs the act of all its intrinsic loneliness. Coitus with the fist.

Sugu wouldn't understand that. So I had to choose ugly but straight language. 'Do you masturbate?'

He nodded.

'What do you think of when you are doing it?' I probed.

'All kinds of things,' he shrugged, embarrassed.

'What about men, Sugu?' I asked quietly.

He hung his head and refused to meet my eyes.

Poor Sugu, I thought, to be stuck in a little place like Ongallur, condemned to sexual frustration and ridden with guilt for his secret fantasies.

It seemed almost a cliché. A situation that is frequently dealt with in magazine 'Dear Doctor' columns with great aplomb. And as Sugu would have discovered if he had written to them, they would have told him his headaches were a result of mental strain and pent-up sexual energy. They would have advised him to take up yoga and go for long early-morning walks. But I wasn't going to fill him with such drivel. The only way to heal him would be to make him confront the truth about his sexuality. But first, I would have to prepare him mentally and physically.

Early next morning I gathered handfuls of pitabhringi from the garden. A common enough herb with a tiny yellow flower that flourishes amidst clumps of grass. I crushed it in a vial of oil and left it to steep. Then I pulled out tiny shankupushpam plants and cooked the creeper—roots, leaves, tendrils, and blue shell-shaped flowers—with milk and cumin.

In the evening I gave Sugu the oil to rub on his forehead and the mixture to drink. 'The oil is for your headache and the brew for mental strength,' I said. Sugu didn't need the herbs to cure him, but they wouldn't harm him either. As the *Atharvaveda* says, there is no substance in the world that isn't medicine. But I needed an excuse to see him every day. And thereafter, every evening for a week, I gently broached the subject of his leaving Ongallur.

I told him of the vaster experiences a city could provide. Of how in a city one could be assured of anonymity no matter what one did. In a city he would find it easier to find others who felt the same way as he did. And then I told him why he shouldn't feel guilty about how he felt. I told him what precautions he would have to take; I told him everything except the word 'go.' For that was a decision I wanted him to arrive at himself. I never saw him after that one week. I heard that he went to Trivandrum.

Why is it that I can't maintain the same distance with you, Mukundan? I don't expect you to accept or even understand what I feel; I don't understand it myself.

I lean over and look at my wife Damayanti and our child sleeping in the crook of her arm. Once the two of them were my universe. The sum total of my existence. I would look at their sleeping faces and feel a great sense of tenderness wash over me. No matter what, I used to tell myself, I have the two of them and that was enough.

Tonight something seems to have changed. The restfulness that bound me to them seems to have lost its power to hold. I am troubled. I am confused. I feel fear as though there are strange, disruptive forces at work, plotting and scheming to take away everything I hold precious.

All evening, as we ate our dinner and prepared to go to sleep, I noticed Damayanti watching me from the corner of her eye. She thinks it is something that she has done. I wish I could tell her that it isn't her fault that I feel so dispossessed.

She tries so hard to please me. Even when she sleeps. She knows how much I detest the fancy nighties the women in the village wear around the house all day and sleep in at night. Garish gowns embellished with cheap lace and sleeves stained with cooking and the aftermath of a hundred chores. So she gave away all the frilled and smocked nighties and instead covers herself with a cotton mundu.

Once, and only with her, I transgressed the line. I let myself get involved but it was a deliberate meshing of lives, and I have never regretted it. But I swore to myself that I would never allow another person, another patient, entry into my life.

I stroke her hair. Beneath the thin cotton of her wrap, her breasts heave. Lit by the night. Shadowed by the moon. Matt-textured fullness hiding what secret longings, what secret fears? Once they were engorged with the anguish of loss. Breasts so full of milk that the women in her family claimed that not even the spine of a hibiscus leaf could slide between them.

Damayanti, I don't wish to raise from the grave the memory of those horrifying days. But I want you to remember what it felt like to be confronted by a twist of fate. A destiny that redefined your entire life and the pattern of your dreams.

Do you remember how your brothers came knocking at my door late in the night? They insisted that I go with them. They told me of the truck that mowed down your husband and six month-old child. They said they knew there was no medicine that would bring back the dead. But their worry lay with you, their living sister. They wept, sorrowed by your sorrow.

'What do you want me to do?' I asked, unable to comprehend how I could help.

'Come with us and you will see for yourself why we came seeking you,' your brother said, wiping the tears off his cheeks with the corner of his mundu.

You sat on a bed in a dimly lit room. You sat there as if all life had seeped out of you. You sat there, a body of suffering trapped in a skin of stillness.

Your hair hung to your waist: lifeless, unkempt hair. Your eyes were vacant pools that reflected nothing. Your lips were dry and cracked. Mouth half open, jaw slack, limbs disarrayed. There is nothing beautiful about sorrow. There was nothing beautiful about you then, Damayanti.

As I stood there watching you, I saw milk taint the fabric of your blouse. I saw your body reach out for the mouth of your hungry child.

'Do you see that?' your mother whispered. 'The first two days after the death, we had to manually squeeze the milk out. But since yesterday, she won't let anyone touch her.'

'There is an injection that will stop the milk,' I said.

'The doctor came here to give her the injection. But she grabbed the syringe from his hand and threw it away. He left some pills behind, but she refuses to take them either. I don't want to force them down her throat. But what are we to do? Shankar from the tea shop suggested that we call you in. He said you would know what to do.' Your mother began to sob.

You reminded me of the boulder that had drawn me to Kaikurussi. You had the same sense of stillness; a clenching within. And I knew that I could heal you. No matter how unorthodox my methods, I would make you whole again. If only to stake my claim on that stillness some day.

'Leave me alone with her,' I said.

Your mother and brothers looked at me indecisively.

'Please,' I said. 'If you want me to help her, you have to let me do it my way.'

I closed the doors and went to sit by your side. Do you recall what I said to you that night?

'Damayanti,' I said, 'Damayanti, what can I say to you that'll make this burden of pain any easier to bear? What words do I use to console you? I do understand what you are trying to do. Damayanti, do you think that if the pain in your breasts was greater you would be able to numb the pain in your soul?'

Your eyes lifted and met mine for a brief instant. I felt encouraged to go on.

'Are you racked by the question: Why them and why not you? Are you frightened when you think of how you are going to endure every moment without your husband and child? You understand, don't you, that it was written in their destiny that they leave this world so early, so abruptly. But you are here. And you can't let yourself drift into a state of nothingness, into intentional indifference. Tell me, Damayanti, talk to me. Do you feel guilty that you are still alive?'

For more than an hour, I talked to you, trying to elicit a response. Trying to bring you back from the almost comatose state you had drifted into. Then I saw a lone tear trickle down your cheek and I thought of the underground streams that rise to the surface with the constant onslaught of the monsoon rain.

When I had no more words left, with great daring, I laid my head on your lap. 'Think of me as your child,' I whispered. 'Think of me as a helpless being who has to be nourished. Let me drain the sorrow that has lodged in your bosom. Let me unfurl the rocklike fist and allow your pain to flow.'

Wordlessly you drew my head closer and let me nurse your ache away. The tears that ran down your cheeks wet mine. Milk mixed with the salt of tears in my mouth.

I touched your cheek. You flinched at first and then let my hand remain. I let you cry for a while. Then I stepped out of the room and asked your family to attend to you.

Two years later I married you. And, on that first night as we lay in our bed as man and wife, I lay on my side staring at you as I do now. Your palm cupped your cheek, your knees curled towards your stomach, your hip curved. In sleep you were as still as the summer noon when the earth burns and even the clouds dare not move lest they be trapped between the twin fires of the earth and the sun.

I gathered you to the arch of my breathing hip and sought to steal that wondrous stillness I worshipped. Instead I found warmth; I found a melting down of defenses; I found contentment.

Perhaps, what I seek now is a friend like I have never had before. Someone to share a smoke and my thoughts with. Someone who will see life with the same eyes as I do; experience the same lift of spirit when mine soars. Someone whose destiny is woven with mine even though we are bound by neither blood nor any other tie.

I have asked myself again and again why it is that I have always felt so drawn to you, Mukundan. At first I told myself that it was pity. You were a broken creature that would benefit from my care. When did it turn into a kindly affection? And when did it metamorphose into this need to be a part of your life?

Do you know what frightens me most, Mukundan?

That you will stop needing me as much as you do now. That I will cease to be important to you and others will take my place. But that is a risk I took when I decided to heal your wounded mind and shape your life. For there was in you a being waiting to be born, and only I could help it emerge.

After last night when you exposed the pain, the hurt that you had carried in you like a secret malignant tumor gnawing at your insides all those years, I lay awake as I do now, wondering what celestial powers I could call forth to help you. And when the dawn broke, I knew what had to be done.

We would have to make a journey, I decided. To the meadow that is in the middle of the forest where trees stand brushing trunks, their branches sweeping the skies. Dense green, their leaves are webbed allowing neither rain nor sun to trespass. So much so the villagers have named it the forest of umbrellas—Kodakkad.

Together, you and I must walk through Kodakkad, where even the darkest of skins like mine are touched with a greenish tinge. If you should stumble, I will help you with a hand on your shoulder. And I shall revel in the knowledge that I am there for you. But I must make a promise to myself that in no other way will I reveal to you how important you are to me. In the meadow, where dew collects through summer and winter, I know the mandukaparni thrives. And it is with this celestial herb that I will find my place in your system, in your thought stream, in your life.

As if you are a child who has to be taught to walk, to talk, to understand the vagaries of this world, I will take it upon myself to show you who you can be once you have shrugged off that persona you wear as an invisible cloak to protect yourself from further hurt, further pain.

Mukundan, you will be the man you were meant to be. A man capable of love and happiness.

Perhaps that is the reason why I feel this dread. For as you discover what you can accomplish by yourself, you will realize that you don't need me any more. Rejection will drain my power to heal. Distance will exhaust the lode of strength you awakened in me. And I fear that I shall be reduced to who I was when we first met: Painter Bhasi. One-screw-loose Bhasi.

15

The Forest of Umbrellas and the Womb Jar

When Mukundan opened his eyes, Bhasi was sitting by his side. For a moment he wondered what the painter was doing there by his bedside so early in the morning. It was barely light. Every morning around this time, his full kidneys knocked at the passageway of sleep, demanding release. Some mornings he pissed and crawled back to bed, half-asleep. Some mornings he rose with a leap of energy that he tamed with a flurry of activity. Dusting his precious belongings, cleaning the tape heads with a swab of surgical spirit, arranging his tapes in alphabetical order.

'Wake up, Mukundan,' Bhasi whispered. 'Wake up, we have work to do,' he urged, shaking Mukundan's shoulder gently.

Mukundan looked at Bhasi, not really seeing him. He groped for his glasses and put them on. What nonsense was this man talking? Then suddenly it came back to him: the events of the night before. Did I really do that? he groaned inside. Reveal to this creature the festering wounds of my soul? Allow him a glimpse of my fears, my pain, my suffering? What have I done?

'Get up,' Bhasi's voice slithered over him. 'This morning and every morning for the next six weeks, I want you to come with me in my quest for the mandukaparni. Within it is locked your cure.'

'I don't know,' Mukundan hesitated. 'I don't think we should rush into anything.'

He rose from the bed and walked towards the bathroom. At its door he stopped and said, 'It was just the liquor talking. Whatever I said last night,' he shrugged, trying to dismiss the happenings of the night before with a little toss of his shoulder, 'was just a drunken man's ramblings.'

When he came out of the bathroom, Bhasi was still there. 'I think you should go,' Mukundan said, allowing his irritation to show in his tone.

'Mukundan, how long will you continue to run away from yourself? Look at you, the pitiful creature that you are. Fifty-eight years old and still floundering in a swamp of uncertainty. Afraid of your father. Haunted by guilt. Shying away from relationships,' Bhasi said, coming to stand before Mukundan.

'I say, you can't talk like this'—Mukundan protested, shaken by the effrontery of the younger man's words.

'Let me help you, Mukundan,' Bhasi put his hand on Mukundan's shoulder and peered into his eyes. 'Give me just six weeks, and I will heal you. Six weeks is all I ask.'

In the darkness Bhasi's eyes glinted behind his thick glasses. Mukundan felt mesmerized by them. A wave of electricity that coiled around his legs drained him of his resolve to not give into the painter's persuasive words, and rendered him powerless.

'What do you want me to do?' he asked weakly.

'Put on a shirt and come with me,' Bhasi spoke as if he were addressing a child. 'I want to reach the meadow before the sun rises.'

'But how can I leave the house like this? I haven't had my tea or a shave or a bath,' Mukundan mumbled, folding the sheet he covered himself with at night.

'Just this once, break a habit,' Bhasi coaxed.

. 'I can't,' Mukundan said. 'How can you expect me to break a routine that's probably as old as you are? I wouldn't feel awake till all this is gone,' he said rubbing his palm over the faint sprinkling of stubble on his cheeks and chin. 'And what if I have to go to the toilet a few minutes after we leave?''

'Fine. Please try to finish all your ablutions in about fifteen minutes,' Bhasi sighed and sank into a chair.

A breeze lifted off the slopes of the Pulmooth mountain and rustled past them. Mukundan shivered. Where was this man taking him? His tongue felt wooden and heavy. In his haste he had gulped down the hot tea, scalding his mouth. Luckily his razor was one of the disposable kind, or he would have cut himself too.

'Where are we going?' he asked trying to match his stride to Bhasi's brisk one.

'Kodakkad,' Bhasi said taking his glasses off and wiping them with the hem of his lungi.

Mukundan stumbled over a clod of earth. 'Here, hold my hand,' Bhasi said. 'I'll lead you through the fields and the forest till we reach the meadow.'

Mukundan ignored the outstretched hand and murmured, 'It's all right. I'm not as young as you are, but I don't need a walking stick either.' He paused to get his breath. A few beads of sweat sprang up on his brow and on his upper lip. Once again he wondered if he was being foolish. Why had he let himself be persuaded by this madman? After all, in the village they called him One-screw-loose Bhasi.

The trees clung to one another like a band of desperate souls huddled together. As if by doing so, whatever it was that threatened them would balk and turn away. Mukundan felt his heart beat faster. Even as a boy, in his most reckless moments, he had never dared to venture into the forest that the villagers said was inhabited by a yakshi who liked to feast on the blood of virile men. They said she would suddenly appear from between the trees, tempting men with her luscious curves and sweet, helpless voice. She would lure a man deep into the forest and sink her fangs into his throat, and when she was replete she would disappear, leaving behind a pale corpse drained of blood and soul.

Mukundan cleared his throat. The leaves crackled beneath his feet. A feathery branch brushed against his face. Mukundan jumped. 'Bhasi!' he screamed, his voice a strangled cry.

From beneath the leaves a pair of hands clutched at his feet. Fingers entwined around his ankles, wedging between his toes. 'Bhasi!' he screamed again. 'Something's grabbed my feet!'

Suddenly Bhasi was at his side. 'There, there,' he soothed, untangling the vine. 'It's just a plant. Nothing to be so scared about.'

'Mukundan,' Bhasi's mouth was twisted in a wry smile. 'Allow me to guide you through this forest. I know the way through these trees.'

Mukundan reached for the younger man's hand uncertainly. He felt a strange sense of unease. As if the callused palm and the slim supple fingers so much in contradiction to one another were trying to pass on a secret message to his brain. He flinched when he felt Bhasi's grip tighten. 'Why do you cringe when you feel my skin against yours?' Bhasi asked softly.

Mukundan pretended not to hear him and inquired with a little laugh, 'How is it you know all these places? I was born here, and yet you are more the native of this village than I can ever hope to be.'

Bhasi kicked a fallen twig from the path and said, 'When I began my study of medicinal herbs, I had to seek them in the most unusual of places. I first came into this forest because someone described a tree to me that sounded like the *saraca indica*.'

'What's that?' Mukundan asked curiously, wondering if it was going to be part of his cure.

'The asoka tree. Not the slender narrow tree found outside the governor's residence and in parks. This is a beautiful tree with dense foliage and orange-red flowers. The most interesting thing about it is the wartlike protuberances on its bark.' Bhasi pouched his fingers to a five-pointed tip and studded the air with a column of warts as he described the tree. Mukundan watched, entranced by the image Bhasi's words created in his mind.

'The asoka tree,' Bhasi continued, 'is used to treat excessive bleeding and depression in women. What has happened is that Ayurvedic drug companies, quacks, and all kinds of people have methodically stripped almost every single tree of its bark. Unlike leaves and fruit, the bark of the tree is never replaced. So I was most excited when I heard that I could find a specimen of this tree here. Do you know something else? 'Sita was supposed to have sat under an asoka tree when Ravana held her captive. There is yet another legend that says Buddha was born under this tree. But the nicest of the stories is the one about how the tree doesn't bloom unless a virgin kicks it with her feet. But the feet have to be decorated with henna first.'

Mukundan was impressed. Into his mind swam yet another frame. Of Bhasi in the light of a flickering lamp poring over ancient Ayurvedic treatises written on palm leaves. 'Where on earth do you find such information?' he asked.

'Amar Chitra Katha comics,' Bhasi said in a matter-of-fact voice.

Mukundan felt deflated. How on earth could he take this man seriously? Whoever heard of anyone except children believing in what they read in comic books?

'Isn't it peaceful here?' Bhasi remarked a few minutes later. 'The solemn trees, the chattering insects, the singing branches; I can even hear your heartbeat.'

Mukundan laughed. A little nervous laugh. 'I don't know. I just find it a little unnerving.'

They walked in silence, and then abruptly the forest opened out into a small clearing. A grass bowl with a streaky sky for a lid.

Mukundan stood there at the edge of the clearing, too astonished to speak.

Bhasi strode into the meadow: prince regent surveying his domain with pride.

'Mukundan,' he said, bending down to wet his palms on the dew-soaked grass. 'Think of that dark gloomy forest as your past. What your life was till this moment. Guilt clung to your feet. Fear brushed your cheeks. But with me at your side, you found your way to this clearing, toward escape, this purity of light. Kneel down and gather the dew from the grass in your palms. Cleanse your eyes. Open them wide. Look around you now. This is how your life will be henceforth. This is how you will be as long as you live.'

As if in a trance Mukundan moved towards the grass and did as Bhasi asked him to. He raised his wet cheeks to the skies waiting for some sign, some signal from the heavens. A gentle breeze laden with moisture and the fragrance of invisible flowers caressed his skin. After the sullen steamy forest, the breeze was a benign blessing sent down from the vault of heaven. Mukundan felt a great peace fill him.

'Mukundan,' Bhasi's voice penetrated the perfect stillness of the moment. 'Come, see this,' he gestured. Mukundan walked towards one side of the clearing dotted with a few trees and a rocky outcrop. Wet mud squelched beneath his rubber slippers.

'Careful. The ground is a little damp in this spot,' Bhasi cautioned.

'My slippers are all dirty. I'll have to wash them. And look at my clothes. They are ruined; splattered with mud. The stains will never wash away,' Mukundan complained, hiking his mundu to knee level and adjusting it so that it wrapped his thighs like a skirt.

'There is much cleaning to be done. Your footwear, your

clothes, but most of all, it is your mind that will have to be cleansed of the debris of your past. And it is this mandukaparni that will accomplish it,' Bhasi murmured pointing to a slender creeper. 'Look at this herb. Would you ever think that in it flows such celestial powers? *Centella asiatica.* Charaka called it the anti-aging plant. The Chinese use it as a brain tonic.'

'Did you read that too in a comic book?' Mukundan blurted out.

Bhasi stared at him. 'Do you think I am some kind of a lunatic? This is the result of several years of study. With the juice of its leaves and a powder of the whole plant, I shall unwrap the various anxieties that have strangled your real self.'

Mukundan looked at the plant suspiciously and hoped it wouldn't give him diarrhoea. 'Are you sure this is the one? It seems very ordinary,' he finished lamely. What if, instead of being a brain tonic, it turned out to be a brain scrambler?

Bhasi smiled. He paused in the middle of uprooting the plant. 'This meadow is the mandukaparni's home. Where the dew rains by the night and the sun rages by the day. Where the ground sucks at your feet and the skies cause your eyes to crinkle. Don't worry, I know what I am doing.'

Mukundan nodded. His eyes wandered over the landscape, and suddenly he began to feel reassured and even hopeful.

On their way back Mukundan asked Bhasi, 'But if you knew the plant was here, why did you bring me along?'

'Because your mind demands that a ritual be enacted. Because your mind will be receptive to change only when along with your body it participates in this walk from darkness to light.' And then under his breath Bhasi muttered, 'And because I wanted you to be with me.'

Four weeks after Mukundan had begun his early morning

excursions to the heart of Kodakkad, Bhasi woke him up one afternoon. Mukundan opened his eyes sheepishly. 'I didn't mean to sleep. I dozed off in the afternoon heat.'

Bhasi, like Achuthan Nair, he thought, probably didn't approve of afternoon naps. Not that Achuthan Nair did as he said. He slept through most of the afternoon with his mouth open, snoring. And yet, as he sipped his four o' clock tea, he would tell Mukundan, 'I'm eighty-nine years old. How old am I?'

Mukundan would murmur, 'Eighty-nine years old.'

'My body needs the rest. But you shouldn't let sloth take you over. Aren't you sleeping enough at night? And what about you?' he would ask, fixing his gimlet eyes on Krishnan Nair. 'When did you start this habit of sleeping in the afternoon? I wanted a glass of water, and there was no one here to fetch it for me. Everyone was fast asleep. As if you had been working in the fields all morning.'

'How do you feel?' Bhasi asked, intruding into Mukundan's thoughts.

'Fine,' Mukundan replied, wondering what Bhasi had in mind next.

'It's time to begin the next phase of your treatment,' Bhasi began. 'Do you believe in me now, Mukundan?'

'Yes, of course.' Mukundan smiled.

'Enough to do as I ask?' Bhasi questioned. 'Even though it might seem foolish and maybe even insane?'

'Why? What is it this time?'

'I can't explain it to you. Just have faith in me. Remember that I don't stand to gain anything from this. I have only your well-being at heart.'

'I know that,' Mukundan began. 'But—'

'There are no buts. Come with me, Mukundan,' Bhasi said, shutting the main door. 'Please tell Krishnan Nair we are not to be disturbed.'

'Do you think we could have some tea? It's almost time,' Mukundan said, looking at his watch.

'No,' said Bhasi firmly. 'And take that watch off. We don't need the device of time controlling us where we are going.'

'And where is that?' Mukundan asked petulantly.

'Your attic.'

'What?' Mukundan yelped in surprise. But Bhasi had already begun to walk toward the staircase room.

Mukundan followed the painter up the steep wooden ladder that led to the attic. Krishnan Nair had frowned when Mukundan said he was not to be disturbed. 'But what are you going to do in the attic? No one has stepped in there for years now. The last time someone went up there was to replace some rafters the termites had chewed up. Even the civet cat no longer comes there.'

'Krishnan Nair, please,' Mukundan held up his hand to silence the old man. 'I have no time to stand here and chat about the attic. Please don't disturb me.' He paused and added, 'Not even if it is my father who wants to see me.'

The trap door, thick with dust and stiff with disuse, opened reluctantly. Bhasi climbed up into the attic and offered a hand down to Mukundan. Why did the younger man insist on treating him like a doddering fool? He could very well manage to heave himself into the attic without any assistance. Mukundan looked at the painter impatiently. But when he stepped onto the last rung of the ladder, the hole in the ceiling seemed miles away. So he clung to the painter's hand and hoisted himself up.

'Frankly,' Mukundan grumbled, 'when I said I was willing to be treated, I didn't expect to have to go to such foolish lengths.' He wiped a frond of cobweb from his mouth and spat on the dusty floor.

'Mukundan,' Bhasi said with a patient expression, 'you probably think all this is foolish. But it is necessary.'

Mukundan sighed and looked around him in disbelief. The attic was strewn with huge wooden boxes; green-tinged, cracked, bronze vessels; and a pair of enormous clay urns.

As a little boy he had questioned his mother about the urns. She had drawn him to her lap and said, 'Long time ago when there were very old people in the family, grandmas, granduncles, grandaunts who grew older and older, smaller and smaller as they shriveled up with age but still continued to live, then the person would be taken up to the attic and coaxed into the earthen urns. When the old man or woman was inside, the mouth of the urn would be sealed, and there it would remain till someone went up to the attic to clean the place. When the urn was unsealed, guess what was inside?'

'What?' Mukundan had asked, his stomach turning at the thought of the sick, putrefying flesh.

'Well, a little tree frog would jump out!'

'How?' Mukundan had cried in surprise.

'The old person turns into a little frog. So now you know why, once the monsoons begin, you find so many tree frogs. They are all relatives who refused to die.'

'Amma,' Mukundan had promised solemnly, 'I swear never to kill a tree frog again. It could be someone we know.'

'These days, of course, I use the urns to store tamarind balls,' she had laughed.

'Mukundan,' Bhasi's voice levered itself into his thoughts. 'I want you to get into one of these,' he said pointing to an earthen jar. 'They are a little dusty but quite clean. I looked inside.'

'You must be mad if you think I would do something like that,' Mukundan shouted in shock.

'I know it sounds preposterous. But all you have to do is think of it as another form of meditation. An exercise to strengthen your mind and exorcise your past. Look at the shape of this jar. It could be a woman's womb; your mother's womb. To rewrite your destiny, we have to start with the beginning of your existence.'

As a child Mukundan had often longed to hide in one of the gigantic jars to escape his father's wrath. That was many years ago, but just this once there could be no harm in doing as Bhasi asked. I would at least have done one thing that I wanted to in life, he thought.

Bhasi patted the rounded belly of the urn. Mukundan stepped closer and touched the cold clay of its flanks gingerly. What mad potter had fashioned such a gargantuan shape? Had he, as he moulded and shaped it, known that someday a man would seek its confines to be born again? Had some voice whispered in his ear: a little narrow to the bottom, more round, widen the mouth, heat the kiln now. . .?

Mukundan stepped into the jar. There was no room for him to sit or even squat on his haunches. Knees against his chest, arms wrapped around his legs, Mukundan crouched in the womb with the clay walls. Bhasi's voice flowed over him. The fluid that would nourish the new being that sought to grow within him.

'Mukundan, it is time you released your mother's soul. To cling to the dead is to curse them to exist without a body. Let her go. Let her find the destination that every soul is headed towards, from the moment it is separated from the Greater Soul. You don't need her any more. Within you are the genes of your ancestors. Of men and women who let nothing trample them down. Let the genes of your ancestors talk to you now.'

Crouched in the womb, Mukundan called forth his genes. He reverted to his original form—a single cell. Bit by bit the embryo of this new man developed. Eyes. Nose. Ears. The three sensory organs. Two hearts fused into one. Budding limbs. Bones. Genitals. Lulled by the warmth of the jar, fed by the soothing drone that washed over him, Mukundan felt himself dissipate. He closed his eyes to shut out the light.

Surrounded by blackness, he felt himself split into several selves. All of whom had no claim to the one that had stepped into the urn. Disembodied, he was no longer anything that he had been before. He could separate himself endlessly so that he could be anything he wanted to be. A new man, a new life. Afraid no longer. Capable of so much more than he had ever dreamed of.

16

A Few Battles

Twin coals feasted on Mukundan's back, devouring tendon, muscle and bone with a rapacious appetite that left a ragged-edged hole as they proceeded along. Fierce red tongues that dismissed the density of his being by boring a pathway through skin and sinew. Four eyes. The outer ones puckered and dead. And yet they too stood up in rapt attention, compelled by the fires with which their inner companions burned. Twin coals. Burnt umber eyes. All-pervading. All-seeing. Demanding to know.

Mukundan's fingers, dancing over the typewriter keys, faltered under the steady gaze of his father. He shifted a little to the side as if to evade the intensity of Achuthan Nair's eyes. But they shifted with him. Mukundan took a deep breath and let his fingers fly over the typewriter keys once more. Two more lines to go. Two more lines to endure, he told himself, and let the click-click of the typewriter depose the oppressive silence of the room.

'I thought you were an assistant works manager when you retired,' Achuthan Nair's voice boomed over his shoulder.

'Yes, that's right. I retired as assistant works manager, grade II,' Mukundan said, savouring the feel of the words as they formed. He felt that familiar pride surge in him.

'So how is it that you type with the speed of a clerk who does nothing else all day long? Who does what all day long?'

'Type all day long. I've always typed my personal

correspondence,' Mukundan tried to explain, wondering why he did so.

'Huh!' Achuthan Nair grunted.

What did that 'Huh' mean? Disbelief? Acceptance? Indifference? Mukundan removed the completed letter from the typewriter and put it into a plastic file.

Then he turned around and looked at his father. 'Do you want to see my retirement notice? It says clearly who I was and what I retired as.'

A flicker of surprise washed over Achuthan Nair's face at this display of spirit. Then his eyes began to burn as they sensed the challenge in Mukundan's words. He sat up straight, his back as unrelenting as ever, and glared at Mukundan. How dare you! his eyes flamed. Twin coals. Burnt umber eyes that had always reduced Mukundan to a state of tongue-tied nervousness.

Mukundan stared back. He felt that familiar fear rise in him. A loosening of his bowels. A clenching of nerves. A choking of the throat. He swallowed convulsively.

Remember what Bhasi said, he told himself. In you is the strength to stand up to anything and anyone. You can choose how to live your life. You don't have to cower and run away any more. You can do what you want.

Achuthan Nair's eyes dropped. 'What is that letter you were typing? he asked.

Mukundan pulled out the sheet of paper and handed it to his father. Achuthan Nair grabbed it from his hands and peered at it. 'Read it to me. I can't see anything without my glasses.'

Mukundan took the letter back and cleared his throat.

26 Sept 1997

The Executive Engineer
Kerala State Electricity Board
Cherplasserry Division

Ref Meter Number 678950
Sub: Fine for illegal connection

Sir,

Apropos the letter from your office dated 22 September, 1996, stating that I am being fined Rs 650 for tapping electricity through an illegal connection.

I wish to inform you that no such illegal act has been committed. It is true that I did take an extension from my residence to another building. But the building, which houses the post office, belongs to me and is part of the same plot of land. Moreover, the line was extended only for the purpose of providing a light at the post office and that, too, only as a temporary measure.

I had explained all of this to the lineman, one individual named Mr Sathyan. However, he refused to accept my explanation and was extremely rude to me. In fact, he had the effrontery to tell me that since most of the villagers of Kaikurussi are related to me, as per my logic, all we needed to do was extend our individual lines from one point, namely, the electric pole.

I wish to state that this is also a letter of complaint. As a public servant, he needs to treat consumers with more amicability. I have been given to understand that if I had paid him a bribe, none of this would have occurred.

As a retired Class I gazetted officer who has devoted almost thirty-nine years of his life to the service of the country, and as an honest citizen who has been paying his taxes regularly, I consider it unjust and morally wrong. And a harassment of the worst sort. What's more, though I pay Rs 200 as a slab rate, what with intermittent power cuts, load shedding, or a burst transformer or a line fault every few days, I must be consuming hardly half of the electricity I pay for. So I believe there is absolutely no justification for this fine. I hope you will look into this and do the needful.

Thanking you,
I remain

Yours sincerely,
Mukundan Nair

'Huh!' Achuthan Nair snorted, knocking his cane down onto the floor. Mukundan ignored his father and put the letter back in the plastic file.

'Do you think this letter is going to be of any use? Give that lineman a bribe. That is the only thing that will work. What will work?'

'A bribe. But no, I don't intend to,' Mukundan said firmly. 'I'll pay the fine if necessary, but I refuse to bribe anyone.'

'Well, then, you will be sitting in darkness very soon,' Achuthan Nair chortled in malicious glee. 'What will you be sitting in?'

'In darkness,' Mukundan answered out of habit. Then his mouth twisted, 'But what's new about that? My life has always been shadowed by your tyranny.'

'What did you say?' Achuthan Nair rose from the chair furiously. 'Who's been teaching you to talk back to me? That One-screw-loose Bhasi, I suppose. Do you think I don't know what's going on?' he spluttered in rage.

Mukundan stared back at his father. For the first time in his life, he realized he was at least a head taller than his father. For the first time, he saw his father for who he was. An aged bully. A has-been despot. An old man clinging to the ghost of his past glory.

Mukundan swallowed a retort, turned on his foot, and walked out of the room. With every step he took, he realized with a little leap of joy that he was no longer afraid. His father no longer ruled him. He could be anyone he wanted to be.

One morning, a few days after Mukundan mailed the letter of complaint, the lineman came on his moped and removed the fuse. 'How can you do this without any prior notice?' Mukundan protested.

'We sent you a notice with adequate time to pay the fine. I don't have time to stand around here and argue with you. Pay the fine today and show me the receipt, and I'll replace the fuse. I'll be passing this way around four in the evening,' the lineman smirked as he rode off on his moped.

'What did I tell you?' Achuthan Nair said from behind. 'So what is it you plan to do? Fan yourself all night? Ho-ho-ho,' he laughed, vastly amused at the thought of his son tossing and turning in bed, bitten by mosquitoes, and stifled by the warm humid night.

Mukundan wished he could stuff a handful of coconut fibre down his father's throat. Instead he walked to Shankar's Tea Club.

Bhasi looked up from his glass of tea and remarked, 'I suppose the lineman caused trouble. I saw him go past this way, looking very satisfied with himself.'

Mukundan sat across the table. Shankar gestured to the boy to bring a glass of tea. 'What do I do?' Mukundan asked, sipping the tea without even tasting it.

'Pay the fine. Do it right away like the lineman asked you to,' Bhasi advised. 'Tomorrow is a holiday, and the electricity office will be closed. You don't want to spend two days without power in your house, do you?' he said, seeing the hesitation in Mukundan's eyes. 'Some other time you can get your own back. But this time let him win.'

Shankar listened to their conversation with great interest. 'That lineman is an arrogant son-of a-bitch. He knows he has you at his mercy. But anyway, I don't think you should go to the electricity office and give him the pleasure of seeing you stand in line. Che Kutty is going to Cherplasserry to pick up some stuff. I'll ask him to pay the fine for you. But the next time you see him, spare a few minutes to chat with him. Che Kutty tells me that you avoid him as if he were a stinking drain.'

'Oh, I didn't mean to offend him. It's a pure misunderstanding on his part. I have just been a little preoccupied lately,' Mukundan said weakly.

'That's all right. Che Kutty is a good chap. Quite an unusual man, like our Bhasi here. In fact, I have wondered why you two never became friends,' Shankar asked, turning towards Bhasi.

'I am everyone's friend,' Bhasi said quietly.

' I don't know about that. But you two are thick, I hear,' Shankar too had been told about the early morning excursions and the late evening visits.

Bhasi gulped and rose hastily. 'I'll see you then,' he murmured to Mukundan on his way out.

Mukundan sipped at his tea slowly. Why was it that the whole village speculated on his relationship with Bhasi? Couldn't a man choose his own friends without consulting his neighbours about it?

Shankar examined his fingernails and said slowly, 'You shouldn't take it amiss, but I think I have to tell you this. Bhasi is a good man, but you shouldn't let him get too close to you. He is just a housepainter, after all. By spending so much of your time with him, you are lowering your standing in this village. Someone of your status should be friends with someone like Power House Ramakrishnan sir. Now there is a good man for you.

'Why, even the other day he was asking about you. He wanted to know if you had settled in. If you ask me, you should call on him one of these days.'

If you really want to know, I think Power House Ramakrishnan is an absolute phony. Bhasi might be a housepainter but he is a fine and cultured man. Even if you were to roll twenty Power House Ramakrishnans into one, you still won't be able to get a Bhasi. Do you know why? Power House Ramakrishnan is a social climber, a status seeker, a snob, and an opportunist. I don't wish to have anything to do with him. Nor do I wish to hear anything more about the goodness of his heart. What's more, I will be grateful if you will desist from telling me whom I should be friends with. Anyway, what gives you the goddamn right to advise me? The words struggled for release. Mukundan bit back the retort that scalded the insides of his mouth and swallowed it down meekly with his tea. After all, he was obliged to Shankar for taking care of that unpleasant 'electricity fine' business. Besides, he didn't want anyone in the village to hear of how he had been found bickering in the tea shop like some illiterate lout. It didn't befit someone like him.

Every evening at half-past six, Mukundan bathed in cold water. Then, with the droplets still clinging to the end of his nose and with only a wet towel wound around his hips, he would rush to the pooja room. He would light the lamp and say his prayers, eyes closed and hands folded. He'd forgotten all the prayers his mother had taught him. Over the years the prayers had turned into a monologue that closely resembled the numerous official letters he had written in his service years:

Dear God,
This is to inform you that I have tried my best to follow all your dictates. As you probably know, it is my constant endeavour to be a good and honest man.
I will be deeply obliged if you will continue to take good care of me. Protect me from illness and sorrow. Kindly grant me peace of mind and blessings.

Sincerely and devoutly,
I remain

Your humble devotee
Mukundan

Dressed in a white sleeveless vest and mundu, Mukundan
would turn the pages of the morning's newspaper till the
clock struck seven. When the TV burst into the signature
tune that preceded the news, Mukundan would look at
Krishnan Nair's face and say with a laugh, 'It's time I
started my second round of pooja.'

Krishnan Nair seldom bothered to look up or say
anything. Some days he asked Mukundan for a drink and
then he tossed it down his throat and made a face as if he
had bitten into a bitter melon. But other days the old
caretaker sat in front of the TV and with rapt attention
watched the world go about its business. Earthquakes.
Killings. Accidents. Strikes. Politicians. Film stars. Poultry
farming. Panel discussions. Krishnan Nair hated it when
something came between him and his beloved TV.

Mukundan rarely watched TV. God knows why he had
bought one at all when he lived in Bangalore. When it was
time to leave for Kaikurussi, he had sold his old TV to the
office peon. However, when the truck carrying all his
belongings drove up into Kaikurussi and began unloading,
Krishnan Nair waited for the TV to be unpacked and fixed.
'You'll need an antenna that's extra tall to get a good
reception,' he told Mukundan. But when he realized that
there was no TV forthcoming, Krishnan Nair let his
disappointment show. 'A TV is more than just to tell you
what's happening around the world. It's a status symbol.
Everyone's going to wonder why you don't have a TV in
your home. They'll think you probably can't afford to buy
one.' And so the gibes had continued until one day
Mukundan succumbed to the constant pressure. He bought

a colour TV with a hundred channels, stereophonic sound, and a remote control. Never mind that, without a dish antenna, all they could receive was just one channel—the national channel, Doordarshan. But Krishnan Nair was happy.

Why on earth did Krishnan Nair want to know what to feed a farrowing sow or when to wean a piglet? Mukundan wondered in amusement. He waited for Krishnan Nair to lose himself in the swirl of images. Then he would carry the bottle, glasses, water, ice, and a plate of salted peanuts to the veranda outside. Bhasi had taken to joining him in the evenings. But he almost never drank. Instead he would nurse a glass of ice water while Mukundan drank his daily quota of two pegs.

Mukundan waited eagerly for this evening rendezvous. 'What do you talk about all evening?' the caretaker cocking an eyebrow, asked one day.

'This and that,' Mukundan said.

'What is this and that?'

'All kinds of things. Village news. World news. Trivia, actually,' Mukundan said, peering from the window to see if Bhasi had arrived yet.

'If news is what you want, why don't you watch TV?' the old man said. He thought Mukundan gave the painter more importance than he deserved.

Mukundan ignored the old man and walked outside. How could he tell Krishnan Nair that he shared with Bhasi a companionship that defied description? Bhasi alone was privy to his every single thought and deed. And if he didn't spend time with Bhasi every day, the strength that he had discovered within himself might begin to ebb.

Their evenings together began always in the same manner, with a slight awkwardness that Bhasi tried to shrug aside with a little snippet of gossip. A new development to some already twisted story; a fresh tidbit of news, a stranger in the village. Mukundan would listen and then begin a narrative of his own. Oh, how Mukundan loved to dredge from the vast coffers of his memory experiences embellished by age and time. And so they would talk till Mukundan poured himself his second drink. Then Bhasi would bring to life one of Mukundan's many ghosts.

Later that night, at quarter to nine, Bhasi rose to leave. Mukundan put down his empty glass feeling completely at peace. 'I think I'll go to Cherplasserry tomorrow. Someone I used to work with very long ago lives there,' he said. Then he stood up, stretched, and yawned.

Suddenly Mukundan was struck with remorse. Earlier in the day he should have stood up for Bhasi when Shankar had made those seemingly-harmless-but-loaded-with-vitriol statements. But it had really been one of those situations when the best thing to do was to keep quiet. Which is what he had done.

'I don't know if it is the rum or your company, but I feel like I am back in Bangalore again. With my friends and a familiar world.' Mukundan uttered the first thing that came to his head and immediately felt better for it. What was the point in defending a man in his absence? He would never know how much you cared for him. It was a thousand times preferable to tell him to his face how highly one thought about him. But in return Mukundan was rewarded with a look of pain that shadowed Bhasi's face.

'Have I offended you by putting you on a par with alcohol?' Mukundan asked, touching the younger man's arm. 'I didn't mean anything offensive. But it is the truth. Spending time with you makes me feel good. As if everything in life is the way it is meant to be.'

Bhasi held Mukundan's arm and said quietly, 'I am not offended at all. I just feel very—' he paused and added, '—touched.'

Mukundan gathered the glasses to fill the silence that had

crept in between them. He knew Bhasi was watching him. He knew Bhasi was waiting for him to bridge the silence. But he didn't know what to say. For a moment he wondered if Bhasi had heard about how Shankar had denounced their friendship and how Mukundan had not spoken one word in defense.

Bhasi sighed and said, 'I must leave. I have things I must attend to at home.'

'Same time tomorrow?' Mukundan asked anxiously.

'Yes, same time tomorrow,' Bhasi promised, and walked to the gate.

Mukundan wondered why Bhasi never spoke about his wife. It was as if he had drawn a veil over that part of his life as a husband and father. If he hadn't seen Damayanti for himself, he would never have believed that Bhasi was married. And to a woman as beautiful as Damayanti.

17

Sweet Joy This

She had clear grey eyes rimmed with a thick line of kohl, and a long braid of hair that hung to her thighs. Her skin was the colour of the flesh of the sapodilla plum. A smooth brown with a faint tinge of red. In a pale blue sari speckled with tiny white flowers, she sat on a ledge built into the wall of the veranda, correcting a sheaf of what looked like exam papers. Mukundan smiled at his old boss and wondered who she was. K.M. Nair had no children of his own. Had he married again after his wife died some years ago?

'So you finally found your way here! Why did it take you almost four months to come and visit me?' K.M. Nair greeted him with a complaint.

'I've been meaning to. But you know how it is. One thing or the other keeps cropping up,' Mukundan murmured in apology.

'Well, I'm glad you are here now. This is my niece, Anjana,' the old man said, introducing the slender woman at his side. Then, turning to her, he said, 'This is Mukundan. He began his career as my juniormost clerk. Not any more. Now he is an assistant works manager. He's settled down in his old ancestral house in Kaikurussi.'

Mukundan smiled at her and said, 'I'm retired, of course.'

Cherplasserry putting down the sheaf of papers, got up saying, 'I'll bring you something cold to drink.'

'A lovely girl,' K.M. Nair said, watching her retreating back. 'Married to a no-good creature. Luckily her parents were wise enough to educate her. So she has a job as a teacher in a school in Ottapalam. She visits me most

Saturdays and leaves only in the evening,' the old man rambled.

Mukundan sat back in the chair feeling as if his insides were churning. *Anjana*, he said the name silently.

'I hope you will stay for lunch,' she said offering him a glass of orange squash.

He sipped at the icy cold drink and nodded, 'If it isn't too much trouble.'

He watched her from the corner of his eye as she hovered around the dining table at lunchtime. She was serene as the evening sunshine and just as pleasant. She would never have bad breath, perspiration patches, or cracked heels. There was something about her that suggested smooth, rounded edges; a golden wholesomeness.

'Some more rice, Uncle?' she asked.

For a moment, Mukundan thought, she was addressing him. I suppose I do seem old enough to be called uncle, he thought despondently. And yet he didn't feel that way at all. He looked up from his plate and found her spooning rice into K. M. Nair's plate.

'Serve Mukundan some fish, dear,' the old man urged. 'He's a bachelor,' he explained to her.

Mukundan smiled shyly. She served him the biggest piece of fried fish on the plate and asked softly, 'So how do you manage?'

'Not very well,' Mukundan shrugged, hoping it would arouse some sympathy in her. 'The family caretaker does his best, but somehow it doesn't seem enough.'

'Well, then, this is your chance to make up for it,' the old man guffawed, smacking his lips.

Mukundan smiled across the table at Anjana. When he began to hiccup, she poured him a glass of water from a big jug.

'Eat slowly. What is the hurry?' the old man said.

'The next time you hiccup in the middle of a meal, I'll remember to tell you that,' Anjana said with a smile.

Mukundan felt a queer warmth steal over him. A sensation as if she'd just caressed his brow with her long, rose-tipped fingers. *Anjana!* His soul leaped.

When the dishes had been cleared and the table wiped, Anjana came to join the men on the front veranda, where they sat smoking. K. M. Nair stubbed the cigarette and rose from the planter's chair with its long arms, stilling a small yawn. 'You'll stay for a while, won't you? There's a bus at quarter past four. The same one she takes up to Nellaya. You can go in it to Kailiad. Meanwhile, let me take a nap.'

Mukundan looked at Anjana. She met his eyes for a brief instant and then, averting her gaze, said, 'Do stay. This bus is very convenient.'

The old man took with him to bed his belches and the easy camaraderie he spread around him with his wicked comments and loud laughs. Mukundan felt as if the drawbridge of conversation between him and Anjana had been raised. A silence shadowed the space between them. A lopsided silence weighed with unspoken words. A crashing of waves as the desire to reveal to her his secret thoughts rose and fell: Shall I take a red, a yellow, and a blue string and tie in each one three knots saying your name, *Anjana*, as I tie the knots? Then shall I bind them together and wear them around my wrist so that you will not be able to resist me?

Or should I pare my nails, grind them to a fine powder, and steep your tea with it so that you will be seized with desire for me?

An ice cream vendor stood at the gate and honked the horn three times. 'Aaaice cup. . . ice cone. . . ice. . . chocobar. . . tutty-frutti. . .' His cry resounded through the afternoon air, ripping the silence between them.

'Do you want an ice cream?' Mukundan blurted out, and then wished he could have bitten off his tongue.

Her eyes widened in surprise. Then she smiled. 'Why not? I haven't eaten one for many years now.'

Mukundan walked back to the house holding the two ice cream cups carefully.

He held one out to her. 'I asked for chocolate. I hope you like it. '

'I do,' Anjana murmured, removing the paper lid from the cup. 'Didn't he give you any spoons?' she asked.

'Here,' he fumbled. As he fished for the tiny wooden spoons in his shirt pocket, the ice cream in his hand dropped with a soft plop to the floor. A puddle of Sweet Joy lay heaving on the red oxide floor, swiftly melting into a viscous stream of running-away joy.

'Never mind,' she said giving him a sidelong glance as she dug into her ice cream with the tiny spoon. 'You can have some of mine.'

And so Mukundan stood there entranced by the vision she made.

Her plait hanging over one shoulder. Her feet tucked under her as she sat cross-legged spooning the ice cream into her mouth. Her left hand curled around the rim of the ice cream cup. The thumb and forefinger of her right hand creating new landscapes of the ice cream universe as it dug, patted and shaped. Lips parted, her eyes dancing with the promise of sharing.

Sweet joy this, he thought.

Mukundan looked at his watch one more time. In just fifteen minutes' time they would close the counter. And there were at least twenty persons standing before him in line.

'How long has she been chatting on the phone?' he asked the man in front.

'For a very long time. If I don't pay the bill today, these monsters will be at my doorstep tomorrow to remove the fuse,' the man complained.

Behind him Mukundan heard murmurs. Someone

muttered, 'Why doesn't she do her canoodling on the phone during the lunch break?'

Someone else sighed, 'What do they care? As long as they come in and sign the register on time every morning, their jobs are safe. And when they retire, they get a good pension for having twiddled their thumbs during their working years. I tell you this country's going to the dogs. What we need is a dictator. Military rule!'

Mukundan shifted his weight to the other leg. He needn't have come at all. In fact, he could have paid the bill by sending a postal money order. But he had wanted an excuse to come to Cherplasserry on a Saturday.

Mukundan turned around and said to no one in particular, 'We should protest about this nonsense. So many of us have been standing here for more than an hour. First she went off to drink tea. Then she was chatting to someone. And now this!'

'Oh, we can complain as much as we want to. But nothing's going to come of it. If we don't manage to pay the bill now, we'll just have to come back in the afternoon or on Monday,' a man in a striped shirt spoke up.

'As if we have nothing else to do but make daily trips to the electricity office,' Mukundan snorted in disgust.

'That's the way it is. There is no point in us trying to change anything,' Striped Shirt said.

Mukundan felt a wave of irritation flood over him. What did he mean by saying: 'That's the way it is'? 'I'm not going to stand around here doing nothing. Let me see if I can get her off the phone,' he said to Striped Shirt and then added, 'please hold my place. I'll be back.'

He walked up to the counter briskly. The rest of the line, mostly men, watched him curiously. Mukundan planted his forearms on the wooden counter and said loudly, 'Excuse me, madam.'

The woman's eyes darted toward him, but she rattled on oblivious to his presence, 'In fact, Girija said every time she sees you, she thinks of Jayaram. What? No, not the doctor at the government hospital, the actor Jayaram! So I said, Jayaram is just a film hero, but you are a real man.'

Mukundan cleared his throat impatiently and rapped on the counter.

The woman tucked a stray curl behind her ear, cupped the mouthpiece of the phone, and frowned, 'Can't you see I'm busy?'

Mukundan snorted, 'Busy doing what? Can't you see that there is a line of people waiting to pay their electricity bills? Why don't you first finish with us, then you can flirt on the phone all afternoon.'

The woman stared at him and snapped, 'Who are you to tell me what to do? If you have a complaint, go tell my HOD.'

Mukundan snapped back, 'That's precisely what I am going to do. Such arrogance!'

As he walked back, he heard her giggle into the phone, 'An old ape trying to teach me how to do my job.'

'So were you successful in getting her off the phone?' Striped Shirt smirked.

'No. But I will,' Mukundan retorted. 'I'm going to talk to her superior, the head of department.'

'I really think you shouldn't make such an issue of it. If we antagonize them, they'll turn nasty and make our lives even more difficult,' Striped Shirt said with an I've-been-through-all-this-before look. 'Why don't you smoke a cigarette or drink some tea to calm yourself?' he suggested.

Mukundan shook his head in refusal. 'Just hold my place for me.'

Mukundan walked up to the first floor. A peon was standing by the door reading a newspaper.

He gave Mukundan a quick lookover and asked in a surly voice, 'What do you want?'

'I want to meet the divisional engineer.'

'Do you have an appointment?' The peon demanded, removing a beedi from behind his ear.

'Why do I need an appointment? I just want to see him for a few minutes,' Mukundan said in exasperation.

'You can't see him just like that. There's a procedure. First you meet the office superintendent. He'll tell you whom to meet. The junior engineer or divisional engineer. But there is one way you can avoid all that,' the peon said wiggling a finger in his ear. Looking away, he said softly, 'Give me some money for tea, and I'll see to it that the DE meets you right away.'

'I don't pay bribes,' Mukundan said furiously.

'Bribe! Pah!' the peon spat out, 'Did I ask you for a thousand rupees? All I wanted was some tea money. Go away. The DE doesn't meet anyone at this time.'

'Then I'll talk to the office superintendent,' Mukundan said and walked past the peon.

The walls of the office room were an indeterminate colour between grey and pistachio green, smeared with patches of flaking plaster. The windows were half open, and from the ceiling hung two fans that rattled noisily as they whirred. Olive green filing cabinets lined the wall on one side. Adjacent to them was a row of grey metal shelves stacked with box files. Across the length of the room ran a bridge of tables. Six metal tube chairs with plastic wire mesh backs and seats and solid wooden armrests stood behind each table. Chairs that hinted at permanence, Mukundan thought to himself, as his eyes scanned the three occupants of the room: a man and two women who were so deep in discussion that they didn't even notice him at first.

Mukundan wondered what to do next. Then he spotted a cubicle at the farther end of the room created by cleverly placing two filing cabinets at right angles to each other away from one wall. A little brown wooden board on the table announced a title: Office Superintendent.

'Excuse me,' Mukundan addressed the trio. 'I'd like to

speak to the office superintendent.'

'Puroshottam sir is on long leave. You can speak to Sethu sir here. He is the in-charge now,' the younger of the two women said.

Sethu sir preened in his chair. Mukundan studied the lean-cheeked, light-skinned man with an almost sparse moustache and began, 'I would like to make a —'. He was cut off in mid-sentence by the other man, who gestured for him to wait and said, 'Please take a seat. I'll attend to you in just a minute.'

Mukundan sat on the visitor's chair. A lesser twin to the office chair, with a sagging seat and no armrests lest the visitor got too comfortable. He looked around him and then at the clerks, or so he assumed they were. Had the women in his office dressed as garishly?

Both women wore several gold chains around their necks and gold bangles on their wrists. The younger woman now perched on the in-charge's table wore a sari that had a print of several tigers chasing several antelopes, round and round her legs and thighs, up her belly and over her breasts before running over her shoulder and down her back into a flowery grave. As for the older woman, she could have taught geometry by just standing up and pointing to the prints on her sari.

Sethu sir's hair shone with oil and care; his face with contentment. 'Do you think we should go to Alukkas Jewellers or Alappat Jewellers? I don't want to spend all afternoon going from one jewellery shop to the other.'

Mukundan eavesdropped on their conversation with a growing sense of outrage. I was never like this in my working years. I did my duty conscientiously and diligently, Mukundan began to fume. So why should I tolerate it in others? 'Excuse me,' he said standing up.

Sethu sir looked at Mukundan's outraged face and then, focusing at a point somewhere between Mukundan's nose and chin, said, 'Didn't I tell you I will attend to you?'

The older woman shook her head and grumbled, 'They are all the same. They think we have nothing else to do but wait on them.'

A silver bead of mercury shot to his head and burst. 'Madam,' Mukundan growled, 'I've been waiting patiently for more than ten minutes, and what is it that you have been doing meanwhile? "Should I go to Alukkas or Alappat?" he mimicked the in-charge's reedy voice. 'Is this what you mean by doing your duty? Let me tell you, I was a government servant for more than thirty-nine years, and I did my duty faithfully. Not like you people! You should be ashamed of yourselves.'

'You can't walk in here and pick a fight. Please behave with some decorum,' the younger woman sprang to defend the in-charge.

'Decorum! Don't you dare talk about it,' Mukundan exploded. Little beads of sweat stood up on his brow and ran down his face. 'Look at you! Dressed in clothes that would be more appropriate for a street dancer. And what is that you have tied your hair with? Your daughter's underwear?'

The younger woman touched the lace-and-satin scrunchy in her hair, suddenly conscious of its crinkled-panty resemblance while the in-charge butted in, 'I say, I say—'.

'What is happening here?' a stentorian voice boomed. Mukundan turned around and saw a neatly dressed middle-aged man eyeing him.

'Sir, this man has been behaving in a most inappropriate manner with us—' the younger woman began.

'Please,' he held up his hand to silence her. 'Sethu, see me after the lunch hour,' and then turning to Mukundan, he said, 'please come with me.'

Mukundan sat across the table in the divisional engineer's room and tried to explain. 'I'm not saying that every minute of office time has to be spent working. But they have to do their duty first.'

'What is it you wanted?' the divisional engineer asked patiently, twirling a paperweight and letting it spin a few times.

'I wanted to pay my bill,' Mukundan said.

'Give me the bill and the money,' the divisional engineer said and pressed a buzzer. When the now-cowering peon rushed in, he gave it to him and barked, 'Pay this and bring the receipt.'

'Sir, it is not just me. There were others in the line.'

'Mr Nair,' the younger man sighed standing up, 'I can help you but I can't help everybody. Then I would have to do the work of this entire office all by myself. Please wait here. The peon will bring you the receipt.' He paused on his way out and added kindly, 'The next time, just send a money order. You don't have to come personally. No one has to. Which is why we have that facility.'

Mukundan sat in the room all by himself. He needn't have come in person to pay the bill. He knew that. But how else could he see Anjana again?

Mukundan walked down the steps of the electricity office slowly. He hoped he wouldn't run into anyone he recognized. Particularly the man in the striped shirt.

The veranda was deserted. The counter hatch was closed, and everyone seemed to have disappeared into thin air. Mukundan glanced at his watch. Nearly one. K. M. Nair's house was about a kilometre away. He would take an autorickshaw. Mukundan stood there on the last step of the staircase when he saw his old enemy Lineman Sathyan driving up on his moped.

Mukundan waited for the lineman to enter the building. Then he hurried to where the moped was parked under a tree. Mukundan surveyed the terrain to see if anyone was around and quickly yanked out the tube from the petrol cock. The petrol gushed out, in a flood. Full tank. Good, he thought in relish. Mukundan watched a while as the petrol dampened the earth, feeling a tremendous sense of satisfaction. You might have won that round, Lineman Sathyan, but this one I win.

Triumphant and excited, Mukundan hailed an autorickshaw from outside the gate.

'Where to?' the driver asked.

'Sweet Joy.'

'Never heard of it. Is there any landmark nearby?' the driver demanded peevishly.

'Just stop by the Blue Star Hotel,' Mukundan mumbled and sank back into the cushioned seat of the vehicle.

As the autorickshaw glided over the bumps and potholes of the road, music blaring, the chromium-plated rods at its side flashing, Mukundan decided that in the evening he would hire one of these gilded chariots with three wheels. And in it, he would seat Anjana. Shoulder to shoulder, thigh to thigh, they would travel together. Till they reached her doorstep and it was time for him to go on. Alone, reluctantly.

18

The Sermon of the Shrimp Heap

Anjana held the shrimp in her left hand and twisted its head off with her right hand. She peeled the shell and then pulled the legs away from the body of the crustacean, tugging at the tail to release it from the rose-tinged flesh within. When the shrimp was cold and naked in her hands, she ran the nail of her thumb down its back as if it were a blade. The flesh parted, revealing the thin black vein nestling within. She edged her nail under the vein and deftly inched it out so that it didn't snap. She dipped her fingers in a pail of water and tossed the shrimp into an earthenware dish where it joined its other innocuous cousins. Deprived of their powers to curdle the human intestines, loosen the bowels, cause the skin to rise in a million bumps, and ring the eyes with little pink pouches, they lay there, shorn of their weaponry; defenceless and dead.

Anjana pushed back a strand of hair with the curve of her elbow and took a deep breath. The aluminum vessel was heaped with an army of shrimps replete with their full suits of shelled armour, long lancelike tentacles, and thin streaks of evil within.

'Is that all you have done?' a voice asked from behind. The stone she was perched on wobbled dangerously as she turned in surprise. She straightened her back and stilled the stone, then she looked at the man framed in the doorway: shirt open to his waist, lungi gathered between his legs as he stood there leaning against the door, one arm raised as it rested on the door jamb. She saw the nest of snakes in his armpit, the matted fleece on his chest, the vicious porcupine quills of his moustache and shuddered. Thin black filaments of brutish callousness. Evil veins more mephitic than a whole ocean of shrimps roamed and thrived all over his body in the guise of hair. Who was this man? This stranger she allowed entry into her house, her life, her body?

On the day Anjana turned twenty-seven, she resigned herself to a state of eternal spinsterhood. She had become, she thought, with a little bitter smile, one of those old maids destined to remain at home. Unloved, unwanted, unfulfilled. Long in the tooth, with sunken cheeks and vacant eyes.

Her parents hid their anxiety when no suitable marriage alliance came about. They encouraged her to study and keep herself occupied. Soon the house was littered with the papier-mache dolls, ashtrays and baskets she had made. Cushion covers she had cut, sewed, and embroidered were propped up in every possible place. She learned how to milk the cow and what to do when the rose plants were afflicted with a disease that turned their leaves brown and caused them to curl. She experimented with recipes she found in magazines. She fashioned shopping bags out of plastic wires and gave them away to friends and relatives. She painted virulent sunsets, lonely shepherds and chubby-cheeked gods on the back of glass and had them framed. She even made a little palace using sheets of glass and tiny injection vials. And still no prospective groom appeared on the horizon.

Then the marriage broker brought a proposal. 'Ravindran is thirty-five years old and works for a pharmaceutical company as a medical representative,' he said. 'His parents are no longer alive, and his only sister is married and lives in Jamshedpur. No family responsibilities, well-to-do, good looking, and the horoscopes match, too. If I were you, I'd close my eyes and go ahead with this alliance,' the marriage broker assured her parents.

They looked at each other uncertainly. The marriage broker, long used to identifying such incertitude, pounced on their thoughts and said, 'Don't worry. He doesn't have a character flaw or a secret vice. I know the family very well.' And then he flashed his trump card, 'Have you thought about how your daughter feels? She is getting older by the day, and while all her friends are married and settled with children, she is still in her parents' home.'

Anjana pretended to be unmoved. The families met formally. He smiled at her. She smiled back. But she didn't dare let herself hope. 'What do you think?' her mother asked as she cleared away the teacups and plates of banana chips and cakes.

'He seems all right,' she said, unwilling to commit herself to anything more.

Yet at night, like the Bethlehem lilies she nurtured in pots, her secret hopes blossomed. A quiet unfurling of dreams fed by the loneliness that leafed within her. Furtive silent desires that only the breeze, the moon, and the bats that prowled through the night skies glimpsed.

A week later the marriage broker came back with a beaming face and a demand that they bring out something sweet to celebrate the glad tidings he brought. Only then did Anjana let her mask slip and reveal how relieved she was. She smiled. She laughed. Her shoulders straightened. Her breasts stood proud and erect. Her hips swung. Her eyes danced. Anjana let herself be a desirable woman once again.

After the wedding Anjana and Ravindran went to live in Kozhikode. Anjana had never been to Kozhikode in her life. But she gathered information from wherever and whomsoever she could find. From childhood textbooks came a page of history—Vasco da Gama landed at a beach in Kozhikode and thus opened doors to colonial greed. A neighbour described the silvery fish one could buy there, plump and still tasting of the ocean. East Hill, West Hill, plump dates, busy streets, Bombay Hotel, the Mananchira

Pond right in the heart of the city. . . Anjana's heart beat faster as the train drew closer to Kozhikode City.

The house was small and part of a housing colony in a little suburb called Beypore. No. 27, Garden Colony. Anjana sighed in satisfaction. As Ravindran drew out a key and opened the door, she looked around her in satisfaction. The narrow strip of ground in the front, the two coconut trees and one papaya tree, the tiny well, all enchanted her. Roses here, hibiscus there, begonias in hanging pots, curtains with scalloped edges for the windows, cushions for the sofa and chairs, rubber mat on the doorstep . . . Anjana began to make plans even before she had stepped into her marital home.

Late in the evening, bathed and dressed in a pink cotton sari with tiny white flowers on it, and a matching pink blouse she had made herself, Anjana went in search of Ravindran. Pink suited her more than any other colour did and she so very much wanted to look her best. She wanted him to feel that he had made the right decision in choosing to wed her. And so even before the actual wedding, she had planned to wear the pink sari the first time they were alone and together. He was sitting on one of the two plastic chairs on the front veranda, flicking through the pages of a magazine. He had been away from the house most of the day. In the morning, he went out and came back laden with bags from the market, 'There is a chicken and some vegetables in the bags. Someone will deliver all the groceries in a little while. I need to go out now,' he said.

'Will you come for lunch?' she asked hesitantly.

'I don't think so,' he said. 'I'll be back soon,' he added as an afterthought.

When he returned, it was dark. Anjana had been much too busy to even bother about eating lunch. She had unpacked the two trunks she had brought with her. Swept and mopped the house till she was satisfied. Stacked the groceries in the kitchen shelves. Examined the backyard and even exchanged a word with her next door neighbour.

Anjana cleared her throat and pulled the other chair closer to him. He looked up at her. She waited for him to say something: You look pretty; you smell nice. But he merely went back to flicking through the pages of the magazine.

'I had a bath,' she said hoping he would take the cue and start a conversation. He is shy, she decided, when he continued to sit there in silence.

'The coconut palms seem like the quick-yielding hybrid variety. If we water them well and feed them with this special fertilizer, I'm sure in a year's time we'll have plenty of coconuts,' she said, unable to bear the silence between them.

'We won't be here next year,' he said, tossing the magazine to the floor.

Anjana stared at him, puzzled. What did he mean by that? She would find out later. He seemed irritable. Probably he didn't have much of a lunch. 'Shall we eat?' She asked, wondering if it was an empty stomach that was making him testy.

When she had covered the surface of the table with food she had slaved over all evening—steaming puttu, fragrant ishtoo, deep-fried chicken, she called out to him. A look of distaste crossed his face when he saw the spread before him. 'Is this what you have cooked for dinner? I prefer rice for the evening meal,' he said piling his plate with pieces of puttu and drowning it in the thick white coconut milk of the ishtoo.

'What is this?' he demanded, picking out a piece of okra from the gravy. Anjana felt the smile freeze on her face. 'It gives it a special flavor. That's how they make ishtoo here in Kozhikode,' she tried to explain.

'I don't like it. It's slimy. It's slippery. If you ask me, it's quite disgusting,' he said meticulously heaping the okra pieces, ginger strips, slit green chillies, and curry leaves on the side of the plate. 'Why did you have to go and do something like this? It's killed the taste of an otherwise delicious curry.'

Anjana felt her eyes fill. She bent her head and began pushing the food around on her plate. She wished there was some way she could discover his likes and dislikes. All she wanted to do was please him.

When she had cleaned the kitchen and showered and changed into a frilly white nightie, Anjana crept into bed to lie beside the man who was little more than a stranger to her. She glanced at his profile, the closed eyes and slack lips, and felt gratitude flood through her. He had married her. He was her husband. It was up to her to see to it that he was happy, always.

She moved closer to him. He lay there unmoved by her presence. Was he asleep or only pretending to be? She waited for him to touch her, caress her. When he didn't, she snuggled even closer. Other newlywed couples, she had observed, tried to prolong the intimacy of the nuptial bed even when out of it. With covert glances, furtive touches, stealthy brushing against each other's bodies. Eight days of marriage, and she was still a virgin. Night after night she had gone to bed expecting him to remedy the situation. Dawn after dawn, she woke up with her hymen intact and self-esteem in shreds. Does he find me unattractive? she worried. But why would he have married me then? she rationalized.

In the middle of the night she woke up to feel him push the nightdress above her thighs. He stuck his tongue into her mouth, squeezed her breasts, and shoved his knees between her legs. When he thrust into her, the rudeness of his pumping hips made her gasp in shock, in pain, in anguish.

Wide eyed, she watched this man, her husband, grunt and moan as his hips ground into her. Glassy eyed, she watched his face clench in concentration as he sought release. Wet eyed, his wetness flooding through her at last, she saw him collapse on her even as she lay there bruised in spirit and body, unsatiated, and feeling strangely empty. Was this the ecstasy poets and romantic novels promised?

Three months later he was still a stranger to her. A man she cooked and kept house for. A man who used her body when the impulse took him. There was little conversation between them and hardly any companionship. When she tried to talk to him about his job, he dismissed her queries with a careless wave and said, 'You won't understand what I'm talking about.'

After several rebuffs, she gave up asking. When she tried to discuss the neighbourhood happenings, he looked bored. 'Isn't there anything else you have to talk about?' he asked, not bothering to stifle his yawns. She said she would like to go the beach. He said it was too crowded. She wanted to go shopping. 'What for?' he demanded. 'Don't I buy everything you need for the home and you?'

'I just want to see the shops,' she said.

'I'm much too busy today,' he said.

He took her to the movies, though. He liked the dark cool interiors and the larger-than-life panorama unfolding in front of them. Quick money schemes worked. Buxom heroines swooned and fell in love with the nearly always impoverished hero. The good men thrashed the bad ones. There was about the celluloid life a predictable pattern that he thought evaded him in real life.

Four months after the wedding, Anjana's mother slipped and fell in the bathroom and broke her hip. Anjana rushed to her parents' home to nurse her mother. Even as she packed her bag, she felt relief course through her. She would be petted, loved, cosseted once again.

Ravindran accompanied her to her parents' home. Two days later, when he had made suitable clucking sounds of sympathy and bought his mother-in-law a mandatory bottle of Horlick's, a packet of arrowroot biscuits and a dozen oranges as a token of his concern, he left by the early morning bus to Kozhikode. The night before, as he smoked his post-dinner cigarette, he had told Anjana, 'I'm giving up the house. I think it would be best if you stayed on here. I'm planning to quit my job and start a business of my own.'

Anjana gaped. She dropped the shirt she was folding and went closer to him. 'What do you plan to do?'

'I'm going to start an agarbathi factory. Making incense sticks doesn't need much investment. Wages are low, raw materials are cheap, and margins are high. And I have some very good contacts in the distribution channels.' It was the longest speech he had ever made to her.

Anjana touched his arm. 'Are you sure it will work?' she asked anxiously.

For the first time, he put his arm around her and said, 'I know what I'm doing. Trust me. I've even decided on the name: Anjana Agarbathi.'

'What?' she asked, unable to believe her ears.

'Yes. Anjana Agarbathi. The fragrance of love. The fragrance of joy. What do you think?'

Anjana nuzzled her cheek into his shoulder. Anjana Agarbathi. She felt all her uncertainties dissolve. He did care for her. 'When will you return?' she asked.

'As soon as I can. In about ten days' time,' he said, running his hand idly through the fleece on his chest.

Anjana saw his eyes glaze over and knew that she had lost him again. She shook her head in amused resignation and went back to folding the dried clothes. That night when he began to squeeze her breasts, she felt a flame flicker in her loins. A sensation that made her want to arch her body, wrap her legs around his hips, and match the movement of his body with a rhythm of her own. That was the night Anjana felt truly married.

In the next two years he visited Anjana nineteen times. He seldom stayed for more than four days; by the morning of the third day he would be restless to leave. At first Anjana complained. He ignored her. When she persisted, he was furious and snapped, 'Why don't you give me some peace? When I come here, I want to be greeted with a smile. Not with a glum face that looks like an entire colony of wasps have stung it.'

She tried to be patient. She tried to be understanding. After all, he still sought the comfort of her body. He even pressed some money into her palm before he left. That much she had to be grateful for. If only she could have a child, perhaps she wouldn't be so lonely.

One morning Ravindran drove up in a little van packed with boxes of incense sticks. Two headload labourers followed closely behind on foot. Anjana rushed to the veranda to find Ravindran arguing with them. 'You can't unload it yourself. We will do it for you, and you pay us the wages for it,' the younger man, in a red and silver INTUC badge, proclaimed with the unquestionable authority of a man who knows he has the backing of a strong trade union.

'I tell you, I don't need help to unload this van,' Ravindran protested.

'In that case you can ask the van to return with the load,' the labourer said, planting himself between Ravindran and the van.

Ravindran wiped his face in exasperation and tried again, 'Why do you need two people to do this little job?'

'How can you decide that?' the young man argued. The old man stood at his side unconcerned, turning the end of a match in his ear. 'I tell you,' the younger man added, 'I am incapable of doing this all by myself.'

Ravindran walked away in disgust shouting at the top of his voice, 'Why stop at two? Call that entire swarm of labourers hovering around the bus stop. Ruin me! Do what you want.'

'What is the matter?' Anjana asked, twisting the end of her sari nervously in her hands.

'It's problems like these that made my business fail. The union leaders are everywhere, demanding their rights. Do you know that there are thirteen thousand trade unions in the state of Kerala alone? And if you remind them about their duties, they start calling you names—"bourgeois vermin", "capitalist pig". Luckily I managed to get out of it before I was totally ruined. Never again will I burn my fingers trying to manufacture anything in this stupid state that breeds trade unions like it breeds mosquitoes,' Ravindran said, fanning himself briskly. 'Fetch me something cold to drink, will you?'

'What? How?' Anjana asked, with a sinking feeling in her stomach.

'I'm now going to represent a mattress company in Malabar,' he said with a weak smile, pretending not to see her consternation. 'The commission is excellent, and the market is just ready for a product like that. Meanwhile I brought back all the excess stock of incense sticks.'

From mattresses he switched to red oxide floor colourings. Then it was a special kind of industrial stapler, then an inverter. Over the years Ravindran's field of dreams was sown with several seeds. Each time a dream came to naught, he couldn't understand why he wasn't more successful. He possessed all the necessary attributes for success, he thought. A way with numbers. An ability to see beyond the needs of the time. Dynamic energy. He was a go-getter. But his wife would have said differently of him: Where is the memory for names and faces? Can you talk about anything at length, let alone start a conversation with a stranger? Can you see people as human beings and not as pawns to be moved around and used?

As the dreams failed to bring the promised riches and were abandoned one by one, his visits became less frequent, and the wad of notes became thinner. Only his appetite for hate seemed to grow.

One morning she walked into her mother's kitchen wearing a palm imprint on her cheek. Her father and mother exchanged looks.

'When I gave you my daughter's hand in marriage, it was with the hope that you would love her. Cherish and protect her for the rest of her life. If all you intend to do is hurt her, and make her unhappy, then there is no need for such a relationship. My daughter can manage very well without a husband like you. If you ever hurt my daughter again, I'll throw you out of this house. Do you understand?' her father told Ravindran.

Ravindran was never again violent, but he found a new vent to express his anger. Anjana, who had graduated from numbness to rapture now, discovered torment. He used her body with a brutality that scared her. Pushing, punching, pummeling. Some nights when he had finished with her, she wondered what heinous sin she was paying for.

Once again her head drooped, her mouth slackened, and her shoulders slumped. Her parents worried about her. What had their precious child done to deserve such unhappiness? Her father decided to buy her a teaching job. Discreet inquiries revealed that a place could be found for a lump sum of twenty-five thousand rupees. So he sold the land around the house and paid the amount. Anjana was encouraged to occupy herself once again.

When the schools reopened, Anjana had a new routine. There was no more of that endless waiting. Suddenly most of her time had a purpose, the hours of the day were accounted for. At the school, when other teachers asked her what her husband did, she smiled and said, 'He's a businessman.'

'Any children?' someone asked.

'Not yet,' she smiled. She wondered what they would say if she told them the truth. My husband is a failure who can't provide for me in any way. As for children, if you can conceive a child by swallowing sperm or feeling the flat of a man's palm against your buttocks or having pain inflicted on you in several different ways in the name of connubial rights, then I, like the *Mahabharata's* Gandhari, would have been the mother of a hundred sons by now.

A new contentment filled her life. She had a job she enjoyed, she had friends she could talk to, and she had an income that made her feel no longer like a destitute. In the evenings, when she came back from work, there were other things to look forward to. Books became her comrades and the transistor radio her baby. She carried it with her from room to room, holding it to her bosom or letting it hang from her hand as if it were a child learning to walk. It sat on the dining table when she ate a meal, waited outside on the doorstep when she had a bath, and at night it slept next to her so that it was the first thing she saw when she woke up in the morning.

She moved the dial searching for the sounds of life. Music. News reports. Radio features for farmers. Children's programs. Plays. Anjana listened to it all with the same appetite she devoted to the printed word. She read everything and anything. Wall paintings to toothpaste cartons to scraps of newspapers used to wrap a handful of green chillies. By losing herself in other people's lives, she tried to escape the grimness of her own reality.

The only reminder that she was married came in the evenings when, after his prayers, her father lit the incense sticks Ravindran had stacked up in one corner of the storeroom. Anjana Agarbathis, with a single glowing eye, burned steadfastly. The fragrance of joy, the fragrance of love, wafted around her in circles; wispy smoke disappearing into nothingness. Anjana Agarbathis. A dead marriage dwindling to ashes.

Her parents died. The seemingly endless supply of incense sticks was finally exhausted. The years went by, and one morning Anjana woke up and realized that in spite of being married, she could very well be termed a spinster. Unloved, unwanted, with sunken cheeks and vacant eyes. That was the day Anjana decided that she would dress the part as well.

She gave away her colourful saris and took to wearing starched cottons in shades as insipid and dull as her life. She locked up all her jewellery in a safe deposit box at the bank and swept all her fripperies away into the wastebasket. Only around her eyes, as if to echo the bleakness of her life, she drew heavy lines of kohl. Grey irises rimmed with black. The children at the school took to calling her 'cat eyes' behind her back. She wasn't hurt or even enraged. Instead she felt replete and safe. She hid behind a shield of drabness and plainness that no man would ever want to break through.

But there was one part of her body that she could never tame. Anjana's hair refused to accept that she had enveloped herself in the comfort of middle age. Fed on sorrow and pure coconut oil, it grew black and luxurious till it wandered beyond her hips. Anjana often thought of chopping it off to an innocuous waist length. How dare her hair behave with such wantonness? But when she took the scissors in her hands, she felt a strange reluctance. It was all that was left of the young, desirable woman she had once been.

Anjana twisted the head off a shrimp and snapped, 'Yes, that's all I have done.

'You know that if I eat late, I can't sleep too well,' Ravindran grumbled, scratching his back.

'You should have thought of that before you brought what seems to me all the shrimp in the shrimp farm you are director of now,' Anjana said, inflecting the word 'director' with special emphasis so that he knew exactly what she thought about his claims.

'I like shrimp. So I brought some. Why are you making such a fuss?' he growled.

'The next time you want to eat shrimp, get someone to clean it for you first,' Anjana said abandoning the shrimps and getting up. Was this her talking? This nagging, shrewish voice? Look at me, look at what you have turned me into! she wanted to scream.

'Sit there and finish it. I want my dinner in one hour's time, and I want the shrimps cooked in a coconut gravy with sliced aubergines in it. Do you understand?' Ravindran said in a quiet voice.

Anjana stared at his menacing expression and sank back onto the stone. She recognized that look. It meant pain, physical pain at its worst. In every which way his depraved mind would choose to inflict it. Now that there was no one to hear her cry out, he seemed to derive a greater pleasure from making her scream louder and louder. It was as if her tortured cries awakened some raging demon in him. A chill ran up her spine. What bravado had made her fight him? What recklessness drove her to oppose him?

The alarm trilled at half-past six. Wake-up time for single schoolmistresses. Adequate time to clean the house, cook breakfast, pack lunch, bathe and dress, and still reach school long before anyone else did. Anjana woke up with a start. Her mouth felt dry. She licked her lips and turned her head sideways. The bed was empty. When she had finally fallen asleep, he had been there lying on his back, smoking. Now all that remained of his presence was a slight dent in the pillow.

She straightened her nightdress and rose from the bed. She went to the kitchen and put a saucepan of water on. A faint odour of cooked shrimps hung in the kitchen. But for that and the rawness between her legs, it was as if he had never been there.

She poured the tea into a glass and took it to the veranda. The chairs stood there vacant and lifeless. He had already left.

On the days when he was pleased with himself, with her, with life, he waited for her to wake up. Sometimes he tugged at her hair playfully to wake her up. He would crack jokes, wander from room to room filling them with hollow words: fulsome praise for his latest business partners, the vast scope his newest venture promised, his hopes for it, for them. She would listen stony faced, without a flicker of emotion. She had heard it all several times before.

There were times when nothing was right. The radio was too loud. The curry was too salty. The neighbour's dog barked too loudly. She didn't offer him any support. Other wives sold their jewellery, land, and even the houses they lived in to aid their husband's business ventures. She was much too selfish and arrogant. He would sit morose and mute, finding fault with everything around, waiting for the time when she was his captive in bed. In the morning he would be gone, with no words spoken, no money left on top of the dressing table, and no indication of when he would deign to come visiting next.

Anjana sipped her tea. What did he want from her? If I knew what it was, I would give it to him. And then suddenly she wondered if she really would.

For there was Mukundan now. Quiet, gentle Mukundan, with his caring ways and love she could see he disguised as a deep affection, afraid to reveal anything more. Several times she had wanted to take his hands in hers and say, 'Tell me what you really feel about me.'

But how could she be the one to voice those forbidden thoughts? What if she was mistaken? What if all he felt was just plain concern for her and nothing else? What if he thought she was a brazen woman offering herself to every man? What if he left and never came back again? Under a slowly mounting heap of what-ifs, she buried her dreams and waited for some miracle to happen that would make him seek her out.

But this morning Anjana felt a strange restlessness. She straightened the cushions. She changed the sheets on the bed and washed the kitchen floor with warm soapy water into which she had emptied several capfuls of Dettol. She wanted to erase all traces of her husband. Banish him from her life once and for all.

When there was nothing left to do, the restlessness turned to emptiness. What is the point? she asked herself. I am still the woman I was. Unloved. Unwanted. And then she felt a great desire to be held. A chest she could lay her head upon and cry. A pair of arms that would wrap her around with caring. A voice that would whisper, 'Please don't cry.'

She let her mind dwell on that first time Mukundan and she had met. He had looked at her basket crammed with books and magazines and observed, 'I see you like reading.'

When she had nodded mutely, he began telling her about the library he had run. She remembered the note of solicitousness that had crept into his voice when he described how the books were covered with thick plastic sheets, indexed and arranged in glass-doored bookcases to protect them from silverfish, moths, and the sweat-stained fingers of the people who came directly to the library after playing badminton all evening. Her liking for him was based on that rare compulsion that made him want to protect his charges, even if they were only books.

She thought of the telephone in her neighbour's house. She bit her lip. She thought of the telephone again.

19

Serenading Anjana

Through the warp and weave of her silky plait, his fingers slithered; long, pale, and bony. Gently, so that not even one gleaming strand of that lustrous hair snagged at her scalp, he undid the plait. He'd dreamed of doing it the first time he had seen her. When she had turned to walk away from him, her hair had trailed down her back, seemingly endless. He had wanted to undo that plait since then.

Mukundan felt her hair ripple through his fingers in exultant joy, tumultuous freedom. When her plait lay unwound, skeins of silk washed by the dew, dried by the moon, he gathered a handful of it. And with reverence, with a thumping heart, he buried his face in it and breathed deep of its fragrance.

Always plaited, always restrained, brushing her thighs this way and that, her hair alone, he thought, had inflamed his numbed senses. Awakening his catatonic soul with a sweep of desire. To love. To live. To hold her in his arms.

She turned, still asleep, to lie on her back. He stretched on his side and propped himself up on his elbow. He ached to touch her face. To trace the curve of her eyebrows with the curve of his palm; brush her eyelids with his lips; cup her chin; dip his forefinger in the well above her upper lip . . . Like an uncertain moth his hand hovered over her face.

For a while now, he had wooed her with cunning and stealth. It had begun the day he had accompanied her from her uncle's house to her home. She had unlocked the gate and asked over her shoulder, 'Why don't you step in for a while?'

Mukundan stood by the autorickshaw, unable to make up his mind. Did she really mean it, or was she just mouthing a polite nicety? He cleared his throat and laughed, 'Not this time. Maybe next time.'

Now it was up to her to take the cue and respond.

She stopped playing with the keys in her hand and murmured, 'I hope you will. I reach home from school by four in the evening.'

Mukundan felt his heart do a little dance. 'I certainly will visit you,' he promised.

He began calling on her once a week. He knew how such comings and goings would be observed and speculated upon and so he decided the best course would be to not have a fixed pattern. One week, he went on a Monday at half-past four. The next week it was a Thursday at five. But each time he took care to not stay for more than an hour.

He didn't know where it sprang from—this deep well of tenderness. Of wanting to protect her, cherish her. Over several plates of golden yellow jackfruit chips, plump cupcakes, banana fritters, and cups of tea made the way he liked it—with no milk and only a squeeze of lime—their relationship acquired a new dimension.

One night as he and Bhasi sat under the cloudless moon, he knew he could no longer shy away from the truth. He had been in a state of denial all this while. He loved her, he knew. Mukundan loved Anjana.

All these years he had never been stirred by any great emotion. He had thought it was his nature to be phlegmatic. He took pride in his equanimity. Now he had found a woman who could awaken in him such an excess of sensations. Where did it all stem from? These strange and wondrous feelings that cascaded in his mind when he thought of her: I don't know what I want from her. A look. A word. A gesture. The warmth of her embrace. The feel of her skin. And if she were to respond, I don't think I would know what to do. I ask myself, would it be enough if I could just be with her? Share a silence. Walk through her dreams. Lead her through life.

'To love someone is to enter a solitary world. Bhasi, it is a lonely world that I am exiling myself into. Where I don't even have the solace of knowing what she sees when she looks at me,' Mukundan spoke aloud, giving vent to his tumultuous thoughts.

'You sound very poetic. What is the matter, Mukundan?' Bhasi's eyes narrowed.

'Anjana.'

'Well, what about her?'

Mukundan tried to describe to Bhasi his relationship with Anjana. 'It's like a long corridor,' he said suddenly, as if he had just divined it. 'A long endless corridor where we are walking hand in hand. But Bhasi, I'm getting tired of it. Not knowing what I will find at the end of it. Not knowing if the end is in sight at all. Tell me, Bhasi,' he blurted out, 'what do you think will happen?'

'What do you think should happen?' Bhasi asked armoured by the shadows.

'I don't know.' Mukundan shrugged. 'There are so many factors involved. Her age for one. She is twenty-two years younger than I am. And she is married. What can one do about that? I know she feels something for me. But what if it is only that she feels safe with me? I feel all churned up,' he said, gulping down a mouthful of rum.

'Are you taking the herbal compound I made for you? And what about the meditation? Or in the throes of all this excitement, are you neglecting it?' Bhasi asked sternly.

Mukundan peered into the corner where Bhasi was seated. He blinked. The shadows hid Bhasi in their arms. Night after night Bhasi sought the shadows. Night after night only his voice escaped the veil of darkness and spoke to Mukundan. A disembodied voice that was teacher and pupil, master and slave, companion and stranger all at once.

'Will you stop slinking in the shadows and sit where I can

see you?' Mukundan gestured towards the chair next to him.

Bhasi smiled. The shadows smothered his smile. He rose from the corner and shifted to the chair. 'That's better,' Mukundan growled.

'You didn't answer my questions.' Bhasi said.

'I do. I do take the herbal preparation,' Mukundan said running his fingers through his hair. 'But—'

'Mukundan,' Bhasi said, reverting to the role of teacher once again. 'Are you going to let all that hard work go to nothing? Ask yourself what you want from her. Then try and make it happen. What is the worst that can happen? She'll say no. So at least you will know that you have come to the end of your corridor and that it is a dead end.'

Mukundan sighed. 'You make it sound so simple. Let's not discuss it any further. Things will happen as they are ordained to,' he finished enigmatically.

Mukundan retreated to the solace of the tea-time rendezvous, where his secret longings found an unusual vent. The salt of the tapioca became the salt of her skin on his lips. When the cupcakes sprang under his fingers, he imagined it to be the smooth young flesh of her body. The honey of the banana fritters flooded his mouth with the taste of her saliva. And then like a strong dose of reality the tea would appear, scalding his mouth, scorching his fantasies, and leaving him with a sense of discontentment.

She never talked about her husband, and there were no signs of his presence in the house: slippers, razor in the bathroom, shirt hanging from a peg on the wall. Yet he existed in the prefix 'Mrs' that adorned her name. A phantom husband who flung handfuls of chalk dust and drew a line between them. So that every time the gate creaked open or a pair of footsteps bounced up the steps, they started. She with fear, he with guilt, in spite of the breadth of a table between them. Until this evening even when his feelings had hammered in his heart with an intensity that frightened him (was he going to have a heart attack just when everything was beginning to go right for him?), he had never transgressed that chalk line.

The telephone call came when he was still in a stupor from his afternoon nap. 'This is Anjana,' her voice had trembled. 'Could you please come to my home right away? I need to see you.'

He had replaced the receiver with a sense of deep stillness within. As if everything would come back to life only when he knew what she had to say.

The veranda was empty, and so was the big front room with its wooden sofas, straight-backed wooden chairs, a tallboy in the corner with a brass vase of artificial flowers, and the TV placed against a wall. 'Anjana,' he called, wondering where she was, the emptiness of the room spawning nameless fears.

'I am in here,' her voice, still wet with tears, crept in on stealthy feet.

She was huddled up on a bed in one of the inner rooms. He stood in the doorway, not knowing what to do. Should he go towards her or should he just stand there? When she saw him, his comforting bulk, the tears began to flow. Unable to bear seeing her weep, he rushed to her side and put his arms around her. 'Please don't cry,' he whispered as he patted her head. But she continued to weep wordlessly, flooding his shirtfront with hot tears, molten feelings. He held her to him in an embrace that he told himself was avuncular and nothing else. When her tears stopped, he made her sit down and brought her a glass of water to drink.

'Do you feel like talking now?' he asked gently, patting her arm reassuringly.

She smiled a weak, watery smile and whispered, 'He came back last evening. After more than eight months. This morning, he left without speaking a word to me.'

'And?'

Mukundan prodded, certain that there was more to this.

'Just because we are man and wife in the eyes of law, he thinks he can treat me as he pleases. As far as he is concerned, I am merely a servant who doubles as a whore. No, I'm wrong there,' she said, lowering her head. 'I think a prostitute has more rights than I have in this marriage. At least she gets paid for her services, and she can say no if she wants to. I have no such choice in the matter.'

Mukundan sat at her side, his palms clasped tightly in his lap, trying to stem the rage that rose in him. She began to cry again, and this time there was no awkwardness, no hesitation. He gathered her in his arms and began to rain little kisses on her face. 'He's not worth it. Listen to me, you are better off without him,' he whispered.

Her body went still. For a moment he wondered if he had gone too far. Then she laid her head on his chest. With one hand she began to unbutton his shirt. When the shirt was open, she wrapped her arms around him, nuzzling her face into the side of his neck. He clenched his teeth and tried to remain unmoved by the sensation of her skin against his. To give in now would be to profit from her vulnerability, to take advantage of her fragile self-esteem.

'Anjana, my dear,' he whispered, 'I think you should lie down. Rest for a while.'

When he rose from her bedside, she clung to him. 'Please don't leave me,' she whispered.

He lay there wishing he could slow his recalcitrant heart. The tears drained. The sobbing quieted. Her eyelids drooped. He lay there with her head on his chest as if it were all a dream. Into his mind sauntered a careless thought: When she woke up, would she still feel the same way?

Her eyelids opened. Mukundan felt the gentle sweep of her eyelashes on his chest. Her nostrils flared. Breath rustled her nerve ends. Her lips parted. She licked her lips.

Mukundan drew in his breath and held it.

Then he felt her touch the side of his face. Her tongue licked the salt of her tears away from his chest. Her hair coiled around him.

Mukundan looked down into her face. She was watching him intently. She met his gaze steadily. He exhaled.

Anjana raised her head from the warmth of his chest and cupped his face in her hands. 'Tell me, what do I mean to you?' she whispered.

Mukundan thought his heart would burst with its furious hammering. What was he to say to this woman he was completely and madly in love with? 'You know that I care about you very much,' he said brokenly.

'Is that all?' Her breath unfurled tiny buds on his earlobes.

'No, that's not all. I love you. I want to spend every moment of my life with you. But you are a married woman. And,' his voice lowered to a self-deprecating whisper, 'I'm so much older than you.'

'I have never ever felt like a married woman in all these years. I feel married when I am with you. In these past few weeks you have given me more affection, shown me more consideration, than my husband has in the last nine years of marriage. I'm going to speak to a lawyer and start divorce proceedings. I decided that early this morning, and that's why I asked you to come,' she said and suddenly, as if the thought had just burst in on her mind, she asked, horrified, 'Do you think I planned all this?'

'Don't be stupid,' he said, putting his arms around her. He smiled. I must be in a trance where there is no reality, he thought.

'I don't care about how old you are or what the world thinks. If you will have me, that is all the happiness I need,' she murmured into his chest.

'Anjana,' Mukundan said. 'You must listen to me. I know you think I am a good man. A gentle man. Someone you can depend on completely. I don't know if I am that man you make me out to be. My mother begged me to rescue her and take her away. But I didn't. I was afraid of my father, and so I made excuses. If I had done as she asked me, perhaps she might still be alive. That is the kind of man I am. A weak and undependable creature. Do you want to be part of such a man's life?'

'All of us have our weaknesses, but we seldom have the courage to accept them. Or even declare it as you have done now. To me, that makes you braver than anyone else. I love you. My love tells me that this is right; you are right for me.'

It felt so complete, so right, the spread of their flesh against each other. Her breasts flattened against his chest. His paunch pressing into the slight swell of her belly. Legs entwined. Her hair raining around them like a benediction.

As the crows returned home to their perch, filling the skies with a shower of hoarse croaks, in that betwixt hour, Mukundan realized that this was enough. He closed his eyes and trembled in anticipation of the promise she bore.

The taste of her touch as she explored his body with eyes, with hands, with skin. The sensations that coursed through him. The imprint of her soul on his body.

This was that moment of magical happiness. This was where all roads ended.

20

An Unsuitable Love

On the ledge that flanked one side of the kitchen were two copper cauldrons filled with water, and a coconut scraper that stood on its head in the manner of an amateur yogi, supported by the wall. On the wall opposite, sagging wooden planks pockmarked with time and grease held a wealth of once-consumed delicacies, an inventory of past habits. A tall Britannia Biscuit tin with a square top and a round lid you pried open with the end of a spoon, now filled with wheat flour, stood cheek by jowl with a palm-oil tin rustling with lentils. A squat Polson's butter tin nudged shoulders with a can of Farex. Peppercorns had replaced butter, and dried fish had deposed baby food. From the ceiling hung two giant pumpkins and several green and gold cucumbers. The floors were edged with vessels of stainless steel and bronze, and the walls were smudged with the memories of countless meals cooked. In that grim, soot-encrusted kitchen with neither running water nor much daylight, the only gay spot was the wood fire that crackled occasionally with flames of laughter, only to be beaten down by the overall gloom into a smouldering silence.

Meenakshi, girl cousin, childhood companion, and once best friend was perched on the ledge alongside the coconut scraper still in the throes of shirshasana. Her hands, clasped loosely, sat on her lap; prissy children not given to boisterous movements or high-spirited pranks. Her mouth, yet another prim child, waited for him to speak first.

Mukundan drummed his fingers on the tabletop. He

darted a quick look around the kitchen and smiled at the copper cauldrons. 'I was going past this way, and I thought I'd drop in for a little chat. It's been quite a while since we last met,' he said glossing over the embarrassment of their last meeting. For a long time afterwards Mukundan had dwelt on that incident with a sinking feeling in his stomach. How could he have been such a presumptuous idiot? He had avoided her, afraid of the scorn he would read in her eyes. But now he needed her.

As a man grows older, there comes a certain point when he begins to solicit the attention of others living around him. As a young man he may scoff at society and shun it. But with age he seeks out the world and invites it to step over his threshold into his home. For with age he remembers that he needs a show of strength for the two most important occasions left in his life: A child's wedding, and his own funeral. He wants attendance. He wants crowds. He wants it to be known that he was respected, admired, and liked. That his happiness is the world's happiness, his death is the world's sorrow. So he will revive old friendships, attend every betrothal, wedding, and house-warming he is invited to, call on the ill and rush to condole when he hears of a death. His single most important preoccupation becomes the wooing of the world he lives in.

Mukundan didn't have a daughter of a marriageable age, nor had he begun to think of his own death yet. But he did want the support of his relatives, the acceptance of the villagers, when he brought Anjana home. As soon as her divorce papers came through, he intended to marry her. But he didn't want to wait until then to start living with her. In four months' time when her school closed for the summer vacation, they would exchange garlands in a temple and be married in the eyes of God, if not the law. Later, there would be time for it to be legally registered.

When Anjana came to his home as a bride, he wanted her

to be welcomed by the women in his family. He wanted a lit lamp, burning camphor, and the red kurudi water made by dissolving turmeric and balls of lime in a brass plate containing water. He wanted the hustle and bustle of cooks and large cooking vessels in the backyard; the officiousness of well-meaning relatives and wailing babies. Mukundan wanted his bride and their union to be blessed and accepted. So he began his campaign to reinstate himself into the lives of the people he had earlier ignored or kept at a distance.

'I'm glad you decided to come by,' Meenakshi said. 'I'm leaving Kaikurussi.'

Mukundan's hands paused in their drumming. He stared at her, wondering if he had heard wrong.

'I'm finally leaving Kaikurussi, Mukundan,' she reiterated slowly the magic words that had eluded her tongue so long.

'But why? How?' he spluttered. On the wood fire, the aluminum kettle hissed. Meenakshi looked from the one to the other and decided to attend to the kettle first. Men come calling when they have ulterior motives. Water is propelled by the fluidity of its own nature. Men will remain as long as they stand to benefit. Water evaporates into nothingness. Men will wait. Water won't.

She placed in front of him a glass of tea that smelt faintly of wood smoke. Then she sat across him and said, 'Do you remember our mothers' cousin who lives in Shoranur?'

Mukundan nodded, vaguely recollecting a plump woman with a face forever spliced in laughter. 'What about her?' he asked.

'Have you ever met her sons? Quite a bunch of remarkable boys. But why do I call them boys? They are all strapping men now. Striding around as if they own the whole earth. In fact, as soon as their father died, the first thing they did was to change the name of Murugan Talkies to Murugan Picture Palace. Anyhow, they know everyone who is anyone in the district. A couple of months ago, I asked them to help me find a job. They promised they would. I didn't really think it would come to anything. But I was mistaken. I have been offered a place in Thrissur. As the matron of a hostel for working women.'

'But what about all this?' Mukundan swept his arm around in one broad, encompassing gesture to indicate the enormous old house and its inmates who had leeched on her forever.

'Haven't I given them the best years of my life?' she countered. 'There is nothing left of me to give any more.'

Mukundan peered into the glass of tea. The very idea of Meenakshi going away made him feel uncomfortable. It was like being told that the Pulmooth mountain was going to be levelled. Some things and some people suggest permanence.

'I'm tired, Mukundan,' she said quietly. 'If it wasn't this, I would have found something else. Perhaps an ashram that would have me.'

Mukundan looked up from his glass with clouded lenses. He wiped his glasses carefully. When he put them on, he thought he saw, for the first time, the fatigue in her eyes, the droop of her mouth.

'For so long now, I have been the one coping and managing. I have borrowed money from everyone I know and then borrowed some more to pay off my more pressing debts. The villagers treat me with the contempt they reserve for a hustler, and people cross the road or pretend not to see me when they spot me. I have neither friends nor well-wishers in this village. I am tired of being disliked.

'Let my son cope from now on. His wife can manage the house. As for my husband and mother, they can look after themselves. No one here is weak or helpless. If I don't leave now, I will never be able to.'

Mukundan watched Meenakshi's face for some show of emotion. Only her hands moved, loosening and clasping, loosening and clasping, as if to stem the eruption of anguish accumulated over a lifetime.

'And,' she added in a low voice thick with unshed tears, 'it is when I am around that the rhythm of their lives falters. I am a constant reminder of everything each one wishes to forget. Unhappy daughter. Abandoned wife. Wheeler-dealer mother.'

Mukundan felt the words jumble in his mouth. He had come to renew old friendships, strengthen old bonds. 'I don't know what to say,' he mumbled helplessly.

Meenakshi smiled at his confusion. 'There is nothing for you to say. In all these years, do you know what I envied about you the most? Your solitude. Your ability to exist without being enmeshed in other people's lives. That is what this respite is all about. One of these days I will have to return, but until then there will be this quiet content. No expectations. No heartbreaks. I will read. I will sew. I will watch some TV and I will sleep. I won't think of anything or anyone else—except myself.'

Mukundan licked his lips. He pushed his glasses up his nose and cleared his throat. The lump wedged there refused to move. 'When do you plan to leave?' he asked in a tight voice.

'Soon. By the end of this week.'

Mukundan ran his hand over his face, undecided on whether he should tell her about Anjana. Ever since he and Anjana had become lovers, he felt this compulsion to describe to everyone he knew the minutiae of their relationship. Most often his natural restraint prevailed. But Meenakshi was different. He decided that he should be the one to tell her about Anjana, and that she should know before anyone else did.

Meenakshi leaned towards him and took his empty glass. She put the used glasses in a gigantic aluminum basin that doubled as a kitchen sink. When it was full, she would take it outside and scour the vessels with ash and a handful of coconut fibre. In that thrifty household, nothing was wasted. Neither water nor ash nor time.

'Mukundan, what about you? Is this how you plan to live out the rest of your life? Like a snail, retreating into your shell the moment you sense something is expected of you,' she mocked half in jest, half in anger, for he had had the chance to have lived life differently and yet he hadn't.

'There have been some changes in my life as well,' he said with deliberate slowness and was rewarded by the glimmer of interest in her eyes. It was true, after all. Women were insatiably curious. He waited for her to question him. 'Tell me about it,' she urged.

He said in his most matter-of-fact voice, 'Some time ago, I met a lady at a friend's house. Her name is Anjana.'

When he had finished, she was quiet for a few minutes. Then she said, trying to soften the harshness of her words, 'Isn't she rather too young? Twenty-two years—Mukundan, she could be your daughter.'

'She doesn't mind the difference in age,' he shrugged defensively.

'That is now. But in about ten years' time, you will be nearly seventy—an old man. Whereas she will still be a woman in her prime. Have you thought of what that will be like? There is also the physical part of marriage.' The coyness of her tone underlined the unmistakable meaning of her words.

'Oh, be quiet, will you!' Mukundan burst out, flushing in embarrassment. Didn't she care that she could be overheard? 'I'm still healthy and fit. I don't see why I can't have a fulfilling married life. Besides, sex isn't the only thing in marriage, you know,' he whispered furiously.

'When you don't have enough of it, it becomes the most important part of a marriage,' Meenakshi said quietly.

'I can't believe this is you talking,' he said, shocked by the nakedness of her need. She drew circles on the table with her index finger and murmured, 'I have been there. You haven't. I know. You don't.'

Mukundan stood up, irked by her arrogance, by what he thought was her patronizing manner. 'I must be going,' he said. 'Come by and see me before you leave.'

'I don't know if I will be able to,' Meenakshi said. She scrutinized him as if to remind herself that she had once carried an image of him in her heart, woven dreams around him. 'Mukundan, I didn't mean to hurt you. Be happy.'

He didn't reply. At the doorway he hesitated. It seemed to him that they could no longer meet and part amicably. Remnants of their childhood squabbles were always bubbling to the surface. He turned to look at her, and proffered, as a peace offering, 'You be happy too.'

They smiled at each other as, together, they remembered a time once, long ago, when they had sought change in their lives atop a mountain with a peak as flat as a football field.

'Someday, I'm going that far,' she said and pointed to the horizon that shimmered in the heat.

'Me too,' he whispered back.

They sat in the shade of a cashew tree recovering their breath.

'Do you think that life will be different elsewhere?' Meenakshi voiced the doubt that had been niggling in his mind ever since he glimpsed heaven from the top of Pulmooth mountain.

'I don't know,' he said thoughtfully. 'But it must be infinitely preferable to this.'

'I guess we will never know until we leave and find out for ourselves.' Meenakshi stood up. It was time to go.

From the moment that Mukundan walked out of Meenakshi's kitchen, he was pursued by one ghoulish thought. The suitability of Anjana as his wife. He didn't mind that she had been married once. That she had slept in another man's arms or that she would bring into this marriage the dowry of her past as another man's wife. What concerned him was the difference in their age.

Twenty-two years. She had grown up knowing for certain there was no man on the moon. Unlike him, during her school years she had stood to attention when she heard the *Jana Gana Mana* and not *God Bless the King*. Her favourite movie heroes were men he couldn't understand or identify with. He would have to carry the burden of those twenty-two years alone. There would be no mating of memories, no joint reminiscences. Where he felt nostalgia, there would be a blankness on her part. How does one feel for what one hasn't experienced?

But it wasn't the past alone that gripped his mind in a query. There was the future too. The time when age would tyrannize him and make her its protégée. When his teeth would reside in a china cup and hers in her mouth. When his flesh would cease to obey the dictates of his mind. When his mind would seek the serenity of the earth and hers in turn would reach for the ecstasy of the stars. Times of impotence and incontinence, of twilight days and the silent ebbing away of life. And there she would be, twenty-two years younger and tied to a wreck of a man. Resenting his every breath. Hating even his shadow, for it meant that he was alive and she was trapped.

Mukundan climbed up into the attic. Since that time with Bhasi, he had never come up here again. Bhasi had said that once was enough. A man could be reborn just once. Otherwise the ritual had no meaning to it. But Mukundan felt he needed the solace of the womb jar one more time. So he crept into the earthen urn. *Anjana*, he whispered to the clay walls. What am I going to do about her?

From the cobwebs streaming from the rafters and the dust of the floorboards, from the long bars of sunshine and the cracked walls, from the pores of the clay skin and the ticking of his heart, answers marched forth:

Nothing in life comes free. Everything has a price tag, including love. Everything has to be paid for. In one form or another. In the end, even when she is yours and you rest alongside her, cocooned in happiness that here lies what is yours, there will be moments when you will know uncertainty. When it is not thanks for this blessing that will form on your lips but prayers to redeem you from your fears. But is that price too much to pay when you know that, as long as you live, you need never be alone again? She will be there to love, to laugh with, and to share the rest of your life with.

When Mukundan stepped out of the urn, his mind was made up. He wouldn't let anything deter him now. Anjana would be his wife, and he would do his best to make her happy. He would blot out the ugliness of her past and erase all the doubts that slithered into his mind. He would begin with placing an order for their marriage bed.

There were six beds in the house. Teak and rosewood beds, fourposters, intricate carvings, spindles, and brass jointings. Dust ribbed their edges and memories crouched in the wood—a stray snatch of happiness. Orphaned laughs. But mostly it was tears, fears, loneliness, and the stillness of death. Mukundan wanted none of it.

He and his bride would lie on a bed that had no memories save of the time that it was a tree. He would lie with her on it and kiss her breasts. She would arch her spine and caress his back. It would be the gasping of their breath and their groans of pleasure that would seep and gather in the grains of the wood. Perhaps in time the bed too would acquire eccentricities of its own, creaking a protest when they moved in a certain way. Perhaps in time it would begin to wear the patina of age that all things organic are destined to, but it would be seasoned with only their happiness.

Mukundan looked at his watch. It was half-past five. Bhasi ought to be home by now. In this new Kaikurussi that Mukundan barely recognized, every single person possessed the power of the written word, and rights were claimed vociferously. Artisans, labourers, and all daily wage earners had a routine like that of an office employee. Beginning work at nine in the morning and finishing at five in the evening, with two fifteen-minute tea breaks and a whole hour for lunch.

Mukundan met Bhasi outside his gate. 'I was just coming to see you,' Mukundan said, closing the gate behind him. 'I want you to come with me to the carpenter's house.' He waited for Bhasi to smirk and say something about ordering a strong nuptial bed.

Instead Bhasi ignored the grin on his face and put his hand on Mukundan's arm as if to restrain him and said, 'We need to talk.'

'We'll talk as we walk. I want to order the bed this evening itself. You know how these carpenters are. They'll promise to deliver on a certain day, and then when that day arrives, you'll discover that they haven't even bought the wood.' Mukundan guffawed, walking briskly down the dirt track.

The carpenter's house was near the old ruined temple at the foot of the Pulmooth mountain. Bhasi walked alongside, dragging his feet. Mukundan watched him from the corner of his eye. He was unusually withdrawn. He's probably quarrelled with his wife, he thought, dismissing Bhasi's sullenness.

'I've decided to tell my father about Anjana. There is no point in hiding it from him any more,' he said in a strident voice. Bhasi's silence goaded him to add, 'But first I thought I would order a bed. A new beginning deserves a new setting. She and I will bring into each other's lives only our love for each other. We won't let our pasts burden us.'

'Why can't you accept that you are free of yours?' Bhasi snapped from between clenched teeth. 'I thought you had come to terms with your mother's death. You have told me on several occasions that you feel absolved of the guilt of her death. So what is this all about? Are you trying to make up for what you didn't do for your mother by rescuing

Anjana from her sordid marriage?'

'What nonsense!' Mukundan exclaimed coldly. This was the second time in one day that his love and his dreams were being repudiated by people who claimed to have his best interest at heart. 'What do you want me to do? Sneak into her bed at dusk and sneak out at dawn? Damn it, I'm in love with her, and I want to be with her. Is there anything wrong with that?'

Bhasi rubbed his temples as if to calm himself. A pulse beat there. 'There is nothing wrong with it,' he said trying to keep his voice calm and unruffled. 'Tell me, why do you need her? Just in order to believe you are alive, you are free, and you are worthy of love?'

'I was wondering when you would start bringing up your textbook psychology,' Mukundan said knowingly.

'Please,' Bhasi put up his hand, not wanting to argue any more. 'Forget everything I have said so far. All I ask now is, what is the need for this hurry? You hardly know her,' he finished lamely.

'Ha! So that is it!' Mukundan tossed a malevolent laugh. 'You are the one always accusing me of rationalizing too much—of being dull and stolid. You keep advising me to follow my instincts. You keep telling me that I should learn to trust people. And now when I do, you question it.'

'I'm not questioning your ability to distinguish the good from the bad. All I said was, don't rush into anything,' Bhasi said, staring into the horizon. 'You must do what you think is right.'

'That I will,' Mukundan muttered in irritation. Sometimes Bhasi could be as condescending as his father. And just as bull-headed.

21

An Abacus of Words

In the twilight silence Achuthan Nair sat on a bench in the backyard, rubbing warm oil into the crêpelike folds of his skin. Under his palms, the skin rolled. Once it had been a glistening sheath that had clung to his muscles. Now its limpid looseness filled him with distress. He raised his forearm and clenched his fist. His biceps tautened. Achuthan Nair felt the hardened muscles and sighed in satisfaction. He might be old, but he wasn't decrepit. At least, not yet.

From behind a clump of bamboo, the devi bird called: poo-ah, poo-ah; let's go, let's go. Achuthan Nair bent down, gathered a fistful of pebbles, and hurled them in the direction of the bamboo. 'Get away varmint!' he screamed in rage. 'I'm not ready to go anywhere yet.'

'What's wrong with you? Why are you sitting out here in the cold instead of going in for your bath? Do you want to catch a chill? Perhaps you think doctors and medicines come free? Or is it that you think that your son will contribute to the expense of looking after you? No one will. No one ever has. I have to do everything by myself.'

Achuthan Nair stared at his daughter wordlessly. His and Ammini's daughter, Shanta. As a baby she had dribbled honey syllables. Her burps had been milky consonants and her yawns gilt-edged vowels. He had held her to him, sat her on his knee, and crooned to her so that the words flowed out of her mouth. Thick, golden, and sweet as the molasses from the palm tree. But it seemed to him that he no longer had the power to make her happy or ring her breath with sweetness. It was as if adulthood had injected into her words the venom of frustration. Everything she said was tinged with bitterness and anger. I gave her everything I could. Love, money. My time and attention. Why then is she so angry all the time? Achuthan Nair wondered unhappily.

In the dingy bathroom that clung to the back of the house like a burr on a dog's fur, Achuthan Nair dipped the plastic mug into a bronze cauldron of hot water and poured it over himself. He groped for the soap and thought longingly of Mukundan's bathroom. It had pale blue tiles on the wall, a niche for the soap dish, and hot water that ran from the tap. It also had an electric light so bright that you could see every hair in your moustache when you looked at yourself in the mirror that hung above the washbasin. He lathered himself with a tiny shard of Lux. He needed a new bar, but the thought of Shanta letting loose another stream of vitriol made him hesitate. He didn't deserve to live like this. Did she treat him so unfeelingly because she thought he was helpless? he mumbled to himself as he reached for the towel.

Achuthan Nair wrapped the towel around his hips and went back to his room. He pulled on fresh clothes. A fine white undershirt and a mundu, and on top of the undershirt a light flannel shirt. If Mukundan didn't buy me clothes, I'd probably be wearing rags, he told himself as he buttoned the shirt. 'Shanta,' he said hovering at the kitchen door. 'Where is my Rasnadhi powder?'

'It's finished. I used it after I washed my hair earlier today,' Shanta said, stirring something on the stove.

'Oh,' Achuthan Nair said and retreated to his room. She didn't like him in the kitchen or anywhere else in the house. He was expected to keep to his room. He felt the beginning of a sneeze stir at the back of his nose and water glugging in his eardrums. The Rasnadhi powder rubbed into his scalp would have helped to alleviate the malaise. A shiver swept through him. He got into his bed and pulled the blanket over his shoulders. Perhaps if he covered himself well, the cold that threatened would go away.

Achuthan Nair stirred the spoon around in the bowl of gruel. It tasted like warm ashes in his mouth. 'Why aren't you eating?' Shanta asked from across the table.

'I'm not hungry,' he murmured. 'I'd like a cup of Horlicks instead.'

'It's finished.'

'What do you mean, it's finished? Mukundan gave me the bottle just ten days ago, and I have only one cup every morning,' Achuthan Nair said impatiently, forgetting to hide his annoyance as he usually did when he spoke to her.

'You are such a selfish old man,' she snapped. 'There are other people in this house. My three children like Horlicks too, and when he comes back tired after a day's work, I give him a cup of Horlicks,' Shanta said with a tilt of her chin, indicating the empty chair where her husband liked to sit.

'But it was meant for me. How can you just finish it off like that?' he blurted out in anger.

'Ask him to buy you another bottle. He's a rich man, isn't he? One more bottle of Horlicks isn't going to turn him into a pauper.' Shanta tossed the words at him. 'Besides, who does he have to spend all his money on, anyway? If he had any decency he would be looking after you instead of plonking you here.'

'No one plonked me here. This is my house,' Achuthan Nair said quietly.

'No, it isn't your house. It never was. It was my mother's house, and after her death, I inherited it. And if you don't like the way I run my house, you are welcome to leave it any time you choose to.'

Achuthan Nair felt rage spiral within him. He thought he would like to curl his hands around her neck and throttle her till the ugly sounds that fell off her tongue like flaky soot would cease forever.

He curled up on the bed and pulled the blanket to his chin. He lay with his eyes closed, fingering the weave of the blanket Mukundan had given him some years ago. By the early hours of the day, his mind was made up.

Achuthan Nair planted his stick firmly into the ground and, holding on to it for support, stepped over the stile alone. 'What are you gaping at?' he growled at his little grandson. 'Give me my things.'

The little boy crept closer and whispered, 'Muthacha, I'll bring them across to you.'

'No,' the old man spat. 'I don't want any of you doing me any favours. I'm going to my son's house. My real son. Not a bastard like your mother is. You can tell your mother that. What will you tell your mother?' he asked, staring at the little boy.

'That she is a bastard and you are going to your real son's house.'

'Good. Now give me my things,' Achuthan Nair said.

An old leather valise. A blanket and a pillow. A triangular wooden box with brass edgings and a clasp. The walking stick. Mukundan surveyed his father's belongings with a sense of trepidation. What did this mean?

Achuthan Nair sat in the armchair, gaunt with exhaustion. 'Bring me that wooden box,' he said.

Mukundan took the wooden box to his father and placed it by his side on the ledge. Achuthan Nair put it on his lap and pressed a secret lever so that the lid sprang open. 'This is the jewellery I had made for your mother,' he said, letting his fingers glide over the gold ornaments that nestled on a piece of satin. 'After her death I kept them with me. It wasn't as if you were a girl to be given your mother's jewellery,' he added defensively.

He watched Mukundan's face as he spoke. 'These must be worth thousands and thousands of rupees now. Here, take them. I give you all of them. To sell or keep or do as you please, but—' he paused and a crafty gleam entered his eyes, '—there's one condition. You must look after me as long as I live, and when I die, arrange a really splendid funeral feast.'

Mukundan slumped against the wall, ignoring his father's outstretched hand.

'What must you do to earn all this jewellery?' the old man queried. Mukundan stared at a beam above his father's head. 'Father,' he said quietly. 'I'm your son. You don't have to bribe me to look after you. I don't need this or anything from you,' he said, pointing to the jewellery.

'Keep it,' Achuthan Nair urged, pressing the box into Mukundan's side. 'You might need it some day. I don't want to be a burden on anyone or to be treated like one. What is it that I don't want to be?' Authority rang once again in his words.

'A burden,' Mukundan murmured, taking the box of jewellery. What was he going to do about Anjana? This is my house. I can do as I choose to, he reasoned. It wasn't as if his father's moral standards were unimpeachable.

Krishnan Nair followed Mukundan into the house, barely able to restrain his excitement. Achuthan Nair had looked at his once-trusted lieutenant and asked, 'Do you have any objections to my coming to living here?'

Krishnan Nair had wrung the towel in his hands nervously. 'Achuman,' he said, reverting to the familiar form of address of the past, which he had not used since Achuthan Nair left to move across the road, 'how could you even think of asking something like that?'

'I have to. After all, you are the one running this house,' Achuthan Nair growled.

Mukundan waited for Krishnan Nair to catch up with him and asked, 'Which room do we put him in?'

'What a question to ask! His old one, of course,' Krishnan Nair said, walking towards the biggest room on the ground floor. Mukundan watched him fling the windows open. What if this had been my room? Would he have suggested that I give it up because my father has chosen to return?

Krishnan Nair wiped his hands on his towel and said brightly, 'I'm going to see if I can find a chicken for him. Achuman always said that I made the best chicken curry he's ever tasted, and we need to make him feel that he's truly welcome here. God knows what indignities he's had to suffer in that harridan's house.'

'I suppose I should be glad that he finally acknowledged me as his son.' The bitterness in Mukundan's voice stopped Krishnan Nair in midtrack.

'That's all in the past. Forget it. He has just a few years left. Make them happy for him.'

What about me? What about what he turned me into? The unscrupulous waste of my youth, of a lifetime? Mukundan wanted to scream. He took a deep breath and said, 'That I will. Go get the chicken. The sheep that strayed away has returned to the flock. We mustn't make him feel he isn't welcome here.' He couldn't help the sarcasm that crept into his tone.

Krishnan Nair appraised him thoughtfully and then walked away.

Chicken curry! Mukundan dragged a mattress and pillow into what had once been his parents' bedroom. Every time he'd asked Krishnan Nair to cook him his much-famed chicken curry, the old caretaker had had an excuse. No one was selling fowl these days. Not the free-range kind, anyway. Or the bird was too old. Or it was too scrawny. But for his father, Krishnan Nair would produce a miracle. A free-range fowl just the right size and age. He would wring its neck and pluck its feathers without complaining about having to pay for this villainous taking of life with an extra term in hell. He would chop it, wash the pieces, and drain and wrap them in a plantain leaf so that the meat wouldn't dry out.

He would take handfuls of coriander seeds and dried chilli pods and roast them well till they made him sneeze. Then he would pound them with a mortar and pestle. He would fry coconut slivers till the air was fragrant with browning coconut and grind it all with a few drops of water till the paste rolled off the stone. A reddish brown ball to dress the chicken in.

The old bronze urli would be dragged out and cleaned. It would be kept on the wood fire to warm its belly. A cupful of coconut oil. Shallots, ginger, and green chillies sliced fine would hiss and splutter in annoyance till the curry leaves joined them. Then ground paste, the chopped chicken, rock salt, coconut milk, and a cup of coconut water.

Krishnan Nair's chicken curry would bubble with the weight of emotions. He would stand there by the cauldron till he knew for certain that every drop of it tasted of joyous welcome. And Krishnan Nair would do all this for a man who had treated him little better than an imbecile or a slave all his life.

How does he do it? How does my father gather adulation and deference, respect and reverence, as if they were his due right? And I, who strive to be nice and kind, can never inspire such devotion.

Now that my father's here, perhaps Krishnan Nair will find the elusive woman to cook and clean, Mukundan told himself and began making the bed in readiness for his father's afternoon nap.

Achuthan Nair held the chicken bone in his hand and gnawed at it with his still-strong canines. He licked the gravy from his fingers and continued to worry the bone like a militant dog.

'Achuman, please eat a little more,' Krishnan Nair said, spooning another huge helping of curry onto Achuthan Nair's plate.

'Mmm, I think I will,' Achuthan Nair grunted, licking his lips. 'I have always said, and will continue to say, that

Krishnan Nair can be forgiven for any crime as long as he makes a curry like this one. The finest curry I have tasted. What is the finest I have tasted?'

'My chicken curry,' the old caretaker gushed. It was a treat to cook for a man who relished every morsel with such blatant delight.

Mukundan observed the little scene unable to decide if he was amused or disgusted. The master-and-slave routine would soon become tedious to watch. He toyed with the food on his plate, barely tasting it. He had to tell his father about Anjana. It couldn't be postponed any more. But how was he to begin? And what was it that he should say?

Father, the impossible has happened. I have finally found a woman, the woman I wish to spend the rest of my living moments with. Her eyes are the colour of October skies, and her skin is like tea into which four drops of milk have been added.

When I am with her, I feel complete. As though I have finally reached the destination I have been seeking all these years. A magical joy that makes my nerve ends vibrate with a resonance I have never known before. And so when I'm away from her, I feel a caving in of my strength, an unbearable loneliness, a cringing of hope. Father, Anjana is the woman who makes all this happen, and it is her I wish to bring into this house. And, oh yes, Father, she is thirty-seven years old and is married.'

The words played on Mukundan's vocal chords. A child with an abacus. Three yellow beads this way. Two green beads that way. Up and down. Left and right. In the end Mukundan said, in a voice cracked with the strain of trying to make a cohesive pattern of red, blue, yellow, and green beads, 'Father.'

'What?' Achuthan Nair raised hooded eyelids. He didn't approve of conversation while eating.

Mukundan felt his insides quell. He would tell his father about Anjana in a couple of days' time. When he'd settled he told himself. 'I'm going to Cherplasserry. Do you need anything?' he asked, swallowing the coloured beads and replacing them with the dull brown ones of filial duty.

'A bottle of Horlicks and a packet of Marie biscuits. And some Rasnadhi powder to rub into my scalp after my bath,' Achuthan Nair enumerated his list between sucking on a bone.

At the gate he bumped into Bhasi. 'I was coming in to see you,' the painter said. 'I heard your father has returned to your home.'

'You heard right,' Mukundan sighed, marvelling at the speed of the village grapevine.

'So shall I come by later in the evening?' Bhasi said. 'I have to tell you what happened at Shankar's Tea Club this morning.'

'Actually I was just going to come over to your house to tell you not to. I know my father doesn't approve of anyone drinking, and I don't want to upset him,' Mukundan said, trying not to be annoyed by the manner in which Bhasi's face fell. 'It's just for a few days, until he and I can establish our individual routines,' Mukundan added. 'Then we can get together as usual.'

Anjana watched Mukundan surreptitiously. Something was the matter. He had been preoccupied all evening, and now he sat in the living room smoking. Even when they had made love, he had done so with no particular joy. What was wrong, she wondered?

She poured tea into two dainty white cups, placed them on their matching saucers, and took them to him on a pretty tray. 'What is wrong?' she asked, going to sit by his side on the sofa.

Mukundan looked at her blankly for a moment. Then he stubbed the cigarette in an ashtray. 'My father has come back to live in my house,' he said. 'That ruins all our plans.'

'Why do you say that?' she asked, placing his cup of tea before him.

'When he lived across the road, it didn't matter to me what he thought of you and I living together before we were married. Legally, that is. I still don't care, but with him in the house, it might get a wee bit difficult for you when you move in there,' Mukundan tried to explain.

'Oh, come, come,' Anjana said, brushing his fears away. 'What can he do? He is not going to gobble me up.'

'If that were all I was scared of, we could have handled it by putting a muzzle around his mouth,' Mukundan tried to joke.

'Is he really such a monster?' Anjana smiled, thinking that Mukundan was merely exaggerating.

'That he is. With clipped claws and blunt fangs, but a monster nevertheless! Would you mind very much if I waited for a while before I broke the news to him?' Mukundan added as an afterthought.

'Is that what you were worried about? That I was going to be upset?' Anjana laughed. 'Oh, you dear man! You were the one in such a hurry. You said the people around here were already looking at you suspiciously.'

Mukundan smiled in relief. 'You are truly not upset, are you? I don't want you pretending just to make me feel all right,' he said a trifle anxiously.

'No, I'm not upset at all,' she said, taking his hand in hers.

'I was worried you would think that when it came to the crunch, I proved to be a coward,' Mukundan said.

'Do you still dream about your mother?' Anjana asked suddenly.

'No, I don't any more. Bhasi and you have cured me of all that. I have buried my mother where she belongs. In the past. Bhasi said that all this while, I was paralysed by a fear of intimacy—' Mukundan broke off, and as if he had said too much, he began sipping his tea.

She watched him for a moment. Even though there was

nothing they didn't know about each other, any display of emotion still made him shy. 'I'm glad that you have come to terms with your mother's death,' she said. Their relationship was in any case fraught with many impediments: the age difference between the two of them, her husband, his father—the last thing they needed was his mother's ghost.

A little later, as he rose to leave, he held her to his chest and murmured into her hair, 'I wish I didn't have to go. I wish I could spend the night with you.'

Anjana embraced him, murmuring, 'It won't be long now. My lawyer said he has already filed the divorce papers.'

'That's a relief.' He smiled into her eyes. 'I'll give my father a few days to settle in, and then I will tell him all about you—and us.'

22

The Taunt of the Banana Stalk

Even now, ten years after the lottery ticket had changed his life, Power House Ramakrishnan often woke up drenched in sweat, a hollow fear hammering in his gut.

Despite the rubberized coir mattress he slept on and his renovated house. Despite the 2 HP motor that sucked up water from the intestines of the earth and filled the huge plastic drums in the newly built, tiled bathroom. Despite the black Ambassador Nova parked in front of the porch for everyone to see, and the acres of fields he had accumulated like an avaricious bee gathering honey. Despite all this Power House Ramakrishnan still felt the sting of poverty and hopelessness in his dreams.

It was always the same disjointed dream. Of the time he had run a petty shop between Lenin's Gate and Karthiayini's Gate. It began the same way, everytime. With him putting his hand into one of the several glass jars that crowded the front counter of the shop and coming up with nothing but crumbs of coconut barfi. Mortified, he thrust his hand into another jar and came up clenching a fistful of air. Each one of the jars in which he stocked his wares stood glassy flanked and hollow bellied. The sacks flopped; the cans held nothing but echoes. The shelves stood empty, and the only sounds were the petrified beating of his own heart and the dismal clanging of a lone coin in the biscuit tin in which he kept his money. When he looked up, even the banana stalk that hung from a hook in the rafter was shorn of all its fruit, swinging in the air like an inverted question mark. What will you eat tonight? What will you do to buy fresh stock? Who is left for you to borrow from? What will you do? What will you do?

On the mornings Power House Ramakrishnan woke up with the chant of the banana stalk echoing in his ears, he was driven by the need to consolidate his fortunes. It had after all wafted into his lap on the back of a lottery ticket. How could one trust such wealth? Easy come, easy go.

Two million rupees and an air-conditioned Maruti car wouldn't last forever. He had sold the dainty, toylike car and in its place bought a reassuringly solid Ambassador. He seldom used it himself, but hired it out as a taxicab. As the black car jumped and leaped over potholes and wove its way through the many roads of the district, everyone could see for himself or herself the legend 'Power House' inscribed on the rear window.

Power House Ramakrishnan didn't believe in banks. In locking his money up where not even burglars could lay their hands upon it. For him the single most joy came from touching his wealth every so often.

He slid his hands along the walls of his house and felt the solidity of his wealth in its brick and mortar. When the handle of the passenger door of the car gave him an electric shock, instead of sending it to the garage, he revelled in the feeling it aroused. He bought land and planted teak saplings himself. He bought a small but yielding rubber plantation and insisted on helping the labourers when they put the rubber sheets out to dry.

His favourite food was biryani. Hours after eating it, he could still feel it hanging in his belly. The fragrance of the rice clung to his fingertips and the fat coated his palate. And then, there was his mistress.

Power House Ramakrishnan had much affection for his faded, lumpy wife. But Saroja, his mistress, bloomed with a youthful vigour that he hungered to touch. She lived in a little town across the river from Shoranur, on the way to Thrissur. Power House Ramakrishnan visited her in the afternoons twice a week, and most of the time all he did was touch her. He coiled his legs around hers and lay there on the bed caressing her nose, her eyebrows, her lips, her plump breasts, her rotund belly, her rounded hips, as if to etch in his mind the fact that his fortunes would never forsake him.

Power House Ramakrishnan woke up that morning with the familiar dirge of the banana stalk in his head. He groped at the edge of the bed, pushing aside the sheet. When his fingers stretched to span the eight-inch thickness of the mattress, he felt reassured that it was all there. None of it was a dream.

He mopped his brow, drank a glass of water, and increased the speed of the ceiling fan. Power House Ramakrishnan lay there thinking, and then he hit upon the idea of building an edifice that would be a testimony to his wealth. A monument that would be part of the village topography and, in time, become a part of village lore. Power House Ramakrishnan decided to build a village community hall.

Later at breakfast as he ate his broken-wheat upma—for with wealth had come a whole host of illnesses: high blood pressure, diabetes and gout—he aired his plan to his son, Venu.

'Right now, when there is a wedding in the village, what do people do?' he asked Venu artlessly.

Venu shot him a what-on-earth-is-wrong-with-you look. 'They go to the temple at Guruvayur or Pattambi or Cherplasserry,' he said, wondering if he should ask his wife for some more iddlis. The old man, he decided, was going senile.

'Well, they soon won't have to,' Power House Ramakrishnan announced, triumphantly thumping the table for effect.

Venu looked up quizzically from the little puddle of chutney he had dipped his fingers in and was licking at while he waited for the iddlis to arrive.

'I'm going to build a Community Hall,' Power House Ramakrishnan explained. 'A place where marriages can be held, political meetings can be conducted. . . . Why, I might even hire it out to a ballet troupe if they desire to perform in this village.'

Venu licked a drop of chutney off his forefinger. 'You won't make any money on it. The Hindus won't hold their weddings where the Muslims do. As for political meetings, they'll want the place for free. Oh, and the ballet troupe! What ballet troupe would come to this village?' he smirked.

Last month, when he had asked his father for some money to take his wife to Thekkadi for a holiday, the old man had flung his hands up and said, 'Two thousand rupees! Do you think money grows on trees? Just because it floated down into our laps, there is no need for us to spend it so carelessly.'

Venu spooned some more chutney onto his plate and added with a sly grin, 'You'll probably get a record-dance artist during the pooram time. You can be sure all the men in the village will be there to see her throw her clothes off in tune to some loud disco music.'

Power House Ramakrishnan sipped at his sugarless tea, and maintained a stony silence. Venu's wife, Valsala, watching from the kitchen doorway, bit her lip. What was he going to say next? Sometimes she wished she could sew her husband's lips. Power House Ramakrishnan rose from the chair and, on his way to wash his hands, he said aloud to Valsala, 'Are you sure all that coconut that he eats is good for him? If his mouth doesn't get him killed one day, the cholesterol from the coconut will finish him off.'

The truth was, though he had pretended to be furious about his son's rebuttal of his idea, Power House Ramakrishnan felt quite cheered by his objections. By now he had learned how to deal with his son's opinions and did precisely the opposite of what he advised. It had begun with the name Power House itself.

At first, after the lottery results were announced, Ramakrishnan had been in a dream-like trance. He had wanted to renovate the house and name it Dream Land. Then his son, Venu, who worked as a mechanic and objected to everything his father said as a matter of principle and means of asserting his adulthood said, 'That sounds like we intend to sleepwalk through life. We need something that is much more forceful. When you become one of the village dignitaries, our house ought to represent power. Besides, the fruit-juice stall opposite Murugan Picture Palace in Shoranur is called Dream Land.'

And so Ramakrishnan decided on the name Power House. When the new telephone directory for the district was released, he was thrilled to see his name listed as Power House Ramakrishnan. It has a certain ring to it, he thought with pride. He underlined his name in red pencil and left the directory open at that page so that anyone who came in to use the telephone would see it.

That everyone wasn't so impressed by the name came to his attention the night the power went off and the phone rang. A giggly voice on the phone asked, 'What time will the power be back?'

'This is not the electricity office,' he snapped.

'Isn't this the powerhouse?' the voice giggled some more.

'Yes,' he said.

'Then don't you have anything to do with power?'

'Not the kind of power you are referring to,' Power House Ramakrishnan said sharply.

'Oh, maybe then you should call yourself "Powerless House". Hee-hee-hee.' The line went dead. Thereafter each time the power went off, all kinds of crank calls came in. Power House Ramakrishnan often wished he had stuck to the name Dream Land.

Since then, each time he had taken his son's advice, he had regretted it. Now he merely used it to test the veracity of his own instinct. Power House Ramakrishnan knew a community hall in the village would be a success. Apart from the rentals, his reputation as a philanthropist would be established. Most important of all, it would be a constant reminder to his stubborn unconscious that failed to recognize him as Power House Ramakrishnan and still thought of him as poverty-stricken, petty-shop Ramakrishnan.

He sank into the easy-chair in the drawing room, as he called the front room of his house, and began to build in his mind the mighty portals of Power House Ramakrishnan Community Hall. However, when he had painted the walls a creamy white with a chocolate brown trim, he realized he ought to start with the actual location of the community hall.

Where should he build it? Not in the city, with the tea shop, rice mill, tailor shop, and other small shops huddled together, he decided. But it had to be close to the bus stop and must be located on the main road itself. Power House Ramakrishnan unfurled his umbrella and set out to find a suitable place to build his dreams. As he walked towards the city, he realized with a little stab of disappointment that there wasn't any appropriate place. At Shankar's Tea Club, he accepted a glass of tea and stood outside sipping it.

There had been a time when Shankar's father had run the tea shop at Kaikurussi while he himself had worked in a restaurant in Pattambi. In those days Power House Ramakrishnan had often sat at the tea shop stretching a glass of tea and a beedi for hours at a time. Waiting for a moment when he could plead with Shankar's father for yet another loan.

For a while after Power House Ramakrishnan came into his wealth, he had avoided the tea shop. But when Shankar's father died a year later, and Shankar took over its running, things changed. He no longer felt embarrassed to stop by. The old man had taken with him to his grave the memory of a grovelling Ramakrishnan.

But he still wasn't very comfortable sitting in the tea shop. For one thing, it brought back memories of his past. Second, it didn't befit his current status in life. And finally, if he stayed there for too long, someone would touch him for a loan, promising to return it in a week's time. Power House Ramakrishnan knew, just as the borrower did, that most of these loans would never be returned. The trick was to quickly finish whatever he had set out to do and then go his way. Power House Ramakrishnan placed the half-full glass of tea back on the counter and began to walk down the dirt road that would soon be a real one.

He stood at the end of Mukundan's compound and looked at it speculatively. It was by the fields, which meant the water table would be high. The existing trees would have to be cut down. But after the building was complete, he would plant a row of teak on one side and quick-yielding coconut palms on the other. Five thousand square feet was all he needed. There was land here. Plenty of it, and more than one man (a bachelor at that) needed.

Mukundan stole a glance at the clock. It was five past seven. He wished Power House Ramakrishnan would leave. Mukundan liked the comfort of his daily routine. It upset him when he had to deviate from it, and Power House Ramakrishnan was instrumental in making him do just that. What on earth did he want anyway? This was no social call.

The upstart had sauntered in a few minutes earlier with a beaming smile and outstretched hands. 'I've been wanting to come and meet you these past few months. But I've been tied up with work at the estate,' he gushed.

Mukundan shook hands cordially and wondered if it was solid gold fillings that glinted so brightly in Power House Ramakrishnan's mouth. He watched him look around the room, quickly assessing the value of things there as if to reassure himself that he still was the richest man in the village. You are the millionaire two times over. I am just a retired government servant with a pension and a gargantuan house, Mukundan was tempted to say. Power House Ramakrishnan began talking about labour problems and corruption and various things that Mukundan sensed were just a prologue to the reason why he was there. Why doesn't he just say it and leave? Mukundan thought, irritated with the other man's assumption that he had nothing better to do but listen to him ramble on.

But when he had walked in, Mukundan had not been alone. Achuthan Nair and Krishnan Nair were there, eyeing him suspiciously. He knew that the old caretaker had still not forgiven him for buying the paddy fields from Mukundan. Besides, Achuthan Nair had the power to reduce him to a cowering creature, and with him in the room there was no way Power House Ramakrishnan dared broach the subject of the land he had identified as the ideal place to build the community hall.

'Maybe we could move out into the veranda,' Power House Ramakrishnan said, sidling up to Mukundan. 'Our conversation will be a hindrance to them,' he said, indicating the TV set whose volume had been turned down.

'I was just going to suggest that,' Achuthan Nair said. Achuthan Nair, like Krishnan Nair, had discovered the world of television, and in the evenings they watched it together. Mukundan seldom joined them. While they sat glued to the TV screen, he went up to the terrace and sat there with Bhasi, chatting and drinking.

Power House Ramakrishnan sank into one of the plastic chairs placed on the veranda. He slowly steered the conversation to the problems of maintaining huge properties, but before he could bring up the community hall, Painter Bhasi walked in, with the casualness of a constant visitor. He decided to postpone what he had to say and was getting ready to leave, when Bhasi asked him, 'Will you be going to Thrissur any time in the next week?'

Power House Ramakrishnan felt the cold hand of fear grip him. The reputation he had built for himself in the village now rested in this mad man's hands. Why did I let myself be tempted, he groaned inwardly.

Power House Ramakrishnan was extremely careful to conceal his visits to his mistress's house. He gave her money to buy whatever she desired, but he never took her anywhere himself. Until the day she told him about the biryani in Hotel Aroma in Thrissur. 'Shall we go there for lunch today?' he had asked, unable to resist the thought of tasting such heavenly fare as she made it out to be. There he had been sitting, shovelling spoonfuls of biryani into his mouth while his left hand played with the gold bangles on her wrist: eating, talking, touching. Then he turned to his side, and at the farther end of the room he spotted Bhasi seated all by himself He hurried Saroja out of the restaurant, swearing to never again make the mistake of being seen in public with her. He waited anxiously for several weeks to see if Bhasi would say something. A couple of months later he dismissed the incident from his mind as a case of mistaken identity. How could One-screw-loose Bhasi afford to go to a place like that anyway?

But now, seated opposite the painter in Mukundan's house, he realized with dismay that slowly dissolved into dread that it *had* been the painter he had seen the other day. Or why else would he ask with a brazen gleam in his eye and what seemed a smirk, ' I thought if you are going, I could come with you. I wanted to buy some books. I could save myself a bus journey that way.'

Power House Ramakrishnan felt his mouth go dry. He sniffed. The double sniff that was more a twitch, which came on when he was nervous. He avoided Bhasi's eyes and mumbled, 'Not in the next week or two.'

Bhasi smiled, a tiny lifting of his lips that had little to do with mirth and had more to do with condescending superiority, Power House Ramakrishnan thought. He continued to sit there wishing he could leave. But he was reluctant to do so until he could get an inkling of what Bhasi intended to do. Power House Ramakrishnan sniffed once again, and suddenly his mind was made up.

He would have to effect Bhasi's removal from the village. If it meant a change of plan on where the community hall would stand, if it meant greasing of palms to rally support, if it meant moving earth and heaven—he would do anything to run Bhasi out of the village. After all, he was Power House Ramakrishnan.

He stood up and said, 'I must be going. We must meet once again when you are less occupied.' And not surrounded by eagle-eyed old men and jackal-faced riffraff, the pause implied.

'Yes, yes, we must,' Mukundan murmured in relief and ushered Power House Ramakrishnan to the door. When he had gone Mukundan said to Bhasi, 'I wonder what he came here for.'

'You can be sure he has something on his mind,' Bhasi said quietly. 'And I have a strange feeling it has something to do with me. Did you see how he reacted when I asked him if he was going to Thrissur next week? I haven't been to a bookstall for more than six months, and Thrissur has some very good ones. He was looking at me as if I had done him some grievous harm.'

'Now you are imagining things,' Mukundan laughed. All of a sudden he felt good about life. His father had been behaving rather well. Anjana had slaved over a delicious lunch for him and then had given him the run of her beautiful body. Now Power House Ramakrishnan had come seeking him. By tomorrow morning everyone in the village would know that even Power House Ramakrishnan held him in high esteem. Or, why would he have made the first move and called on Mukundan at his house?

'Come in, have a drink,' he offered.

'I think tonight I will,' Bhasi said, sitting down in his usual place.

Part IV

23

The Density of Power

For some days now, there has been a strange density in the air. A heaviness that weighs down words, leaving sentences unfinished and conversations riddled with pauses. Even the snickers that have always snapped at my heels through dark alleys and from around corners seem unusually subdued. A pack of dogs that no longer wish to worry carrion.

The denseness gathered around me has begun to prey on my dreams as well. The weight of hefty leather-bound tomes fills my palms even as I sleep. A tautness that inches its way up into my elbow as I struggle to hold the books aloft. A helplessness I try to resist as I fight the heaviness; to hold and hold and not let go.

Damayanti says that I always read deep dark meanings into perfectly ordinary situations. She laughs at times that I let my imagination run away with me. Sometimes she is not so kind. Then she uses that ugly word 'paranoia'. Usually I ignore her.

But once, I don't know why, the word rankled and I snapped, 'Do you know what paranoia means?'

She snorted in reply.

'Let me tell you what paranoia is. It is a condition of the mind characterized by delusions of persecution. It is often accompanied by hallucinations. Do I accuse you of poisoning my coffee? Do I stare at shadows and cry: Someone's holding a knife to my throat? Do I look at everyone suspiciously?' I asked her.

She stared at me with an aggrieved expression. 'Just forget that I mentioned it. I'm sorry,' she said, and walked away.

But this morning I knew for certain that there was something mysterious happening in Kaikurussi. At Shankar's Tea Club, where I am normally greeted with friendly jibing, a peculiar silence descended when I walked in. Eyes were averted, and no one joined me at my table. And then in Shankar's face, I saw the same withdrawal. A smattering of guilt at knowing something that I didn't. A wariness at how I would react when I found out.

What was it, I wondered, that had brought about this opaqueness, this wanting to disassociate?

I left my glass of tea unfinished and walked away pretending that I hadn't noticed anything disturbing in their behaviour toward me. What devious hands were working silent strings to spring the trap? What devilish breath had this power to turn friends of many years into disinterested strangers? I felt an overpowering presence loom over me. I was afraid.

I entered my home and crawled into bed. I lay there with my arms crossed behind my head. I could hear Damayanti talking to our son as she bathed him. I could hear him splashing water and squealing in delight when it slopped over the side of the red plastic tub. I went to the backyard and watched them for a while. Then I returned to the comfort of the bed.

I wished I could air my fears. Unravel its fabric thread by thread, so that when I got caught in its twisted darkness, I would be prepared. Once upon a time, I would have rushed to your side, Mukundan. I would have unburdened my fears to you. But a distance has sprung up between you and me.

You have discovered a landscape of your own. The songs of that land only your heart can hear, the water and fruit of that region only your soul can savour. The stars that shine above it are visible only to your eyes. It is a country that you allow me to glimpse with picture-postcard-like tiny but tantalizing word pictures. But when I question you about it, you clam up. As if talking about it would invite some disaster to swoop down upon that precious land of yours.

Mukundan, you are no longer who you were. It seems to me that a monarch, whose ascendancy over you is complete, governs you. Even your mind that I helped to free from the shackles of a lifetime of fear and guilt has switched its allegiance to its new master—your penis.

Night after night it is this erect stalwart who sits across from me, oblivious to everything happening around it but its own pleasure. Incapable of listening, unseeing, all it can do is spew out its own secretions. Rapturous outpourings of the hue of her skin, the texture of her voice, the miracle of her touch.

The penis has no heart, no mind, no sense of the world around it. All it has are nerve ends like a jellyfish. How does one befriend a jellyfish? How does one confide in it? One can watch it for hours at a time, mesmerized, and then one goes on with one's life.

How did she bewitch you so? What ruse did she employ to coil herself around your heart and enter into the veins that run the length of your body?

'You are still here!' Damayanti exclaimed, coming into the room with our son in her arms. There was concern in her voice, a tinge of fear too.

'What is the matter?' she said. She put the baby down on the bed and began to dust him with talc. The powder puff moved briskly between the folds on his neck, on his belly, around his groin. Then she turned him on his stomach and started on his back. I watched my son with his petal-soft baby skin transform into a sweet smelling, chalky organism. 'Why do you smother him with so much talcum?' I asked.

She pretended not to hear me and felt my brow. 'Are you unwell?'

'I'm all right,' I said. 'I just feel a little feverish. There is some kind of viral fever in the village.'

She dressed the baby, spread a mat on the floor, and left the baby on it with some toys. 'Keep an eye on him, will you?' she said and went out of the room.

'Drink this,' she said bringing me a glass of coffee. I could smell the aroma of dried ginger in it. I smiled at her.

'You probably caught a chill sitting out in the open last night. It is almost the end of November, and winter has set in, even if it is still warm during the day,' she said, sitting by my side on the bed.

'Probably,' I mumbled, sipping the coffee. In the winter months, nights are filled with the noiseless pattering of dewdrops. Dew rains down, washing the leaves of trees and bushes, soaking the grass, dampening the earth. In the morning a thin mist clings to the sides of houses and to the branches of trees as if all night millions of spiders have been at work, relentlessly spinning gossamer veils that only the fingers of the sun can lift and cast aside.

'Do you have to go there every night?' she asked, pointing to where Mukundan's house was, across the dirt road. 'We shouldn't be too friendly with people who are not our equals,' she said.

I looked at her curiously. She continued, choosing each word with care, spelling each thought with caution. 'As long as we have something to offer, they will never perceive any kind of difference. But the day they realize that we are of no more use to them they will begin to see us as inferior beings and will want to have nothing more to do with us. They treat us like curry leaves in a gravy—to be used and discarded. Ultimately we will be the ones to get hurt.' She turned her face away and added, 'You must do as you think right. I just said what I feel.'

So my Damayanti was jealous. My Damayanti resented the hold you have over me. My Damayanti would like me for herself. Suddenly I felt cheered.

In all the time that I have known her, she has always held herself aloof. As my wife, as the mother of my son, she has been an exemplary woman. But every time I have tried to reach within her, she has evaded me deftly. Several times I have wondered if I was married to the shell of a woman and the real living Damayanti resides in some other plane that I would never be able to access. She is so self-contained that it used to scare me. Not any more.

In some sense I know that you have outgrown me. I realize, Mukundan, that I have less and less to give you. Probably it is because of this that the tempo of our friendship has slowed down.

'What are you thinking about?' Damayanti asked me, worried by my silence. 'Nothing,' I smiled. 'Do you feel lonely when I go out every night?' I probed. 'A little,' she said quietly. Other women would have complained much earlier.

Not Damayanti, my paragon of restraint.

'I'm sorry,' I said and pulled her into my arms. I rubbed my cheek against hers. She looked at me with startled eyes. I'm not usually given to making gestures of affection. 'For some time now, I have been worried that you no longer care for me. That somebody else has taken my place in your heart,' she said.

It was my turn to be startled now. Have I, Mukundan, been so wrapped up in your life?

'As a painter you go in and out of several homes. You meet women there—fresh, blooming, and untouched. Whereas I was a widow when you married me.' A tear trickled down her cheek. I think I fell in love with her all over again. She would always need me. She would never outgrow me. I would always be the most important person in her life.

It was a little past five in the evening, and already the skies were tempered with grey. I decided to go into the backyard and take an inventory of the herbs and medicinal plants growing there. I have over the last several years tried to cultivate as many plants as possible. Some of them are weeds like the lajjalu (*mimosa pudica*) and pitabhring (*wedelia*) that thrive only when neglected. At first I tried cultivating them in pots, like I did the punarva and the shatavari, but they wouldn't grow. With a stubbornness I couldn't help but admire, they stayed alive until I reluctantly flung the half-dead plants away. Then with great enthusiasm they took root and began to breathe and grow with remarkable speed. So I leave most parts of my garden untended. If neglect is what will make them flourish, then so be it.

In fact, the kantakari (*solanus xanthocarpum*), for some peculiar reason, prefers to live in a ditch that borders one side of my compound. With its ovate leaves crusted with sharp yellow thorns on either side, and pretty yellow globular fruit with white and green longitudinal veins running all over it, the kantakari is an extraordinary hedge plant. Decorative to look at and armed with thorns that keep away cows and burglars.

But those are not the reasons why it is part of the flora of my garden. To me, it owns its place there because of its roots. The kantakari is a fertility inducer in women. It helps a woman's womb release an egg that would make the man's seed seek its embrace. And let the resultant effect of that union take root in the woman.

Every time I have felt restless, my plants have offered me solace. Not tonight.

There is something afoot in Kaikurussi that I fear threatens the very fabric of my life here. And I know I cannot confront it alone.

Damayanti came up to me and whispered, 'There is someone here to see you.'

'Who is it?' I asked, not particularly wanting to see anyone just then.

'It's Power House Ramakrishnan,' she continued to whisper.

Power House Ramakrishnan had opened the gate and

stood leaning on his umbrella in the front garden under a tree. His car was parked outside by the gate. He was, I saw, eyeing my house and garden with a speculative gleam. When he saw me walk towards him, he called out, 'Why don't you get someone to pull out all these useless wild plants growing here and burn the whole lot?'

I didn't bother to reply. What did he want, I wondered. If there was a painting job to be done, his driver usually left word at Shankar's.

'How big is this compound?' he asked when I drew closer. I tried to read his expression. What was all this leading up to?

'Twenty-two cents,' I replied. 'Why do you want to know?' I asked after a moment's pause.

He ignored my question and began to prod the ground with his umbrella. 'Almost a quarter of an acre, I see. How much did you pay for it?'

I began to get angry. 'Why do you want to know?' I snapped back.

'Whatever you paid, I'll pay you double and throw in another lakh of rupees towards the house,' he said.

'I'm not looking for a buyer,' I said.

'I know you are not looking for a buyer. But I want this piece of land.'

'I am not selling.'

'Look here, Bhasi.' Power House Ramakrishnan was no longer pretending to be polite. His face wore a menacing expression. 'Don't try to pit your strength against mine. I normally get what I want. It would be in your best interest to sell me your land.'

'But why my land?' I didn't understand his sudden desire to own my home. Was there some secret treasure buried there? 'What is so special about it?'

'Because no other land is as suitable for me to build my community hall on,' Power House Ramakrishnan said, as if he were explaining a universal truth to an idiot.

'What community hall?' I began to babble stupidly.

'Soon Kaikurussi will have a community hall of its own. Power House Ramakrishnan Community Hall. Weddings. Political meetings. Cultural events. All of it will be held there,' he gloated. 'And to house the community hall, I need land that is on the main road, close to the bus stop, and yet not in the middle of the market. Your land is just perfect,' he finished triumphantly.

'Where can I go if I sell you this land? There isn't a square inch of land that can be bought anywhere in Kaikurussi. Besides, even if there were, I wouldn't be able to afford it. What with this new road coming up and these Gulf chaps willing to pay escalated amounts, land prices have shot up,' I tried to reason.

'Why do you have to live in Kaikurussi itself? It's not as if you were born here or your family lived here. Why not a few kilometres away? You'll probably get a bigger plot of land and house for the price I'm offering you,' Power House Ramakrishnan retorted.

'I'll have to think about it,' I said finally, wanting to get rid of him and his outrageous proposal.

He stared at me wordlessly for a long moment, and then he rubbed his chin thoughtfully and said, 'Don't take too long over it. Take my advice. Sell me the land. I have the support of all the VIPs in the village. The temple board. The masjid committee. The village officer. The political parties. The Young Men's Association for Culture. Everyone who is anyone in this village will back me. So if you don't sell me the land, I'll tell them why the community hall can't be built. I don't need to tell you what the consequences will be. All I will say is, there will be no more work for you in this village. Besides, I know that you still owe the Namboodiri at Plashi Mana some money for this land. I also know that you've been extending your loan for a long time now. All I have to do is put some pressure on him.'

Then I understood the strange density that had weighed

down the air around me. Each one of them at Shankar's Tea Club, my everyday cronies, had known about Power House Ramakrishnan's ploy to take control of my land and they had wilfully kept it from me. Even Shankar, whom I have always liked and trusted. In the final reckoning they were all natives of this village, bonded by birth and banded together. While I was the outsider. The one who could be dispensed with. But they were not going to get rid of me so easily. Kaikurussi might not want me. But I want my land, my house, the pattern of life I had wrought for myself here.

So, Mukundan, the time has come when I need you to give me the comfort of your strength. I need your support. You cannot fail me now when I need you most.

24

A Glimpse of Fragility

The cough seemed to come from under the eaves of his rib cage. A bellowing of air, a grinding of bones, a bruising of tissue filled the hollows of the house in spasmodic thrusts. Mukundan heard the cough as if in a dream. Far away on the outer fringes of his consciousness, the cough lurked. Knocking impatiently. Demanding attention. Calling for what—help, maybe?

Mukundan stirred uneasily in his bed. The cough plucked at his eyelids. A demanding child unable to accept that someone, anyone, could be oblivious to its presence.

He sat up still half-asleep and pawed the ground with his feet for his slippers. He groped for his glasses that, as always, seemed to have walked away by themselves to crouch under a pile of magazines on the bedside table. He put on the light and walked into the belly of the house, where his father slept and now coughed.

Achuthan Nair was sitting up in bed propped up by several pillows. When he saw Mukundan, he greeted him with a fresh spasm of coughing. Loud enough to display distress and violent enough to be accusatory—Where have you been all this time? Couldn't you hear me coughing away to death?

Mukundan stood helplessly by his father's side. He had to search for some recess of compassion in him that would tell him what to do. Krishnan Nair appeared at his elbow with a glass of warm water.

'Drink this, Achuman,' he said gently, putting his arm around Achuthan Nair and holding the glass to his lips.

The old man sipped at the water, letting the warmth soothe the turmoil that racked within. 'Do you have any Vicks? I could rub some of it on his chest and back,' Krishnan Nair murmured in a low voice to Mukundan, who remained motionless, unable to reconcile himself to the idea that his father, the all-powerful Achuthan Nair, could be ill.

When Mukundan brought the jar of Vicks Vaporub from his room, Krishnan Nair gestured for him to take his place. 'Here, you do it. Let me fill the thermos flask with hot water just in case he needs another drink.'

And so for the first time, Mukundan held his father in an embrace. Dipping his fingers into the blue plastic jar, Mukundan scooped out the balm, while with his other hand he supported his father. Cautiously, as if he were fastening a muzzle around a particularly vicious dog's mouth, Mukundan began to massage the balm onto his father's chest. Beneath his fingers, the skin felt old and fragile. Tired, loose muscles pouched. Mukundan felt a great wave of tenderness flood over him. His throat filled with a gigantic lump, and his eyes stung with the salt of dammed tears.

A strange image floated into Mukundan's mind. That of Karna, the valiant hero of the *Mahabharata*. He had sat thus, suffering excruciating pain in stoic silence as a vicious insect feasted on his blood. Only so that his teacher, the short-tempered Kshatriya annihilator Parasurama, could sleep undisturbed. Yet when Parasurama woke up and discovered the extent of his pupil's dedication to him, he chose to curse Karna. He remembered only how he had been deceived. For Karna had claimed to be a poor Brahmin boy. And no Brahmin, Parasurama ranted, could endure such pain.

My pain is no less, Karna, Mukundan said to himself. My father is as unappreciative of my devotion as Parasurama was of yours. They see only what they want to see. And when it doesn't match their expectations, they are as unforgiving in their disappointment as they are in their anger.

What is it that you expected of me, Father? What deeds of valour did you require me to perform? What lines of duty did you expect me to toe? What battles did you demand I fight? What hopes did you expect me to fulfill? What kind of man did you want me to be?

'Father,' he whispered, feeling the syllables as they formed on his tongue. If only you had let me know what I meant to you. If only you had recognized that in me you had a son. An extension of your hopes and dreams. If only you had loved me and found in me the comfort that you come seeking now, when there is little I can offer you.

Achuthan Nair slumped against his son's shoulder and went to sleep abruptly, like a baby. Mukundan let his father's weight rest against his neck. His father's breath blew on the skin of his throat. Mukundan looked down at his father's face and felt a certain heaviness descend on him: something akin to responsibility. He had never felt this way before. In fact, he had consciously evaded responsibility by choosing to be with people who could take care of themselves and who demanded nothing of him.

Krishnan Nair helped him settle his father into bed. 'I'll remain here with him,' Krishnan Nair said in hushed tones. Suddenly Achuthan Nair opened his eyes and sat up as if he had seen someone. 'Paru Kutty, Paru Kutty, where are you? Fetch me my watch and handkerchief. I'm going for a panchayat meeting.'

Mukundan and Krishnan Nair rushed to his side. They pushed him back onto the pillows, and Mukundan began gently stroking his father's brow. 'Go to sleep, go to sleep,' he crooned from memory of the many times his mother had calmed him when he'd woken up screaming from a nightmare. After so many years of unnatural silence, why was his father suddenly thinking of his mother?

Outside the room, Krishnan Nair passed a weary hand

over his grey stubble and said, 'He's not his usual self.'

'What do you mean?' Mukundan asked haltingly, with a sinking sense of dismay.

'The usual thing that comes with old age,' Krishnan Nair said slowly. 'His mind seems to be slipping. Yesterday he asked me if I had started plouging the western field. Then he demanded that I leave for the fields immediately and finish the job. When I told him that all the fields the family owned, including the western field, had been sold ten years ago, he looked at me as if I were the one losing my mind.'

'What do we do?' Mukundan asked, peering at his father, who lay against the pillows breathing heavily through his mouth.

'There is nothing one can do. Except perhaps make him as comfortable as we can,' Krishnan Nair muttered. 'It won't be very long now. Can't you see that his body too is giving up on him?'

Mukundan felt a chill enter his heart. A mounting dread that once again his carefully structured plans for his future were about to crumble. He wanted his father alive and well. And approving of his plans. He wanted his father's stamp of sanction so that everyone else in the village did the same. For what Achuthan Nair had permitted, no one had yet condemned.

Mukundan stood outside the gate waiting for Bhasi. The doctor had come by on his way back from the Primary Health Centre. He had examined Achuthan Nair and prescribed a course of antibiotics for his cough. When Mukundan explained to him about Achuthan Nair's incoherent words, the doctor shrugged and snorted, 'No one's found a cure for jealousy or baldness or old age yet. He's almost ninety years old. It's a perfectly natural thing for senility to set in. I'm surprised that it's taken so long.'

Mukundan stared at the young man with dislike and

wondered how it was that men such as this cold-blooded creature, who didn't have a shred of compassion in him, chose a profession that was built on the foundation of concern for fellow human beings. He suddenly remembered what Bhasi had told him about the doctor. On the second day of taking charge, he had made it known that he had little time to spend at the Primary Health Centre and preferred to see his patients in the privacy of his quarters. There, on the table alongside the BP apparatus, the thermometer in a bottle, the impressive array of half-filled medicine bottles and colourful pamphlets, a table clock and a pen stand—all pharmaceutical company giveaways—a pink plastic box rested. Between collecting the prescription and walking to the door, you were expected to drop fifteen rupees into it. House calls were double that fee, of course.

'I suppose he has to earn back the money his father must have invested to procure that medical seat. Donations, bribes, whatnot. A medical seat costs as much as two hundred thousand rupees these days. Perhaps when he has earned back all that money, he may consider doing the job he's been hired to do,' Bhasi said wryly, and then added with a smirk, 'but because he is not a hard-hearted man, his prescriptions can be filled at the Primary Health Centre pharmacy.'

In his mind Mukundan heard the click-click of knitting needles. Mrs Luthra and Mrs Arora in his office had been chronic knitters. Every free moment the steel of their knitting needles clicked and darted, turning yellow and brown wool into sweaters, red and black wool into mufflers, pinks and blues into baby booties and cardigans. They had made him a grey sleeveless pullover with a band of red diamonds running along the hem.

Mukundan looked at his father's wan face and thought of the women and their knitting needles.

Was the mind a piece of knitting held between two needles—age and thought? Did dropping a few stitches mean that there was no longer any hope for the mind and that it had to be abandoned? Is ultimate unravelling its only future course?

'But, Doctor,' he tried again, 'Isn't there some compound? Some medicine that'll knit his mind together?'

The doctor shook his head. 'I don't know of any. At least not in allopathic medicine.' Then he added with a malicious gleam in his eye, 'Perhaps you should ask that One-screw-loose Bhasi. He's a great one for alternative medicine, I hear. But you probably know all about it. I have heard you two are good friends.'

Mukundan ignored the doctor's caustic comment and paid him his fees. Perhaps, as the doctor had said, Bhasi would know what to do. Why hadn't he thought of speaking to him earlier?

'Why are you standing here in the dark?' Bhasi murmured later in the evening when he dropped in as usual and found Mukundan by the gate.

Mukundan ran his fingers through his hair and sighed. 'I wanted to speak to you before you came in.'

'What's the matter?' Bhasi asked quietly.

'It's my father. I didn't want him to overhear us. Let's go upstairs to the terrace. You go straight up, and I'll follow you in a few minutes,' Mukundan said in a low voice.

'Listen, if it is such a bother, I'll come by in the morning,' Bhasi said, feeling decidedly uncomfortable at the thought of having to sneak into the house like a thief. 'No, there's no problem. I'll explain it all. Go on to the staircase room while I talk to my father and Krishnan Nair,' Mukundan urged.

Achuthan Nair lay back in the armchair and watched television. Occasionally he coughed, but he looked more like himself again. 'How are you feeling now, Father?' Mukundan asked.

'Not too bad,' the old man grunted.

'That's good,' Mukundan said, and gestured to Krishnan Nair to follow him. 'I'm going upstairs for the usual. Don't let him know that I'm drinking,' he whispered. Krishnan Nair smiled. 'No, I won't.'

Then with a crafty gleam in his eye, he asked, 'Do you have any brandy? I could mix a small peg in a glass of hot water, squeeze a lime into it, and give it to him. He'll have a good night's sleep.'

'Give me a glass.' Mukundan was secretly appalled and delighted at the thought of his father, a sworn advocate of temperance, drunk.

'Make that two. I will also have some,' Krishnan Nair said, sounding as nonchalant as he could.

Mukundan poured himself a stiff drink and gestured to Bhasi to help himself. 'No, not today. I don't feel like it,' Bhasi refused.

'I'm almost fifty-nine years old, Bhasi, but I have never given a thought to old age. I always thought I'd sail from perfect health to a perfect death. No fuss. No pain. Just an effortless passing through,' Mukundan said thoughtfully.

'What has happened to change that?' Bhasi asked from his usual place in the shadows.

'My father,' Mukundan murmured, taking his glasses off and massaging the bridge of his nose. 'My father, who for as long as I can remember clung to his dignity as if it were his most precious possession, is losing it. And there is nothing he can do to prevent it from happening. My father's turning senile. The doctor had a name for it. "Senile dementia."'

'The return of childhood. Where the old adult body houses a child's mind. A mind that doesn't understand the concept of shame or honour. Childish things delight it, and its needs are as basic as a two-year-old's. Tidbits of food, short naps, and the moon to grab and play,' Bhasi explained as if he were reading aloud from a medical textbook. 'The person becomes increasingly egocentric, irritable and difficult, intolerant of any change and suspicious of things. The patient has difficulty following a conversation and tires easily. Delusions that others are out to steal his possessions are a common manifestation. Any sudden change in the environment may precipitate a severe persecution complex.'

'Isn't there anything you can do?' Mukundan asked, leaning towards Bhasi. 'The doctor said I should ask you.'

'He doesn't like me very much. He thinks that I'm out to steal his patients. There's very little one can do to stop time taking its toll on the body,' Bhasi said guardedly. He took out a few mint leaves and began chewing them to gain some time while he thought of how to tackle this sensitive issue.

'I'm sure there must be something you know. Take my case. Only you could have helped me change the way I have,' Mukundan said, unwilling to accept Bhasi's reasoning.

'I can't promise anything, but I shall certainly try,' Bhasi said, wondering if he was being foolish. Lazy minds could be woken up. Fractured psyches could be set. But what was he to do with a mind that had already regressed into a state he had no control over?

'Power House Ramakrishnan came to my home yesterday evening,' Bhasi said a few minutes later.

'What did he want?' Mukundan asked carelessly. He was a little peeved with Bhasi's noncommittal answers.

'He wants to buy my land.'

'What does he want it for?' Mukundan cocked an eyebrow.

'He wants to build a community hall,' Bhasi said. 'He said if I didn't sell him the land, he would see to it that I never work in this village again.'

'No, no. Tell me exactly what happened.' Mukundan said.

'Last evening I wasn't feeling too well, so I was at home,' Bhasi began, and narrated how Power House Ramakrishnan had called on him demanding that he sell him his land.

Mukundan gazed at Bhasi's worried expression and felt his earlier anger disappear. 'Idle threats! That's all there is to it,' he tried to reassure him. 'If I were you, I would just ignore it.'

'How can I? He's got money and the backing of the whole village. What do I fight him with?' Bhasi looked at him expectantly.

Mukundan nodded. 'That is true!'

'Mukundan,' Bhasi said desperately. 'Will you help me?'

'But what can I do?' Mukundan asked, not knowing what was expected of him or whether he wanted to do it at all.

'Talk to him. Talk to the rest of the village bigwigs. They'll listen to you. For them, you and he are equals. Your words carry as much weight as his,' Bhasi pleaded.

'I can do that,' Mukundan said. 'Of course I will do it for you,' he added as an afterthought. Secretly he wasn't so sure that he should confront the leaders of village opinion. Bhasi was expecting too much of him.

Bhasi's expression lightened. Mukundan watched the transformation and felt a rare power swell within him. He could be anyone he wanted. He could do anything he wanted.

Tomorrow I will tell my father about the woman in my life, he decided.

'Mukundan,' Bhasi asked, 'Will you do it as soon as you can?'

'Of course I will,' Mukundan lied, shifting from one foot to the other. 'Just let my father get better, and I'll handle this upstart scoundrel. And then I also have to tell my father about Anjana,' he elaborated on the spur of the moment. It was a trick he had learned in his years of government service. When someone presents a problem to you, present one back to them in return. So that they know you are otherwise occupied. Moreover, it gives you a valid excuse to explain procrastination or even sheer indifference.

He waited to see what effect his words would have on Bhasi. But the painter's face was expressionless. Instead he stared at the ground as if trying to understand the implication of what Mukundan had stated. When he looked up, his face was clenched as if to prevent it from crumpling into a visage of defeat.

'This morning while I was out, he sent someone over to my house to measure the land. It is as if he refuses to accept my no.' Bhasi's voice was heavy-bottomed with a plea.

'What nonsense!' Mukundan expostulated. 'He's got no business doing anything like that. This is an outrage on a person's fundamental right. The right to private property. I'll sort this out once and for all. Don't you worry, Bhasi.' Bhasi stood there looking unconvinced.

'Cheer up,' Mukundan said, clapping Bhasi on the back. 'No one's going to take your home away from you. At least not as long as I can help it.'

'I think,' Mukundan resumed after a few moments of silence, 'I will go over to his house the day after tomorrow. I don't think we should postpone it any longer.'

'What will you say?' Bhasi's eyes glittered in the moonlight. Like some wild creature hiding in the undergrowth and peering out cautiously before it went its way.

'I know exactly what I'm going to say. I will make it very clear that he can't bully anyone into selling his or her land. I will tell him that you have as much right to remain in the village as any of its natives. And that by making threats, he hasn't frightened anyone. Besides, there are courts and laws to prevent any such arm-twisting. After that I intend to speak to what I call the opinion pockets of the village and explain pretty much the same thing to them,' Mukundan said enjoying the power of his rhetoric. 'If my father were well, I would have summoned that Power House Ramakrishnan here. Now you see, don't you, why it is imperative that you help my father to get well again. He still wields so much authority in the village.'

'I'll try, Mukundan,' Bhasi said carefully. He knew what Damayanti would say if he were to repeat this conversation to her: 'They always want something in return. Nothing is offered from the goodness of the heart.' She would toss her head impatiently with barely concealed anger.

Achuthan Nair was in the veranda when they went down the stairs. He was leaning on his stick and calling out to Krishnan Nair, 'Krishnan Nair, hasn't Mukundan come back from school yet? I'll give that boy a much needed caning when he gets home today. The impertinent cur! He must have gone fishing again with those scoundrel classmates of his.'

Mukundan and Bhasi exchanged glances. 'Who are you?' Achuthan Nair asked.

'I'm your son,' Mukundan said clearly, as if he were talking to a child.

'Of course I know that, you fool. What do you think I am? A doddering idiot? I asked, who is this?' he demanded, pointing toward Bhasi.

'The painter,' Mukundan mumbled.

'I didn't know painters worked this late in the night. You must be a peculiar one. What kind of a painter are you?'

'A peculiar one,' Mukundan answered as he normally did his father's rhetorical questions.

Bhasi shot a reproachful look at him and hastened to add, 'A house painter.'

Achuthan Nair stared at them and then walked away with a grunt.

'Most of the time he's very lucid. Then abruptly he goes back to a time when my mother was alive, I was a boy, and he was in complete control of our lives.' Mukundan's voice was quiet.

'I will try my best, I said.' Bhasi squeezed Mukundan's shoulder to comfort his friend. But as he walked out into the

night, a sixth sense told him that something had changed
forever that night.

25

A Committee of Notables

Mukundan fidgeted. Power House Ramakrishnan's drawing room, as he called it, was a museum of conspicuous consumption. The floor was speckled mosaic; the fans, a chocolate brown so that its gold trimmings stood out in relief. The sofas were plump and upholstered in red velvet, and the built-in shelf was burdened with a row of wooden elephants; a garish Kathakali figurine; a brass stork with its beak in a pitcher and six black-and-gold cups placed upside-down on their heads on the saucers. On the coffee table, which had ornate carved legs and a Formica top, a ceramic ashtray stood with its gaping mouth spotlessly clean. At the far end of the room was a peach coloured washbasin. Mukundan wondered what it was for. Perhaps for washing your face if you were overwhelmed by the room's opulence. Or maybe it was there, he sneered, to throw up into if you were nauseated by the magnitude of bad taste.

Power House Ramakrishnan came into the room wiping his glasses on the hem of his mundu. 'I'm so glad that you decided to come today. They will all be here shortly.'

'Who?' Mukundan asked, feeling stupid.

'The community hall committee,' Power House Ramakrishnan's voice rolled up like shutters in surprise. He stared at Mukundan's blank expression and said, 'When you called yesterday to say you were coming, I called for a meeting. It might be difficult to get everyone together at the same time another day.' Then with a puzzled look, he added, 'But didn't Krishnan Nair tell you? I called back to say that this meeting had been fixed.'

'No, he didn't,' Mukundan said. 'We had a rather upsetting day yesterday, and Krishnan Nair must have forgotten.'

'Nothing serious, I hope?' Power House Ramakrishnan probed with the right amount of concern to make it seem as if he wasn't probing. It made Mukundan want to grit his teeth.

'No, nothing serious,' Mukundan replied, unwilling to reveal anything to this man who made his flesh crawl. He didn't know what it was about him that made him dislike him so much. He tried to rationalize it. Did he feel a certain amount of resentment for the position Power House Ramakrishnan held in the village? After all, Power House Ramakrishnan had in many ways usurped his rightful place, Mukundan told himself with a mutinous expression as he sipped at the orange squash. 'So what is this community hall committee all about?' Mukundan asked, trying not to let his dislike show in his voice.

'Well,' Power House Ramakrishnan began, reclining on a velvet sofa and putting his glasses on, 'as you can see for yourself, this village lacks a place where everyone can get together. As a native of Kaikurussi and being in a position to do so, thanks to the blessings of the gods and my ancestors, I have decided to build a community hall. This is purely an act of charity, but to pay for the maintenance, I intend to collect a small amount as rental charges, no matter what occasion it is hired for. To ensure that no one's sentiments are hurt by the nature of functions held, and to uphold the moral and cultural values of our village, as the community hall's founder and builder, I thought a committee was necessary. The committee will in turn decide to whom and for what purpose the hall can be hired out, etc. etc.'

'Oh, I see,' Mukundan muttered. 'Who's on the committee?' he asked with a frisson of excitement curling up his toes. He had felt the same way when all those years ago at the General Body Meeting of the Recreation Club, someone had nominated him for the club secretary's post. He had lost the election. But the defeat hadn't rankled too much because he had been unanimously declared the club librarian.

'Parameswaran Namboodiri from Plashi Mana. Haji Suleiman from the masjid committee. Abu Seth.'

'Who?' Mukundan asked. The name meant nothing to him.

'Abu. Remember hook-nosed Abu who sold fish? Some years ago, he went to the Gulf and came back a very rich man. He has tremendous sway over the Muslim community in the village, and his presence on the committee will encourage them to hold their weddings at the community hall,' Power House Ramakrishnan explained. 'I have also asked two other people whom you don't know. Youngsters who were probably little more than babies when you left the village. And then you, of course.'

'What?' Mukundan half rose from his seat, incredulous.

'Yes. Why do you sound so surprised?' Power House Ramakrishnan asked. 'It was a foregone conclusion as far as I was concerned. How can anything so important be constituted without your presence? You might not have lived here for many years, but the villagers look up to you. They respect who you are, the lineage you represent.'

Flattery dripped. Mukundan lapped it up with the thirst of one who has only heard about it but has never tasted it.

But the innocuously smooth, transparent droplets that fell as though from the side of a rock were as venomous as a giant lizard's urine. They ate into the skin, gnawed at the locks of evil within, causing blisters to rise, badness to unfurl and escape.

The cars arrived, one by one, the sun glinting on their fenders. The horns heralded the identity of each personage.

The 1925 Bentley, in the manner of a mythical beast, emerged rarely from its lair-like garage. Parameswaran Namboodiri from the Plashi Mana clung to the vestments of the past, and so, the Bentley with its cherrywood panelling and papers that said it had once belonged to the Raja of Nilambur, was more than a car. It was Parameswaran Namboodiri's sceptre of power and hence his right to royal privileges. It demanded awed attention, subordination of viewpoints, and the overruling of one's conscience.

The haji and Abu Seth, as expected, arrived together in the latter's brand new Mahindra jeep. The haji was a wise man, a scholar, but he had no sons draining the oil fields of Arabia. So when it was required, the rich Muslims of Kaikurussi rallied together to provide and protect. 'Let money not be the reason why our haji Suleiman is treated as a less important man,' the Islamic brotherhood maintained.

Professor Menon was not a native of Kaikurussi, but his wife was. He worked at the Pattambi College and was the head of the department of Economics. He seldom used his car, but this morning he knew that if his opinions were to have any impact, they needed to arrive on four wheels and with an automobile heart. So he washed his cream-coloured Fiat that didn't really need any washing, and lit an agarbathi stick in it.

Behind him, as befitted someone who held a party card in the Communist Party, Comrade Jayan rode up on his Hero Honda motorbike. Comrade Jayan could tell anyone who asked, on what points Lenin differed from Trotsky. His belief in the principles of Communism was implicit and unshakable, but that didn't prevent him from seeking refuge at Mata Premanandamayi's feet, every now and then. Her blessings were not something to be trifled with. His position in the party was ample testimony to that. She had, in her own way, guided his political career to where it was today. In fact, he hoped to persuade her to make a stop at the village once the community hall was built. His stock in the village, he knew, would definitely soar if the miracle worker chose to accept his invitation and grace Kaikurussi with her presence. At least once.

Power House Ramakrishnan stood on the veranda of his house greeting each one of his guests volubly, vociferously. He glanced at Mukundan out of the corner of his eye to see if he was suitably impressed. He felt a deep surge of power rush through him. These are the people who are supporting me in my endeavour, he wanted to tell Mukundan. They who hold the reins of this community. And you, who are a mere nobody, an insignificant retired government servant, think you can sway the support I have.

Power House Ramakrishnan watched Mukundan shift in his chair. He had been expecting Mukundan to call on him. He knew that Mukundan would try to persuade him to change his mind. He had planned ahead in preparation for the time Mukundan would come to plead Bhasi's case.

Power House Ramakrishnan operated on a simple theory: Every man has his price. In some cases it was a little more difficult to settle on. The currency was intangible, the exchange rate high, but he was yet to discover a human being who couldn't be bought. All you had to do was figure out at what price principles began to erode. Based on his theory, which had never failed him, he plotted his stratagem to buy Mukundan's complicity in the building of his dream. The Power House Ramakrishnan Community Hall.

The Namboodiri sat by himself in the three-seater velvet sofa. Whoever heard of a king sharing his throne? The yellow creaminess of his skin reflected the reddish tinge of the sofa, suffusing his cheeks with a fiery glow that would quell even Comrade Jayan's doubts about whether a man should be allowed such authority merely because he had been born into the Brahmin community.

The rest of them, ministers of state, flanked him on either side. Power House Ramakrishnan, radiating energy and pride, introduced Mukundan to each one of them. 'Achuthan Nair's son, Mukundan. And a very good friend of mine.' He sensed Mukundan's head jerk in surprise but he ignored it and went on, 'His family is, as all of us already know, the oldest and most respected tharavad in the village. I think we should all be honoured that he has agreed to be on our committee.'

He saw the battle in Mukundan's face. The flush of acknowledgement, the satisfaction of recognition, tussled and grappled with his reason for being there. Uncertainty churned to the top. Power House Ramakrishnan let it rest.

'Yes, yes, we all know who Mukundan is,' Parameswaran Namboodiri said, eyeing Mukundan with a glint of amusement. 'Where is Susheelan from the Young Men's Cultural Association?'

'He should be here any time now,' Comrade Jayan murmured, stealthily fingering the velvet he sat on. He liked the sensation, but he wasn't sure if he should approve of it or of Power House Ramakrishnan who represented the bourgeoisie with his acres of land, rubber plantation, and a car-hire service. Comrade Jayan darted a covert glance around to reassure himself that this was a project meant for communal welfare and didn't mean a corrosion of party beliefs.

'Make yourself comfortable. The sofa won't bite,' Power House Ramakrishnan guffawed.

'Will they expel you from the party for being here?' Abu Seth gestured, with a sweep of his hands. The gold watch glinted, and his armpits sprayed the air with the reek of Aramis toilet water.

'Of course not,' Comrade Jayan said, in that self-righteous tone that crept into his voice when he took the dais. 'The party understands that certain projects need the backing of capitalistic enterprise. The party encourages us to support such ventures. At least then some of the bourgeois wealth will reach the needy masses.'

'Stop making speeches, Jayan, and sit down,' Professor Menon called out, as if he were repressing an irascible student in the classroom. Jayan had been his student some years ago, and a mediocre one at that.

Mukundan surveyed the room with a growing sense of ease. Soon they would be his friends too, these men of distinction and power. Father, I am as much a personage in this village as you are. Father, you might not think so, but they value my presence like they did yours. Mukundan felt warm and protected. As if an invisible ring of hands surrounded him with affection and camaraderie. Then a little voice at the back of his head reminded him of Bhasi. Have you forgotten about him and that he needs your support? Have you forgotten why you are here this morning?

Mukundan cleared his throat. All heads turned except Power House Ramakrishnan's. Instead, he sniffed. The double-twitched sniff that alone expressed his inner agitation.

Mukundan began in an uncertain voice that would have irked both Bhasi and Achuthan Nair had they been present. 'This is about the land the community hall is going to be built upon.'

'Yes, what about it?' the Namboodiri asked in his most imperious manner.

'Well, does it have to be located there? I mean, it doesn't seem right that we take away a man's land even if it is for a good cause,' Mukundan said apologetically.

'Power House Ramakrishnan sir isn't taking anyone's land away. He's offering a very good price for it,' Abu Seth interjected.

'Painter Bhasi can buy himself a sizeable plot of land anywhere he chooses to, and build a house better than the one he's living in right now,' Haji Suleiman explained, trying to take away the sting of Abu's words. He had heard that Mukundan and Bhasi were friends.

'But there isn't a single square inch of land for sale in Kaikurussi,' Mukundan said weakly.

'Why does he have to live in Kaikurussi? It isn't as if he is a native of this village. Whether he lives here or in another village can't make any difference to him. Look at me; I wasn't born here. But I feel completely at home in Kaikurussi,' Professor Menon said loudly and clearly. A teacher, they say, can never stop being a teacher.

'Mukundan,' Power House Ramakrishnan said in a quiet voice, 'besides all this, there is one more reason. When I invest so much money in a project like this, I have to at least break even. I'm being completely honest here. I hope you can appreciate that. I don't want to make a profit but I can't run into losses either. If it is located anywhere else, its commercial prospects will be nil. Would anyone hold a wedding in the middle of a market? Would anyone attend a concert in a hall that's next door to a toddy shop?'

Mukundan nodded his head in agreement. Power House Ramakrishnan was right. Why was Bhasi being so stubborn? He should just take the price offered and look for another piece of land.

'Perhaps you could explain this to him,' Power House Ramakrishnan murmured. 'I know he respects you and will listen to you.'

'But . . .' Mukundan stuttered.

'I think you should,' Power House Ramakrishnan insisted.

'Yes, yes, you should,' they all said, one by one.

Mukundan glanced around him. He felt himself flush with pride. He had never realized how highly the people of Kaikurussi thought of him and his influence on others.

'Where is that Susheelan?' the Namboodiri suddenly demanded. 'I have to be elsewhere by half-past twelve.'

'I hear that he's tangled in some kind of a romance with that milk woman Nalini Amma's daughter,' Abu Seth murmured.

The Namboodiri and Power House Ramakrishnan exchanged looks. 'We can't have that,' Power House Ramakrishnan said. 'In fact, when we were talking about forming the committee, one thing we instantly agreed upon was that all committee members had to be citizens above reproach. With pristine reputations and no skeletons in the closet. Like Mukundan, for instance. Can any one in this village point an accusatory finger at him for any reason?'

Mukundan felt his heart still. What would they say if they knew about Anjana? He felt dread rock his insides. He couldn't afford to lose their friendship. It meant too much to him. This was what he had longed for all his life and he didn't want to jeopardize it in any way.

Power House Ramakrishnan saw the distress crouching on Mukundan's face. So the rumours he had heard about a woman were true. He smirked. He had Mukundan in a cleft stick. Mukundan wanted so much to belong. To feel important. To be appreciated. That was his price. Look at him, as he fawned over everyone. 'I can take over the bookkeeping if you like,' Mukundan gushed. 'I used to be in charge of the administration of the recreation club when I worked in Bangalore. I know how these things are done.'

'That would be a great help,' Power House Ramakrishnan said. He smiled at Mukundan. 'You will stay for lunch, won't you?'

'I . . . I . . .' Mukundan hesitated.

'I would be honoured if you did,' Power House Ramakrishnan said in his most humble manner.

'That is very kind of you,' Mukundan said and lapsed into silence. There was nothing to do but explain the situation to Bhasi. Sometimes Bhasi got the wrong idea about people, and then he clung to it like an iguana on a rock. That was the trouble with young men. They didn't understand that life, and reality, exist in shades of grey. They insisted that everything was either black or white, left or right. The middle path had no meaning for them.

Mukundan waited for Bhasi, camouflaged by the shadows. He knew Bhasi would soon be there, eager to find out how his meeting with Power House Ramakrishnan had gone. He poured himself a drink and formed appropriate phrases in his head.

He clinked the ice cubes in his glass and stared at the night sky. He heard footsteps and the surreptitious clearing of a throat. He avoided Bhasi's eyes as if he were ashamed, embarrassed, and guilty. But guilty of what? Instead he looked at the glass and spoke to it. 'I tried to talk to them, Bhasi.'

'And?' Bhasi asked sharply.

'And they explained to me why it had to be your land and nowhere else. Bhasi, why are you being so stubborn? It isn't as if Power House Ramakrishnan isn't giving you a good price for the land and house.' Mukundan's voice was brusque and his eyes were still shifty.

'How would you react if they asked you for your land in return for a good price?' Bhasi snapped, unable to contain his anger.

'There's a difference,' Mukundan said. 'I was born here. I am a native of this village. My ties to this land exist in my blood. But you are just a settler. And a recent one, at that.'

'So is that what it has been reduced to? That as a native you have certain rights, and as a settler I don't. I love this village, this land, more than anyone else in this village does. I love it as if it were a living being. But because I am not a native, I'm dispensable.' Bhasi's voice shook. 'How am I going to make you or any one else understand what Kaikurussi means to me? What can I say to you who sees this land merely as mud, grass and trees, of the bonding the land and I share?'

'You are being irrational,' Mukundan said quietly.

'How dare you say I'm irrational!' Bhasi's voice rose.

'Yes, listen to me,' Mukundan said, glancing at his watch, and cutting him off in mid-sentence. 'If I were you I would accept the offer as quickly as possible and scout for some land to buy somewhere around. Abu, I hear, has some land to sell in Mannur. That's only four kilometres away. It can't be any different from here.'

'How do you know?' Bhasi demanded, suspicious by now.

'They were all there when I went to meet Power House Ramakrishnan,' Mukundan murmured.

'They?'

'Yes. The committee that's responsible for the community hall. After all, the community hall is for the welfare of the village and so every group's sentiments have to be taken into account.' Mukundan gestured airily.

'What are you talking about?' Bhasi asked. He didn't recognize this Mukundan. A Mukundan whose words bore the eloquence and hollowness of political promises.

'Power House Ramakrishnan has constituted a committee of opinion leaders of this village, and each one of them said the same thing. That you shouldn't be stubborn and should take up the offer graciously.'

Bhasi stared at him uneasily. 'Who's on this committee?'

'Parameswaran Namboodiri from Plashi Mana. Haji Suleiman. Abu Seth and some others,' Mukundan was evasive.

'Who are these *some others*?' Bhasi persisted.

Mukundan frowned for a long moment, took his glasses off and, under the pretense of wiping them, looked down and said, 'Comrade Jayan, Professor Menon. Susheelan and . . . I.'

'And you, Mukundan?'

'Yes. I mean, I'm sorry that I couldn't do more to help. But aren't you happy for me? This is everything I have always wanted. The village has finally recognized me as a worthy man. I'm no longer just Achuthan Nair's son. I'm seen as a man who can make a contribution to the betterment of this village. My opinion counts, you see.'

Mukundan's voice rose in excitement.

'When did the opinion of these people or your position in the village become so important to you?' Bhasi asked standing up, no longer bothering to hide his bitterness.

'You are the one who said that I have to emerge from my father's shadow. That I have to be my own man and make a place of my own in this world,' Mukundan said angrily. 'And now, when I do so, you are telling me it isn't important. I don't understand you any more. I suppose you would have liked me to remain a nervous wreck so that you could continue to exercise your power over me!'

Bhasi looked at his feet for a while. Then he looked up at Mukundan. 'You are right,' he said. 'I'm being irrational. What is so special about Kaikurussi? One piece of land is like another . . .' And then he said, 'You can tell your *new friends* that I'm willing to discuss the matter with them.'

Mukundan pretended not to hear the inflection. 'I will do that,' he said. With a self-confidence he had never felt before, he continued, 'There is something else, Bhasi. Parameswaran Namboodiri brought up the matter of the loan. It seems he needs the money now for his daughter's wedding, and with the principle and interest, you owe him quite a bit. So you might have had to sell your land anyway. But I'll tell you what I can do. I will see to it that the payment is made as soon as possible. I will also insist that till you find a house or land to buy, they find you a house to rent, perhaps in Kailiad. What do you think?'

Bhasi shrugged. 'I can actually get a loan from the bank to repay the Namboodiri. I don't need to sell my land. Will you stand as my guarantor?'

'Me?' Mukundan laughed, a mock laugh. 'I am a retired man. No one will consider me for a guarantor.' Mukundan had decided he would do nothing that would jeopardize his new standing in the village.

'That's fine,' Bhasi said in a tight voice. 'I'll find another way. I have other friends, you know, people I can count on.

They will be happy to oblige, I'm sure.'

Mukundan examined his nails, pretending disinterest. He didn't like Bhasi's tone of voice. Just because they were friends, it didn't mean Bhasi should forget who Mukundan was. He thought of what his father and Krishnan Nair would have said: 'If you take a leech and put it alongside you on your bed, do you expect it to lie there quietly? Of course it's going to fasten its little leech teeth into you and bleed you dry!'

'I'm off, Mukundan,' Bhasi said. Mukundan watched him walk away. Suddenly he called out, 'Have you been able to find any medicine to help my father?'

'No, not yet,' Bhasi replied.

Mukundan chewed his lip thoughtfully and muttered, 'Perhaps I should simply accept that this is inevitable and that this is the beginning of the end.'

The next day, when Bhasi returned home after painting a shop at Kailiad, Che Kutty was waiting on the front veranda. He didn't meet Bhasi's eye when he walked up to him.

'Did you get my note, Che Kutty?' Bhasi asked. In the last few months, Che Kutty and he had become more than acquaintances. They often met at Shankar's and chatted for a while. For a toddy-shop owner, he was remarkably cultured and well read. But what Bhasi liked most about Che Kutty was his sense of discretion. He rarely gossiped, and you could trust him to keep a secret. Which was why, when Bhasi decided to take a loan from the Co-operative Bank, he asked Che Kutty to be his guarantor.

'I don't think I can stand surety for the loan you want to take,' Che Kutty said, looking away.

'Is that all?' Bhasi said with a little laugh. 'Don't worry about it, I'm sure Shankar will help.'

'No, no one will help. Neither Shankar nor anyone else in the village.'

'What are you saying?' Bhasi demanded, frightened by

the implication of his words. 'All of you know why I need this loan. If I don't pay it off, Power House Ramakrishnan will take my house and land away.'

'I wish I could help. All of us wish we could help in some way. But we are all indebted to Power House Ramakrishnan in one way or another, and he has said that if any one of us stands surety for you in the bank, he'll no longer be there for us,' Che Kutty said quietly. 'There is no way people like Shankar or me or Barber Nanu or anyone else can exist in this village without his help. No bank will give us loans. He has always lent us money when we have asked him for it, and he's quite lenient when it comes to repayment. There is nothing we can do.'

He was right. There was nothing he or anyone else could do. Bhasi looked at him, not knowing what to say. Bhasi knew Che Kutty wanted him to assuage his guilt. Absolve him and everyone else of their betrayal. But he couldn't do it. Bhasi felt betrayed. He felt that they had cast him aside. Just as Mukundan had.

When he realized that no more words were forthcoming, Che Kutty began to walk away. At the gate he stopped and said, 'Why don't you give him what he wants?'

26

Verdigris on Love

Mukundan opened the wooden jewellery box and looked at its contents speculatively. Which one of these would Anjana like? He glanced at his watch. It was almost half-past two. If he set out right away, he could be at her house in an hour's time. He drew out a necklace of coral beads and pearls set in gold to take with him. The necklace would delight her. After all, which woman wouldn't succumb to a gift of jewellery? Besides, he had to explain to her about the new turn in their relationship.

He had thought about it for a long time and had come to a decision. There was nothing to do but wait until everything could be made legal and aboveboard. He didn't want even a whiff of a scandal tainting his reputation at this very important juncture of his life. It was going to be difficult to persuade Anjana to see his point of view. That much he was sure of. But he had to make her understand why he couldn't call on her as often as he used to, and that the divorce would have to come through before they could begin to live together.

Anjana sat on the veranda of her house, flanked by bronze vessels of various kinds. Mukundan walked towards her with a grin. 'What is this? A classroom?' He bent down and picked up a bronze saucepan. He tapped the side of the saucepan. A hollow clang-clang echoed. 'Tell me, my dear teacher,' he joked, 'do you hear the same sound when you tap the sides of your students' skulls?'

She smiled obligingly. She always did, no matter how asinine his jokes or how silly his quips.

'I thought you said you would be coming only tomorrow,' she said in greeting.

'I couldn't stay away from you,' Mukundan said, putting the vessel down and reaching out to brush her cheek with the back of his palm. I never knew I could talk like this, Mukundan marvelled at his own capacity as the glib words sallied forth effortlessly. Maybe it isn't really glib talk. I do love her, and she is very important to me, and I did want to see her, he told himself as a faint sense of shame began to tinge his conscience.

Anjana's eyes dropped. She felt a peculiar tightness constrict her throat. He always made her feel she was his most cherished possession. She cleared her throat and pushed aside the vessels as though they were a group of unruly children. 'Let me clear a place for you to sit down.'

'What are you doing with these vessels?' Mukundan asked curiously.

'I thought I'd try cleaning them. Some of them have gone a peculiar shade of green,' Anjana said, examining the insides of a bronze kettle.

'Verdigris.'

'What?' she asked.

'That's what that green layer is called. In the big cities like Bangalore, Bombay, Delhi and Madras, people pay thousands of rupees for vessels like these. They are considered to be antiques. Objects of art to be displayed in posh living rooms with special stands and lights so that everyone who comes in knows a huge price has been paid for them.'

'You must be joking,' Anjana giggled. 'I wonder what my grandmother would have said if she knew her spittoon and this kolambi, her chamber pot, would be treasured and given pride of place in a room with expensive sofas and carpets.'

'People who have money to throw away are always looking for new ways to spend it,' Mukundan said, picking up a betel-nut box.

'I knew old furniture fetched a good price, but this . . .' She laughed again. Little things amused her these days. Happiness was so easy to find when one is well loved. The world's a charming place where chamber pots with verdigris become rare finds and one's lover comes calling a day early because he couldn't stay away. Time is treated with the disrespect it deserves, because love can't be constricted by the hands of a clock.

'Perhaps I should sell it all and bring the money with me as dowry,' she said peering at him covertly.

Mukundan watched the laughter in her eyes frolic and felt fear dribble down his chest. How on earth was he going to break the news to her that until her divorce came through, there was no way they could have a future together?

'I had an appointment with my lawyer yesterday. He said the divorce could take longer than we expected it to. I told him I didn't care how many months it took, as long as I could be free of that man. It doesn't really matter to us, does it?' She paused and then resumed, 'Have you thought of what is to be done with all these things, this house and its belongings when I . . . you know . . . come to your house,' she finished in a rush, embarrassed.

In reply, he began gathering the vessels. 'Where do you normally keep these?'

'What are you up to?' she asked, trailing him into the house with an armful of babies streaked with green.

'Just show me where to put them,' he said standing at the doorway.

She gestured towards the storeroom adjacent to the kitchen. He stacked the vessels and then went back for the rest. 'Put away the ones you are hugging to your bosom and wash your hands,' he said soaping his hands at the washbasin. He sniffed his hands to see if there were any traces of the metallic stench that old unused vessels seemed to wear as a halo. He washed his hands again.

He decided that he would have to convince her the only way he knew how to. He waited till Anjana washed her hands, then he took the towel from the rack and carefully dried her hands. Parting her fingers and sliding the towel between them. Gentle and abrasive. Moustache and mouth.

'What is all this?' she murmured as she let him lead her into the bedroom.

'This is about how much you mean to me,' he whispered as he drew the curtain across the window.

Anjana had made some changes to the room since that first time they had wedded their feelings for each other. She had begun by taking down the square wall clock, yet another wedding gift. In their early months of courtship, when Mukundan came calling on her once a week, she had watched him cast surreptitious glances at the old clock that hung in the front room. As if to reassure himself that he was not overstaying his welcome. In this room, in their new-found togetherness, she didn't want clock hands measuring the passage of their love. The coat stand that had stood laden with her clothes had been shifted to another room along with the chest-of-drawers and the tall almirah. In that enormous room with huge windows, the bareness evoked a virginal purity. An unsullied simplicity that suggested new beginnings, fresh starts, and holy unions. And yet, in it was a sensuality that stoked their senses without making their passion for each other's bodies seem sordid or clandestine.

She made new curtains for the windows. Thick cotton that lit the room in a soft light and yet shielded them from the eyes of the world. Anjana had moved out the double bed her father had bought for her wedding and replaced it with the old four-poster her parents had cradled their marriage in for almost half a century. The bed had been polished till the old wood gleamed with the sheen of satisfaction. The sheets and pillowcases were always freshly laundered, always a pale pastel shade. She wanted no remnants of the past in this room. Besides, Mukundan hated dark-coloured bedlinen. Only the walls of the room remained unchanged. Always a pale cream, their only ornament now was the almost five-foot tall mirror framed in wood.

Anjana could see herself reflected in the mirror from where she stood silently. Since the first time, they had made love exactly eight times. Enveloped in clothes, cloaked in darkness. Each time, desire and restraint had coupled so that even as they lay exhausted and satiated in each other's arms, she still felt afraid that none of it was meant to last.

She leaned against the bedpost. Free-falling hair and sensual curves. Parted lips and heaving breasts. She looked at his profile, the light glinting on his spectacles, his sensitive lips, and his fingers as they fumbled with her clothes. She watched him accord her the reverence priests reserve for deities. This was some sort of a ritual. That much she understood. And she felt fear shoot through her. Something about him portended an end. A closing act.

The fan whirred noisily. She could hear the splash of water in the pond next door as children swam in it vigorously. Anjana wanted to cover herself. With splayed fingers and crossed thighs.

'No, don't,' he whispered.

He drew out the coral and pearl necklace and trailed it over her. Her skin bloomed terracotta beads. He turned her so that the curve of her back faced him and then he clasped the necklace around her neck. His hands cupped her breasts, touching, searching . . . Then he pushed her gently onto the bed and loved her with hands and eyes, skin and mouth, touch and thought. Till he felt her quiver, and her fragrance scented every inch of his consciousness.

The evening glided in but he wouldn't let her rise. 'Not yet,' he murmured coiling a lock of her hair around his fingers.

'Where did you get this?' she asked, touching the necklace.

'It's my mother's,' he said, caressing the gentle swell of her belly absently.

'Was it in a safe deposit box?'

'My father gave it to me,' he said and sat up abruptly. 'Anjana, there's something I have to tell you.'

The fan's breeze felt unpleasantly cold now that the warmth of his bulk no longer pressed against her. She drew a sheet upto her chin. 'Have you told him about us?' she asked.

'No, I've yet to tell him about us,' he said in a low voice.

'But you said you were going to tell him this week,' she reminded him quietly.

'I wanted to, but he is in a strange frame of mind. When he's a little better and back to his usual obnoxious self, then I will talk to him about us,' Mukundan said stiffly. 'But there is something else I need to talk to you about.'

'Has that man been bothering you? He'll do his best to prevent this divorce. But my lawyer said he has no real grounds to contest it,' Anjana said, frightened by the aloofness in Mukundan's tone.

'It is not about your husband, though he is connected to the problem. There is this man Power House Ramakrishnan in the village,' he said in a low voice.

'What about him?' she asked, relief taking the guise of a languidly trailing finger down his back.

And so Mukundan told her about the community hall that was to be built. The committee that had been formed. He spoke to her about how the committee members were expected to guard their reputations and of how he had been held up as an example and because she was still married in the eyes of law, they would have to postpone their plans for the future for a while.

Anjana listened to him quietly. When he finished, a stony silence weighed down the space between them. She lay back against the pillows and closed her eyes. The necklace curled stiffly to one side of her neck and bit into her skin.

'But is this committee so important to you?' she asked.

Mukundan swallowed convulsively. He had known it wasn't going to be easy. In fact, he had feared this confrontation more than the one with Bhasi. 'It is not so much the committee as the chance to be at the helm of village affairs,' he said turning towards her. 'It has always been my greatest desire to take my father's place in Kaikurussi. An ambition that I thought was going to remain unfulfilled till this opportunity came up. Besides, it isn't as if your divorce will take forever. In a few months time, a year at the most, you will be a free woman and then we can go ahead and get married,' Mukundan offered in a conciliatory tone.

'Are you ashamed of me?' she asked suddenly.

'Don't be silly,' he said brusquely.

'I don't know.' Her voice rose. 'I get this feeling that when I am a free woman as you term it, you might want your committee's approval before you marry me.' Her voice was tight with tears.

Mukundan bent towards her and pressed his lips to her brow. 'I love you.'

'Then why don't you tell them about me and make them understand how important I am to you?' she asked, letting her hurt explode into anger.

'I don't think they will understand. They are a very conservative lot. And have you thought about Ravindran? What if he chooses to come to my house? From what you tell me, he will think nothing of making a scene and drawing everyone's attention to our relationship. In the eyes of the world, we are committing adultery,' he said, straightening the necklace so that the pendant lay between her breasts. A plumb line of lust.

'From thy heart to thy loins, I worship thee. With the fullness of my being, with every pore and follicle, I love thee body and soul,' he murmured trying to distract her attention with poetic words and exploratory caresses.

'Is that why you brought me this necklace?' she demanded, thrusting his hand away. 'As if I were a child to be appeased with a present.'

'Anjana, please,' he pleaded. 'Why are you being difficult? Why don't you understand how I feel?'

She looked at him for a long moment. Then she took the necklace off and thrust it into his hands.

'When you told me that you were a weak and unreliable person, I told myself that I was fortunate that the man I loved was someone mature enough to know his own limitations. Someone who wasn't afraid to admit it. I was wrong,' she said, pulling her clothes on. 'You are a coward. A smug and completely self-absorbed coward who puts himself before anyone else and then uses his own feebleness of character to excuse it. What a great trick that is! To admit to your frailty so no one will condemn you later on. You disgust me. Please leave,' she said quietly. 'If the committee members hear of your visits, they might throw you out of that precious committee of yours. We don't want that to happen, do we? After all, this is the culmination of your life's dreams.'

Mukundan put the necklace into his wallet and pulled his clothes on. Maybe Meenakshi had been right after all. An older woman would have behaved with a great deal more maturity. Understood his viewpoint and even been supportive. But there was no point in thinking along those lines. He did love Anjana, and someday they would have a life together. But she would have to learn to wait and curb the impetuosity of her youth.

In a few days' time, when her temper cooled down, he would visit her and they would reconcile their differences. There was nothing in this world that couldn't be accomplished if one set one's mind to it. That much Bhasi had shown him.

Part V

27

Fireflies Are Not Stars

Perhaps this is the way it was meant to happen. When all has been said and finished, each word and sensation examined and dissected, cauterized and analyzed, loose ends tied, rhythms equalized, I sit here staring at the darkness. Trying to restore my pulsating heart to its previous state of numbness. Trying to trample to ashes the embers of a relationship you wish to revive. Trying to trash a friendship that has no place. Trying to memorize the words you spoke, the look in your eyes. Trying to seal the memory of that secret joy that gushed in me like an underground stream. Trying to stifle the anguish of remembering that our affinity has no more substance than a mirage. Though you claim otherwise.

But I want you to remember how we parted the last time. It was the twenty-eighth of December when you came looking for me. An evening that was slowly dwindling into night. 'This is the cheque for the land and house. And this is the key to the house in Kailiad. The rent has been paid for four months, after which you will have to either find your own accommodation or pay the rent yourself,' you said, giving me an envelope and a key ring, severing forever the bond that had held us together.

Once again I felt the taste of failure coat my tongue. An acrid grey wash of disillusionment tainted my mouth with bitterness. The back of my neck began to hurt. The muscles in my shoulders were taut. My hands shook. I clasped them together to stop their frenzied dance. My throat felt parched and dry.

At what point does a man allow failure to take root? At what point does a man realize that where eyes meet the horizon, only despair awaits him? Perhaps every man has his own line of realization. An imaginary line that divides green fecundity from brown barrenness.

Ever since I began to live in Kaikurussi, the landscapes of my life have been green valleys, green meadows, endless green fields lush with hope, blessed with peace. My horizon stretched, bearing the promise of greater fertility. But you, Mukundan, pulled out the tufts of green from beneath my feet that night and showed me the menacing rocks that had been biding their time till they could cut my feet and bleed my dreams dry.

How could you be so oblivious to my anguish? Could you really not see that you were building your dreams on the dust of my hopes?

'What have you decided?' you asked me when I took the envelope and the keys from you silently. Did you expect me to dismiss this uprooting as one of life's many unexpected turns and accept it quietly? Or did you think that I had resigned myself to leaving this village for good?

'I don't know,' I said. I really didn't know. For until that moment I had thought that our friendship would prevail. That you would realize that I was being driven out of this village and would do something to prevent it. That you would find a way for me to stay on.

You looked at me belligerently. I knew you thought that I was being deliberately reticent.

'I suppose you are angry with me. I suppose you resent the fact that I'm part of the community hall committee.'

'Did I say that?' I asked.

'You don't have to. I'm not a fool. Do you think I haven't noticed the change in your behaviour? That's the problem with you youngsters. You don't understand the priorities in life. If something doesn't happen the way you want it, then you are quick to reject old ties, old relationships. Anjana is the same,' you said, a frown crinkling your forehead.

I knew then that Anjana too had been sacrificed on the altar of your quest for self-worth.

'I'm not angry or resentful. I'm still in a state of shock,' I said baldly. I wasn't trying to make you feel guilty. Or maybe I was. You were supposed to be my friend. My ally. Now you are neither.

'I don't understand why you are going into these histrionics,' you said furiously. I realized then that you really meant every word you said. You thought you were in the right and that I was being wilful and difficult.

'I didn't want to come to Kaikurussi, but circumstances forced me to return. And so I made a new life for myself here. You are still a young man. You can't let yourself be defeated by a small setback like this. Look at it as a new beginning. An opportunity to make something of your life,' you said imperiously, conveniently blanking out the extent to which you had hated this village. Till I decided to step in and change your life. That hurt more than anything else did. For what you had done, Mukundan, was to diminish my life's work to nothing.

'So then, it is goodbye,' I said.

'It doesn't have to be goodbye,' you said. 'It isn't as if you are going to the end of this world. You are just going to Kailiad, and that's barely half an hour away by bus. We will see each other again. Soon.'

I shrugged. I wasn't listening to you any more. I wanted to slam my fist against something hard and let my pain flow.

The night swirled around me, rubbing its face against my skin. The earth, damp and loose, cushioned my feet, inviting me to rest a while, and heal my bruised spirit. The leaves of the jamun tree whispered soft murmuring sounds. They knew me. They responded to my pain. The earth, wind, water, skies, and energy of this land. They saw in me someone who loved them unconditionally. And it was this land that has always been my haven and salvation that you, along with those others, forced me to sell.

The fireflies flickered. Glowing beads that sought to replicate the starlit skies at mortal heights. I trapped one in my palm. The lines criss-crossed my skin, and the course of my destiny lit up for a while. Then I let it go.

I had tried to play God. I had made myself the impresario of another man's fate. I had let myself believe that I could shape a man's life as surely as God does. That in me resided a superior power that allowed me to fashion a future course that even God hadn't known how to. Like the firefly trying to match the brilliance of the stars, I had let the limits of my knowledge rule me.

Man cannot change the movement of the planets with a sweep of his hand. Every man is guided by a force that is individual and unfathomable. Man can heal, but a little. Man can aid self-discovery, but only a little. No man is the master of another man's destiny. For man is not God. And fireflies are not stars.

28

A Paying of Dues

Nellikka hung from the tree by the post office. Giant clusters of waxy green, glistening fruit, tart and delicate and so irresistible to boys who walked on the road. In each school bag was a screw of paper that held chilli powder and salt cut into each other. In their pockets were pebbles that, when flung with a sure hand or a catapult, sliced the stalk of the nellikka cluster and let loose a rain of golden green rounded drops. To pick, to dip in the chilli-salt mixture, to pop in the mouth till their tight little bellies and hungry-for-adventure minds were satiated.

Mukundan sat at the dining table sipping his evening tea. Through the window, he saw his father flit across the back yard into the garden. He waited for the rattle of pebbles as they fell on the tiled roof of the post office, the excited cries of the boys, and the rustle of leaves as his father rushed towards them. Flapping his arms, screaming curses, and seeking to crush their young spirits as he had once done with Mukundan. But the boys only saw an eccentric old man who could be preyed on for excitement. They waited for him to arrive, an ancient stick insect with spindly legs and arms, to torture and derive amusement from. The meeker ones made faces and called him names. 'Old Fool; Ancient Ape; Brown Hopper . . .' they chanted from the cover of bushes.

The braver ones darted around his legs picking the fallen fruit and stuffing it into their pockets while Achuthan Nair pranced around, waving his arms and stick, incoherent with rage. Wanting to slap them, kick them, and subjugate their soaring voices into whimpers of fear and pain.

Mukundan sipped his tea and wondered what he was going to do. He didn't know how to handle his father any more. He wished there was someone he could talk to. Bhasi no longer visited him as often as he used to. As if to keep the pretence of that friendship, he called on Mukundan once a week and then left after a few minutes. There was no more exchange of confidences, no more of the camaraderie they had shared once.

As for Anjana, she still clung to her anger and hurt; still unwilling to see Mukundan's point of view. At first he had wondered if the estrangement was going to be a permanent one. She sent back the two letters he wrote her, unopened. Unwilling to accept defeat, Mukundan went to her house. If she refuses to see me, then I will never return again, he swore to himself. No woman should be so arrogant, so full of pride. But she didn't turn him away. Instead she treated him as if he were some passing acquaintance. She received him in her front room, asked about him and his father's health politely. Served him a cup of tea and then waited for him to leave.

The committee members called on him when they had the time, which wasn't often. Power House Ramakrishnan dropped in once to show him the blueprint of the community hall. 'This is where the foyer with the nameboard of the committee members will be, and the hall will be here,' he said tracing a line on the graph sheet with his finger, while Mukundan looked at the drawing uncomprehendingly.

Abu Seth drove up in his Mahindra jeep one day to invite him for his brother's housewarming and Susheelan came in with a receipt book as part of his fund-raising activity for the Young Men's Cultural Association annual celebrations. What could he tell these people about the fears that racked him? Or of the helplessness he felt when he saw his father?

In less than a month his father had regressed into a

confused, malevolent child. He drew on the walls with a piece of charcoal. Abstractions that made him chortle in rude glee. He scratched the wooden doors with a safety pin—rows and rows of hieroglyphics only he knew how to decipher. He wandered around the house speaking to invisible companions. He spat out the food he didn't like and had to be cajoled into having a bath. He would enter the room reserved for the souls of the dead ancestors. He would take out his penis from the folds of his clothing and like a child who's been forbidden to handle a knife, he would stealthily examine it, fold, crevice, and glans. And when he had played with it enough, he would aim it at the wooden pedestal that was meant to be a homing place for the souls of the ancestors and pee. Giggling in delight as the arc of urine rose and splashed the wood.

But when he saw anything tinged with the promise of beginnings—buds, calves, children—his mind rallied forth with the hatred of an old man who saw his own life trickling away at a pace he could no longer control. Achuthan Nair leaped up in manic rage. He slashed buds off bushes with a stick; threw stones at any calf, chick, kitten, or puppy that dared wander into the compound; and rushed at children with an upraised stick. When he had vented his anger, he would curl his lip at Mukundan and say, 'If you don't show them who is in control, they will try to assert their power.'

Mukundan would shudder, thankful for the years that sat on him.

Mukundan as he was had no place in Achuthan Nair's mind. Achuthan Nair remembered him as a boy. It was as if his mind had chosen to freeze time so that it wouldn't know the coming of its own end.

Mukundan heard the cycle of sounds: pebbles falling, boys shrieking, his father roaring . . . and then there was silence. He waited for his father to return to the house almost frothing at his mouth with rage. But there was no sign of him. Mukundan examined his nails and wondered if his father had wandered into the kitchen.

These days Achuthan Nair made a beeline for Krishnan Nair as if he were a favourite uncle who could be relied on to produce a treat. Mukundan often found his father crunching sugar or chewing on freshly grated coconut. Once Mukundan had seen him licking at milk powder cupped in his palm while Krishnan Nair watched, anguished by the deterioration of a man he had once respected and feared. 'Eat slowly, Achuman,' he pleaded, 'you'll choke on the milk powder. Shall I put it in a little bowl for you?'

'No, no,' Achuthan Nair shook his head and stuffed his mouth as fast as he could. When he had finished, he asked slyly, 'Will you give me some more tomorrow?'

But when he peeped into the kitchen, Krishnan Nair was all by himself, staring at the fire, deep in thought. Krishnan Nair had lost the ebullience, the friskiness that had marked his tenure there till the time Achuthan Nair had come back. He had become very quiet, and withdrew from the room when father and son were together. From his father-uncle-older-brother role in Mukundan's life, he had retired to plain caretaker. Manager of the house, provider of meals, a presence that allowed father and son to dwell comfortably under one roof.

'Have you seen him?' Mukundan asked.

Krishnan Nair stared at him blankly and then murmured, 'I thought he was with you.'

'I saw him rushing towards the post office to chase the schoolchildren off. But that was a while ago,' Mukundan said, beginning to feel anxious.

Krishnan Nair stood up. 'We should go look for him,' he said.

Achuthan Nair had taken to wandering outside the gate. He would cross the road, stand outside the stile of his mistress's house, and demand in his most imperious manner, 'Who dared build a house on my land?'

When he spotted his daughter or grandchildren, he threw stones at them, hollering, 'Get away! Get away from my land, you scum! I don't want whores and bastards living on my land.'

Mukundan had led him away three times already. He would hold his father's arm and gently tug at it. 'Come Father, we have to go.' When the old man resisted, Krishnan Nair stood across the road and waved a toffee in the air. 'Look at this, Achuman. Look at this,' he lured and Achuthan Nair rushed towards him, greedy for the little treat. Once Mukundan had glanced at Shanta's face and then had looked away quickly. He could see that she was hurt and angry, bitter and resentful. She was his half-sister, but he had never ever spoken a word to her in his life. And he wasn't going to start acknowledging her existence now. They might have the same father, but he knew that the only thing they shared was an unmitigating hatred for each other. He had heard from Postman Unni that her poisonous tongue had been busy at work.

Postman Unni had been on his way to Mukundan's house when Shanta hailed him. 'Do you have any letters for me?' she asked, wiping her hands on the pallav of her sari and walking towards the stile.

Postman Unni smiled and shook his head. 'None,' he said. 'Maybe I should start writing you some,' he added coyly. When she didn't bite his head off at his audacity, he felt encouraged enough to stand there and chat for a while.

'I suppose they have several letters coming in every day,' she probed, with a tilt of her head at Mukundan's house.

'That's true,' Postman Unni agreed. 'Letters, magazines, wedding invitations—he must know several people.'

But Shanta wasn't interested in Mukundan's mail. All she wanted to do was air her venomous thoughts. 'When my father left home, he was sound of body and mind. God knows what he did to him, but my father no longer even recognizes me,' she told Postman Unni.

'No, no, you are mistaken,' he waved her accusation aside. 'Achuman is almost ninety years old. This was bound to happen.'

'So why didn't it happen before? He must have asked that Painter Bhasi to prepare a herbal potion that addles the brain. They are great friends. The painter is always in and out of that house, as if he's a family member. While I, his sister, have never even stepped into that compound.'

'That was in the past. They are not all that close these days. There was some misunderstanding over the community hall, and the painter is leaving the village,' Postman Unni said, shuffling the bundle of letters in his hand impatiently.

'Then that's exactly why he wanted my father out of the way. Now that he's on the committee of the community hall, he probably doesn't want any to-ings and fro-ings between my house and his.'

'Why would there be any to-ing and fro-ing between his house and yours anyway? Achuman left your house swearing never to return, didn't he?' Postman Unni said brusquely, trying to extricate himself from the unpleasant turn the conversation was taking. Later he had narrated to Mukundan every single detail—from how she had raised one eyebrow when she had asked about Mukundan's mail to the manner in which her lip had twisted downward when she had talked of the community hall.

'That one should be watched,' Postman Unni had cautioned Mukundan. 'Don't have anything to do with her at any cost.'

It was this that Mukundan remembered when he saw Shanta. He walked away hastily. He was scared that if he remained there any longer, she would try to start a conversation with him. Probably even quarrel with him.

Mukundan and Krishnan Nair searched the house, checking to see if Achuthan Nair was skulking in one of his favourite places. 'Maybe Achuman is still standing by the nellikka tree,' Krishnan Nair suggested, when they realized he wasn't in the house.

They found him at the bottom of an old pit that had once been quarried and then abandoned. There had been some vague plans to fill it up but somehow it had never got done. He lay there on his side, whimpering amid dried leaves, broken twigs, and sharp-edged rocks. Eyes glazed, helpless and stricken. Mukundan and Krishnan Nair looked at each other horrified. 'What do we do?' Mukundan asked in panic.

He walked around the edge of the pit searching for a way down into it. Some way of reaching his father without breaking his own limbs. 'Mukundan,' Krishnan Nair called. 'Wait, you won't be able to help him. I know what to do.'

Mukundan stopped. What did he mean by that? 'I may be old but I'm still much younger than you,' he began angrily.

Krishnan Nair held up his hand, 'Please,' he said. 'This is not about you or me. We need help here. Strong young men who can go down to your father and bring him up without hurting him any further. Let's not argue about this.' He paused and took a deep breath. Then, at the top of his wavering voice, he shouted, 'Help! Help! Someone please help!'

Mukundan stared in amazement and then joined in. 'Help!'

Several men rushed towards them. Mukundan saw a blur of faces. He heard the trampling of leaves and the snapping of twigs. A chorus of voices rushed towards them asking, 'What happened? What happened?'

Two of the young men rushed to the house to bring the planter's chair. Someone else rushed to the Primary Health Centre to fetch the doctor. Mukundan stood there, numb and shaken, while they gently eased his father into the chair and carried him back to the house.

His face clenched and loosened. His brows crinkled, and his nostrils flared in agitation. Achuthan Nair's thoughts tossed and turned. Mukundan stood by his father's side watching him impassively. He felt something akin to pity wander into his heart.

The fall had cracked a bone. A simple hairline fracture. 'A younger man would have been up and about in three days' time,' the orthopaedist at the American Hospital in Ottapalam said. 'But with the elderly, everything becomes that much more difficult. Bones don't knit. Bruises don't heal. I would recommend you get a home nurse to attend to him. I'll give you an address you can contact for help.'

The doctor at the Primary Health Centre in Kaikurussi said much the same. Except that he added, 'You are not all that young yourself. So don't take on too much. Get a home nurse like the orthopaedist advised you to.'

Mukundan swallowed convulsively. Just because he had to have his blood pressure checked every month, it didn't mean he was a dithering, decrepit creature. The young and the old were alike in their manner with the middle-aged, Mukundan decided in irritation. The young tried to slow you down. They found it inappropriate for a person of his age to ignore the passing of time and stride ahead in life. As for the old, they resented the strength that was still there in him, living and breathing. They wanted him to embrace infirmity and be like them. Resigned to the thought of aging and dying.

Achuthan Nair moaned. The home nurse who stood by the table rearranging sentinel rows of bottles and swabs, looked up. Usually she sat in a chair near the window reading, except when Mukundan came in to check on his father and then she hastily stood up and began fiddling with the bottles. She walked to the bed and with expert hands moved Achuthan Nair. A few pink spots already dotted his back. Her lips pursed, and a tiny frown appeared on her forehead as she daubed Vaseline on the raw areas and dusted baby powder on his buttocks and genitals. Mukundan felt a slow, mounting horror. 'Is that a bedsore?'

he asked, forgetting to whisper.

'Yes,' she nodded, gesturing for him to lower his voice.

'Can't you do anything to prevent it?' he whispered furiously.

'I'm doing my best,' she shrugged. 'But when a patient lies on his back all day and all night, there will be bedsores. The only thing I can do is keep him dry all the time so as to try and minimize it.'

When the nurse went to the dining room where a hostile Krishnan Nair served her dinner, Mukundan sat in her chair flipping the pages of a magazine. Someone had to keep watch constantly at his father's bedside.

Achuthan Nair's chest rose and fell. The room hummed with the effort of that laboured breathing. Mukundan put down the magazine and stared out of the window. How much longer would his father fight? He battled on, unwilling to surrender, even though he knew death already perched on the foot of the bed with a noose and a sack to snare his soul.

Mukundan counted the days in his head. Fifteen days had passed since his father had let go the reins of his life and ended up at the bottom of a pit. Fifteen days of lying in bed in a semi-comatose state, ready for death and yet reluctant to leave. Fifteen days of having his past confront him as shadows on the wall and from the corners of the room.

Achuthan Nair began muttering in his sleep. 'What do you want, Paru Kutty? Leave me alone. Don't you have anything else to do all day but whine? Get out of my sight! I'm sick and tired of you.'

Mukundan felt anger swamp pity. And with it a certain realization. Perhaps he could finally find out how his mother had died. He walked to his father's side and gently shook him awake. 'Father,' he whispered. 'Father,' he said with a growing sense of urgency. 'How did she die? How did my mother die? Tell me, Father, tell me who killed my mother?'

'What are you doing?' the nurse asked in a horrified voice. She stood at the doorway taking in the scene. 'He's heavily sedated. And his mind is wandering. There's no point in trying to get a deathbed confession out of him. He's beyond all that now.'

Suddenly Achuthan Nair's eyes flickered open. He blinked. For a fleeting moment, remission set in. The mind leaped over the formidable barriers of age and chemical compounds and sought to reinstate itself in that dying body. He remembered who he was. He recognized the debilitating state he was reduced to. His eyes were clear and contemptuous as his voice tried to emerge from his cracked lips. A cracked voice, royal nevertheless in its decree, said, 'Do something. Don't let me rot away like this. Let me die in dignity.'

'He's sinking,' the nurse said quietly. 'Perhaps it is for the best. From what Krishnan Nair tells me he would have hated to die like this. There is nothing noble about death. But it is worse to be trapped in a state between life and death.'

Mukundan continued to sit by the side of the bed. He licked his lips and adjusted his glasses.

'Hush, hush,' the nurse soothed his father.

His father would have preferred to have fallen down a staircase and broken his neck rather than suffer the indignity of reverting to infancy in a withering body. Fed with a spoon, mush that would slip down his throat easily. Shitting and peeing into a bedpan someone thrust beneath his bottom at regular intervals. Watched over day and night. Except that this was a vigil kept reluctantly and with a fervent hope that it would end at the earliest. All of them—Krishnan Nair, Mukundan, and the home nurse—waited for him to die and release them from the painful duty of trying to keep him alive.

'I have been a nurse for a long time, and I have nursed several people through the last moments of their life.

Sometimes I think there is no place called heaven or hell, or an afterlife. There is only one life, and that is here and now. You reap your goodness or pay your dues before you die,' the nurse said in a sepulchral tone from her chair.

Mukundan felt sorrow cloud his anger. What did it matter how Amma had died? How would anything in his life change by knowing whether she was pushed down a staircase, or had slipped and fallen? His father was no longer who he was. Every part of him was caught in the machinations of time. A mind that bolted like an unruly horse. A body that bore the stench of rot. A conscience that tormented every breath he took. Pricking, prodding, reminding, torturing, so that there was no escaping his past.

Just before he died, Achuthan Nair's eyes blinked open. His head thrashed, his mouth gasped, the tendons of his neck tautened and stood out in stark relief, a fish struggling to remain alive on land, as his throat, tongue, lips tried to form words. One last command? A cry for help? Regret? Sorrow? God knows what it was he saw in that last moment of his life, for his face crumpled in fear, and from that mouth that had known only how to issue orders and exude authority, a plea escaped: 'No, no. Oh, please, no!'

How do you mourn a man you had always wished dead? How do you mourn a father who bound your mind and crippled your spirit?

How do you grieve for someone who never once looked at you with love or smiled at you with plain affection? How do you grieve for a tyrant who held your happiness in a vise-like grip and taunted you with fleeting glimpses of it?

How do you weep for one whose stench clung to your nostrils; a cloying, sickly sweet odour peculiar to power and old men—bile, phlegm, saliva, urine, excrement, eau de cologne, talcum powder, rubbing alcohol, rotting flesh, trickling life, age, authority, corruption? How do you do it? How?

Under a canopy of dried palm leaves held aloft by bamboo poles, three hundred people sat at the last feast in honour of Achuthan Nair. To appease his departed soul, to fill a thousand bellies and earn their gratitude so as to allow the soul easy entry through the doors of heaven. Six hundred had already eaten and four hundred more, including the cooks, helpers and beggars who lined the compound wall, were waiting to do so.

Mounds of fat brown rice; vats of curries—creamy white, deep brown, startling yellow. Drumsticks, eggplants, yams, pumpkins, beans, melons, bananas, lentils, cooked individually and cooked together, so that there were seven different curries to choose from. Pickles, chutneys, and two payasams made of palm sugar and coconut milk. Never a milk payasam. That was for births, marriages and auspicious beginnings.

Mukundan sat huddled in a chair, wondering who all these people were. He had never seen them before. Krishnan Nair seemed to know everyone, though. 'Distant relatives, your father's well-wishers, people who looked up to your father. I've never seen such a turnout for a funeral before,' he said in an awed whisper. 'Achuman was no ordinary man. He inspired respect. There will never be anyone like him again.'

'There never will be anyone like him again.' Mukundan's bitterness spilled over. 'He was the worst father anyone could have had.'

'Lower your voice, Mukundan,' the old caretaker urged frantically. 'Devayani's sons are in the next room. They are waiting to speak to you before they leave.'

'I was a good son. I did everything he expected of me and more. I didn't even marry because I wanted my wife to be someone that he would approve of. I spent my whole life trying to please my father. And I never did.'

Krishnan Nair mopped his brow with his towel and sighed, 'Did he ever say so?'

'No,' Mukundan said. 'But you know him. He never said anything. He simply bristled with dissatisfaction.'

Krishnan Nair touched Mukundan's elbow. From under the canopy, the sounds of people eating, drinking, slurping, burping and talking permeated the room. The sounds of one thousand men, women and children gathered to hoist Achuthan Nair on that last leg to eternity.

'Mukundan,' Krishnan Nair said in the voice that he had used only once before, almost forty-seven years ago, on top of Pulmooth mountain, when he had understood that Mukundan's disappointment was the result of the boy's own unwillingness to look beyond what he wanted to see.

'I never meant to tell you this. It is not my place to do so, nor is now the time for me to say it, but you make me sick. Take a good look at yourself. Do you have anyone to share your sorrow with? Anyone you can call your own? A wife? A friend? And yet you sit here on judgment on a man whose death is mourned by hundreds of people. I'm not saying he was perfect. He had his faults. Several of them, in fact. He was callous, brutal, and a tyrant. But he also had the courage of his convictions. When he believed in something, he let nothing come between him and his purpose. He stood by it no matter what the world thought of him. Do you have that courage, Mukundan? Do you have the strength to pursue happiness? You cling to your old grievances like someone adding up the same set of figures day after day, expecting a different answer each time. Get a grip on yourself, Mukundan. Grieve for your father, mourn his death. Then go on with your life and make something of it. If you think you are a better man than him, let us see it. You can't use him as an excuse for your ineptitude any more.'

Mukundan sat in the room with his head in his hands. He felt shaken and ashamed. Krishnan Nair had never used that tone of voice with him before. Nor had he ever reproached him.

All these years he had done nothing with his life. What

have I accomplished because I wanted to do it for myself? The thought whirled and pirouetted in Mukundan's mind. He felt completely alone. And insignificant. What am I going to do, he asked himself again and again. He no longer knew who he was. It was time he confronted the truth about himself. He could no longer hide behind the layers of self-deceit that had been the costume he had worn to fit the role he thought he had been given. Who was he? A better man than his father or merely an extension of who his father had been? That was what he had to discover.

Mukundan walked into the bathroom and examined himself in the mirror. He stared at his reflection, aghast. The nakedness of his self challenged him unabashedly. He saw for himself who he really was. A creature who had hidden his inadequacies by using his father's domineering methods as an excuse to explain his own weakness of character. A selfish being whose world and happiness revolved around the appeasing and nurturing of his fragile ego. A timid man who used his niceness as a facade to deflect attention from the fact that he had made nothing of his life. He was no better than his father had been. Selfish, insensitive, brutal, incapable of loyalty or love . . .

What do I do next? Mukundan asked himself despondently. How can a man evolve into what he desires to be? How can he stand taller than his father and create a new line of vision for himself? How can he set himself free of his father's presence?

There was still life left to live. Who did he have to share it with? He had betrayed the only two people who had loved him and given all of themselves to him—Bhasi and Anjana. He had used them and discarded them because it suited him to do so.

He was no better than his father had been. Perhaps he was the lesser man.

29

A Better Man Than His Father

Mukundan walked up the road towards Shankar's Tea Club. The sun shone down fiercely, a harbinger of summer. There was hardly any breeze to move the heat that pressed down upon him. Mukundan felt as if he were caught in a pile of several wet blankets. Layers and layers of heat and steam.

'It's only February, but summer's arrived early this year,' a voice broke through the pile of sodden wool. Kesavan Kurup, the retired schoolteacher who until now had merely been on nodding terms, offered in tones that were solicitous and cordial.

Mukundan smiled politely.

'I hear you are on the community hall committee.'

Mukundan nodded. His stomach rumbled.

'It's good to be preoccupied with some activity when one has retired. Otherwise you become prey to all kinds of illnesses, real and imaginary. What they say about an empty mind being the devil's workshop is a hundred per cent true,' the schoolteacher said as he walked along with Mukundan to Shankar's.

Outside Shankar's, Kesavan Kurup put his hand on Mukundan's arm and murmured, 'Those upstarts Mad Moidu and Abu Seth think that money is everything. It is good that there is someone like you in our midst. A cultured man. When my son wrote to me last, he was complaining that he finds it very difficult to handle the corruption levels in the hospital he works for. So I wrote back to him that he should consider returning to the village and setting up a clinic here. I told him that with people like you around, Kaikurussi is a very different place from what it used to be.'

At the tea shop Mukundan sensed again the breath of a new camaraderie. Of villagers who, it seemed, had accepted him as one of their own. Of a breaking down of barriers. Of a new openness. One by one, they walked up to him and spoke to him: regret at his father's death, astonishment at the number of people who had attended the funeral, appreciation of his involvement in the community hall project. Statements. Comments. Questions. Opinions. And finally, when Shankar put down a plate of vellappam and masala curry in front of him, he said, 'You should consider standing for the panchayat elections. This village needs a man like you.'

Mukundan stared back at him wordlessly. Then he tore a piece of the soft, cushiony vellappam and dipped it in the curry. He heard a wave of voices wash over him. He felt as if he were in a glass bubble that allowed him to see but not to feel. No matter what they said, there was a distance that couldn't be transcended. They stirred no emotions in him except perhaps a faint anger. For weren't these the same people, the villagers of Kaikurussi, who had been willing to accede to Power House Ramakrishnan's decree that no one stand guarantee for the bank loan Bhasi had wanted to take? They were just as responsible as he was for making Bhasi leave the village in desperation. And it was to win the approval and appreciation of this fickle lot that he had so readily cast aside both his friend and lover. He had never been so alone in his life.

The day after his father's funeral, Mukundan was greeted in the morning by the sight of Krishnan Nair seated on the ledge on the veranda, with all his belongings packed into a cloth bag. 'Where are you going?' Mukundan's brow crinkled in surprise.

'Home,' Krishnan Nair said in a voice that revealed no trace of emotion.

'What?'

'It's not just you who's been living in the past,' Krishnan Nair stated baldly, resuming the strain of their last conversation the day before, 'I'm guilty of doing the same. I ignored my wife. I neglected my family. All these years, I was caught in some absurd slavish love. I squandered the best years of my life, but perhaps I can still make up for it. A lifetime is what I wasted.' He paused as if stung by memories of years of yearning, of vain hopes.

'I don't know what I'm going to say to my wife or how she's going to respond to me. But I know that I have to try. In the few years left to me, I'm going to try to make her happy, and in the process find some happiness of my own,' Krishnan Nair concluded slowly and clearly. He had thought of little else in the days after Achuthan Nair's death.

'Will you come this way when you have the time?' Mukundan asked, stricken by the thought of Krishnan Nair's departure.

'I will. But not for a while,' Krishnan Nair said. He stood up and picked up his bag. 'There's tea in the flask and breakfast on the table. From now on you will have to look after yourself. Maybe you should find yourself a wife,' the old man said, with a smile hovering on his lips.

Then, abruptly, as if he had remembered something, his expression changed. 'Mukundan,' he added, choosing his words with deliberate care, 'I think your father was more successful with your upbringing than either he or you realized. Do you remember what he told you day after day when you were a child? If you wish to survive, you need to think of yourself first. The moment you start thinking of others, there is no way you'll ever reach anywhere. In this world, no one can be responsible for any one else. Protect yourself first. Then if it doesn't involve risking your life, you can help someone else. A survivor is someone who is selfish. It isn't true, Mukundan. What is the point in surviving if you have no one to share your happiness or grief with? Don't make the mistake I did. Don't throw away your life.'

Mukundan watched the old man leave. One by one his roles in life were being stripped away until all that remained of him was the insignificant man he was. Mukundan the man, native of Kaikurussi, the last remaining scion of a long pedigree of distinction; retired government employee. No one's friend. No one's beloved.

'Have you seen Bhasi lately?' Shankar asked.

'He came home the day after the funeral,' Mukundan said quietly.

'I saw the obituary in the newspaper,' Bhasi had said, standing outside in the veranda, presuming nothing more than the right of an acquaintance. 'I thought I must come here and express my condolences.'

And Anjana. She had called him on the telephone and mouthed stilted words a telegram would have conveyed with as much feeling. Mukundan knew that he had no one to blame but himself.

'I suppose you won't be attending the pooram in our temple,' Shankar said from behind the counter.

Mukundan pushed aside the half-eaten vellappam and stood up. He took his glasses off and wiped them. 'Have the festival preparations begun?'

'The kodi-kura,' Shankar mimed the movement of a flag going up a pole, 'went up yesterday. Which means the pooram festivities will be held on the eighth day.'

Mukundan took out his wallet to pay.

'I know you are in no mood to be a part of all this pooram fever, but you should come to the pooram ground and join in the celebrations,' Shankar said, counting out the change.

'Maybe I will,' Mukundan said and began to walk away.

He ambled down the hill deep in thought. Moved by some impulse, he walked past his gate and paused outside what had once been Bhasi's land. He stood outside the dirt track and stared at it with anguish. The wilderness in which

Bhasi had seen cures and miracles had been ruthlessly tamed. The branches of trees bled, the stiff carcasses of plants lay outstretched. The land that had spread, lush and reckless green, had been dug up and turned over. Where flowers once bloomed, rectangular walls of bricks stood. A cement mixer and rods of iron. A rubble of dreams.

In a little more than a month's time after Bhasi's departure, the community hall and its annexe of rooms had already reached window height. He had known that Power House Ramakrishnan was moving at tremendous speed. That he had been eager to have it ready for the wedding season that began in April. But Mukundan hadn't expected such a drastic and rapid transformation.

A miasma of loathing filled his insides for the hollow structure, for Power House Ramakrishnan, who had destroyed one man's dreams to build an edifice to his own ego. For the villagers who had been prepared to forsake Bhasi to pander to a powerful man's whim. But most of all, it was the shame he felt for what he had done that crippled him.

He had been mesmerized by the image of a structure that had a paved courtyard and a hexagonal pond in which an upright cement fish let water cascade from its open mouth. He had been flattered by the thought of the shining brass plaque that would hang in the foyer of the building with the names of each one of the committee members. He had wanted to be part of the welcoming committee when the district collector arrived for the inaugural ceremony. And be seated in the front row with him as one of the village dignitaries. He had imagined the letters he would write to friends in which he could, with studied carelessness, mention: The other day when I was with Mr Guha, our district collector . . .

His greed for recognition and acceptance, importance and adulation, had blinded him to everything else.

This is what I sacrificed my integrity for. This heap of

bricks and mortar is what I held more precious than two loving souls. Mukundan felt weighed down by guilt and regret.

There had been men such as him before, Mukundan thought with a pang. The mythologies of all religions were peppered with stories of souls that let the weakness of their character rule them. Judas, weary acolyte, who sold his faith for thirty pieces of silver and a temporary happiness that he too was capable of accomplishing something worthwhile. Of being of use to someone. Dronacharya, the recognition-hungry master of the Pandavas and Kauravas, who sought to make a mark by pleading his allegiance to the blind king Dhritarashtra even though he knew some day he would have to wage war against his own conscience. How did they live with themselves? Mukundan wondered. How did they die?

In the brief instant before death galloped away with the last vestiges of their breath, were they racked with guilt and regret? Fear and a great desire to make amends, to have lived life differently?

If only I could rewrite the course of events of these past days. If only I could do it all differently, Mukundan told himself as his leaden feet took him home.

The soil still bore the traces of death's departure. The spot where Achuthan Nair's funeral pyre had burned, shooting giant flames into the sky.

The trees stood around disapproving and silent in their stillness. Birds called lazily. The soporific heat had dulled their voices too. In the distance he heard the pelting sound of pebbles as they rattled within a wooden drum pulley as the rope rushed to the dank bottom of a well. Deep. Deep. Deeper. Mukundan could feel the splash of cold water as the iron bucket broke the surface. Crystal droplets that cleansed and smoothed the furrows of his troubled mind. The sweetness of clarity. The bucket twisted, turned, and danced to the top. Mukundan felt the awakening of hope.

One last time he sought the confines of the earthen pot high in the attic. Cradled in its stillness, he called forth the man he knew was there somewhere within him. That being that had eluded him all these years. I will be who I want to be, he chanted again and again, surrounded by blackness. The confusion of his tortured spirit churned until what rose to the top was the means to his release—an end to the repugnance he felt for himself. And when he climbed out of the urn, he kicked it on its side and smashed it to a thousand pieces.

Mukundan knew he would never need it again. In this world, in this life, there was room only for one man. The one that had been born in the urn.

This new Mukundan was plagued by no uncertainties, reined by no inadequacies. He called the water diviner and had him mark a fresh spot where water could be found. In that village where land couldn't be bought because everyone clung to it as a living vestige of their ancestry, Mukundan sent for the document writer and had him make out a deed. A quarter of an acre around the spot where the water diviner's stick had promised water was gifted to Bhasi with immediate effect.

'Do you realize what you are doing?' the document writer questioned curiously. 'No one sells their ancestral land. It speaks of disrespect to the dead and the family tree.'

'Is it against the law to make a gift of my land to anyone I choose?' There was a hint of steel in Mukundan's voice.

'I didn't say that,' the writer cowered. 'The villagers won't like it.'

'Do the villagers look after my well-being? Then what business is it of theirs what I choose to do with my land?' Mukundan asked, and realized that was exactly how he felt. And thus he set the seal for what the rest of his life in Kaikurussi was going to be like. From now on he would do only what his conscience told him was right. Between the individual and society, he had made his choice.

The document writer saw the determination in Mukundan's face and shifted uneasily. He recognized that look. He had seen it before on another man's face. Achuthan Nair. Not that it's surprising, he told himself as he walked out with his pens and sheaf of papers. Like father, like son.

Later in the evening he would visit Bhasi, Mukundan told himself. He would wash his hands with water ritually, so that Bhasi would know that he had severed his past self forever. And then he would offer the land deed to Bhasi and plead with him to return. To forgive him and once again resume his life in the village, in the land he loved.

The carpenter who came next on Mukundan's list stared in shock. 'You must be joking. How can I finish the bed in five days' time?'

Mukundan touched the planed planks of teak and rosewood. 'When I paid you the advance, you promised to deliver it in a month's time. Do you realize how many days have passed since that date?'

'Everyone knows that no carpenter delivers on the date he promises.' The carpenter was surly.

'I don't care what everyone knows. I need my bed completed and delivered on the day before the pooram. Do you understand?' Again the steel glinted.

The carpenter nodded with a sullen face. He had heard that Mukundan was close to all the village notables. 'What is the hurry?' he asked. 'It isn't as if you are getting married!' He tried a little joke.

Mukundan looked at him as if he were a termite that had crept out of the woodwork. Deserving to be crushed. 'That is none of your business,' he said as he turned to go.

Later in the night Mukundan went looking for Bhasi at his house in Kailiad. He stood outside the gate and called, 'Bhasi!'

Bhasi heard Mukundan's voice and felt a strange twisting of spirit. Then he remonstrated with himself; he called forth suspicion and distrust to watch over him.

'Bhasi!' Mukundan called again. Bhasi heard the hesitation in his voice.

When Mukundan saw Bhasi framed in the doorway of his house, he opened the gate and went towards him.

Bhasi waited for Mukundan to say what he had come to say. Bhasi wanted to ask Mukundan how he was faring all by himself in that gargantuan house of his, if he had made up with Anjana, and whether his new-found friends still rallied around him now that they no longer had any use for him. Bhasi wanted to know if Mukundan was happy and well. But he chose to remain silent.

'Could I have some water?' Mukundan asked.

Bhasi brought a glass of water. Is that why he had dropped in? To quench his thirst?

Mukundan poured the water on his hands. Bhasi looked at him, unable to understand what he was doing. Was this some kind of a sacramental rite? But what was it meant to convey?

Mukundan then opened the handbag that he always carried and took out a paper. It was a photocopy of a document written on stamp paper. He held it out to Bhasi.

'What is this?' Bhasi asked. 'I have already signed all the papers for the registration.'

'Look at it,' Mukundan said softly.

Bhasi read the document and understood the meaning of the earlier ritual. He felt a tremendous sadness take root within him. Why had he waited so long? 'Why?' he asked.

Mukundan said, 'I was foolish. I let my own lack of self-esteem rule me. I was so besotted by the idea of being someone important that I didn't realize how important you are to me. This is the only way I know to make amends.'

Bhasi took a deep breath. 'Mukundan,' he said. 'I want you to know that I am overwhelmed by this gesture. But what is once broken cannot be repaired.'

'No, don't say that,' Mukundan said. 'You were the one

who taught me that everything can be repaired, all breaks can be mended. All that is necessary is that you must want to do it. Accept my land, Bhasi. Come back to the village, and the land you love.'

'Do you realize what the committee of notables will do to you once they know that you brought me back to Kaikurussi? You will no longer be one of them,' Bhasi said quietly.

'All my life I wanted to be my father's equal. But now I want more. I want to be better than him. I want to know what it is to love and to give. And, in turn, be loved. I don't want to wake up one morning and discover that I have frittered away my life chasing after ephemeral dreams. I want my dreams alive and living beside me. I will leave it to you to decide whether you wish to return or not. But the land is yours to do with as you please. But nothing would make me happier than to have you living alongside me. I will wait for you, Bhasi,' Mukundan said.

Bhasi thought of the person Mukundan had been when they first met. And he wanted to shake him by the shoulders and demand: Tell me, Mukundan. Tell me who exorcised the ghosts that haunted you? Tell me who cleared the darkness that clouded your life? Tell me who taught you to free yourself from the hands of the clock and meticulous routine? Tell me who made you understand, accept and even appreciate imperfection? Tell me who did it, Mukundan? Who?

Let me share the glory of this magnificent being you have evolved into. Let me know that my life has not been in vain. And that the man you are now is the result of what I did for you.

Bhasi swallowed his feelings that rose like bile into his mouth. In some ways he had won. And in some ways he had lost. Bhasi had made Mukundan the man he was now. But somewhere along the lines of his growth, Mukundan had become who he was all by himself, growing beyond Bhasi.

Shifting the balance forever.

The boundaries of their lives had shifted. And with them the levels of what could fill them with hope and what could bring happiness.

'I need to think about returning to Kaikurussi,' Bhasi said, knowing that deep inside him he wanted to return. To sink roots afresh in the land that he loved. To restore the rhythm of their mutual esteem.

'Yes, I do realize that you need to think about it,' Mukundan said quietly. Then he looked at Bhasi for a long moment. As the clouds lifted off the moon, Bhasi glimpsed his face once again. He saw in Mukundan's eyes the strength of resolution. As if he had made peace with himself.

The next morning Mukundan visited Anjana. One last time and then never again, he told himself. He would ask her, plead with her to forgive his trespasses and accept him again.

Anjana looked at him in disbelief. 'Are you sure?' she asked.

'I'm sure,' he replied. He had never been more certain of anything in life. Her place was with him.

'The villagers won't approve of it. Or me. You will be kicked out of the committee. They will ostracize you. You won't be invited to anyone's wedding or housewarming or be included in any of the village's activities. They might not even give you the time of day,' she said quietly. Even then his emotional well-being was her primary concern.

'Would it bother you?' he asked, although he knew the answer. All through their relationship, she had been the one to take risks, to forge ahead while he had walked a step behind, afraid, unsure.

'No,' she said, slipping her hand into his. 'But you are the one who wants to be accepted by the villagers. You are the one who craves recognition,' she reminded him, still a little unforgiving, still a little hurt by his betrayal.

'Not any more. As long as you are with me, I don't care if I'm not invited to a single housewarming or even if the villagers never talk to me again,' he told her, excessive in his declaration, for reconciliations are built on such foundations.

Probably there would be snide references to his father. Comparisons drawn about how they chose to flaunt their mistresses shamelessly. He didn't care. His father had survived it, and as long as he lived, no one had ever managed to drag a word of regret from him. Mukundan would survive it too. One way or the other.

'I have a few more things to finish before I take you home with me. I will come back the day after the pooram. I want you to be packed and ready,' he promised as he kissed her brow. I shall let everyone see that I love Anjana, he told himself. But, more important, he would no longer allow his past to dam his passion. If he had to, he would retrace the steps of his spent years and live them all over again. So that when he cupped her chin in the hollow of his palm, he would remember only what she had taught him. The splendour of loving and giving.

And then there was only one more thing left to be done: the community hall. As long as it stood, the community hall was a statement of his weakness, his cowardice, and his lack of integrity.

With every brick placed on its growing walls, with every slap of cement reinforcing its strength, the community hall entombed failure. His failure as a friend, as a lover. As a man. The new Mukundan wanted no such remnants of his past staring him in his face day after day.

The whole of that night he pondered what he was to do. At the crack of dawn, he heard distant rumbles. He looked out of the window to see if it was raining. The skies were streaked with red and the promise of a heat wave. Then it occurred to him what the origin of the rumble was.

All over the district, various temples were celebrating

pooram with the vedikettu. The ritual of explosions. Of cylinders packed with gunpowder and ignited. The power of explosions and its deafening thunder, it was believed, would wake up the deity of the temple and beckon her to preside over the festivities and bless her devotees.

He walked out of the house to the land that was now Bhasi's. He had a fence put up. A border of frangipani stumps. After the first rains in April, the stumps would bud leaves and branches. And waxy white blossoms with yellow centres. Once again their friendship would know no boundaries, and the only barriers drawn would be a line of flowers that scented the daytime and glowed in the moonlight.

Mukundan searched among the bushes around the spot where the well-diggers had already started work. The water diviner had claimed that water would be struck at a depth of thirty feet. At ten feet, slabs of rock had greeted the well-diggers. Pale creamy rock that couldn't be cut through and could be crumbled only with gunpowder. The layers of rock would get harder and more difficult. Or they might strike water beneath this first layer of rock. Who was to know what cosmic music the layers of the earth danced to?

The gunpowder was kept in a tin trunk in a hollow under a bush. Mukundan opened the trunk and touched the black grain gingerly. He slid his hand into the pouch, and the powder slipped through his fingers unconscious of its own might. He took a palmful and held it. A surge of electricity shot through him. You need to know explosives and the explosives need to know you. Mukundan and the gunpowder understood each other. Within everything rests a power to ignite, to explode, and to change the face of life. All that was necessary was to kindle and set it alight.

Epilogue

It was the last hour of his vigil. He dared not close his eyes. For as the night intensified, he knew that soon it would be time.

They were all there, the people of Kaikurussi, thronging the temple grounds. Mountains of puffed rice, yards of jasmine, rows of glinting glass bangles, shimmery satin ribbons in rainbow hues, trinkets, toys, mouthwatering savoury murukkus, the stamp of feet, the straw-stuffed pairs of bullocks that were the lure of the pooram. He had heard as the rest of the villagers had, the call of the drums and the cymbals, beckoning them to the grounds. The annual festivity that the Devi of the temple demanded as part of her payment for protecting the village from plague, pestilence, drought, flood, and earthquakes.

Mukundan sat on the terrace with his fingers tightly clasped. His thoughts kept him company. A stream of thoughts bounded in and out like guests at a wedding, devotees at a temple, revellers at the pooram. Eager, exuberant, chaotic thoughts.

Mukundan had waited. Patiently. Patience is easy to find when one knows the end is in sight, he told himself with an inward laugh. On the day before the pooram, all work in the village had come to a standstill. Shutters were pulled down, shops were boarded up. The carpenter delivered the bed and assembled it in the room Mukundan had chosen as his nuptial chamber. The well-diggers left in the evening, promising to return two days later.

The morning of the pooram dawned. Mukundan woke

up, his heart hammering loudly. Over and over again, he had rehearsed the script in his mind. All that was left was the actual performance. He went to the construction site of the community hall. It was deserted except for the watchman. 'I was going past this way and came to check on its progress,' Mukundan told the watchman.

'No one's working because of the pooram,' the watchman said. 'Not even the construction supervisor.'

'Oh,' Mukundan said in a disappointed voice.

'But you can look around if you want to.'

'I think I will,' Mukundan said and sauntered into the building. The watchman went back to his seat by the gate.

On his way out, Mukundan drew out a fifty-rupee note from his wallet and gave it to the watchman with a wink. 'Have a good time at the pooram,' he said. The man clutched the note fervently and grinned slyly. 'I will. I will. Thanks very much.'

From the terrace, Mukundan could see the glow of lights that bathed the pooram grounds. Mukundan licked his lips and cleared his throat. He hadn't talked to anyone for more than ten hours. His voice felt strange and unused. It didn't matter, he thought. Tomorrow there would be time enough to talk, to laugh, to make amends . . . But first he had to do what he had to do. Tonight. Alone.

His hands felt cold and clammy. A bird screamed, flapping its wings. The bamboo copse began its reedy music. The branches of the jackfruit tree rustled. The civet cat had landed. Night after night it traced a path down from Pulmooth mountain, swooping through the night sky, gliding from tree to tree till it reached the jackfruit tree. For as long as he could remember, Mukundan had heard the plop of the civet cat reaching its destination. And its scurrying movements till it set forth again on its aerial route. He felt comforted by the familiarity of its arrival.

This was to be his karma. To reverse the process of his destiny. As it was the civet cat's to forage among the trees every night. There was no escaping the forces of one's karma.

For the first time Mukundan was struck by the magnitude of what he was planning to do. What if he failed? What if he was spotted? What if all his plans came to naught?

Mukundan took a deep breath. He thought of the promise of tomorrow. Of all that it held. Of happiness and harmony. The ripening of contentment and the fullness of living.

There would be no tomorrows if he didn't have the courage to go through with this night.

The Burmese clock that Achuthan Nair had taken with him to his mistress's house began striking the hour. One, two, three, four, five, six, seven, eight, nine, ten, eleven . . .

In half an hour's time the ritual of explosions would begin. The deafening gyrations of gunpowder as it lit and burned in the flame of its own heat. Soon he would have to walk, in the cover of the night, to the community hall. The watchman, like everyone else, would be at the grounds. Or at Che Kutty's shop.

Mukundan counted the ticking of the clock in his head. In ten minutes' time he would rise and walk out of the house. The metamorphosis that had begun nine months ago when he returned to this village would finally be complete. Unbidden, the memory of that first day as he drove into Kaikurussi tumbled into his mind—the wetness of June, the patina of thunder that hung in the air, the slump of his shoulders, the hopelessness of life. Mukundan realized with a strange sense of calm or, perhaps it was relief, that there was no going back now.

In his pocket was the pouch of gunpowder stolen from the tin trunk. He had already marked the place where he would dig a hole and bury it. Then he would stuff the hole with granite pieces that lay around the building site. He would insert a thin long wick into that pit of power. A wick that would trail him to what was to have been the foyer of the community hall.

And then Mukundan, who as a boy had feared firecrackers and had crept under the bed to hide from their wrath, who as an adult had stuffed his ears with cotton to block out the violence of explosions and the roar of their power in his head, would light the wick.

In this month of golden dryness there would nothing to deter its path. The flame would run up the wick till it found its destination. A body willing to be ignited. The air would fill with the acrid smell of gunpowder and the earth would tremble, heave, and shake. The edifice to the man he had been would no longer exist. This was the moment that had eluded him all his life. When he would become a man. A better man than he ever had been.

Mukundan felt his destiny flicker, leap, and change its course.

Glossary

Agarbathi: Incense stick.

Beedi: Cigarette made of dried leaf, instead of paper, and tobacco.

Biryani: Savory rice-and-meat dish.

Cent: 440 square feet; 100 cents make one acre.

Champakam: Flowering tree that blooms only at night. A popular myth states that a person who plants a champakam will not live to see it flower.

Dalit: "Politically correct" term for the untouchable castes of India.

Ezuthachan: A caste name.

Gandharvas: According to Hindu mythology, immortal celestial men who seduced virgins with their handsome looks and melodious singing. Gandharvas entertained the gods with their singing and brewed liquor for them to drink.

Ishtoo: Stew made of onions and potatoes cooked in coconut milk; probably inspired by Irish stew.

Iddlies: Round, steamed cakes made of fermented rice batter; a very common breakfast dish eaten with a coconut chutney.

Jaggery: Palm sugar that is brownish in color and has a distinct flavor.

Jubbah: Collarless long-sleeved shirt.

Kanji: Rice gruel.

Lakh: One hundred thousand.

Lungi: Colored sarong, worn by both sexes in Kerala.

Macch: The lower portion of the built-in wooden granary that is part of all traditional Hindu homes in Kerala. Usually the macch also has a resident goddess who is referred to as macchilamma—mother of the macch.

Masjid: Mosque.

Mundu: White cloth sarong made of cotton or silk, worn by both sexes in Kerala. A mundu represents dignity and hence is worn by the upper classes of all religions. Women drape a white shawl-like cloth over their shoulders as a mark of modesty, and this is called a vesthi.

Musaliyar: A learned man of the Islamic community.

Odiyan: Practitioner of black magic.

Onam: Annual harvest festival of Kerala, which usually occurs in the months of August and September.

Pooja: Worship of Hindu deities.

Panchayat: Local government body at the village level.

Palakka Modiram: Traditional heavy gold necklace studded with green and red stones.

Puttu: Steamed dish made of rice flour and grated fresh coconut; it is eaten with Ishtoo or Kadala Curry—a spicy sauce made using lentils.

RSS: Abbreviation of Rashtriya Swayamsevak Sangh, a Hindu political group.

Rasnadhi: An ayurvedic powder rubbed on the scalp after a bath to prevent colds.

Sanyasi: Mendicant.

Tharavad: An ancestral Nair house; since Nairs follow the matriarchal system, the tharavad defines the lineage and hence the pedigree of a particular person. Nairs use their tharavad name as a point of reference rather than the father's name.

Toddy: Coconut or palm sap collected in the morning in mud pots and left to ferment. By evening, it turns a milky white in color and has a high alcohol content.

Upma: Breakfast dish made of boiled semolina or broken wheat and sautéed with chopped green chilies, onions, and mustard seeds.

Vellappam: Fluffy pancake made of rice batter that is fermented by using fresh toddy.